The Wrestler from Montreal

prophecy for a separate man

by Arnold Holtzman

ISBN 0-7414-4028-8

Published by:

INFINITY
PUBLISHING.COM

1094 New DeHaven Street, Suite 100
West Conshohocken, PA 19428-2713
Info@buybooksontheweb.com
www.buybooksontheweb.com
Toll-free (877) BUY BOOK
Local Phone (610) 941-9999
Fax (610) 941-9959

Printed in the United States of America

Printed on Recycled Paper

Published November 2007

for Esther

PART ONE

1898

(1)

The village never had a name. Some families from Kresnatshov, which was only a few miles to the north, had made their homes there when salt seeped into their wells. It was thought that everyone would eventually follow them, but most of the others left for towns or more distant villages. So to everyone, it had always been just "the village," and when it died, it is doubtful that even a ghost had lingered there for very long.

Between the road and the shallow creek along which the village had risen was a flat rock into which an epitaph was carved. Some said that it was carved by Hezkel the ironmonger for a dog that he had buried beneath it; but Hezkel was himself long in the ground so it was impossible to know. Still, the words were an apt elegy for everyone and everything that had ever been there. It read simply:

Whatever he once was
Is lost to the hard clay.
Who remembers
If he once was and is no longer?

There was no name. Also nameless were the thirty or so Poles from the old mining town of Baslavek, five kilometers to the east and next to the railway tracks (but where the train no longer stopped), who had ridden into the village on the very coldest day of what turned out to be its last winter. They proceeded to tear down a few homes which they then broke up into manageable pieces for firewood; this, and all the strewn furniture made of wood they hastily loaded onto their large sleds and withdrew.

Old Duvid Hazan was done in when he wouldn't move out of the path of a cherubic seventeen-year-old. Charged with intoxicating authority, the young boy had driven his axe with great determination into the old man's head. There was a moment, then, of uncertainty, when the Jews shrieked and the butchered body lay dead on the ground. But looking down at him, another Pole had said almost to himself, "I swear, that face looks exactly like my armpit." A roar of raucous laughter from his partners then exploded into the wailing, and there were no further disruptions.

In the spring the snow had melted far too quickly and it rained without letup for days on end. Soon, violent and unnatural rivers began whipping down from the Carpathians, and a few of the low-lying homes were lifted away from their supports. The topsoil around the village surrendered its hold, and the land that once had been rich, black, and fertile lay barren and slashed to its rocky substratum.

Milk cows had to be slaughtered for food, but even so, the unsettling bite of hunger soon fell upon the people. The chickens had succumbed to disease, and the eggs from those that still laid them had such thin shells that it was almost impossible to lift them without their breaking. But then some children playing near the forest came upon a field where a lot of rotted lumber had once been discarded, which now was thick with fine mushrooms. A young couple saw this turn of fortune as an omen to marry, and all the villagers were ecstatic in the certainty that this delicious abundance marked "paid" to whatever debt the Almighty had had a mind to collect from them.

Not quite. On a Friday in July, a dozen heavily panting, frowning, ferocious-looking horsemen, accompanied by dogs of similar countenance, rode into the village and ordered that a criminal from Warsaw be turned over to them. But Varshova was so distant from them — virtually another planet, altogether more than 600 kilometers away! There were questions and answers. It seemed that a young Jew had run off with the horse, carriage, and daughter of a wealthy and titled financier from the House of Radizvilli, who had employed him to give his daughter lessons on the piano. They were traced to Lublin, and from there to Jaruslav. There were eyewitnesses in Jaruslav who swore that they had seen the carriage racing out of the town along the road that led to Kresnatshov and Baslavak and the Ukrainian border, and Baslavak — being directly on the border, perhaps even across it — had to be where the Jew passed through with his plunder. Moreover, they trusted the dogs' noses.

The militiamen were told that they were the only outsiders to pass this way in many weeks. No such Jew was seen, certainly not one with a Christian mistress, and they could see for themselves that there was no fine carriage anywhere about, let alone the sort of horse that could pull it so far.

Straining their leashes, the dogs were barking and snarling hatefully. They had cast their judgment, it seemed, and the officials quickly became infected with their mood. Beyond the village was a forest leading into the Ukraine; there, neither their uniforms nor their dogs would make much of an impression. No, their search had to end at this village; the captain would not have his party return without something concrete to report.

"You are all making criminals of yourselves," he lashed out at them. "Give him to me, and I promise that the time I have wasted here will not cost you."

The villagers were cornered and helpless. Women wailed. Children cowered. Some men offered gold. Whoever this fleeing Jew was, they hated him. To think, of all the villages in Poland, theirs had to be the one to pay for a crime perpetrated by someone whom they had never seen, in a city not one of them had ever been to. This couldn't have happened *stamm*. Clearly, God wasn't done with his accounting of this community — and who knew what remained to be extracted from these wretched folk.

There were more words. Pleas and desperate explanations poured from one side, orders, curses and the most malevolent threats from the other. It might have been a scene from the grossest theater, with a number of acts which had yet to be played out before the final curtain would fall. But only the dogs were impatient — the dogs and possibly a few militiamen, as well.

"Enough!" their leader finally shouted. "If you Jews must be more loyal to the criminals amongst you than to the motherland that, for no good reason, feeds and tolerates you, you deserve to know what can happen when this goodwill is removed."

He then turned to his party and gave them orders. They were to assume that the wanted Jew was hiding in one of the houses. To flush him out, the houses were to be burned to the ground. Fortunately, they had brought along a few urns of coal oil and a number of bulrushes which they soon had aflame. In the spring there was no end to the rain, but now it had not rained a drop in more than three weeks. The days were hot, and all the wood was old and dry. It took no great effort to burn the houses down.

When the flames were high and still spreading, the unearthly cry of a beast was heard. It was Zemel the peddler's old horse. Again the cry was heard. The militiamen began to shout excitedly among themselves that they had caught up with the Jew, when suddenly, maddened and blinded by the fire eating into its hide, the horse tore itself out of the furnace and pounded across the stream. The beast's agony only ended when it charged into the stump of a dead and tinder-dry oak and there let the fire consume it. But somehow, the fire carried itself from the stump deeper into the thick of the trees, and four days later, 300 acres of imposing forest were reduced to black-and-silver smoking ash.

(2)

The team of Ukrainians sent to investigate the fire found the villagers on the road to Lvov. Suffering their accent and crude provincial Russian, the Ukrainians heard out their tale of woe, but the explanation of the fire was too confusing and contradictory to set in their report. The villagers, it seemed, were not of one mind. Most blamed the Polish gendarmes whom they claimed had set fire to their houses. Others remembered a horse. Still others made it seem as though the fire had spread to the forest directly from the houses, and this led the Ukrainians to suspect that the fire had actually been started in the forest and spread later to the village. They suggested that the villagers had originally set fire to the forest to clear new ground for more homes, but that the fire had escaped their control.

This was vigorously denied, but the Ukrainians insisted that all the villagers must stay where they were until the chief of inspectors himself would come to make the report which would take a day. In the meantime, food and water were to be dispatched to them and would reach them by morning. The Jews were suspicious.

And for good reason. At sunrise, as many as thirty or forty Cossacks, most in white jackets and tight leather boots, suddenly appeared; bayoneted rifles were strapped across their backs, while those in animal skins and black shirts had long curved blades affixed to their saddles. Their horses were wet and nervous, and even the civilian Ukrainians seemed surprised by their arrival, or at least by the air of urgency they generated.

A paper was presented. It was studied and returned. To the villagers — most of whom were still trying to trap some warmth between their bodies and the cold of the night — the Cossacks seemed anxious to get back on their way. But in an instant, the air was full of flashing, slashing steel — the unforgiving props of a familiar ritual. Shots were heard, and thick smoke was everywhere. There was no letup. The horses raced toward the Jews and reared above them, striking out. The blades whipped at their bodies, and the rifles knew no charity. Slowly, the earth swelled with blood as it reclaimed its own.

* * *

"Press close to me, my children — your mother trembles.

"I have seen the winter rise before the sun and engulf the summer for a day. I have seen an old tree with warped fruit, and though this fruit was hard and green and far from seed, it

fell suddenly to the ground, overripe. Rich with maggots, they were not for gathering, and neither did any germ of a root ever lodge in their decay.

"This I have seen and more. Though the tree in its crisis surrendered itself to the winter, the frailest of arteries rising in its stem locked stubbornly onto the two last fruits — and these were spared. These were also the smallest fruits, the very greenest. Yet the wrath of the winter was not appeased until it rent even this single artery, so that each existence grew separate, apart from and unknown to the other.

"Oh, my children, a fearful hour rushes upon us, and this is your inheritance that I deliver. Measure it not against the marble and cedar of kings, neither alongside the rags from your father's cart, for these and all else on this earth crumble in their day. But the winds — the winds of resurrection — are forever.

"Your inheritance is the grace of an eternal covenant — a covenant of vengeance, but vivid with love. Know this, my children, for you have been blessed."

* * *

Their work done, the Cossacks poked through the belongings of the dead, but except for a blanket or two and several pocket watches, they found little that interested them. Some were anxiously nursing strained wrists or examining with some concern the tears in their garments. An argument broke out between the leader of the Cossacks and the one in charge of the team of investigators, who until now had followed their work from a distance — who would attend to the bodies? The Cossacks had their orders, the investigators theirs, and neither included anything about burying dead.

At one point, a Cossack raised his blade and an investigator produced a pistol, but then someone pointed out that in any case, neither team had any shovels, so the responsibility would have to be handed over to the local authority. What of the diseases that the dogs would carry? And the gas that would spread if the burial were delayed? Once again, that would be the problem of the local authority. With the matter comfortably settled, they all rode off. The day was growing hot, and flies were beginning to swarm.

Miraculously, Avrum Vishinsky, age nine, and his brother Hershel, seven, found themselves still alive. Close to eighty people had been killed, and no tricks or devices had saved them. By curling themselves tightly under some thick blackberry bushes, the two boys had somehow escaped notice. They had come within a hair's breadth of being trampled by the horses, but that didn't happen, and they didn't look up until long after the horses had galloped off and the men's voices had thinned to nothing. Even then, they had remained fearful and hesitant. Dust and rotted leaves stuck to the heavy sweat on their faces and got into their eyes, but nothing could blur the picture of impossible horror that spread out before them.

It was a sight that had no part in this world, and if their eyes recoiled, the clouds of flies going about their business impressed on them the reality of it all. They found the crumpled bodies of their mother and father, but horror upon horror, they seemed more like strangers now than the people who had shared with them the same warm rooms and hard table. Avrum tore crazily at his hair and clothes. He would have torn the flesh from his bones if his lungs did not have to struggle so for air. Frail Hershel clung desperately to Avrum's shirtsleeve, his fixed, unblinking eyes exposing an impossible madness.

* * *

"As for the rest of us, I see us deep into the gates of the most awesome and terrible night, and I, Hassia, from the house of Neiditch, eldest daughter of the great Hassid and visionary reb Mendel Sheinman, shamefully cannot harden myself at this hour of final judgment.

"Yet your blessing is no less mine, for it signals my cleansing, and thus will I prostrate myself at the feet of the Blessed One, whose name is sanctified. Cling to this vacant heart, my children, and fasten yet to these words, for this is the manner in which you shall go forth into alien lands.

"Hershel, kin to the timid and unquiet deer, will be chased by the rustling of leaves and the timeless echoes of the prophets. Your very unrest shall be your armor, and you will let no station rise around you. For your heritage is the shifting sands of Sinai, and the restless stars that paint the skies will yet deliver you to the mountains at Paran.

"And Avrum . . . Avrum, my firstborn — you are a multitude of one and a multitude apart. Your heritage will be delivered unto you violated and defiled, for it is the Land of Canaan. Then the pestilence born from their dogs will overtake your armor, for your shield that was resignation and your sword that was perseverance shall wither. But until that day, you shall proceed not by mortal will, but by distant design. Let not disparate incidents and separate calamities blind you to this design.

"And then . . . only then shall you shed your tired armor and embrace what you have learned from you enemies. And you shall smite them. And on that day, the artery that was rent shall be healed; the tree shall find its ancient roots, and you shall have inherited the land.

"This is the gift and the burden of your deliverance, my children. And whoever shall venture to abort this pledge from on high shall be stricken. This is the Word."

(3)

Hershel collapsed at his mother's side. His fists pulled at her dress, and his wailing cracked the still air. It was a wailing to provoke the hills and the heavens, but these were long inured to the suffering of men. When finally he lifted himself away from her, his face was awash with the thick humors of grief, and it was like a mirror for the earth to know itself.

Avrum looked down at his mother. Alone in the ocean of mutilated bodies, hers seemed clean and entirely untouched. The soil was dry around her, and yet there was no mistaking the heavy mask of death that had bonded to her face.

It had only been an hour, perhaps two, since she had awakened them and frightened them with her urgent and mysterious words. It was a mad woman — another creature altogether — and not their mother who had pressed their faces into her wildly heaving chest. As the words issued from her lips, he remembered thinking strangely that the voice was not in the least familiar. It was as if the tongue of another had replaced hers, and that the mild and retiring woman he knew as his mother was not there with them. Truly, he would have sworn this. And yet, it was as though she had never spoken to them at all, for her image was now overtaken by the blur of the carnage.

Now as he stood over her, her words escaped him entirely. He raised his hand to his neck: the thin silver chain she had placed around it even before uttering a word was still there. There was one for him, and another for Hershel. Each carried a talisman in the form of a *mezuzah*, which was thinner but about as long as his little finger. Even in the dark of the night, he remembered seeing how she brought the silver oval capsules to her lips before slipping them over their heads.

There had been more than words that reached into Avrum's terrified heart, however. From an impossible distance, repeated bursts of light as though from within his eyes had dissolved into a frenzy of gray, ethereal images that appeared and disappeared with the flow of her words. The images seemed to be not of this world nor of this time, but it had been her words that delivered them, and that fit them into the weave of the darkness that draped the earth.

The giant tried the door, but it was locked. Over the talk and the laughter inside, someone asked who it was. The answer came from a heavy boot, which drove into the lock and splintered the rotted frame. The door swung away. A sudden, electrified silence froze everything where it was, but a moment later, a pack of faceless gray dogs — wild-eyed, needle-haired, and fangs in drenching froth — sprang to their feet. A hundred pulsing knives separated them instantly from the giant at the doorway, who stood frozen in silence. Towering above them, he studied the room. One of the dogs, crouching low and inching forward, motioned for the others to spread out. Very slowly, it approached the giant, turning its knife slowly over and over in the flat of its paw.

"What the freaking hell you think you're doing here, mister?"

Was Avrum hearing words, or was it the wind and the crackling of leaves?

The images dissipated into nothing — but only for a moment. Again, they fitted tightly into the flow of his mother's words.

The giant grabbed a chair.

The dog shouted for the others to attack. A few lunged forward, and the chair slammed into two of them. First blood had been drawn. The giant kicked the third in the chest, but the fourth slammed a broken, jagged-edged bottle into the giant's chin and neck. Turning, the giant lifted the writhing animal off the ground and threw it like a broken toy against the wall. Blood was beginning to drain beneath the giant's shirt now, and his face wore a grotesque mask of madness.

The images suddenly shattered into fragments, and from fragments into dust. Avrum had felt his mother's trembling arms clutching him more tightly to her bosom; her breast thumped against his cheeks.

The most fearsome of the dogs, the largest and darkest one, made its move. Spitting and snarling, it threw a bottle at the giant's face, hoping it would distract him long enough to close in with its knife. The giant sidestepped the lunge and caught the dog by its carpals. An instant later his massive hand closed over its muzzle. With a sudden, savage, and unforgiving smash against the edge of a table, he shattered its bones. The knife dropped to the floor. The beast howled. The giant broke a leg off the chair and hammered it unmercifully against its mouth and toward those trying to get at his back. They fell like flies, and those not on the floor raced to get out.

Above him were only the night and a foreboding silence. Avrum felt his mother struggling to catch her breath; with the tension in her arms and the desperation of her clutch never abating, Avrum knew that the life he had known up to that moment would never more be. He lent himself to the rocking of her body. The images again emerged from the darkness. He was partner to their world now.

Another single blow demolished the dog's nose, flattening the bone and cartilage so that the animal's face lost every semblance of natural proportion. The shapeless, disfigured mass dropped to the floor, unconscious. The giant wouldn't let up the fury of his attack, and delivered a vicious kick squarely between the hind legs of the crumpled, broken, prostrate body. A large pool of blood quickly collected where the body lay.

A knife plunged into his shoulder near his neck and stayed there. The giant caught the arm that had driven it, and instantly broke it at the elbow. It snapped like a dry twig. He worked the bottle out of the hand of another dog, and threw it hard at the animals rushing for the door. It caught one of them on its ear; when the bottle fell, the side of the dog's face was half torn away.

The chain came down on his back again, and another knife cut into his arm. The giant was able to latch onto the dog who wielded the knife, and with his free hand, removed the knife that was still in his shoulder. He was bleeding profusely. The dog in his grip howled and pleaded for its life. Lifting it over his head, the giant hurled the animal across the room into the one who still had the chain. Both crashed heavily to the floor.

There was then no one left moving in the room but them, and the giant kicked at their heads and bodies, until they, too, stopped moving.

* * *

The boys sensed danger in staying where they were. The calamity of the horror that had befallen everything and everyone linking them to their lives would forever bind them to this place and this time. And the air that now rushed in and out of their heaving chests promised no legitimacy to their continued existence. It was calamity that delivered them to a seething ocean of fear that swelled to impossible heights and dropped to the most terrifying depths. How could it be that among all the mutilated bodies, they did not discover their own slashed and bloodless corpses?

Under his breath, Avrum muttered that the Cossacks might return at any moment and find them alive. They would come back with their dogs, he thought — dogs that could stiffen a body just by baring their teeth. They would make sport of their torture. The boys had to put a great distance between themselves and this place. There was nothing but black smoldering ashes where their village once stood, so there was nothing to go back to, nor was there a soul anywhere in the world who might know them and might be waiting for them. The hard, cracked, and dusty road beckoned them, and Avrum pulled on Hershel's sleeve. Hershel didn't resist.

There was the great synagogue in Lvov — this they knew from their father's accounts. On one occasion, he had even been there, but truly, he might have been describing a castle above the clouds. Still, it was where the villagers had hoped to find refuge. Neither boy had been to any city before, and in their minds Lvov loomed as a distant and foreign land — foreign and forbidding, with army men, violent Cossacks, and hard, aggressive Christians who would make their presence a glaring contradiction to the temper of the city. But they would worry about what they'd find in Lvov when they reached it. Now they had to move on.

Wary of being found on the road, the boys climbed into the hills, but not so far as to lose sight of the road. They followed its direction, and the trees and rocks hid them. Thorns cut into their skin and branches slapped at them. Their jackets were full of pine sap; they wished they could discard them, but the ragged garments remained the only protection they had against the flies and gnats. They would have nothing else to cover them in the night.

After every bend in the road was another one farther ahead. One hill led to another, and the road seemed to go on forever. There was no hint of a city; nothing disturbed the dust on the road. Persistent pangs of hunger and thirst reminded them that starvation was a death, too.

Just when the evening gray made the hills, the sky, the trees, and the road all melt into one another, they were able to make out the speck of an isolated house about half a mile away. As they got closer, a dull yellow glow gave it an outline, which surely meant that someone was living there. They might have waited until morning to approach. Better judgment would have advised them to hold back until they could see who lived there, but the light was too welcoming, and the strange and ominous noises that night had loosed frightened away all better reason. They made their way down to the road, and there broke into a run.

There was a fence around the house, but it was broken, rotted, and down in parts. They could hear the low clucking of chickens. Yet, just as they were about to pass through the gate, their hopes suddenly deserted them. Their hearts thumped madly. Whoever lived in the house had no reason to be friendly. On the other hand, the boys were plainly no danger to anyone. The house itself was an odd, spindly structure full of shadows. It had a porch, but the three stairs leading up to it were broken, and much of the first step wasn't there at all. The light from inside was unsteady, but it filled the window and framed the door invitingly. They called out.

It was a dog's sharp bark that answered. The boys grabbed at each other in terror. Deep, slow, throaty barks followed, but now they seemed to lack conviction. The boys drew back a yard or two, but didn't run away. The light behind the window began to shake, and shadows darted everywhere until a shutter was pushed open and a lamp thrust out.

"Who is out there?" It was an old woman's loud and crackled voice, but the boys didn't answer.

"Who is out there?" she repeated almost desperately. "Jesus, help me. Come to the front."

"It's us. Just us," cried Avrum, trying to control the tremor in his voice. "Two boys — we're out here by the gate." He was close to choking on the words.

"Who?"

"Just us. We're two boys, and don't want anything. We just saw the light."

"Go away. Away! Away! Do you hear me? Go away. I'll set the dog on you. Go away!"

"Can we have some bread — maybe something to drink?" asked Avrum. A sliver of confidence touched him; she was, after all, an old woman, who it seemed was frightened of them. They could show her that they were harmless and in distress. A woman would be given to compassion.

"Who are you? Get where I can see you."

"We're here. Just me and my brother."

The boys were able to see her more clearly now. She really was an old woman and as horrible and wretched looking as they had ever seen. Her face was knotted and bitten with patches of hair under her chin. Her skin seemed to have been sucked into every cavity in her skull. The butt of a cigarette was in her mouth. Suddenly, she brought the lamp back into the house and a moment later appeared with it at the door.

"Now, you two come closer, but not too close." The dog was behind her. He was an old heavy thing, with little fur and a dragging belly. Still, when he jumped off the porch, the boys ran.

"And stay away — stay away from here!" she shouted after them.

Avrum turned. Still backing away, he called at her. "We didn't want to stay . . . not to stay — just wanted some bread or a potato and a drink of water. It's by accident that we got here. We want to go to Lvov." Then, a flash of pain ripped through his foot when it caught in a fissure in the rock over which the path ran. It had twisted and pulled a ligament. But he stood erect, his muscles tight and ready to outrun the dog if it chased them.

"Where did you come from?"

"From the Polish side, but everything there burned down and everyone was killed."

"Go back to the Polish side. You're not allowed here."

"We want to go to Lvov." This from Hershel.

The woman hesitated. She called to the dog, and with a shake of her head ordered it back into the house. Picking up a stick that lay on the porch and still carrying the lamp, she lowered herself to the ground and hobbled over to the boys.

"Jews!" Again, almost in disbelief, "Jews?"

The boys said nothing.

"Jews and robbers. You can't fool me. Do you think that I'll let you steal from me?"

"We aren't robbers," said Avrum and Hershel as one.

Her body was not much less distorted or disfigured than her face. The sweater she wore seemed to just hang with nothing filling it. But her hips . . . her hips bulged and swelled so that only a bench might contain its mass. And her thick, stockinged legs were literally like tree trunks, without a suggestion of difference between calf and ankle. Her feet spilled from her shoes. Hantshik's mother, who used to live near them in the village, had the same legs, and they were always bringing the leeches to them.

"You'll steal anything you can! Come in the night and steal what you can, eh? But not from me. I can still break your bones."

Hershel began to cry. Avrum shook him to make him stop.

"It's an accident that we're here. That's the truth," said Avrum. "This was the first house on the road, and we don't know how much farther we have to go before we reach Lvov. We aren't robbers. We're lost and need water. Water will be enough and we will go."

"Just water, eh?"

"And a potato, if you have a potato."

She was standing next to them now and the fetid smell of her engulfed them; it was the smell of rancid fat and old flesh mixed with wet hay. Their nostrils had never known anything as foreign as this. They wouldn't touch more than water, either, and even that with reluctance. She walked around them, tapping their bodies with her stick. Plainly, they were no danger to her.

"Did you ever do any work in your life?" she asked, focusing her attentions specifically on Avrum.

"What work?" he replied.

"Work . . . any work — feeding the chickens . . . where you have to use your back." She swatted his shoulder, but not very hard. Avrum stayed his ground. He tested his sprained foot and repressed any surrender to the pain. Hershel began to tug at Avrum's arm, wishing to pull him away from her.

"All right. Come inside, and I'll give you something."

"The dog," muttered Hershel, but Avrum quashed his own hesitations and pulled Hershel toward the house. His strides remained long and sure; if there was a hint of a limp when his weight shifted to the sprained foot, he was still without any conscious experience of pain.

Inside, she set the lamp on the table that stood in the middle of the room. From the door, the boys could see a big black iron stove, and in the corner next to it, a stack of wood that reached almost to the ceiling. There was a chicken standing on one of the logs and about five or six more scurrying about on the floor. Over where they were standing, the ceiling had fallen in and some beams and rafters were exposed, but perhaps that was by design, because to one side was a ladder that led up to it; a great stack of hay filled most of the space between what remained of the ceiling and the roof. The hay was also thick on the floor.

Across from them, a door led to another room. It was half open, but too dark inside to make out what might be there. Almost a dozen different crosses hung on the walls. Some had images of a body draped listlessly across them. A large one of polished wood had a photograph set into it; it was brown and cracked with age, a little faded at the bottom, but still showed clearly the face of a man — clean, lean, and sharply etched. The eyes were not frowning, but they were cold, and his hair was cropped short enough for one to take him for bald. Other crosses were adorned by strings of beads, but over all of them was a think layer of black grime. The stench in the room was heavy, foul, and offensive — so thick they felt it in their eyes, and so smothering that their heads began to turn with dizziness.

She didn't ask them in, but instead handed Avrum a bowl and told him that at the back of the house was a pump. There was a little water in the bowl, but it wasn't for drinking: Avrum was to pour it down the spout before bringing the water up.

"It's dark."

"You'll find it if you're thirsty."

Hershel was across the porch when Avrum turned.

"Avrum, I'm thirsty. Come on." He jumped to the ground, but from the corner of his eye, he saw Avrum take a step and falter.

"Come on. What's the matter?"

"It's my foot." Avrum was plainly favoring his sore foot now, but he got to the ground and they rushed to the back of the house. The dog was behind them — coming from nowhere, but now he wasn't menacing. "It's the foot I caught in the rock."

"There's the pump," cried Hershel. "It's like the one we had in the village."

In a flash, he got it to and began to work the handle. After three or four plunges, he had the vacuum; when water poured out of the spout, he abandoned the handle and raced around to drink it while it was still running. Avrum replaced him and worked the lever slowly. The water poured into Hershel's clothes, but his mouth remained glued to the spout. Then Avrum had his turn, and he, too, got his clothes soaked. They choked on the water and their bodies shook with coughing. Close to exhaustion, both found a dry spot on the ground and remained silent, lending themselves only to their lungs straining for air. The dog lapped the water that had spilled, and the sound reminded them of where they were.

"I'm not going back in there, Avrum. The smell chokes me. And if she gives us anything to eat, it will only be poison."

"A potato has a peel. If we remove the peel, it will be clean."

"Still . . ."

"Look, it won't be so bad. If we stay in there a while we'll get used to the smell. And our clothes are wet. If we sleep outside, we'll freeze. Like this, we'll lie on hay, and our clothes will dry. Maybe we should even clean them before we go into the city. And my foot hurts."

Hershel began to cry again. Avrum turned to face him directly. "Look, tomorrow for sure we'll be in Lvov. How far away can it be? There we'll find the *shuleh*, so tonight is our last night like this."

"Mama . . ."

"No Mama, Hershel. Come."

Avrum was as tortured with trepidation as his brother, but now there was an evil and ominous thumping in his foot. It was swelling inside his shoe — he could feel it pressing. Standing on it sent needles charging through his body. "And I just can't walk, Hershel; I just can't walk. Tonight will pass and it will be better by tomorrow."

"What are you doing there? Looking for what to steal?" The woman shouted from inside the house and banged on the wall with her stick.

"No, no. We're coming in," Avrum shouted back. "We're coming in."

(4)

> *Yet the wrath of the winter was not appeased until it rent even this single artery, so that each existence grew separate, apart, and unknown to the other.*

As they stepped through the doorway with Avrum gripping Hershel's shoulder for support, the woman slipped behind them and began to beat them with a poker. She was in a frenzy, wildly hysterical, shouting, "I HAVE YOU! I HAVE YOU!" with every blow. Blood immediately ran from Avrum's head, and while he stood there stunned, she slammed it again across his ear and hard down on his back. He fell. Hershel had only been grazed and he jumped away, his eyes wild with terror.

"MAMA!" he screamed. "MAMA . . . A . . . A!"

The woman had no interest in him. On the floor, Avrum was moaning and crying, and she stood over him, the poker threatening in her hand.

"I have you. I have you. I have you," she repeated madly. "I have you." She was heaving wildly and snorting uncontrollably.

"Don't kill him!" shrieked Hershel, his body bent over and shaking. "Don't kill him!"

"Get out of here, you—" She lifted the poker over her head and took a half step toward him.

"Waaa . . . a . . . a . . . a!" Hershel panicked and began to dart madly around the room. "He's my brother — my brother."

"I'll kill you and him, you filthy little Jew. Get the hell out of this house."

"AVRUM!!"

"Hershel, she is going to kill me!" And instantly, Avrum felt the poker again, twice, on his ribs and back. He tried to get up. His head was a fearful sight, covered with blood now, and it caught the third blow. A whimper escaped him and he dropped.

"Avrum! . . . AVRUM!"

Blindly and desperately, Hershel threw himself at the woman to push her away. There was little power in his lunge, and less to his push. She tried to grab him, but he fell to his brother's side and tried desperately to pull him out of the house. Then he saw that the poker was about to come down on him, too. There was a white froth at her mouth and nose.

He fell backwards against the wall, and the iron ripped into his knuckles just as he released his grip. But she advanced, and wouldn't let up her murderous charge. Again, he saw the poker in the air and, with only his instincts now to carry him, he scrambled through the door. There he lost his balance, and rolled across the porch. The dog, confused and excited, lunged at him and barked hotly, but Hershel, shrieking in terror and anguish, rushed away into the night.

In fact, he ran only to the hill at the other side of the road. From there, he kept watch on the house, but the door was closed and he heard nothing. Incredibly, he somehow fell asleep, to awake in a rain. It wasn't morning yet. He called out to his brother and waited. No answer. He called again and still no answer. There was nowhere to go except back to the house. If his brother was dead — best that he, too, should die.

From the road, he threw stones at the house. They clattered from the walls onto the porch, and the last one broke through the shutter. The door was thrown open and the woman holding the same evil poker stepped out, cursing as much with her eyes as with her mouth. Hershel wasn't far from her, but he made no move to run. If she hesitated, it wasn't for long, and a moment later, she was upon him. But in her rush to strike him, the weapon flew from her hand. She grabbed his hair and pounded him with her fist.

"He is mine. I have him and he is mine. Dirty . . . miserable . . . filthy Jew, I'll kill you. I'll feed your eyes to the rats."

Hershel was limp and oblivious to the blows. Then he bit her arm, but she caught his neck, pressed him to the ground, and tried to crush him with her weight. Then they heard Avrum.

"Hershel!" he shouted. "Hershel." The cry was weak.

"Avrum! She wants to kill me, too!"

"Hershel, I'm tied to the stove! I can't move. Hershel! Go to Lvov. Run from her. Run away. Go to the *shuleh* in Lvov, or you'll die."

"AVRUM!"

"Hershel! Go!" But how to get there, Avrum himself didn't know.

"Yes, you heard him. Go! Get away from here." Only with enormous difficulty did she manage to struggle to her feet, but she didn't let go of him. "You want to die, you black little thief?" She pummeled his head.

"Leave me alone!" Hershel wailed in insane desperation. "*Loz mir* . . . Leave me alone!"

They were near a rock and she pulled him over to it. "I'll open your head."

Somehow, Hershel twisted out of her grip and backed away quickly. "Avrum!" he shouted madly, choking on his dry tongue. "Avrum! Avrum!" But there was no answer.

The poker was again in her hand. It had fallen near the rock and she had retrieved it. Hershel saw it and knew that if she got near enough to him now, she would surely kill him. He ran to the road, broken.

Hershel again climbed the wooded hill at some distance now from the house, but from where he could still see it. Despair overwhelmed his mind and heart. The hours passed as though they were seconds. He had seen no one entering or leaving the house. The day was gray, and eventually the moon climbed to the heavens. He slept.

But the night was rich with the eerie howling of wolves and the flapping of wings. Hershel awoke in the darkest of nights and felt the earth alive under him. The old woman was standing over him. Was he dreaming, or had he already been delivered beyond the world of mortals? More than he could see her, he could smell her. And even in the darkness, there was no mistaking the iron poker that her hand held high.

"I killed your brother, and now I will send you to hell," she spat at him.

Somehow, Hershel rolled away and raced blindly down to the road. The poker had again flown from her hand as she swung it at him, but now she came after him with only her curses and flaying arms. He ran toward the house and fell over something he had not seen and still could not see. She was over him again, looming in the darkness as large as a mountain. At that moment, Avrum's desperate voice cracked the air.

"Run from her, Hershel! Run! Don't let her catch you! I can't move. Find your way to Lvov. Find your way to Lvov! It has to be on this road!"

Avrum was still alive!

Hershel backed away from her. She didn't move. They stayed that way until the first light of morning. Then he called to Avrum that he would go to Lvov; there was no reply. He called to him again. Only silence. Even the dog was silent.

(5)

She had followed him for a way, but he kept to the road. When he looked back once and saw that she was still coming after him, he threw a stone at her and broke into a run; it was then that she stopped and watched until he disappeared. There was an excruciating pain in her chest. Her heart was pounding so that she feared it might hemorrhage. Her nose had bled the day before, and again she tasted blood in her throat. But the boy was hers. And it wouldn't necessarily be a bad thing if his brain was torn, for it would dull him and it was only his back that she wanted.

Since Stefan deserted her, everything was collapsing. The sick cow he left her with had died, and the hyenas got to it before she could bring someone to skin it and cut it up. She might have sold it or at least smoked some of the meat for herself, but nothing was left of it now. The house was rotting. Please Jesus the roof would hold for another winter, but the floor was falling from under her. There were packs of rats under it. Every night she would hear them, and at times, the scraping sounded as though it wasn't from below any longer. And they would yet get to her feet — her damn feet. The poison that filled them would be rich meat for them; they'd quickly eat her to the bone. She had been too long on her legs yesterday and now they were swelling as if about to burst. She would have to get them up. But if the boy was to free himself while she was unable to move . . . ?

Back in the house, she tested the bonds and was satisfied that they were holding well. She had tied his hands and legs to the stove with all the rope that she had, and, thinking it wouldn't be enough, she cut up some hemp sacks and tied his neck and shoulders to the stove as well. Then she feared that the blood would draw the rats, so she collected the straw that had absorbed it and stuffed it into the stove. On his head, the blood had coagulated and matted his hair; she didn't want the smell of that to get to the rats, either, so she went for her scissors and cut off what she could. That, too, she threw into the stove.

A grotesque blue and purple eruption swelled on his head — with a gash across the length of it — but she pressed around it and the bone was firm. It would have killed a pig, she thought, but not a Jew. No wonder there were so many! It had been months since anyone had called at her place, and of all the travelers on the road it would have to be Jews who would stop to torment her. Stefan would have had a time with them. Pity, she thought, that the little one got away alive. She might have tried to draw the rats out with his body, but the Djerzys were out there, and those bandits would find his body sweeter than marzipan.

Her second chance to kill the younger one had also come to naught. Her hands had once been strong enough to do anything a man's could; now the power was gone from them, and her legs dragged like impossible weights. Legs that once had danced. Legs that now had to be hours in the air after every few steps.

From the second room, she brought in more straw and made herself a pallet opposite Avrum. She needed to rest and she needed to think. His eyes flashed fear and hatred at her, but he lay quietly. He was hers for the moment, but he'd have to be nailed to the floor or have his legs broken to keep from running off. Doing either of course would make him useless to her, and she needed him. Stefan once had a clamp made that was welded to a long chain, which he would lock around his horse's foreleg. That was a long time ago, but if she could find it, maybe it would also fit around the boy's neck.

"Do you hear me, boy? You're going to stay here. You'll be my Stefan number two. Ha!"

She was on her back and her feet were lifted onto a stool. She pointed to them. "Do you think I can do much with these feet? Look at these feet. How can I work anymore with these feet? I'm a cripple — an old cripple."

Then she remembered something, and heaving and wheezing, she stood up again and went to the wall. From there she removed a small brass crucifix, wiped the dust off on a patch of cloth over her emaciated breast, and fit it under Avrum's jacket.

"There. You won't die now." She pointed a finger at her breast. "*I* think of saving you."

Now lying on her back, she shifted her hips to get her legs back on the stool. A moment later, there was only the thunder of her snoring.

* * *

A commotion on the porch and a sharp knocking at the door broke into her sleep.

"Who?" She glared at Avrum, whose eyes were hard and fixed on her own.

"Mada, Mada, it's Iannuk. Open the door, you stinking black skunk."

"Iannuk?" she shouted back. "Good Jesus." And to Avrum she laughed. "It's Iannuk — my old friend Iannuk . . . everything at once." She opened the door and would have embraced the man, but he stretched his arm out stiffly in from of him and held her off. His disgust and impatience were not hidden.

"Crow! Same old decrepit crow! Why did you stop shaving?"

"Iannuk! Holy Jesus, you knew just when to come. A year can pass and I don't see you, but you've come when I never needed you more."

"What's the matter this time?"

"I'll tell you. The matter is inside, lying by the stove. Go in and look."

"When were you ever without headaches?" He turned his head to a side and spat. Then he called to a party of men waiting on the road. "There is a pump at the back of the house. Peter, take the empty skins and fill them, and don't forget mine. I'm going inside for a minute."

"Just water, Iannuk. No chickens. Tell them. No chickens."

"I don't have to. Who doesn't know how cheap and miserly you are? They all know Stefan."

With that, he pushed past her; for Avrum, it was as though a darkness had filled the room. He had heard of giants stalking the land, but he never imagined that anything human could grow into such a massive, hulking body. His shoulders bulged and spread like those of an ox, and they seemed to swallow up his neck. The man was wearing a fur jacket, something brown and gray, and the sleeves were cut at the elbows. But what protruded from them seemed as hard, as black, and as dangerous as iron cudgels.

"Stefan?" She tried to pull him back to her. "You spoke with him? You know where he is?"

"What in the name of Christ is this? What do you have here?"

"You know where he is?" she asked again. "Iannuk, tell me. He has to come back to me."

"His head is still screwed on his neck. He won't ever come back." Iannuk spat his words pulling his jacket out of her grip. "Bad enough you've grown into a freak, but how does a human put up with the smell here? You shit on the floor?"

"Iannuk!" She struck him weakly but in anger. He ignored her. "I'm alone — all alone," she whined.

"Where did this come from?" He pointed at Avrum.

"It's a Jew. I caught him last night. Me. Alone. By myself. I caught him. There was another one with him, too. So I'm a freak, eh, Iannuk? There are still some things I can do."

"What are you going to do with him? You need him to diddle you?"

"I need him to work. That's a pig in your mouth."

"You really expect this child to work? Who was the other one?"

"Even smaller than him. His brother maybe. Look at that," she said, pointing to the broken window. "Just this morning it was in one piece, then he threw a stone through it. If I had caught him, I would have killed him. Where am I going to get a new window now, eh? Where? Where? Where? Where?"

"Cover it with boards."

A chicken squawked in panic outside. An instant later, there was a chorus of squawking chickens.

"They're after the chickens, Iannuk. They're after the chickens! Stop them." She rushed to the door. "Hey! Hey! Leave the chickens," she shouted. "Only water, you said."

"We'll pay you."

"Money doesn't lay eggs," she wailed. "The pigs are gone, and Stefan took the one good cow with him. All I have left are the chickens. What is left for me? Just the chickens!"

She stormed past Iannuk with a hip slamming into a chair. Outside, she shouted furiously and desperately. "Leave them! Good Jesus! Goddamn! Leave them! Iannuk, they're all after the chickens. I'm going to die!"

"Die then," said Iannuk almost to himself.

There was a scuffle outside and some laughter and cursing, but this giant, towering now over the prostrate huddling bundle, looked into the boy's hard and distant eyes. He poked him with his boot and studied the wound on his head, but said nothing. Finally, sure of what he was doing, he bent over and tore the rope and sacking from the stove legs, undid the bonds with a twist and a jerk of his fingers, and in the same motion, lifted Avrum onto the stool by the table. Outside, the commotion still raged.

"What did she do to your head?" There was a sharp smell of whiskey on his breath, and it seemed like the freshest air in the whole dank and foul room. When he spoke, the sounds vibrated in his throat for a long time before they filled into words. And he spoke slowly, unhurried. This man would never worry about interruptions.

"She hit me with the iron." Avrum's breath was rapid and shallow. A massive tremor suddenly overtook his body. His muscles jerked involuntarily. There was a second spasm, then a third. The man terrified him, and he struggled not to swallow his tongue.

"You're untied, but try to break away and they'll have to peel you from the wall." He showed Avrum the back of his hand, and that was convincing enough. "Now, what's your story? I'll pinch out your eyes if even one word is a lie."

"I came with my brother."

"From where?"

"We lived in a village that they burned down. It was next to the Polish side, but everything burned down when the militia came looking for a — a — I don't know . . . I don't know — a horse . . . a crook or something."

"So where are the people from this village? Where are they now?"

"It all burned down. Nothing was left, so all the families together decided to go to Lvov. Everybody together. My mother, my father, my brother, and me."

"I'm asking you again: Where are they now?"

"The Cossacks—" Avrum caught himself. This man might just be one of them. To tell him what they had done might fix in him a notion to finish what they had started. "Well . . . riders came . . . on horses . . . with dogs . . . maybe Poles . . . and they finished everyone with shooting — my mother and father, everyone — and they are all lying there still." He struggled for air. "We were going to Lvov, that's all . . . there was nothing left in the village . . . and right in the morning — it wasn't even morning — it was just yesterday morning, these riders came in . . . maybe Poles because of the fire . . . then they began shooting and swinging their knives and axes — chopping right and left. Everyone shouted 'Stop! Stop!' but they finished with everyone."

"Where was this? It couldn't be far from here."

"I don't know. We left the place and walked for a whole day, until we stopped here for water."

"*We* is you and your brother?"

"Yes."

"Where is he now?"

"I don't know. She chased him and I hope — maybe he got to Lvov."

"They were Cossacks, no — wearing those dumb hats and white jackets?"

"Fur hats . . . yes . . . most of them — some in brown hats."

"And how did you get away? What made you — you and your brother — so special?"

"I don't know. They just didn't see us."

A stomping was heard on the porch, and the woman was back in the room. Her face was flushed purple and red, and the veins in her cheeks were prominent and pulsing furiously. She threw four chickens onto the floor and they scrambled away in a flurry of feathers, clucking and squawking.

"Waaa! He's mine! He's mine! Why did you untie him? I need him. O holy Jesus — mother of Jesus!" she screamed. "Tie him up again — I beg you, Iannuk, I can't lose him." She ran in her grotesque shuffle to pick up the rope and then lunged at Avrum. "Murderer! Murderer — Iannuk!"

In terror of her, Avrum's body suddenly flooded with life. He threw himself to one side, and there was an instant then when everything froze. The door was open and he bolted in blind panic. Outside, the men saw him, and one of them instantly gave chase. Iannuk's voice boomed out, ordering them to stop him, and two others immediately took off. Altogether, this was becoming a fun day for them.

On the road, Avrum ran with a vigor not his own. His legs responded to an energy quite apart from anything his body was generating, and that insulated him from every pain. He couldn't even feel the ground under them. He didn't have to turn around to know that there was someone behind him. The pounding on the road came from more than one pair of legs.

The man just behind Avrum was young and fast, but though only about three yards separated him from Avrum, he couldn't gain on him. The boy was carried by wings, not legs. If he wouldn't let up his furious pace, there would be no catching him. His lungs were more than hinting now that they wouldn't hold much longer. Damn cigarettes and *wishniak* killed his legs. He'd be mocked for a week if the boy escaped. His eyes searched for a rock while he ran, and he was able to pick one up without breaking his pace much. Then he threw it hard, and gave up.

It struck Avrum heavily high on his back. This broke the flow of his stride, making him fall forward. The sand and stones tore through the skin on his hands and ripped through his trousers to cut into his legs. He was about to rise — blind to everything — when a boot drove viciously into his rump. The men laughed and congratulated themselves, and wondered aloud what that freakish woman had to do with this urchin. Avrum lay stiff and silent. Hands lifted him onto a shoulder and he was carried back to the house. His mind still blurred and his body racked by nightmarish shooting pains when Iannuk's hand smashed into the side of his face and threw him into a faint.

Water poured onto his head couldn't rouse him. Iannuk ordered that the boy be put on their wagon, but laid so that his head would be lower than his legs — and one of the men was to stay with him. "And when he wakes up, give him something to eat and drink."

"He's mine. I don't want him on your wagon."

The woman, frustrated and furious, went for the poker. In her desperation, she had a mind to use it, too.

"Jesus took Stefan from me. What can I do here by myself? Give him back to me. You hear me, Iannuk? Give him back." Then, raising the poker menacingly, she shouted: "Jesus sent me the boy . . . Don't you see? Jesus — Jesus! You can't take him from me."

Iannuk withdrew a flask from inside his jacket and was about to throw it at her, when he changed his mind. Instead, he lifted a stool by one of its legs and forced it against her, pushing her to the wall. She swung the poker at him, but he caught her fist in his and crushed it. There was madness in her eyes. Her mouth was open wide and she choked on her tongue.

"Stupid woman. Calm down."

She spit on him and he spit directly back on her. Then he took the poker and threw it out of the house, but, still angry, he lifted the seat of the stool to her face and jammed her against the wall. When he relaxed, she fell to the floor — a broken, misshapen mass of flesh. Froth appeared at the corners of her mouth, and she had to struggle to breathe.

Iannuk took a few coins from his pocket and counted them carefully.

"How many chickens were there?" He asked the men at the door.

"Twelve."

"Twelve? No more?" He set the coins on the table. "You have enough there for the boy, too — much more than he's worth."

The woman didn't answer. Her face was beet red now. Hatred raged in her eyes.

"Crow! How long do you think you'd have been able to hold onto him? Even with me here, he ran away."

"What are you going to do with him?" asked one of the men.

"If he doesn't die, we'll use him to help with the cooking. What do you say, Bohdan? You'll find something for him, no?"

"Boss, if I can't use him, I'll cook him," said the one called Bohdan, who laughed the loudest at his own joke. He was still laughing when the man on the wagon called out that Avrum was coming to. A few of the men walked over to study their new prize.

In the house, the woman, her head scraping the floor, crawled slowly to the table. Iannuk thought she was going for the money, but instead, she reached for the matches, which were under the bag of tobacco. Iannuk watched her with scorn and some amusement, but he didn't move. To the men still at the door he said, "If she wants to burn the house down, I'll help her."

He thought that she really wanted nothing more than to get back to her senses with a cigarette, and if she didn't seem to be so overtaken with freakish diseases, he'd have offered her his flask. Instead, she look two, three, and four matches from the box, and with one swipe lit them all. Pressing her lips tightly against her black gums and baring the few teeth left in her mouth — never moving her eyes from Iannuk — she threw the matches onto the straw. No one moved to stop her, and when the fire found firm roots, a grotesque smile and wild eyes fixed on her face. Iannuk looked at the money on the table and considered leaving it there. Deciding otherwise, he shook his head and returned the coins to his pocket. Then he pushed the men out of the doorway.

“The first sensible thing that she ever did in her life,” he muttered. Then to the men he said, “If there are more chickens around, take them all and let’s move on.”

Just as the wheels began to turn, they saw the rats — gray, black, some of them as big as cats — rush into the field like the flow of a river. But only the rats deserted the house as the rippling crackles and thickening smoke orchestrated its death.

(6)

The thought of owning the soul of a Jew — even if it was as unimpressive a specimen as Avrum, broken and defeated — teased the imaginations of the men. To fill the monotony of the road, they let wild and lurid scenarios of themselves alone with the boy swirl through their minds; their narrow sidelong stares, fixed and unblinking on the boy, augured evil for the chapter in his life which was about to unfold. Some smirked at him. Others joked about him to release the strange and uneasy tension that came over them. They drank continuously, except for Iannuk, who from the start had fit himself into a prone position and fallen asleep. No one spoke of the woman, but someone had said that now Stefan finally had the likelihood of a bigamy charge lifted from him.

Avrum was sitting on the floor with his back against sacks of flour and with the chickens with their tied feet draped over his feet. He was aware of the men’s stares, but his distress was the terrible and gnawing ache in his heart of feeling the wheels carrying him farther and farther away from Hershel. If Hershel somehow managed to reach Lvov, and if God helped him find the *shuleh* there, they’d be waiting for him — they may even go out looking for him — but the two were severed now, severed and lost. God alone knew for how long. For long hours, he wept bitterly within himself.

Later, Zum, the fellow who had run after him and caught him with the rock, washed and painted his scalp with vodka. Avrum suffered its fires with silent, open eyes, but tears soon filled them. The men laughed; one of them said that vodka was the best sterilizer, and the same man abruptly poured some from his bottle over Avrum's head. It burned deeply, but Avrum steeled himself better this time.

"You're wasting it," said Zum. He had made a doughnut-shaped ring from a piece of cloth and held it out to the man. "If you have enough to throw away, spill some on this."

"Use your own." Still, he held the bottle over the cloth.

Zum tipped the mouth of the bottle to the cloth and set it still dripping over the purple black swelling. Where the skin was torn, crusty, and still oozing he sprinkled a sulphur dust, and with another cloth, he wrapped the head tightly. That done, he searched for something in a bag. It was a meat sandwich. He handed it to Avrum along with a pot of water, and Avrum devoured it with two tearing bites. Someone proffered a chunk of bread cake, and when that was also gone, he drained the water. Some of it seeped into the wrong passage and he doubled over coughing. Meanwhile, the horses pulled and the wheels turned.

* * *

The earth was still spongy from the melted snow, but the moss was already thick on the old trees. His mother was on the bench behind the house, scraping the innards of a Sabbath fish into a pail, and she had drawn her collar to the side to let the warm sun flood her pale skin. Scales caked her hands and her fingers were glistening red. Sometimes she'd throw something to Saltche the cat and it would disappear between her claws and jaws.

"Mama," his eyes were fixed on her busy hands, "what part of me is really me?" He thought that a smile had settled at the corners of her lips, but it wasn't a smile at all.

"What kind of a question is that?" She asked.

"It's just a question. Is it my eyes? My head?"

His mother slowly wiped the knife and her hands on her apron and turned to look at him. Her eyes had grown deep and watery, but words didn't come to her at once. Avrum had expected her to say that that was just one of those questions which had no answer. She was always saying that.

"Look at what you're doing to the fish. What part do you have to cut out before it stops being a fish?"

He wasn't sure she was listening. Finally, she said in her soft way, "Skin and bones belong to the dust, my little one. What is really you is the wind God has breathed into you, and the carriage reins he put in your hands for you to make your way in life."

It was an answer that might have fomented another hundred questions, but his mother quickly made them all unnecessary.

"Let me tell you something about this wind, Avremeleh. It is only strong in the man who trusts God to carry him where the Holy Blessed One intended. If he holds the carriage reins in this way, he will own the wind forever. More than this — with a grip on these reins, this man will be able to rise above every cruelty and every evil in the world." Then she caressed his cheek with the back of her hand, but her lips were tight and there was no smile.

* * *

Avrum was to stay with these men for over ten years. They weren't always the same men; every season brought its new faces and removed some of the old. Seven to eight months of the year were spent in the forests of Szambor and Urman bringing down the towering firs. Another two months were taken up with work at the sawmills at Szambor, and when winter was at its heaviest, most of the men would disperse to regroup either there or at Urman sometime between mid-March and early April.

Although the winter months brought a brisk demand for lumber for firewood, keeping most of the mills busy, Iannuk preferred to leave the forests and the heavy snows to sub-contractors. He would mark the trees for them to bring down and they would come with their own teams of lumbermen, horses and heavy sleds. Some of Iannuk's men would stay on with them.

As the first days and months passed, Avrum made increasing references to his separation from Hershel. The thought that his brother might possibly have made it to Lvov always brought with it intense feelings of shame and guilt for having so abandoned him. But from the start, Iannuk made it clear that his only home now was with him and with his men in the forests. This wasn't delivered as a threat, but as simple fact. "Your Hershel," Iannuk would tell him, "would have had to cover a distance of over eighty kilometers to reach Lvov."

In softer tones, he would add that the roads along the way were packed with gangs of highwaymen — that a seven-year-old boy would be ripe pickings for these gangs, who would have had their way with his body before killing him. Some gangs, said Iannuk, were even notorious for kidnapping village children, and showing Avrum his hand, said that he didn't need five fingers to count those that remained alive. There was just no way he could have escaped their attention. Besides, he added, the wolves more likely than not would have gotten to him first.

Avrum stayed with Iannuk through the winters of his first years. Iannuk's home was in Burislev, a town smaller than Szambor; they had to cross a tributary of the Dniester and climb for two days into the Carpathians to get to it. It seemed to Avrum that there were at least a dozen children and half as many women waiting there for him — and these didn't include his wife, who almost ignored his arrival. Iannuk said that something had snapped in her head when their last child was born. And, he'd added, the child also wasn't everything it should have been.

By the end of his fourth season there, it would have been almost impossible to recognize Avrum. Little of the spindly, ashen-skinned nine-year-old remained. He had grown almost two feet in height; his light skin was developing a thick and leathery constitution, while his blue eyes, sunk deep in their sockets, remained clear and focused — even piercing. Etched into his strong angular jaws were tight, narrow lips that swelled delicately at the middle, almost like the buds of a rosebush pushing through unfolding leaves. His chest had filled out and broadened, and his shoulders were taking on a low muscular slant, which already hinted at the power that would soon come to them.

If the men once entertained lascivious or perverted designs on his body, they were cancelled out that very first day, when Bohdan had drunk so heavily that any natural sense of proportion escaped him. To demonstrate his sudden ambitions — "I'm gonna let you see some meat that can do with a little cooking" — he opened his trousers. Spitting, grunting, and laughing stupidly, he shook his pasty organ over the boy's nose. From nowhere, it seemed, a fist slammed into his mouth, and another crushed his ear. It was Iannuk who fell upon Bohdan like a raging behemoth. Bohdan pleaded through his bleeding lips, but he hardly had time to make sense of the pain in his face when he felt a wet coolness over his groin and legs. The coolness didn't last long. Iannuk had taken Bohdan's bottle and spilled whatever vodka was left onto him.

The men roared in convulsive laughter, but later they too stirred uneasily. Bohdan was in a mess of pain. The blow had broken three teeth, which were eventually extracted. He had to wait a whole season before he could get them replaced, and the cost of the gold would swallow up half his wages. Meanwhile, the hole in his mouth set the law unmistakably with regard to Avrum.

When the mills at Szambor prepared for the winter of Avrum's fourth year there, Iannuk told Avrum that he was now on his own — quite free to go wherever he wished, but that he couldn't accompany him any longer to Bursilev.

"It's possible I won't be going to the family this year," said Iannuk. "It's just possible. In fact, I know I won't."

Avrum studied Iannuk's eyes. A sudden chill overtook him, and despite himself, he felt his heart sinking painfully. Iannuk's eyes were warm and his words were uttered in a low, slow, hushed, almost careful voice, but the words delivered a message of cold abandonment. Yet, what claim could Avrum have even on the air he breathed and the food he ate, let alone a claim on Iannuk? That he was spared the carnage of that terrible morning was at once both his punishment and his crime. He had no legitimate license to expectations of any sort in this world.

"That's alright."
"You'll go to Lvov, I suppose."

After so much time had passed, and after all that Iannuk had said so convincingly about Hershel's inevitable fate, did he still give weight to the possibility that Hershel might actually have survived that road to Lvov? Lvov remained a city he had never been to, even though there were the trains regularly hauling coal and lumber there from the station at Szambor. He would see the name "LVOV" in big letters on a sign behind the engine room, and the name would flood his mind with the depressing, if veiled, images of some painful certainty.

"I suppose."
"It's a big city, so prepare yourself. It's not Moscow or Petersburg, but it's a big city. Anyway, you have enough money — just watch that it stays with you. What about next year . . . April?"
"I don't know."
"If you come back in April, we'll talk about serious money. You're smart. You can have a future."
"Maybe."

His heaviest clothes were on his back, and all of his other belongings barely filled one small cardboard valise. But he was a free man. He even had papers, which Iannuk had arranged for him — traveling papers with his name on them. The important one was a slim red booklet, which had his photograph and a dozen official stamps in it. Iannuk called it a "passport," and Avrum knew in his bones that this passport would be the portal to the rest of his life. A great authority protected him now.

(7)

He was less sure about that authority when he stepped through the hissing vapors and smoke, and stood alone on the platform at Lvov. It was a magnificent building with high walls and massive pillars. A bustle of people rushed with determination in every direction; from their dress and demeanor, it was clear that these were not the thick-shouldered, spitting, cursing lumber workers in whose midst he had lived all these years. Occupied only with themselves and entirely familiar with everything around them, they vacated the station quickly. The engine continued to whistle and clang, shake and shudder. Outside, some people piled their bags and valises onto wagons or waiting carriages. Others were met by people who must have been friends or relatives. A few embraced. In minutes, the station was deserted. Beyond it was a city.

Avrum walked the road leading away from the station. It was snowing heavily, and the roads had narrowed to barely passable lanes. Carriages scraped one another, and people could not avoid colliding. His shoulders and valise seemed to get into everyone's way, and some didn't hesitate to hurl a few expletives at him. He was an alien in their world. He stiffened, but the people walked on.

He had an address in Lvov, but it probably led nowhere. One of the men from their party at Szambor had called him over to where he stood with his buddies, and said with affected sincerity that even if the boy was a *Jide*, he was going to help him. That was the day they were paid their wages and the word that Iannuk had freed him reached everyone's ears.

"They say you're going to Lvov to find your brother, eh?" This was Wladek, who had a black patch over one eye and a deep scar leading to his ear from the other — testimony to a less than pacific past.

"I'm sure he isn't alive."

"And you've never been there, eh?"

"No. Never."

"I thought so. Look, I'm going to give you an address, which you'll thank me for. You just go there and say to whoever comes to the door that I sent you. Wladek . . . just Wladek . . . mention the name once, and you got your ticket. Eh? Now get me some paper and I'll write it down for you." The others tried to hide their smirks. Avrum had ignored them and handed him a crumpled piece of paper that needed unfolding.

Wladek took the paper, wet the tip of a pencil with his tongue, and as he scribbled some lines on the paper, said in the hushed tone of an actor onstage, "These uncut pigs would think I'd fix you, eh? But you trust me, boy, eh? I got no reason to fix you, eh? You'll thank me yet. And remember — anything you need." He read the number and street name he had written aloud. Carefully, too carefully, he folded the paper, opened Avrum's heavy jacket, and with a heavy hand stuffed it deep into his shirt pocket. "Next April I'll want to hear all about it, eh?"

It was a game with him meant to play the fool, but Avrum had learned that such games were safest when tolerated quietly until they were played out. A contrary remark from him and Wladek would have changed in the blink of an eye to the more dangerous game of being offended. It was their last day and Iannuk would soon not be there to keep the tight hold he always had on the reins of their tempers and intentions. He had put the paper in his pocket and now as he walked, he could feel it there crumpled almost into a ball. He took it out, unfolded it carefully, and studied it.

* * *

The house closest to the forest and standing apart from the clump of other houses was where old reb Krimmer lived. The shutters were never seen open, and because they were warped and loose on their hinges, they could never be properly closed, either. Mothers would say to their children, "Don't stray past reb Krimmer's house unless you want the forest pits to swallow you up."

The space between that house and the others was the favorite place for all the stick and jump games in the summer and all the sliding races in the winter, so that Krimmer's yard became the children's second home. But no one ever saw the old man enter it or leave it. Still, no one else lived there — that was certain — and even reb Krimmer had to sleep somewhere.

He was a tall, gaunt man, with cheeks like rotted green tomatoes and eyebrows thick enough to hide a cow. Now, in the village, there were other tall and stringy men, and even men whose cheeks and eyebrow's compared with his, but what set him apart were his hands. Reb Krimmer was the village fiddler; he appeared magically at every wedding and at the birth of every firstborn son. Watching his hands was like watching a tangle of snakes, and the word among the children was that the Angel of Death once came for Krimmer but got trapped in those fingers and escaped only by luck — forgetting what he had come for.

Somehow, little Hershel and gotten it into his head that he was destined to become a fiddler, and he busied himself for days assembling a violin. From a stick here and a box there, with glue from the carpenter and polish made from tea leaves strained in goat's milk and mixed with coal oil, he had his instrument. For strings, he tried horse hair, and many lengths of horse hair tied to the ends of a supple branch gave him a fine bow, only whenever the bow would just begin to bring a sound from the "strings," one or more would snap and hang to the floor. Hershel tried using thicker hairs from the horse's tail, and when these tore, he tried doubling them, all in vain.

Hershel moped for a day. Finally, he put his fiddle under his bed and seemed to give it no more thought. A week later, when the family was about to sit down for supper, Hershel was missing. No one had remembered seeing him after he'd done with lunch. Avrum was dispatched to the homes of Hershel's friends while his father started to knock at the doors of their neighbors. No one had seen him. His mother waited for Avrum, and then went to meet him.

"Go to reb Krimmer's house," she ordered. "Hershel is there getting strings for his fiddle."

"How do you know that, Mama?"

"I just know. Nothing will happen to you." She turned him around and pushed his shoulder.

So he went — or, at least, he had started off in the direction of Krimmer's house. But on the way, Nissen Tvitch — the seamstress' oldest boy and, by reputation, a rebellious and vile-mouthed agitator — had crossed his path. Avrum was almost glad to see him.

"Hey, Nissen — I'm looking for Hershel. Maybe you've seen him?"

"Sure. I know where the pimple is, but I can't tell you." Nissen smirked and spat on the ground.

"Everyone at home is worried. My mother thinks he's at Krimmer's house."

"You're wasting your time. For a groshen, I'll tell you."

Avrum, like most of the other boys, carried a "lucky" groshen in one of the cuffs of his trousers. He delivered it gladly.

"You're wasting your time going to Krimmer's house. Krimmer took him halfway to the cemetery. I'm just coming from that direction, and I saw them fornicating with three of Satan's goats. Actually fornicating!"

"A lie!"

"Please yourself."

Nevertheless, instead of continuing on to Krimmer's house, Avrum turned into the path to the cemetery. He was less aware of where he was going than of where he couldn't yet bring himself to go. In his heart, he was sure that even if Hershel was alone in Krimmer's house, he somehow wouldn't be Hershel anymore.

Just before dark, he heard his name being called from a distance. He shouted back, and a moment or two later saw Hershel and his mother running toward them. They had been out looking for him. It turned out that old Krimmer had given Hershel a lesson on the fiddle, and then sent him home with two good strings. Avrum had a million questions.

"What were you afraid of?" his mother asked after he'd undressed and done with his ablutions.

Avrum had no answer at first, but when he finished the reading of the Sh'ma and his mother pinched out the lamp's wick, he blurted, "I believed there was a deep hole behind reb Krimmer's door — that whoever falls in it falls forever . . . that Hershel was in it, dropping away from us, and the same thing was going to happen to me. But, Mama, believe me, I was going to go after him even so."

"Mama — I just needed time to be strong."

* * *

It seemed to be a legitimate address. Avrum was keeping to the main streets; the others seemed almost entirely blocked off by the snow, and even the horses had difficulty getting through.

He showed the address to the keeper of a kiosk, who immediately sneered, but who gave him reasonably accurate directions. Avrum interpreted the sneer as a tic or itch, or perhaps he was trying to get something out from between his teeth. But there was, after all, such an address. He bought hard onion bread from the man, and a sweet cherry juice. The cold was less biting now.

Farther on, at another kiosk, he asked a second time. Directions again were immediately forthcoming, this time without insinuation or nuance. He had to cross five or six more streets, and turn right when he came to a bridge; from there, there were still another five or six streets until on his left he would come to a lane with a green gate blocking it. Not to worry — the gate was always open. At the end of the lane was the street he was looking for.

And Avrum found it. The house showing the number he was looking for was not far away; it was on the second story, and stairs from the street led directly up to it. On this back street, carrying a patched valise and wearing an oversized coat so different from what others were wearing, Avrum was suddenly overcome with the terrible, if familiar, reality of his isolation. He struggled not to surrender to despair. What could possibly be in that house, he wondered. What, after all, could he expect from anyone who knew Wladek? He felt inside his coat for his papers. They were still there. He might go to a police station and ask them to lead him to the synagogue. The papers would protect him. Iannuk had said that with these papers, anyone who would dare molest him would have to answer to the grand commissioner — that Avrum had rights now no less than any born Christian.

He saw the door open — the very thing he might have hoped would happen — and two women stepped delicately out. He waited for them at the foot of the stairs, but until they reached the street, they seemed to deliberately avoid looking toward him. In their black fur boots and high coat collars, they were absolutely the most beautiful and elegant women Avrum had ever seen. The taller and slimmer of the two seemed to radiate a beauty that was not of this world.

His eyes fixed on her. There was the slightest hollow under her cheeks, which were tinted with the warm pastels of angels, and the rich red color of her lips was edged as though defined by a razor. In Iannuk's village, there hadn't been a single woman who might have compared to her, and although he had seen painted lips in Szambor and at Burislav, none defined beauty as richly as did this woman's. She was standing no great distance from him now, meeting his eyes fearlessly. The sweetest scents surrounded him and became the air he was breathing. Begging a thousand pardons, he showed them the crumpled and now stained and torn paper with the address Wladek had scratched onto it and mumbled his name.

The second woman, who shifted herself so that she separated Avrum from her companion, motioned with her head that he was to go upstairs. They seemed to be looking at him quizzically — almost with amusement — and with more than a hint of laughter. Avrum saw that they were studying his valise. The shorter asked coldly if Wladek had sent money with him — money he owed them. Avrum seemed stunned by the question and could only shake his head, but they smiled again and waved him upstairs. Avrum climbed them two at a time. The second woman pulled the pretty one to her; they locked their arms together and they walked away. From the top of the stairs, Avrum watched them go. Neither looked back.

Uncertain of anything except the paper in his hand, he tapped the brass plate with the knocker, but so softly that it might have been the work of the wind. Still, someone on the other side had heard.

"One moment," came a voice — high pitched and belonging to a woman.

When the door partially opened, Avrum found himself standing before an old woman whose hard, thin, sunken lips, set in a field of wrinkles, told him in his heart that he had no business there. Her head seemed perched atop a high stiff collar. Black lace peeked out from under her chin and jaws. But most of her body remained hidden behind the door.

"Well! Come in before we all freeze in here."

Inside, Avrum handed her the paper. There were thick carpets on the floor. Heavy, impossibly expensive furniture lined the walls. The warmth flooded him and a good smell filled his lungs. The walls were red with gold stripes — a dark, inviting red — and Avrum hoped that the people here were good. But the woman's face disturbed him.

"Who is this Wladek?" she asked with piercing, narrowing eyes. "I've never heard of him."

"He said I should mention his name." Intimidated and not knowing where he was or what to expect from this place, Avrum spoke in a voice so low it registered as a mumble.

"What's that you're saying?"

Avrum struggled to find his voice. "Wladek works at our lumber camp at Szambor. And the address you have there is in his writing. The two women who just left knew him."

"I still never heard of him, but what do you want?" Jutting her sharp chin in the direction of his valise, she asked with not a little annoyance, "What is that for?"

"I just got off the train."

"Well, you can't stay here, sir. No one told you that you can stay here. And you don't look to me as if you the kind of money for anything we have to offer here."

"He just said . . . if I needed anything . . ."

"If you can pay for it. But at your age? Please Jesus — I don't think you're looking for what we have, sir. You have ten rubles to leave here?"

"Ten rubles?" He could buy a new fur jacket with ten rubles.

"Fifty if you came to spend the night, sir."

"I made a mistake."

A young girl wearing a flimsy, carelessly fitting housecoat and smoking a cigarette appeared from nowhere. She could only have been two or three years older than him; she walked over to the woman and put her arm lightly around her waist. "What's this?" she asked.

"A practical joke. I'm throwing him out."

"What did you come looking for here?" asked the girl, while sending a cloud of smoke into his face. "You came all this way for nothing if you haven't got the money — just to leave us mud and slush on the carpets."

"I'm sorry."

When she opened the door for him to leave, Avrum told her that he was looking for the synagogue.

"The synagogue?" This from both women as one. There was no mistaking their surprise, tempered with not a little amusement and an equal measure of distaste.

"The *Jide* church? This . . . Wladek told you that this place — this address — was a *Jide* church?" the young girl howled loudly now, her breasts bouncing from side to side under the housecoat.

"No, I'm only looking for it. I have no address. He said I should come here first."

"Out," snapped the older woman, jutting her chin at him. Their high-pitched laughter continued inside, but the sudden blast of the bitter and cutting wind outside the front door brought home to him yet again how total and how abysmal was his isolation in this world. Only now, he had nowhere even to fall.

The door opened again before he descended a stair, not more than a fraction of an inch. He heard the young girl's voice. She didn't show herself, but she said that she thought the first street over to the left of the green gate and somewhere across at the other side — if he walked straight for fifteen, perhaps twenty minutes — past the stable and the fire station — he would see a star in colored glass on the high window.

"It's a big building. Big iron gates."

(8)

Snow had collected on the stained glass window from the sill almost to the top. Still, there was no mistaking from the little left exposed that it was part of a Star of David, and Avrum surrendered to a sudden and powerful rush of excitement. His heart raced maddeningly.

But there was more. What he saw might have been not more than a large shed, but shifting his gaze to his left, he saw that it was, in fact, just outside a large complex of buildings behind two massive wrought-iron gates. He was only a short way from a wide boulevard now. The central building was a towering, massive, dark-domed stone structure — altogether a breathtaking edifice, surely the equal of a number of the churches he had passed that morning that had impressed him so by their magnificence. The gates were hinged to huge, thick square stone posts, and led into a courtyard.

There was no mistaking where he was and what he was seeing. The complex of buildings, the leaded glass windows dominated by the largely snow-covered Star of David, the gates with their rich and intricate metal weave, along with whoever and whatever might be behind it, he felt, were all somehow a part of who he was and where, perhaps, he belonged. It was all so utterly impossible. His heart thumped loudly in his ears. Then the thought of Hershel filled his mind, and he felt a knot of aching and anguish temper his joy.

He banged with his fist on the gates; the sound that issued might have been a peal of thunder. There was no answer. Hesitantly, he tried the handle; it turned, but the gate remained fixed, possibly latched from the other side. He banged on it a second and a third time. Still no response from the other side. To one side of the shed, hidden behind a tree and a broken trash barrel, Avrum saw that there was a narrow space leading behind the gates into the courtyard. Flushed with anticipation, he pressed himself through that space, and from there made his way along a path, where the snow had been cleared to the threshold of what appeared to be a small wooden extension of the main building.

He thought he saw a light flickering behind a dark curtain, so he tried the door and found it open. Even more surprising, there was a man inside — a small man who stooped slightly and whose long stringy hands protruded far beyond the cuffs of his shirt. He was at the far end of the room atop a small stepladder, adjusting some books in a floor-to-ceiling cupboard. With his high, black, cylindrical skullcap, short beard, creased shirt, and gray satin vest, he was a figure right out of the village. Avrum remembered them well, especially the way their ears stuck out under their skullcaps — much like this old man's.

"Yes!" It was a shout, not a question.

"Umm . . . this place — this place is the *shuleh* . . . the synagogue?" *Stupid remark,* thought Avrum on the verge of panic, but he didn't know how to begin to explain himself or his presence here.

"This is a question not even a blind man would ask. Who are you? Am I supposed to know you?"

"But Jews come here, no?"

"Who else should come here?" The man left his books and studied Avrum from where he stood. The lad's height and healthy physical dimensions notwithstanding, he seemed fragile and very confused. More importantly, there was nothing about this stranger that appeared threatening. "So? My guess is that you didn't come here to give a donation. What exactly are you looking for, young man?"

"I just came from Szambor. I worked at the mill there. I came by train in the morning. This very morning."

"Who do I know in Szambor? Nobody."

“I was there for three years — four years. I’m a Jew.” Avrum stumbled over his words which came in a rush.

“You want a medal?” He closed the cupboard and locked it with a long key. Beyond all logic — it was too absurd even to work the picture through in his mind — Avrum felt envious of the key. It had a place where it belonged, a place that was its home. The man made his way to Avrum. He studied him closely for a long moment, and then his eyes flitted nervously up and down, right and left.

“No, but I really and honestly am a Jew. I lost my brother four years ago. We were on the road to Lvov from the village near Baslavak on the other side. He was supposed to come here — to Lvov — and I want to look for him. I didn’t know where to go. There is supposed to be a Jewish *kehila* here in Lvov, so I looked for a *shuleh* — a synagogue.”

“Where is your mother? . . . father? You don’t have a mother, a father, a grandfather somewhere?”

“They are dead. The whole village was supposed to come to Lvov, but they were all killed.”

“They were killed, or they died?”

“Killed, killed! We came with the whole village after all the houses were burned. Then Cossacks stopped us in the middle, and killed everyone with their guns and knives.” There was a pause and the old man, his eyes still shifting in every direction except where Avrum stood, remained silent. Avrum continued. “Only my brother and I got away. We were the only ones left alive. But then — then something else happened and we got separated. He should have come here to Lvov, but it was eighty kilometers from where we were.”

The old man’s face suddenly reddened, and he took hold of Avrum’s coat sleeve with a shaking hand. “From Kresnatshov?”

“Kresnatshov wasn’t far away. Just past Baslavak.”

“Sure! Oh, sure — oh, of course! Take your coat off. Take your coat off. God help us.” He tried to help Avrum with the buttons. “And I remember that there was a boy — a little nothing! I remember. I never saw him myself, but everyone knew.”

"Where is he?" A question Avrum had waited so long to ask.

"That I don't know. But you'll wait here and I'll get someone who does. Weiner! Weiner or someone in his family knows. First, you are going to eat something. Well, it was the worst pogrom. What a fright! What did you do for so many years in Szambor? Who did I ever know in Szambor?"

"I worked in the woods and in the sawmills there . . . three years."

"Then why didn't you come before? There's a train here from there. Everyone a hundred kilometers from here could have told you how to get to the Golden Rose Synagogue."

"I couldn't do what I wanted. I came here today on that train."

"I'm sure you have a story. But put your coat on and come with me now. You can leave the valise here. No, take it with you, take it with you." He went for his own coat and worked himself into it. "You are ready?"

"Yes."

"It's not far. Across the street. Almost upstairs. Come with me. Oh, this is an event!"

Outside, on crushed snow, they turned toward the steps leading into the central building, and then veered right through a small wooden gate, which opened to the very lane Avrum had first come through. Avrum looked back at the building with its three massive wooden doors. Could it really be, he wondered, that he would find himself one with the people who identified with these magnificent structures? After a short walk, a few yards into a narrow lane, they passed through a doorway. A thousand images had flashed behind Avrum's eyes as he followed this old man, but there was no time for them to coagulate into a perception of substance. Avrum struggled to grasp the reality now overtaking him, but the thick, rich smells that suddenly issued from behind that front door enveloped him in the strangest and most distant world he had ever known. At the same time, they somehow delivered a world that seemed as close and as familiar to him as his own skin.

Chaya-Freidle, the old man's wife, was a pale, bleak, and altogether gray creature, who in her printed dress seemed to have stepped right out of the wallpaper. The oversized, tight-curled black wig she wore would have better suited the head of a sixteen-year-old girl. All her color was in her mouth. Avrum couldn't help noticing the quantity of gold locked into her gums, and when she spoke, it was at such a high, almost crystal-shattering pitch that his ears suffered. Still, she must have been a wizard in the kitchen, because the deep bowl of hot, richly fatted soup and the soft boiled chicken mixed into red beet salad was the finest meal, the first luxury that his stomach had known as far back as his memory would reach. No less a luxury was the deep and unbelievably soft couch on which he spread out when they invited him to remove his boots and take a short nap.

He awoke when the first visitors kept slamming the knocker at the door as though they expected to be let into the thick of a carnival. They weren't the Weiners, and as he shook hands with them, stabbing stomach cramps suddenly brought a heavy sweat to his brow. He remembered that he hadn't been to the toilet in more than two days, and now he could feel the soup heavy inside him. He asked Chaya-Freidle to tell him where he could find the outhouse, but she surprised him by pointing to a door behind the kitchen. He had thought that only castles had indoor toilets, and when confronted by the ultra-modern installation, he felt strangely as though he had overstepped his place. Where and when in this world did anyone of his station ever have better than a hole in the ground? And here was this comfortable white stone chair, with a ring of wood over a bowl of water for a seat. He had never known anything like it.

But just as he closed the door behind him, he heard the front door being opened again, and by their voices and footsteps, the people coming in were beyond count. More than that, he realized that the front door hadn't been closed, and that even more were converging upon the house. Their sounds were getting closer and bodies were even brushing now against the toilet door. He could hear voices asking for him. The name *Kresnatshov* was mentioned more than once, and he thought he heard Hershel's name mentioned. Bodies were pressing hard against the door. The house must be packed to bursting, he thought.

Avrum pulled the chain. He knew vaguely how these were supposed to work. There was a slushing and a gurgling in the pipe, but instead of the water going down, as it had seemed to at first, it now seemed to be filling the bowl. The water was coming up . . . rising to the rim . . . and — God in heaven! — spilling over. What had he done wrong? Everything that Avrum had entrusted to the bowl began to drop onto the floor. He tried in vain to hold the pieces back with his boots. The water seeped freely out beneath the door. There was a sharp rapping from the other side.

"Open the door, I'll stop it." It was Chaya-Freidle. "It always does that. I know how to stop it."

Still, there was the embarrassing matter of the tremendous things which were floating around on the floor. If he were to open the door, it would all sail out into the kitchen, and possibly the living room as well. He pushed what he could into a back corner — there was less water there for some reason — and he opened the door, mumbling confused explanations. Chaya-Freidle pushed past him with a mop.

"It's not the worst," she said. Avrum wasn't convinced.

Suddenly: "That's him! That's him!"

"*Ut-ut-ut*, he really looks as if he's been through something."

"But he is big, don't you think? Shoulders like an ox! Do you think he even looks like a Jew? Bring him here — *nu*, bring him here. Let's hear his story."

A rush of voices, pleading, calling, arguing, insisting, and ordering, and hands, pulling, pushing, pinching, and holding, all carried him away. And people were still crowding into the house. Avrum wondered how Chaya-Freidle was managing.

"Well, where is he? Where is he?"

"Maybe those who came earlier will leave now? Maybe they'll give the people who've just come a chance?" cried someone from the doorway.

The warmth of all the bodies quickly melted the fresh snow on their coats, and few had thought of shaking the snow from their boots before stepping into the house. Chaya-Freidle's eyes told a story of rage and resignation when she tried to lift the soaked carpets from under their feet. She used her backside like a bulldozer, and when finally she had the first one freed and raised above her head, a cruel downpour rewarded her efforts. Her wig had slipped over one ear and been ruined, and her best dress would never be the same again. She felt the water run into her corset, but there was no way she could lower her arms.

In desperation, she pushed her way over to the sink and dropped it there, realizing an instant too late that at the bottom of the sink, among other things, were the leftovers from the red beet salad. "Goodbye, carpet," she muttered to herself. That and the used tea leaves that she had cleaned from the samovar would leave stains nothing would remove. Gritting her teeth and carelessly readjusting her wig, she went for the other carpets, which she angrily threw on her husband's bed. Her pleasure showed in the defiant thrust of her chin. Let him dare complain. Unbelievably, more people were still coming through the front door.

"Where is he? Is he in this room?"

"Pick him up, *nu shoin*. Let him stand on something."

"Well, let's see him. Those who saw him should go!"

"Will someone open up a window here? Let some air in."

"My God, you can choke here," another voice agreed loudly. "The window! Somebody!"

A small man reeking of tobacco introduced himself to Avrum as Weiner's cousin by his marriage to Feigel, the daughter of Surel, who was sister to the elder Mendel Weiner. His name was Gans, he said, "Haim Gans."

"With me, everything is *gans git*. Ha, Ha — *gans git*. You still remember your Yiddish, don't you?"

"A little. You know about my brother Hershel?"

"I saw him."

"*Saw* him??" Avrum froze. For a moment, he could not feel his body, and the air rushed out of his lungs. His heart might have lost a beat, but an instant later, began to thump heavily. The words echoed louder and louder in his mind. "You *saw* him? And how was he? Alive? Are you really sure it was him?" His legs could not support his weight now, and he rested against the wall. "How did he get here? Where is he now? Is he here? Do you know?"

"Actually, it wasn't me — at least not me with my own eyes — who saw him. But with my own eyes, I talked to Flomen, Feigel's uncle, who saw him."

"Where is this uncle? Please!"

"These days, in America. Well, your brother Hershel I know is also in America. He was adopted by someone in the Flomen family, and they all went to America."

"America!" Avrum's heart sank, and dizziness overtook him. He felt his mind shattering.

"Yes, America. We are all going to go there, sooner or later. This just isn't a place for tomorrow."

"I saw the boy Hershel."

Avrum turned. Behind him was a taller, gaunt but elegant-looking man sporting a thin moustache. He smiled, and his words were soft and slow.

"I called at their house at least a hundred times. He was fine. Well, maybe not so fine. At the beginning, he was fine. We thought he was fine."

Avrum thought his head would explode in an instant. Was he hearing what he was hearing? Every word burned in his ears, and his heart raced in his chest. At that moment, it was as though there was no one in the room except that man and him, and no other sound reached him but the man's voice.

"He was maybe half your size. No, even less. In fact, much less. Who would have guessed that someone as small and as skinny as him could have a brother who looks like you? And he coughed all the time, but not from being sick — I could say this for sure, one hundred percent. It was a cough with nothing in it." Suddenly, Avrum found himself coughing and he struggled to clear his throat.

The man, who introduced himself as Kalman Fishbein, continued. After they found the boy, he recounted his terrible stories to them; his teeth never stopped chattering.

"This I remember well. They went out looking for you. Ginsberg — he's here, too." Fishbein pointed in the direction of the door and nodded. "That gentleman standing there, still in his hat — he was one of those who went. Meirovitch also went, and he is here, too; we came in together. That's him there," he said, pointing toward a man near the kitchen in animated conversation with a woman, whose blue veil fell from her hat and covered her face.

"Anyway, what I heard was that they found a burned-down house, nothing but a burned-down house — and the bones of somebody. They didn't think it was you, but nobody really looked closely. The authorities said it was a woman — but did they really *know*?" He sighed. "Don't ask about the pogrom . . . We got a message from Kresnatshov — it's what, three years now? Soon four, in fact. We knew about the pogrom and the burning of the village. It wasn't the only pogrom, but it was definitely the worst. Because of them, so many of us are going to America these days, it's only a question of getting the right papers. But the house where you were supposed to be was burned to the ground. And with the bones . . . well . . ."

"I know," muttered Avrum. "That's when I was brought to the forest. It was the woman who lived in the house. She wanted to kill us." Then, in a rush of words, "But how did my brother manage to get here? He was only seven years old — who found him?"

A commotion from the opposite side of the room interrupted them. An old man, apparently the one who had complained about the air, had fainted.

"Air — air — give some air. Reb Yankel is sick."

"Reb Yankel is dying?"

"Dying? Dying? Reb Yankel is dying?"

"Who?"

"Reb Yankel!"

"The reb Yankel from Kiev, or the reb Yankel from Smolensk?"

"The reb Yankel from Smolensk died last year."

"Oh my God — why didn't somebody tell me?"

"Water!" someone shouted.

"Water," came an echo.

"Somebody bring water."

"There's no air here."

"Who is a doctor?"

"A doctor! A doctor!"

"What? A doctor? He died?" cried a multitude of voices.

"And so young."

Something stirred in the old man. Perhaps in the depths of his unconsciousness a spark of life told him that his time had not yet come. And likely, he realized that the only service he would be getting from these people would be a funeral. He half opened his eyes, clutched his heart, and heaving his chest to fill his lungs, the thick, stale air, heavy with smoke, sent him into a spasm of coughing.

Kalman Fishbein added a few more details in a rush of words. "But we will meet again, and I will have more to tell you."

Avrum asked if he could tell him just a little more about Hershel's physical condition. "How did he look? How did he stand? How did he walk?"

"Well, I admit there is more — not about his physical condition — but this is not the place, and now is not the time. I promise you that what I know, I will make sure that you know. I promise you."

The word was passed quickly that reb Yankel was one hundred percent better. All interest in him dropped. Once he was on his feet and after a sip of tea, he was helped with his coat and scarves and then to the door. Reflexively tipping his hat, he stepped outside. Others followed him shortly; minutes later, the rest departed in a wave.

At some point, Avrum was asked to say a few words about what had happened to his family and where he had spent the last years. He looked defeated, unsure of what they expected from him or what memories he should recall. Thankfully, one of the visitors said over the din that this was all too soon for the boy. Most sufficed with a pat on his arm or shoulder before leaving. Avrum still wondered how Chaya-Freidle had managed with his deposits at the toilet.

It was arranged — after some intense politicking throughout the evening prayer service — that the congregation would honor their most righteous, orthodox, and, not unexpectedly, wealthiest of their members (" . . . whether he likes it or not!") with the responsibility of Avrum's care. "If we are not going to look after our own, who will?" For the next week, his benefactor paraded Avrum from home to home to repeat his life story, while the benefactor, a Mr. Leibel Kaplinsky, stood behind him, trying his best to look holy, though his swimming breasts and great belly, in their unending struggle against the buttons of his shirt, somewhat undermined that air. But then, everyone knew Leibel.

Avrum learned that Hershel had been found by an old farm worker still far from the entrance to the city in the countryside, where they were gathering blueberries and raspberries. They had little time for him, but he seemed so sick and beaten — walking and falling and crying — that they sent some of the children there with them to fetch the authorities.

A policeman showed up, but was reluctant to get too close to Hershel, thinking he might be diseased, so that when he heard some of Hershel's mumbling about Jews and about wanting to find a synagogue in Lvov, he had Hershel brought to the town — luckily finding a Jewish textile merchant in a party of travelers on the road. The man was Pinyeh Flomen, whose brother was the city's largest importer of textiles and spices, Aren Flomen. It was Aren Flomen who eventually adopted Hershel, and who, very soon afterwards, took him to America when the whole Flomen family — some thirty people — decided to uproot. It was the Cossacks' murderous pogrom of Avrum's old village that impressed them as the surest sign of things to come, and they couldn't leave soon enough. Many Jews followed, many more planned to. Leibel Kaplinsky, however, trusted the king. "He eats Jewish bread. I know this for a fact."

A few days later, Kalman Fishbein came to the house and told Avrum that it was clear that Hershel had suffered terribly.

"The Flomens found him one day standing in a corner of the bedroom, pressing his head — no, actually, *banging* his head, and really banging it hard — into that corner. They could see blood on the walls. He was crying, maybe shouting things like 'Go away! Go away!' but he wasn't shouting at them. He didn't even know they were there."

"Did he die then?" What was he to understand from these words? "You said he was in America."

"Yes, of course he is in America. And of course he didn't die," Fishbein said softly. He patted Avrum gently, reassuringly, on the knee. "It's just that something happened to him."

"Something happened to him? What?" Avrum's entire body tightened into a knot.

"I also heard that something happened to him — something about his balance," added Leibel Kaplinsky, who was sitting across from Avrum on the other side of their visitor.

"Well," continued Fishbein, "when he turned around and looked at the Flomens . . . for them it was as though he was somebody else — not Hershel, not who he was. There was a fire in his eyes — maybe even hatred."

Avrum shook his head. He couldn't make any sense of what he was hearing.

"The boy shouted, 'I'm Piotr! Call me Piotr. My name is Piotr Piotr. Hershel is dead! Hershel is dead, and I am glad! Don't talk to me about Hershel.' Pinyeh told me that it was horrible — that, in fact, he didn't even look like Hershel anymore. He looked different. It sounds crazy, but it just wasn't Hershel."

Kaplinsky asked, "Did he stay that way for very long?"

"It didn't end there," answered Fishbein. "After a few hours, he calmed down, and he was Hershel again. But now he was talking about how Piotr wanted to kill him. He would throw himself under the bed or hide behind a curtain, crying that Piotr was looking to kill him."

A silence fell over the room. No one spoke and no one stirred. Then, as if talking to himself, Fishbein said, "And a few days later, he said his name was Avrum — certainly he meant you — and that everyone should call him Avrum — and that Avrum would save him from Piotr."

Fishbein then lifted a silver cigarette case from his vest pocket, snapped it open, and offered a cigarette to Leibel Kaplinski. Kaplinski took one and produced a small box of matches. He brought a burning match to Fishbein's cigarette and then lit his own.

"But I can tell you," said Fishbein, rising from his chair and going for his coat, "it's one hundred percent positive that when they left for America, Hershel was Hershel again. And that's the whole story. The good and the bad. Maybe everything is now finished and forgotten."

* * *

Avrum never learned to belong to these people. He sat in a school for a few days, but his presence was disturbing, if only because he was older and physically far more developed and rugged than the others. His lack of "background," let alone a basic education, was repeatedly impressed upon him by the teacher, who turned all his explanations into extravagant theater. The other pupils smelled to him of sour cream, but they were friendly enough, particularly the aggressive little gang that wanted to get him to smoke with them. Kaplinsky eventually hired a private teacher three afternoons a week, and found work for Avrum at the slaughterer's, but later even the lessons were discontinued, and Avrum took to working full time and more.

He insisted on giving Kaplinsky most of his wages, and never came into the house without a fish or potatoes for Nechomeh, Leibel's wife. Though the sights and smells at the slaughterer's violated his senses, he kept to the work regimen. What slowly surfaced in the back of his mind was that he had felt more in his natural environment in the forests with Iannuk than with these people; perhaps he would consider returning to Szambor in the spring after all. Still, there was no way he would permit Kaplinsky and his wife to think of him as a parasite.

When April came, he, in fact, packed his valise and boarded the train to Szambor. The Kaplinskys accompanied him to the station, and there were heavy tears in Leibel's eyes. When the clattering and hissing and whistles grew faint and the cars receded in the distance, Nechomeh Kaplinsky stopped waving her handkerchief and used it to blow her nose.

"He used to eat like two horses," she sniffed. "Where in the jungle is he going to find meals like I cooked for him?"

"Don't worry," said Leibel. "I'm telling you — a man may want to live alone, but no one wants to die alone. He'll get older, and he'll come back. Listen to Leibel — he'll be back."

From his window, Avrum watched the countryside fall away as the train charged ahead. For him, every hill, every tree, and every lonely farmhouse marked his helpless surrender to a vacant future. The train was committed to the knowing tracks, but for him it was the blindest of passages.

* * *

His mother had once said, "A straight head knows the sky is always turning." This was on the day that fat Shloimke Plotkin had tried to drown himself in the creek.

He was asked: "Shloimke, how could you do such a terrible thing on such a special day?" It was the very Saturday of his Bar Mitzvah. "Did some *dybbuk* crawl inside your head?" But the boy only grinned and said that he'd fallen into the water by accident.

Shloimke's older sister, Feigeleh, later told her best friend the true story, and then everyone knew. Reb Shimen Plotkin — who, after Bunim Vinshelboim, was the wealthiest man in the village — thought he deserved a son finer than the clumsy, plodding creature who lived under his roof. The boy could never eat groats without some of the kernels climbing into the back of his nostrils, and then he'd make loud, hideous sucking noises in his throat trying to get them down. He could never walk without getting the cuffs of his trousers caught under his shoes — and one had the distinct impression that there was nowhere for him to walk except behind some horse. The rabbi at the *cheder* complained regularly that what filled the space between the boy's right ear and his left ear could only be a block of wood. But the final straw came when Shloimke disgraced his father that Sabbath, when he was called up to read from the holy scroll. He misread the words, lost his breath in long spells of coughing, and then used the prayer shawl to wipe his mouth. Later, he forgot a whole line from the Kiddush.

Reb Shimen had cornered his son after the guests left and hissed at him through bared teeth. "The real difference between you and me, Shloimke, is that you have me, but I have to have you." Ashamed and broken, Shloimke had taken himself to the creek; there, he picked up a rock and crashed it against his head, and lay down where the water was deepest. On one hand, he wanted to die; on the other, he held his breath, so that when he finally had been discovered, he got dumbly to his feet and grinned impossible explanations. Later, the whole village heard him cry.

"The sky is always turning, but no one can make it turn faster or slower."

It had been Hershel who overheard her, and he asked his mother what she meant.

"I will tell you," she said. "Later, when the time is right."

Then, when the lamp was out and they'd fitted themselves into the caverns of their beds, she pushed the shutters apart and asked them to look out at the night. She began in wistful tones.

"Once, when your mother was as young as yourselves, there was a night when sleep was impossible. For some reason I felt the world had crumbled around me, and I wanted to be outside, alone and at the mercy of the ghosts. I didn't take my eyes from the sky. At first, the moon was huge and resting like a ball of fire on the roofs on the farthest houses. But then I saw it in the middle of the sky, and it wasn't red and burning anymore, but as silvery and as small as you see it now. The stars had also moved — all of them, from one side of the sky to the other . . . some had even disappeared. What I want to tell you is this: Try as I might to see them actually move, I couldn't. To my eyes, everything was frozen where it was, and I would have sworn to that. To my eyes, nothing was changing, yet I knew in my heart that nothing was the same from one moment to the next.

"And all this, my children, is to say that while it seems as though nothing changes, everything changes . . . everything changes all of the time — that in life, nothing is final, even when your eyes tell you otherwise. Shloimke thought his disgrace was final, but tomorrow will have another truth for him. So long as the sky turns, everything turns. But you can't make it turn faster to escape a heavy hour, or slower to keep only good fortune. Remember my words: where even the longest road ends, there is always another that waits to take you in a new direction. However long your trials in life, the heavens will one day deliver you from them. If you trust their wisdom, not even the blindest hours will ever crush you."

Avrum had wondered what there was in the heavens that made the stars move, but he never asked. God, of course. His mother had stepped past him to close the shutters, and when he heard the latch fall, the strangest fear gripped him. He found himself alone on a rushing, clacking, whistling train, like the one he had seen once from a hill near Kresnatshov — only under it were the tops of the trees, and ahead, sinking away, was an ocean of thick, black smoke.

(9)

For the next seven years Avrum lived between the forests of Szambor and Drogovitz, and those near Berezhany, in the vicinity of Urman, where Iannuk had acquired new territorial licenses. He returned to Lvov for a spell every winter, putting up at the Kaplinskys' and then visiting the families who had shown particular interest in him. In the third winter, however, the community had so dwindled that after a day, Avrum had found himself walking aimlessly along the streets, shopping for the year ahead and ruminating with a heavy heart that somehow he would always be alone, fixed outside the pales of all the things that seemed to touch the lives of everyone else.

After all his very life was a stain on the earth and the heavens. How could it be that back there on the hard, cracked wagon road on that wet and black morning, he had not found his own broken and lifeless body? In his mind he could see it clearly, crumpled beneath the body of his mother. That was the only place in the world where his body belonged; this he knew. It would forever belong there. His comings and goings ever since were like the dead and colorless leaves on the forest floor being carried from nowhere to nowhere.

Nechomeh had told him that it was only a question of time before they, too, would leave for America. ("Leibel is stubborn, but it isn't a secret that he is slowly liquidating.") There was no hint of a suggestion that Avrum would be invited to join them. Perhaps it was an oversight. Not very likely. He had no function, and played no role in anyone's life.

For eight months of the year, the sap of the trees seemed to glue the men to each other. The germs of loneliness and isolation filtered into their blood and thickened there. The forest became the mother of them all. But when November and December came around the trains that pulled out of Szambor and Urman, packed with lumbermen, marked the truth. Avrum was under no man's skin but his own.

He suspected also that in his wake he invariably left feelings of discomfort and mistrust. To the Jews he remained an iconoclast in that inasmuch as he acknowledged his faith, he somehow resisted the spirit they drew from it and that structured their lives. When he shied away from their suggestions that he prepare for a Bar Mitzvah ritual, they never really pressed him. Leibel once said, "Any *goy* can make a noodle *kugle* the same as Nechomeh; everything would be the same to the last detail — but it's the *yiddishkeit* that gives her *kugel* its special taste. Go explain it. But this boy, Avrum, —don't ask me why — has a taste like the goy's kugel."

To the lumbermen, even in his respectful deference to them, he remained an enigma, and an unsettling intruder in their lives. He knew how to fell a tree with a talent that equaled Iannuk's, and whatever party he'd made up, that party somehow always produced more. When he'd be cutting away the branches, the fellow on the other end of the saw would find himself pressed to keep up with Avrum's pace.

None of this escaped Iannuk who knew the minds of his men and made sure to keep the boy in his shadow. In the forest, the law was a fragile commodity where the justice of anger and fear left little license for leniency. Perhaps it helped a little, too, that Avrum was Iannuk's favored, if not sole, confident. How far, after all, could the informed be from the ratting informer?

It also seemed to Avrum that Iannuk was becoming more and more inclined to forsake the saw in favor of his papers. He was forever occupied with his accounts, at one point managing three different territories, each about a hundred kilometers distant from the other. And now, he affected thin, gold-rimmed glasses that, on his bulk, lent a decidedly incongruous, almost comical air. Still, one had to be thoroughly drunk to ridicule what the old-timers came increasingly to see as a caricature of the fearsome giant they once knew. When Nikolai, a man as heavy as an ox, was in just such an intoxicated state and tried to remove the glasses to answer a challenge by his drinking partners, Iannuk promptly broke his nose.

No one who saw it missed the look of absolute indifference on Iannuk's face. Nikolai might just as well have been a fly, but his nose would remind him of Iannuk for the rest of his life. Iannuk appeared to regard them all as very near the stuff of trash — entirely discardable after their hour of usefulness. His regard of Avrum in an obviously respectful way only underlined another grating difference between the boy and the rest of the men.

Then there was his friendship with the Doctor, whom Iannuk had brought to the camp during Avrum's third season. He was called "the Doctor" not for any diploma he may have earned, but for the curious bits of knowledge he readily disseminated on almost every subject; these were issued with such conviction that even when the men loudly professed their disbelief, one could still see in their eyes how unsure they were of their own minds. The Doctor was always mocking the men's intellectual limitations. They seemed hugely entertained by his recourse to sophisticated, almost elitist language in his references to them. Or so it seemed.

Avrum was his most rewarding audience, and it increasingly appeared that one rarely moved without the other in tow. The men preferred keeping both of them at arm's length. Even in the heat of work, there was a strained air between those two and everyone else. Plainly, what irked the lumbermen was the Doctor's harsh and cynical judgment of them. They had forgotten their own taunts and provocative stubbornness, but they knew that the Doctor never said what he didn't entirely believe. And here was Avrum continuing to learn, and the Doctor continuing to teach. They were no longer worth the effort of his convincing.

Their irritation only sharpened when they discovered that Iannuk had arranged for the Doctor to teach English to Avrum and himself. They had books and papers, and the impression was that they were going at it with more than just a passing interest. There seemed to be something devious about the secrecy of these lessons, which were timed to the hour the men were usually glued to their cards and bottles. The chasm deepened, but the men never did more than grumble. They were there for their wages and not for any pleasures.

Avrum had a growing suspicion that Iannuk had some hold over the Doctor — that the latter was bound to him for reasons other than contract. First, it was odd that the Doctor should be there at all: at least half the size and weight of everyone else there at the camp, he was probably the last man one would point to as a natural lumberman. Moreover, he seemed to suffer from a chronic nervous condition, with muscles in his jaw and shoulders continuously twitching and jerking. Iannuk had forbidden him to wield an axe from his very first day out. Bad enough he couldn't bring it down twice on the same mark, but he also tired quickly.

Then there was that wild swing, when it flew from his hands and struck one of the men. It struck with the handle and not the blade, but Iannuk was not about to wait for either man's luck to change. The men then had even refused to have him at the other end of their saws. They complained that they found themselves not only pulling the saw through the trunk, but, because he couldn't maintain the rhythm, often pulling him with it, as well, and instead of him pulling the saw back, they had to push it to him. It would break their backs. Nor did he ever get the knack of properly fitting the teeth of the saw into the wood. Either the saw would slide away, biting nothing, or he gave it too much and it would buckle. Iannuk had him team up with Avrum, and Avrum never complained that the Doctor was a burden.

Like Avrum, the Doctor had no commitments for the winter, but an unusual, even strange, exchange between Iannuk and the Doctor had jarred Avrum out of feeling entirely complacent in their company. Iannuk was paying the Doctor his wages, and the latter was unusually moody and downcast. Then, his eyes never leaving the pages of his notebook, Iannuk said to him quietly, "Be sure not to move far from here between now and April. I won't be telling you this again."

"Don't worry."

"It's not for me to worry. We can be straight and clear about this."

"Look, let me surprise you. I was not born an idiot. I am not going to pretend that I don't know what's on your mind. I told you, but I'll not give a damn if you don't believe me. I'll be in Drogovna for the whole of the winter. The trains will take me there, and the trains will bring me back."

"Sure."

"And if at any time it gets into your head that you are doing me a favor — just tell me, and I'll take off." Here the Doctor stared, unblinking, directly into Iannuk's eyes, but a moment later he seemed crushed. Avrum saw Iannuk go around the table to the Doctor, taking a gentle hold of his shoulder. Both walked away together for a few yards. Their whispered exchanges were puzzling, and through it all, the Doctor nodded continuously.

Strange, Avrum had thought. It was then that Iannuk had called him over and, without preamble, asked Avrum if he could possibly stick to the Doctor that winter — as a personal favor to him. It would be a favor that would put additional money in his pocket.

The Doctor accompanied Avrum to Lvov, and while Avrum called on the Kaplinskys and one or two other families, the Doctor went off to look for work. He was back at the Kaplinskys' door the very same evening, and told Avrum that he had found jobs for both of them at a restaurant; they were to begin the following morning. At first, he said that the restaurant was a short walk from the university, and that the clientele were mostly students and artists, but when they were alone he explained that what he had said was intended only for the Kaplinskys' ears. Not that it wasn't a restaurant of sorts, nor that it didn't cater to students and artists. It was just that these nuances made it unnecessary to add that the "restaurant" was in fact a kitchen in a brothel. "Can anyone call me a liar?" he asked, feigning innocence. Avrum had no objections, and the Doctor went on to explain that he was having a problem with his papers, and it was for this reason that he had to seek out discreet employers.

Until then, it had never occurred to Avrum that brothels really existed outside the lurid stories of the lumbermen. These stories seemed to pour directly from the liquor bottles. Moreover, coming as they did from these men, the gross vulgarity, the extravagant lasciviousness, and their individual heroics could not but be totally untrue. After all, every woman had to be someone's daughter. And clinging to this rationale, he had tried to take the unsettling edge off the lumbermen's stories. At times, however, it would surface in his mind that his interest in these stories went beyond their simple appeal as entertainment. He never forgot that first address he had been to in Lvov. The faces of the women he had encountered there remained etched perfectly in his memory, and though he suspected that they were in some way different from other women, in his heart he was certain that there could never be any question of their virtue.

The Doctor was as amused as he was scornful of these sentiments. “There is nothing holy in this world. There is nothing someone may want that another someone won’t sell for the right price.”

In the morning, while on their way to the house, Avrum learned of a detail that seemed to be a condition of their employment. The Doctor had assured the proprietress that his boy was twenty years of age, but suddenly doubtful about Avrum’s ability to carry it off, had added that he was also a deaf-mute. “That means if you say one damn word, we are out of two good jobs.”

Shaking his head, Avrum stopped in his tracks, reluctant to go on. The Doctor slapped the back of his head. “Just wait until you see the place, and then decide if I didn’t do you a favor.”

Outside the door of the house, and with his heart racing in his chest, Avrum heard the Doctor sneer under his breath. “. . . never saw a little girl blush as easily as you.”

Avrum gave vent to his nervousness. “I’m just not comfortable with your plans. This isn’t a place for me.” But the Doctor was already rapping the knocker.

An instant later, the door opened just enough for an enormous woman, who might have been thirty or sixty — it was impossible to tell — to show her face and shoulder. The Doctor quickly pushed Avrum in ahead of him, and she closed and latched the door behind them. “Another freezing day outside,” mumbled the Doctor. The woman didn’t reply.

Except for the strings of beads she wore around her neck and which fell to her waist, she was dressed entirely in black — a mountain of frills, black stockings, and black lace. Even her lips were painted black, as was her hair, which was pulled tightly into a bun at the top of her head. The beads were the brightest orange.

“He is the deaf-mute, I suppose.” It was a dull, caustic observation, which fell on Avrum’s ears as an accusation. She laughed dryly.

“And the truth is that he is only eighteen, madam — so what? What has changed? I wanted the arrangement to go more smoothly, that's all. He is good, absolutely honest, and everything else I said. So?"

The woman pointed at his face and said slowly and coldly, "Let me tell you, whatever your name is: I don't know you, and I am not interested in knowing you. Not you, and not the boy. Never mind yesterday. I had the night to think. You can be who you say you are — you could turn out to be somebody. I don't know, and believe me, I really don't want to know. But I find it really suspicious that you should know as much as you seem to know about us."

The Doctor paled visibly. "If that's what you believe, go call the police. I'll wait here."

"Your bravado doesn't impress me. I don't like you, and I'm not sure I'm going to trust you. In fact, my answer is 'no.'"

"Well, what about the dollars? Can we finish with that — at least that?" The Doctor glanced sideways at Avrum and shrugged his shoulders, but Avrum could make no sense of their talk.

"No . . . no, nothing with—"

"What has one thing to do with the other?" The Doctor was suddenly aggressive and agitated.

"I think you are mistaken about me and about this place. And now I think I know who you are."

The Doctor stiffened visibly. His eyes shifted for an instant toward the door, and he spoke in a rush. "You are a sow turned whore. What is to be mistaken about?"

"Bad mouth you have, mister . . . real bad." She walked with slow, determined steps to the door and opened it. The Doctor was plainly in a rush to get through it. Avrum followed behind him.

The Doctor was visibly shaken, and he struggled to find words. "The maggots in your crotch — they got into your brain, madam," he hurled at the door now closing behind them.

The woman suddenly showed her face again. It had reddened considerably, and there was as much rage in her eyes as in her words. "Come back again — let me so much as see you on the street — and I swear by Jesus, I'll have the boys split your head and spill your brains on the street." With that, she slammed the door loudly behind them, and they heard the latch fall, locking it from inside.

Avrum pulled his coat tighter around himself and raised the collar to where his hat covered his ears. In the silence that filled the moments that followed, Avrum glanced at the man next to him; he felt suddenly that he was as much and possibly more of a stranger than any of the gray, snow-covered figures presently on the streets.

The Doctor grabbed the sleeve of Avrum's coat and pulled him ahead. "The syphilis climbed to her head," he said.

Avrum stopped to fix his scarf over his neck and cheeks.

"We have to get away from here — and fast," mumbled the Doctor under his breath.

"You are in trouble with the police?"

"No. But she has gorilla pimps that I'm not exactly anxious to meet." The Doctor hesitated and then looked back at Avrum with scorn. "You! You're still so green, so wet with milk — it will be years before you know what goes on in the world!" He continued walking swiftly away.

Avrum had no reply.

"Trouble is you fool people. You're only now beginning to grow, and you're already halfway to the size of an ox."

"Well . . . what *are* 'gorilla pimps'?"

"Gangsters . . . killers . . . the people who own these houses and these women. They even own the police. If they smell anyone giving them trouble, they bury them without ceremony."

"Like you?"

"I could make more trouble for her than anyone she ever knew."

"How do you come to her? The day before yesterday, you told me that you had never been to Lvov before."

"I wasn't lying, but it is a long story."

(10)

The Doctor was agitated and restless within himself. They had stepped into a restaurant for tea and a sandwich, but the Doctor was on pins. He froze every time the door opened. He began to crouch and slink whenever it seemed that a face from outside was trying to look inside, and in the end, they left while his glass was still full and warm; his sandwich had not been bitten into more than once. He told Avrum that they would find something to occupy them at Szambor, and that he had no intention of staying another hour in Lvov.

Avrum mumbled confused explanations to the Kaplinskys, but they didn't press him. Clearly, they weren't comfortable with the presence of the Doctor, who was much older than Avrum and a quarter his size, but this showed only in their eyes and the turn of their lips. Nechomeh Kaplinsky gave them half a *kugel* to eat on the train. There was something about the way the Doctor carried himself — with his head and thickly waxed hair jutting ahead of his narrow shoulders, rather than on top of them — that left people with the impression that his entire character was less than upright. A storm caused the cancellation of the regular departure, and they had to put up at a nearby rooming house for two nights. The train left for Szambor at noon the third day, and they were on board.

Avrum found work at the sawmill, which never closed down. The Doctor found work as a barber, and both of them lived together in a small rented room, which was the attic above the barbershop.

The incident in Lvov was not referred to after that first day, and the Doctor seemed to slip back into the character Avrum was more familiar and somehow more comfortable with. But by mid-January, that image had totally come apart; the Doctor had begun to recall past incidents with Iannuk, and injected into them dark overtones of discredit to their employer. Soon they were no longer overtones, but blunt and blatant judgments, which Avrum either contradicted or otherwise refused to accept. This always infuriated the Doctor, and Avrum no longer knew how to react. At least when the talk was tempered with some ambivalence, Avrum could remain neutral, but now he would find himself stung and provoked. Increasingly, Avrum ignored his remarks, sensing that the Doctor was struggling to work something out in his mind. Finally, the Doctor said that he would be going away for a few weeks.

"Where to?"
"Across the country."
"But where to?"
"Wherever I have to be."

Avrum found himself again overtaken by thoughts that lately seemed to be recurring in ever heavier and more crushing waves. Their sediment was the depression into which they invariably delivered him. The months of last winter and most of the winter before that he had spent entirely alone here in Szambor; he had worked for a tailor, and then for a week or two at a butcher's shop. No one had sought his company, and no one asked more of him than his back and two hands. Now he also had to manage his promise to Iannuk.

"Take me along. Nothing is keeping me here."

"What? Take you along? And have you wet your pants every time you smell something not just so?"

"If it's to places like those that you'll be going, then, ok, you can go by yourself." Avrum just couldn't find his footing with this man.

"No, child, I'm not going to 'places like those,'" the Doctor's tongue turned in his mouth as though he was about to spit, "but if you want me to prove something to you about your boss, I'll think about it."

"Iannuk said we should stay together."

"And if he told you to eat dog shit?"

"Well, I want to travel. I have some money."

The Doctor looked intently into Avrum's eyes. "I have never heard you say even once that you wanted something. Never *really* wanted something. Never in that voice. Suddenly, you *want* something. You would go as far as Kiev?"

"Kiev?"

"Almost 400 kilometers. Maybe less. Actually, not so far — maybe 300."

"Distance is no problem."

"I'm thinking of coming back through Odessa. You've heard of Odessa? That would add at least another thousand kilometers. At least. You'd become a cosmopolitan. Imagine: you — an overgrown water buffalo who still doesn't shave — you a *cosmopolitan*. What a joke! Do you really think you are ready for another life?"

Avrum kept his tongue, but it was as though the tip of a knife had suddenly pricked his heart. There was more than a modicum of truth in the Doctor's words, even if not the truth intended. He did want to go to Kiev and Odessa, but could there really be another life waiting for him there — or in any other place?

Somehow, the thought of shifting his life to distant stations unsettled him. It would mean turning his back on the earth into which the blood of his mother and father had drained. His body would be violating his bonds to all the ghosts that never stopped carrying him back to that terrible day and terrible place. And however many years had passed since then, when alone and still awake in the dark nights, he knew his body belonged more to that earth and those ghosts than it belonged to the people and places around him. His legs suddenly seemed too weak to support him, and heavy sweat drenched his underclothes. *Another life.* For Avrum, the idea of inviting another life was not far removed from inviting another kind of death.

Two weeks later, they boarded a train more elegant than any Avrum had ever seen. There were cars with curtains on the windows, polished brass fixtures on the walls, narrow tables, and padded benches. The Doctor had grown a tight beard and had taken to shaving his head, explaining that that was the style in which he preferred to travel. Actually, he would make Avrum shave it for him, saying that this was the price he demanded for being his traveling partner. Avrum quickly grasped that bald and bearded, the Doctor vaguely resembled the barber who had employed him. The Doctor wasn't at all displeased to hear Avrum remark on the resemblance, and he slyly produced his traveling papers, pointing first at the brown photograph inside the cover. In fact they were the barber's papers — "Borrowed, mind you," winked the Doctor, "and only for this trip." Left unsaid and unquestioned was why it should be so critical that he not be recognized.

* * *

"Hershel . . . I hear underneath the wheels a clackity-clacking, and racing madly past the empty stations. Only God knows what is waiting for me at the end of these tracks."

* * *

To help pass the time, the Doctor tested Avrum with word puzzles, but soon lost his patience.

"You've lived so long with those stiff trees," he complained, "you've become one yourself. Where a normal man has brains, you have sawdust."

Avrum suspected that the Doctor's mood was sour because he'd been rejected that morning by a particular woman. The woman was traveling with her infant daughter, and the Doctor did his best to blind her with his brilliance. He was bold and witty, but she turned up her nose. From her expression, she might have been tasting a lemon. Later, when he touched her neck, not even pretending that it was by accident, she told him quietly that if he were to do that again, she would have him arrested.

Forcing an air of aloof disdain, the Doctor moved slowly away from her, and said dryly, "Dear madam, when the nectar goes, the flower fades. The bees fly by without hellos . . . without goodbyes."

But he sulked for hours.

* * *

Windy, sprawling, high-domed, and very gray, the station at Kiev was magnificent — virtually a city unto itself. Winter was probably at its most severe then, but, unbelievably, there were vendors in elegant kiosks selling fresh flowers. Loud noises from the screeching engines, with their bells and shrill whistles, mixed with the rush of shouting people pummeled Avrum's ears. All the sounds reverberated as echoes thumping down upon them from the great central dome. The forests at Szambor and Urman belonged to another planet.

* * *

"Am I looking for you in the cemetery instead of going to Krimmer's house? And would I know you if you passed directly in front of me? Could you look into the face of a Christian lumberman and know he was your brother?"

* * *

"Police are everywhere," the Doctor said under his breath.

Avrum arrested his thoughts and stopped to look around. The Doctor was plainly agitated, but for no reason that Avrum could guess. When they were in a carriage and the Doctor had given their driver the name of a street corner, he told Avrum not to be disappointed if their stay in Kiev turned out to last no more than a day or two.

"The city used to be interesting," he said, "but it dried up. We would be smarter if we spent our time and money in Odessa."

"Why didn't we go directly to Odessa, then? We aren't here for one hour, and you can say it dried up?" Tired and longing for a bath, Avrum found himself overtaken by impatience and stirrings of resentment. "I think that with you, being smart is the other side of being mad."

"Be patient."

They registered at a hotel, washed, and changed into fresh clothes. The Doctor's beard was thick and perfectly trimmed now, and Avrum agreed to shave his head yet again. Wrapped in their heavy coats and thick scarves, and with the thick fur earflaps of their *ushanka* hats pulled over their cheeks and down almost to their necks, they went out into the frigid winter air and walked to another quarter of the city. The Doctor knew the streets well, and, despite himself, Avrum could not repress a surge of gratitude for being with this man. He said as much to the Doctor, but his thanks were depreciated by the back of the latter's hand gesturing that Avrum could keep his distance.

"Believe me," grumbled the Doctor impatiently, "there was no one for me to thank. Everything I learned, I learned with scars on my own body."

Still, Avrum refused to dislike his peculiar traveling companion and sometime partner. They reached a restaurant, and the Doctor chose a table that was set against a sidewalk window. The curtain was pulled tightly closed, but the Doctor fidgeted with it for a moment until he had it parted very slightly where they sat.

They ordered fish and borsht with sour cream, which came with hard-crusted black bread. When Avrum tried to ape the table habits of the other patrons, the Doctor teased him for his bourgeois instincts. "If you eat with your hands and fart loudly, you'll live a lot longer than everyone you see here choking in their tight vests and corsets."

The Doctor kept them in the restaurant long after they finished eating. His eyes never left what he could see of the street. Afterwards, they went back to the hotel to sleep. In the morning, they resumed their places at the same table in the same restaurant, and the Doctor continued his strange vigil. Avrum's questions and expressions of annoyance never met with more than a "Wait — just wait."

Suddenly, electrified by what he had just seen through the curtain, the Doctor half rose from his chair and froze.

"I thought we would have to wait much longer," he said in a rush of words, his voice now thick with a sense of urgency. "Look out there now. Quick! — across the street — on your left . . . two buildings on your left — on the steps."

Avrum had already caught sight of what the Doctor had come all this way to see: Iannuk.

"Iannuk! It's really Iannuk! Holy Jesus!"

"So now you're one with Jesus, eh? Okay, close the curtain."

"But that's not his house. Who lives there?"

"I do," the Doctor said, after the slightest hesitation. "I do. Now, ask me what he's doing there."

"Well . . . tell me — what?"

The Doctor paused. His eyes fixed on Avrum's and his lips twitched in silence, as though seeking to fit themselves around the right words.

"Fucking my wife. That's what."

(11)

Iannuk stepped onto the street and turned in their direction, even crossing the road to their side — and the Doctor stiffened with fright. He seemed just a snap of the fingers away from an apoplectic seizure. He gripped Avrum's wrist hard in his trembling hand, and ordered him in a rush of words to get himself into the washroom.

"If he comes in here, chances are he won't recognize *me*. If he doesn't come in here, I'll go and fetch you. But you wait there — you wait there until I fetch you. I'll fetch you. Don't dare show yourself."

The Doctor then prepared to bury himself in a newspaper and whatever dish sat in front of him. At the same time, from the corner of his eye — even though the curtain was closed except for the thinnest slit where two sections met — he was able to follow the giant figure passing within a yard of him.

When it was evident that Iannuk meant to continue down the street, the Doctor dared part the curtains a hair more. It was then he noticed that Iannuk was not alone. Toddling next to him, all bundled in heavy gloves and thick woolens, was a child. The Doctor could see only its back; still, he knew it had to be Alexander, and it flashed through his mind that he would have to see the child in another fifteen years or so before he could be sure that it was really his.

If she cuckolded me, he thought, *there is no chance that he'll grow into the miserable, emaciated weasel that I was.* "The truth would be known from a mile," he mumbled, shaking his head.

The Doctor would have left Kiev that same afternoon, except that Avrum registered his disappointment in what — for him — were unusually loud and critical tones. The Doctor relented.

"It is madness to have come to Kiev to only stay here less time than it took to make the trip."

"What kind of measure is that?"

"Why panic so about another day or two?"

"There are reasons. I have my reasons."

"You are never short of reasons."

Either the Doctor had no reply, or he had not the heart to force his will on Avrum yet again, when plainly it was so rare for the boy, despite his physical size, to demonstrate even a hint of assertiveness toward anyone. If a person stepped on his foot, it would be Avrum who would beg forgiveness. In any case, the Doctor's attention shifted to what were more painful and critical issues for him; his eyes glistened with tears, and he made no effort to hide them.

"It's still Iannuk that's on your mind. And you've told me nothing."

"That fornicating backstabber robbed me of my whole life. I have to sneak here like a thief in the night to see my family." With that, the Doctor produced a large, crumpled red handkerchief from the depths of a trouser pocket. He dabbed at his wet cheeks and blew his nose loudly.

"See your family? All we saw was Iannuk."

"If you were less a cretin and had a grain of imagination in that porridge you call a brain, it would tell you everything."

Avrum would not be offended. "Maybe I am what you say," he half smiled, showing the Doctor the palms of his hands, "but see who I have for a friend. And who does the brilliant Doctor have for a friend?"

The Doctor welcomed that observation, and his mood changed abruptly. He broke into a laugh that soon had his whole body shaking. He rose from his chair, pulled Avrum to his feet, and embraced him with a passion. With Avrum standing a full head taller than the Doctor and at least eighty pounds heavier, the picture of them together this way was almost fantastic.

The Doctor was reticent about Avrum's request that they go to the theater the next evening. Posters advertising *The Last Soldier* were posted everywhere. Until then, the only performance Avrum had ever seen was a small Yiddish production of *The Dybbuk* in a cellar while staying with the Kaplinskys. It had all seemed so real to him; even now, he could hardly believe that the actors had merely been actors, and that their lines were rehearsed. It was all just too real. However, what commanded his attention at this time was the image on the posters of a voluptuous maiden in scant clothing, appearing terribly forlorn. He mentioned to the Doctor that she very much resembled the girl who suffered *The Dybbuk* and its exorcism.

"Sure. Like my mother resembles Lina Cavalieri."

"Lina Cavalieri?"

"Only the most beautiful woman in the world. She sang with Caruso."

"Caruso?"

The Doctor shook his head and grimaced in the direction of an imagined audience. "Why . . . ? Tell me why am I forced to waste so much time."

"Let's go see it."

"We haven't got clothes for the theater."

"Clothes we can buy today. How much do we need?"

"No. Forget it. And the last time you shaved my head, you left me scarred as though I had the pox. Now it is full of scabs, and there is no way that I'll agree to take my hat off."

"It wasn't as bad as you make it to be. A small nick at the most, and only because you couldn't stop moving."

"You have the hands of a butcher. You bury an axe in my head and call it a small nick."

Instead, they spent a few hours in the sprawling market on Spraga Avenue, and toward evening the Doctor had them in a carriage, taking them across the Dnieper to the farthest quarters of the city, just past the Kiev Circus, where artists and musicians had their booths. They alighted at a shabby amusement center, where a poster advertising what purported to be the world's greatest freaks piqued their curiosity.

Inside, they found a grossly fat and pathetic woman with a wispy beard, a man who seemed to be breathing in the flames of a torch he was holding, and another man whose skin and limbs were so elastic that he could wrap himself around himself, as it were. What was advertised as a snake woman — and pictured as woman from the waist up and reptile from the waist down — turned out to be a whole woman who let a large snake curl itself around her. Avrum was fascinated by the snake, but when they left the place, his mood dropped. They walked along in silence. The snow was falling heavily now and blew into their eyes. Avrum found this strangely comforting. It disturbed him that those unusual people were introduced as freaks of nature. Somehow, he could imagine himself up on that stage with them as one of their number. The barker would invite the crowd to see the physical presence of a man who had died a long time ago and a long way from here . . . a man who belonged nowhere except on a hard piece of earth along a distant road that still waited for his blood and his bones.

They left the amusement park at the Doctor's urging. There were pickpockets busy everywhere, some singly and some in packs of three and four, with no policemen in sight. Avrum had his money and papers strapped to his leg, as did the Doctor, but arguments and fistfights were erupting almost everywhere in the thin pockets of people, and remaining there became decidedly dangerous.

The episode in the restaurant earlier in the day continued to invade his thoughts. Even without the answers to the thousand questions he asked, all of which the Doctor had summarily deflected, there was no way he could erase or otherwise deny what he had seen with his own eyes. That man on the street *was* Iannuk. And caught as he was in a drama, the details of which of which were beyond his best guesses, he had also to suffer the cutting barbs, verbal lacerations, and the acerbic impatience that he had long ago learned were the Doctor's only ways of communicating with the world external to himself. At the same time, he could not escape feeling grateful to this man. The Doctor was his teacher. And more than his teacher: they were partners now — partners to the same days and the same nights. They walked the same streets, rode the same carriages, and suffered the same freezing winds and snow. There were even moments when the sense of separation and apartness that always weighed so heavily in Arum's heart would lift.

"There is nothing else I can tell you." The Doctor seemed not to have a stomach for Avrum's persistent questioning. "And if you've learned anything, it is that very little in this world is exactly the way it seems to be. Iannuk is only one example. Maybe I'm another. How can you know? At Szambor, I told you about Iannuk. You were sure you knew better. Do you still think you know better?"

"He saved my life. I would be dead now if not for him."

"And if you died, would that be worse than the life he gave you?"

Avrum searched in vain for an answer. There was none. The image of Hershel flashed behind his eyes, and no words would come to him.

Earlier that same day, they had the following exchange.

"Now I have only questions," said Avrum. "The first one being why when you saw him in your home and with your wife you did nothing. I was sure you were going to rush right out. Instead you can't leave the city fast enough."

"I have nothing more to do here. It was worth the trip to prove to myself that Iannuk was lying. Didn't you hear him say that he was going to Drogovitch? 'I'll be at Drogovitch all winter' was what he said."

"What will you do now that you know what you know?"

"Nothing. Absolutely nothing."

"Just nothing? All this, and then nothing?"

"Professors go to school for 35 to 40 years. They learn, learn, learn, and learn, and then what do you think they do with everything they learned? I'll tell you. Just what I'm doing — nothing. Absolutely nothing."

"It's not the same thing."

"Sometimes it is an advantage just knowing."

"Will you be going back to Szambor?"

The Doctor smiled. "Of course. One thing has nothing to do with the other."

But then the image of Alexander with his hand locked in Iannuk's clouded his thoughts, and the smile faded.

* * *

In Odessa, Avrum and the Doctor were sitting in a coffeehouse looking out at the huge ships in the harbor. The Doctor was still massaging his legs and knees. To get here they had made their way down the entire 200 Potemkin steps. After the first fifty, the Doctor complained of a massive headache. After the next fifty, his knees started buckling. For most of the last hundred, Avrum had to carry him virtually suspended in the air.

The small cups of coffee were sharp and bitter, and they each had a hot, freshly baked cinnamon roll. Under his breath and almost to himself, Avrum said he could not understand how those massive steel ships out there in the water remained afloat.

"It's simple physics," said the Doctor. "But, of course, you don't know what physics is. When the water that gets pushed away by the weight of the ship weighs as much as the ship the water pushes back. So if the boat is still higher than the water, it floats."

"So if I throw a rock into the water, why does the rock sink?"

The Doctor feigned impatience with the question, but he plainly enjoyed shaking some dust off a few bits and pieces of his education.

"You really are a doctor. How do you know all this?"

"Because a Greek named Archimedes was born before me. It's all a question of the timing of our birthdays. But don't worry, my little ox. If you had my head, it wouldn't do you much good. You were born so that the world could have your perfect face to look at and your strong back to bring down the trees. Brains at this time in your life would only confuse you. Besides, look at me. What greatness did brains deliver to me? Here I am this minute with you. We do the same work, in the same place, and earn about the same wages. I can live no better than you, and if one thing cancels the other out, you are still left far better off than me."

Avrum said nothing.

"And to tell you the truth, I would change places with you like this," continued the Doctor, snapping his fingers loudly. "Your life is all ahead of you and your education will yet come. That's for sure. My own life is all behind me, and all my education is good for wrapping dead fish."

"I don't believe you."

"Believe me."

"Well, I see nothing ahead of me except more forests and more trees to bring down."

"If you were born blind, would you understand an explanation of light?"

"And that means . . . ?"

"It means you'd see better if your dead eyes weren't in the way. Don't ask me to explain. You see everything except what is in front of your nose."

"I wish you could tell me what life I can know outside the forests. What is there that you think I don't see?" Avrum was moved more by the hard bitterness in the Doctor's voice than the aggressiveness in his words. He really wished the Doctor would have an answer.

"To begin with, you don't have to run from a past that's hunting you."

"You're talking about yourself. What do you know about *my* past?"

"Oh, I know about the Cossack murders and I know how you were brought here — at least to Szambor. But the past, rather than chasing you, now gives you the option of becoming the chaser. Consider — if you think you have accounts to settle, you can decide one day to settle them. But there is no one who has a serious mind to settle an account with you. There is no one chasing after you, say, to collect a debt — and not necessarily a money debt."

"And that's why you say I'm blind?"

"It's a weight you are definitely free of — a weight, I assure you, you don't feel and don't even know exists. But I can give you other examples — the list is longer than my arm."

Avrum just looked at the Doctor and waited. There had to be more.

"Look at those ships. You see a monstrous bulk of steel floating in the water — actually, nothing more than iron on iron. You would say it was this long, and this wide, and this deep, yes? But I would measure it very differently. What I see is a promise that I can turn my back on everything diseased and rotten in my life and start out again — a new life in another world — with new lungs, new legs, new eyes, new people, and a new heart."

"In America?"

"Look. We got off the train in Odessa and your eyes almost fell out of your head. You saw beautiful buildings, beautiful people, the richest shops, statues, ships, and you think, *Ah, another world* — as if to live here must be paradise on earth. Let me tell you — have you ever heard of the *Potemkin*? Do you know why those damned steps we were on are called the Potemkin steps? The whole world heard of the *Potemkin*. Let me tell you something."

The Doctor reached for his cup and was disappointed to find it empty. He left the table for the counter and ordered second cups for both of them. A moment later, he returned with the cups; a young boy delivered more cubes of sugar to the table.

"The Potemkin was a warship sitting right out there in those waters you're looking at. It's not even a year. The sailors mutinied because of maggots in their meat. Maggots and worms. It could have been a bloody hell, but the tsar's other battleships wouldn't fire on it! The *Potemkin* got away to Romania, but what did our tsar do? He blamed the Jews of Odessa. The pogrom your mother and father died in was a blink in the night compared to what went on here. What killing and burning! Jews were slaughtered right and left.

"Even the good people — even those who were themselves shot at by the tsar's Cossacks when they came in the thousands to support the sailors — they never blinked an eye. They thought it was a show that they would enjoy for an hour and afterwards forget. And if you think that they are changed now, you are blind. If anything, their appetite for your blood has grown, and I'll tell you why. You Jews are always weeping, always walking around with some mysterious pain in your eyes. When my daughter — I have a daughter, you know — when she used to cry for no reason that I could see, I would lift my hand to her and say, 'If you are going to cry, at least let me give you a reason.'"

"What exactly do you expect me to see?"

"Lummox! What exactly do I *expect* you to see?"

The Doctor was incredulous; he half rose from his chair, jarring their table. They got their hands to the cups before they spilled. Avrum was at a loss trying to fathom the man's mind and the sudden turn in his mood.

"First, I *don't* expect, and second, you need to have eyes attached to something called a brain before you can see. So, let me be your eyes for one minute. While I have to run *away* from something, you can run *to* something. Those ships were made for *you*. There is money in your pockets right now to put you on one of them. Even the papers are with you. With your back, and even with your dulled brain, you could build yourself a fine life anywhere in the world. Your place is on the other side of these waters. Not here. Definitely not here. This land and these times are just for madmen, asses, and dunces like myself."

"The idea isn't new. Many from Lvov are going to America. And don't say you are a dunce."

"Believe me, I am. And if the idea isn't new, then what in the name of Jesus are you still doing here?"

"Let's stop this." Avrum raised his arm as if in tired surrender. "All I know are forests and how to lay down a tree. The only streets where I can walk and not feel that my face is out of place are the streets in Szambor."

"*That* is exactly what I had in mind when I said that the blind know nothing of their blindness. Like blinkers on a horse

— if it can't see to the side, it thinks that nothing is there." The Doctor shook his head and let it rest a moment on his chest. His lips pressed tightly together and his eyes became wet with tears. They told of dark, curdling memories from somewhere deep within him, which were carrying him back to other people, other places, and other times. Avrum turned his chair to the side and looked out at the ships.

(12)

The new men Iannuk brought with him to Szambor introduced a simple but brutal sport that instantly took hold with the lumbermen. They called it "the Quick Boot," and taught several variations, like "the Polka," "the Moldavian Polka," and the "Kazakhstan Straplash." A circle about four yards in diameter would be marked out on the earth, and two men would face off against each other inside it. The first to get his heel down on the boot of the other was the winner, and anyone stepping outside the perimeter more than three times lost by default. (This happened rarely. However, the scorn of the crowd, who'd feel cheated of their blood, must have been harder to suffer than a few bruised toes.)

There were no rounds (but one), no time limit, and no rest periods. A count of three got the contest underway, and a cry of pain would inevitably punctuate the grunts and wheezes and signal its end. Neither "soft touches" (from the toes) nor grazing the sides of the boots counted, and the crowd would wave the fight on. The shoe had to strike with the heel from above — and a certain amount of power was expected to be behind it.

The "Polka" appealed to brawlers. It called for the left wrists of the battlers to be bound to each other by a cloth that left them free play of about a foot and a half. These contests never lasted for more than a few seconds. One of the men would find his forearm pulled across his own face, and while he'd think about it, the other fellow would already be pulverizing his toes. Or else, he would be pulled forward and suddenly released, and at that instant, when he might have stumbled to regain his balance, a waiting heel would crash down powerfully on his defenseless boot. Those who were still holding their opponents off after three or four seconds invariably suffered sharp elbows poking into their eyes, or stiff forearms slamming across their noses. The only moment of drama the Polka afforded, actually, was when the opponents would tense up while their wrists were being tied. The "dances" that ensued were comical enough, but after a time, the men decided that the Polka was too tame.

"Straplash," in contrast, allowed each man his own cloth (usually his handkerchief), which he could flutter in the face of his opponent, and so try to distract him. Here they weren't tied to each other (in the "Moldavian" version of the Polka, each also had his own cloth, but they were still bound as before), and this freedom let each man work out his own style and fighting strategy.

Strategy, as much as speed and strength, now became a factor deciding the contests, and the growing crowd of "aficionados" could analyze the course of each fight almost for hours. But problems arose when "handkerchiefs" were produced that some claimed were tablecloths. There were also those who first filled theirs with sand, which they shook into their opponent's eyes — and all used the cloths to conceal their fists, which were discovered to be the surest distraction. In the end, the popularity of Straplash waned as well, and the serious competition concentrated on the unembellished Quick Boot, where the contestants were not tied to each other and no cloths were permitted. His primeval instincts were all that a man was permitted to carry into the circle.

But the sport took on an unexpected and unpleasant dimension when Avrum became the champion at Szambor. Albeit a wholly reluctant champion, Avrum found no joy in humbling, or worse, humiliating the men. Often, he'd start a round determined to lose, but it just never happened. There was also a flow to the events that could not be reversed. The Jew would not be permitted to disappear until someone would best him. There was no way they could let him step aside undefeated. The men who were thrown against him suddenly found themselves carrying the fighting flags of all their ancestors, and their chain of defeats only exacerbated the collective humiliation. The tension grew explosive.

A catalyst, in the person of the Doctor, allowed neither side to back away; he would goad the men, laugh at them, call scornfully for challengers, and insult them grossly on their defeats. Sometimes he became so delirious he would roll on the ground crying and holding his sides. The men would spit on him. But nothing changed: Avrum went from win to win as every contest repeated itself.

For the first minute or two, Avrum never concerned himself with more than keeping a distance between himself and his opponent. The way to win was to get above a boot that might be on its way down so that every split second was vital, and one tried not to leave a foot on the ground for more than the smallest fraction of an instant after a miss. Avrum's tactics however, seemed to inspire his opponents to show off their bullish aggressiveness in the grandest manner. They may have been moved to believe that he was intimidated by them, and that their victory was only one move away. Snorting and baring their teeth, they charged at him again and again, but somehow they could never find his feet where they remembered them last.

Avrum's springs were electric and instinctive. Somehow it was always easy to force him to within an inch of the perimeter — but impossible to have him cross it. And every failure invited a renewed charge, with the men invariably becoming increasingly careless about the way their feet would come to rest. Finally, the contest would end when dulled, confused, and enraged, the challengers suddenly found their own feet trapped and crushed under Avrum's pile-driving heel. The men would immediately and with vigor renew their challenges. Luck, they called it. Just his damn luck! But sometimes they would hobble and limp painfully for hours.

Lucky or not, Avrum was champion until somebody would produce more than words to defeat him. Ironically, the men had not been entirely serious when they taunted him into testing his skill in the circle that first time. Standing at the side and to the back of them, the Doctor penetrated their smiles; he was more than irritated by the dark malevolence that he saw behind them. The man waiting for Avrum, spitting into his hands and testing his knees, grinned and said he'd have to go easy on the kid. "Don't want the boss down on me for amputating his toes," he said.

The Doctor was as surprised as the last man there when the victory came to the Jew. The "professionals" sneered and shook their heads, as if to say that they had thought they'd seen everything. The chap who was shamed clamored for another encounter, and made a great thing about Avrum not having hurt him. Another fellow took it upon himself to clear the slate for the rest of them and with a confident and quiet shrug he beckoned Avrum back to the circle. It was his mad and vigorous thumping that gave Avrum the idea of biding his time. And he saw that if he had a mind only to escape the charges, he had time enough to get his feet out of the way. Every move opposite him was telegraphed. Finally, when for an instant there was a pause in the man's rush, Avrum's boot came from nowhere to crash down on his. A meteor striking him from space would have stunned him less, and there was no calling back the rich squeal of pain that had escaped him. The man didn't stop drinking that night until the bottle slipped from his hands, the rest of his body following it to the floor.

Avrum quickly became a marvelous club in the Doctor's hands — one he wielded heartlessly. It wasn't long before he promoted his man as the champion of them all, and when he smelled that the response to his taunts lacked enthusiasm or conviction, he flayed them with the shame of their submission to a Jew.

A Jew he may have been, but a sure eye and cold calculation made them appreciate that only Iannuk and perhaps one or two other men were taller than the youth. His neck was not much narrower than the width of his head, and it sank into a powerful back and sloping shoulders — shoulders that had matured into the low, hard, and muscular slant that bespoke natural power. His arms were almost as thick as Iannuk's, and lacked the soft fat that seemed in the last year or two to have collected everywhere around the big man's body. Only his waist might have belonged to a young girl, but this was an illusion brought on by the extraordinary spread of the rest of him. His legs were solid, chiseled, and evidently as hard and as packed for kicking as a mule's. And more than one man envied his clear, fair skin and the smooth lines of this face, which still showed no shadow of beard. Had they been allowed to start off their lives so equipped, they imagined, their lot today would surely have included far better things than what described their present circumstances.

Szambor was combed for anyone who might best the Doctor's Jew. Contest followed contest, and Avrum wasn't permitted to escape them; the Doctor reached the crest of his finest hours. Avrum could not be beaten.

Almost imperceptibly, the men began to not even disguise their solid respect for him. There was something remarkable in the way he coolly handled their throttling persistence. Not one of them could have managed the same psychological pressure without breaking. In their hearts, they knew this well. Still, they also knew that they could not go on for very long calling the Doctor's protégé their champion. So it was with more relief than surprise when the Doctor's body was found one morning tied by the waist in the fork of a tree. An axe had parted his hair and left the most gruesome cleavage.

The contests stalled for two days, but Avrum was challenged again. It was only a glancing blow with the toes, but Avrum conceded and limped away. Everyone knew it was an act for their benefit. There were no contests after that.

(13)

Iannuk was at Urman when the Doctor was killed. When he learned of it a week later, he inquired after those responsible for the murder, but was not perturbed when obliged to stay largely uninformed. One of the men coldly said that he had seen no burial. Indeed, the body had disappeared not an hour after it was found, and apart from Avrum, no one had found it necessary to ask questions. Avrum's questions were answered by silence and shaking heads. Another took the cue and said that he was almost certain he had seen the Doctor pack his bags and leave. He didn't actually see him leave, but was certain he saw the Doctor packing a valise. Iannuk asked if anyone else had seen him leave. A few shoulders shrugged, and Iannuk raised his hands to indicate that as far as he was concerned that was the end of his inquiry.

But Iannuk had registered Avrum's intense disappointment and painful dismay. Later, when Iannuk invited Avrum to his cabin, Avrum complained bitterly that in their midst now was a murderer or murderers, and Iannuk had made no effort to expose them. The man or men who killed the Doctor might have equal reason to target him. Iannuk took his time. Slowly stoking the primus to get a better fire under the coffee, he confessed that he knew the Doctor was murdered, and that he even had a pretty fair idea who the murderers were. He explained, however, that if he were to report this to the police, they would have to come and question the lumbermen. Every last one of those working for him had something to hide from the authorities, and they would disappear in the blink of an eye if they thought they would have to present themselves for questioning.

"Believe me. At least half the men here are here only because the police are looking for them somewhere else. You can take my word for it."

"They were looking for the Doctor, too, weren't they?" Avrum looked directly and unafraid into Iannuk's eyes.

"Possibly, but that's irrelevant now. Don't you think so? The point is that I could live very comfortably without the Doctor. But if these men leave me, my entire operation closes down."

"But tell me, all the same, were they — the police — looking for the Doctor?"

"Yes, they were."

"What did he do?"

"That really is unimportant now, isn't it? The man is right now starting to rot in his grave, wherever in the forest they buried him, and there in nothing you can point to that can show he was here and was ever alive."

"Not really so, Iannuk. Not really so."

"No?"

"No."

Avrum related the episode at Kiev.

"And all this time, you thought I had taken up with his wife? Well . . . don't answer that. You don't have to. It would have been the most reasonable thing to believe."

"Except that he didn't go out to confront you."

"No, he wouldn't. He couldn't. He risked being shot to death — put before a firing squad, or maybe hanged. He legally would have been executed had he been recognized. You could not have known that. Also, the woman used to be his wife. They were divorced a full two years before he showed up here. He tried everything to see her after that, but the papers showed that she was divorced from him. She wanted nothing to do with him. It's a complicated story."

"I lived with him, Iannuk; I traveled thousands of kilometers with him. He is dead now, so who will it hurt if I know?"

"That woman is my sister." Avrum seemed stunned, and Iannuk shook his head slowly. "Yes, you heard right . . . my sister." His voice had dropped to a whisper.

Avrum felt his face redden. The Doctor's blunt remark about Iannuk fornicating with his wife suddenly echoed loudly in his ears. And he had taken him at his word. Iannuk went on.

"Believe me, there was no other reason that would bring me to Kiev. I was there to help her out with all the problems the Doctor had brought upon them. He had a difficult problem of his own — something sexual, and very, very sick, if you didn't know by now. Well, you still don't know about these things. His greatest pleasure was having a woman urinate on him and beat him with a strap. He would steal panties from clotheslines. Do you understand?"

Wide-eyed, Avrum nodded and listened hard.

"Then there was another side to his sickness. Unless he was actually hurting the woman in bed with him, he could never feel quiet. He liked to choke them. Doctors recognize this as a mental disease. My sister would have no part of it, and they divorced. But he always tried to get back to her, and there was no way she would let him. Maybe in some way he was a brilliant man, and maybe he really loved her, but he couldn't change. So he had this relationship with a prostitute who let him do what he wanted to her. It cost him a fortune, but he paid willingly whatever she asked. Then it seems that one day her mood changed, and when his machine wouldn't stiffen, if you follow me, the stupid woman complained that he wasn't a man and never really had been a man. Well . . . the ugly little whore never said anything after that. The Doctor choked her to death in seconds, and then started a fire in the room. The whole damn house burned down."

"Holy Jesus!"

"Yes. Holy Jesus! Three other women were burned to death. The one who ran the house was no small-time amateur. Besides Kiev, he had houses in a dozen other cities — Lvov included, by the way. The Doctor knew they'd be after him, but crazy with fear he ran first to his ex-wife's house . . . and I was there at the time. They had a little daughter, and she was well on her way to delivering a second. She needed help, and now you see that she wasn't getting any from him. If I wouldn't have stepped in, it is very likely that the Doctor would soon have delivered my sister to one of the same houses he frequented. Anyway, we heard the story, and, crazy woman that she was, she pleaded — begged — that I take him into the forest. I had to swear that I would; that is the reason I had him here. He couldn't show his face anywhere. Every day that he lived after that was my personal gift to him."

Almost as an afterthought, he added, "To look at him, you'd have thought he was normal — two arms, two legs — but the truth is that he was a mental cripple from day one."

* * *

The boys played "Battleship" on the creek; they'd take old kettles, fill them halfway with mud and stones so that they'd drift low in the water, and in the spouts, they would fit their "lucky flags," twigs carrying slips of colored fabric. The "ships" were then pushed off not far from the stone over Heskel's dog, and the boys would rush along the edge of the water, heaving rocks at the "enemy" ship. The last one to stay afloat would be the winner.

Berel Smojak, the fishmonger's boy, never lost easily. Whenever his ship was sunk, he'd try to stop the game, or else complain that he'd done it accidentally with his own rock. But he'd only start in with his antics when the other fellows pelted him with their acid verses.

> *Cry and make a storm grow,*
> *The wind is just the noise you blow,*
> *Tell me something I don't know.*

Or, if they were feeling particularly malicious:

> *In your mouth one finger,*
> *In your behind another. Fuy!*

Ordinarily Berel would retort, "Same on your grave. Same on your grave. Same on your grave, too." But one game took another turn. Someone had hurled a stone that nicked his finger, and when he turned in the direction he thought it came from, his eyes fell on Hershel. Without thinking, he charged at Hershel, who started to run a fraction too late. Berel had a rock in his hand, which he slammed into Hershel's shoulder; the force threw him backwards into the water.

An instant later, Avrum was on Berel's back, and they wrestled furiously on the ground. Teeth bit, fists punched, feet kicked. The other boys tried to separate them and succeeded, but not before Avrum had ripped the shirt and fringed garment away from Berel's chest. His own trousers were torn and a tuft of his hair was in Berel's fist, but no one paid any mind to that. Everyone was transfixed by the sight of Berel's exposed chest. There was a vestige of one nipple, but stretching from it across to the other side and cutting down across his belly was thickly layered, twisted, pinched scar tissue. And the color was not of this world.

It was Berel who had broken the silence. "It was a fire. So what? It could happen to anyone."

The boys backed away, and, hastily covering himself, Berel made for home. For a fraction of a second, he glanced at where his ship had sunk. His flag was floating on the surface, split and bent — a partner to his disgrace. Nothing could make him go back to collect it.

Avrum had related the circumstances of the battle to his mother and Hershel had to swear that it wasn't he who threw the stone. It turned out that their mother had helped treat Berel when, as an infant, he had overturned a pan of fat on the stove. It had burst into flames, spilling on him.

She had taken Avrum's hands in her own and he wondered what he would hear. She lifted them to her lips and kissed them.

"He who would forsake his own blood," she began softly, "surrenders his heritage to the Evil One and commits the scar of Cain to his soul. Scars on the body violate only the eye, and easier are these to bear than the scars which violate the earth.

"In your life, you will know people worse off than Berel."

(14)

Iannuk continued to expand his operations. The camp he had at Urman was now larger than the one at Szambor, and Avrum had relocated there. Otherwise, the new season was like every other, until a spate of robberies in the middle of the summer turned everyone's mind to the thief lurking amongst them. Watches, money, bits of gold, and even articles of clothing were disappearing regularly. Searches were demanded and invited. Everyone asked that their own goods be inspected in an attempt to clear their own names; but despite everyone's protestations of innocence and constant alertness, everyone suspected everyone else, and the thieving continued.

Purses with considerable savings disappeared. Crucifixes, if there was half a gram of gold or silver in them, were removed in the night from around their owner's very necks. So it was with watches. No one saw, felt, heard, or knew anything that could put a halt to what was happening. It was as though the entire camp was both the victim of and a partner to some insidious criminal conspiracy.

The oldest friendships became strained, and conversations soon lacked intimacy. Everyone seemed to distrust everyone else, and the angry, enervated men were drained of any zest for getting on with the day's work. Many took to speaking openly about their intentions to shift to other companies. Iannuk was confounded, but utterly helpless. The dilemma began to assume the dimensions of an ominous design, which, in Iannuk's mind, might portend his immediate ruin.

The camp at Urman was directly on the Zolochiv, one of the tributaries that flowed into the headwaters of the Dneister. At about this time, Avrum used to take advantage of an hour or two of the warm sun to swim in the river. He would let the chill and very swift waters carry him for a distance before starting back, straining mightily against the current.

One afternoon, while the waters still commanded him, a stirring a few yards in from the shore caught his attention. As no work was called for in that area, he expected it might be a beast — possibly a bear that was moving about. If indeed it was a bear and could be trapped, his gains in cash and prestige would be enormous. But bears were unpredictable creatures; a few seemed almost to ask to be done in, but the others on the whole were so determined in their savagery that for anyone to become fixed in their line of vision proved too often a fatal miscalculation.

Wladek, who gave him the first address in Lvov, had been killed by a bear just last season, and they said that the only way he could be identified was by the clothes scattered around the sickening chunks of crushed bone and scrapped flesh that had once been his body. His skull might have been the inside of a chicken from the way it was opened and cleaned out. And some men said that they were only convinced it was Wladek when he alone failed to turn out when they left the camp the following morning.

Avrum let the waters carry him to a downwind position, and silently worked his way from there to the bank. The stirring in the bushes was easy to follow, but it was not the stirring of a bear. He heard sounds that were distinctly human. He recognized Peter's voice — Peter, perhaps the oldest man in their company — and Avrum was about to call out a greeting when a sudden, sharp constriction in his throat caused him to hold back. Something was unnatural in the voice, as though fear was curled thickly in his tongue. Avrum waited. Another voice answered Peter; Avrum thought it belonged to Boris, a new man in their company.

"We'll decide if that's the last of it. Meanwhile, old man, you're still alive, so don't look to complicate your life." It *was* Boris, and he spoke in a strange tone, one shifting between malice and menace.

The voices were muffled after that, and the cracking of the underbrush made it impossible to follow their words. But Avrum suddenly heard Boris say quickly and sharply, "We'll cut your stomach open and you'll be carrying your guts in your hands. You'll beg us for a bullet between your eyes."

Peter's stiff promise followed. "No one will know anything from me."

Avrum moved back into the river and slipped below the surface. He plowed ahead powerfully and silently for about a hundred feet before surfacing, and then continued to the camp.

His thoughts raced even as he delivered what he knew to Iannuk. Iannuk embraced him. As much affection as gratitude radiated from his eyes. "If the season can still be saved after this, I'll make you my partner. But damn — was it only Peter and Boris?"

"Those were the only voices I heard there."

"But Boris said '*we'll* decide' and '*we'll* cut your stomach out' . . . there must be someone else with him."

"I think so, too."

"But you don't know who?"

"No. I should have waited longer, but the water was freezing."

"You should have. But it is better this way than risk having them discover you. Anyway, I'm certain that it is the one they call 'Boku.' They make as though they have nothing to do with each other now, but they were friends enough when I took them on. They smelled wrong. Pity it was too late to check them out; I was short at least twenty — and Christ, now I'm down thirty — but it is Boku. It must be Boku who is with them."

"How do you plan to expose them?"

"Exposing them won't be enough. I must get everything returned to the men. Nothing short of that will keep them on here."

The plan Iannuk devised was to get to the site the same way Avrum did, by swimming there, and then to try to uncover where the loot was hidden. Failing that, they would lie in wait for Boris, Peter, and whomever their partner might be to expose it to them.

"You'll need help," said Avrum.

"You'll be with me — but I'll keep you on the side to watch. They won't lift a finger. Boris may try something, but if he does, he'll have to eat with his rump hole, because that is where he'll find his teeth when I finish with him."

Avrum never doubted Iannuk's capacity to do just that. But just as they were on their way to the water, Iannuk stopped a fellow by the name of Grigor who had been the very first victim of the robbers. The man had had a full year's savings taken from his belt. Grigor was invited along, and from the way he shook his head and narrowed his eyes, it was plain that the moment he had waited for was now at hand. He asked to change his clothes. Iannuk did the same and took along a supply of rope. They held their clothes in bundles over their heads, and let the water rush them away. When Avrum pointed out the place, they waded to the bank and concealed themselves in the low overhanging branches there.

After fifteen minutes of silent waiting, Iannuk motioned for them to climb out of the water. Grigor had to be helped. His skin had turned blue and gray from the cold and his muscles wouldn't respond. They dried him and dressed him but when he developed a fit of shaking Iannuk slapped him hard across his back and chest and stretched him out on the ground.

They were alone, but it was evident when they looked about that the clearing they were in was not natural to the land. Leading from it was a narrow but well-trodden path and they imagined that it would take them back to the camp. They overturned rocks, looked behind and into the trees, and stomped on the earth hoping to catch the sound of a hollow, but the loot apparently had been hidden well. Boris, Peter and the third person — whoever he was — would have to lead them to it.

Iannuk, Avrum, and Grigor returned to the site the next day. Iannuk had insisted that they cover the distance in the water again, because it was the earliest part of the afternoon and if they would be seen on the path by the wrong people, their plan would collapse. Grigor wore a sweater in the water and it seemed to help him, but again he was struck by a terrible shaking; this time he insisted on overcoming it himself.

Hoping that Boris and the others would make an appearance by at least late afternoon, Iannuk arranged to ambush them by blocking all lines of retreat from the clearing. He took Grigor with him to a spot where they were distant from the path, but could still see it clearly. The distance was not such that they couldn't cover it in a few seconds. Avrum was instructed to stay well concealed directly on the water line, and Iannuk would throw a stone into the river to signal Avrum of someone's approach.

An hour passed, then another. The sun had moved a long way in the sky. Suddenly, Avrum heard a splash behind him, and so that he couldn't think it was a fish or a frog, or something from a tree, Iannuk sent a second stone after the first. The alert was on, but only after an interminable quiet with all his senses unbearably strained did Avrum hear the first faint voices. These approached and grew louder.

Avrum was not to make a move until the whereabouts of what had been stolen were revealed, and a shout at that time would signal Iannuk and Grigor to rush in.

Boris and Peter came into the clearing, but they just stood there. Peter seemed very restless, and Boris made a few curt remarks while his eyes darted everywhere.

Avrum was struggling to hold down a cough and to ignore a maddening itch on his knee. He thought he saw Boris look directly at him, and it entered his mind to signal Iannuk then and there, but Boris shifted his gaze and Avrum had to control the wild pounding of his heart.

Peter was walking back and forth — clearly very agitated about something — and Boris told him to quiet down. For some reason they spoke in whispers and Avrum was beginning to sense that Iannuk's plan was not coming along as smoothly as he might have wished. Worse, Boris and Peter seemed to have come empty-handed, with no intention of disturbing the cache. Perhaps they were waiting for the third party, but if that was Boku, it was unlikely that he would show up: Boku was down with a fever.

Suddenly, and for no apparent reason, Boris withdrew a pistol from his vest and aimed it at a terrified Peter. There were neither words of explanation nor pleas when the shot dropped the old man.

"Boris!" It was Iannuk shouting from where he was hiding.

"I hear you, Iannuk." Not a trace of surprise crossed his face. Avrum held himself back and tried to make sense of what was developing.

"You are finished, Boris. Gun or no gun, you have had it. Stealing is one thing—"

"Come out, Iannuk," interrupted Boris, "and we'll see who is finished."

"You tried it in the wrong camp, Boris."

"I'm a better man than you Iannuk. Come get me."

"Swine shit."

Then there was silence. Boris crouched low and advanced in the direction of Iannuk's voice, then he stopped and called out, "Where's your army, Iannuk? Who is coming to help you? Where's your sniveling Jew?"

"I'm here, Boris." It was Iannuk again.

Boris crouched even lower, but kept his pistol straight ahead of him. Avrum found a length of wood stripped from a rotted trunk that was lying against him, and he hurled it over his head to fall near Boris, who turned in surprise.

"*Jide!*" he shouted. "You're as dead as your boss."

But that same instant, with Boris still turned, Iannuk rose like a mountain before him, and there was a very real pistol in his hand as well. He had it pressing hard into the back of Boris's neck.

Iannuk shouted, "I'll kill you, Boris. Don't even breathe."

Boris paled, dropped his gun, and raised his hands. Grigor ran over to them and collected the gun. Avrum began to rise, but before he could focus on Iannuk and Boris, his eyes took in the sight of Peter, whose blood was still flowing out of his body. He saw Grigor stoop for the gun, and with that, some of the tension drained from him.

"Who is the third man?" Iannuk asked, still pressing the gun into Boris's neck.

Incredibly, Boris only laughed and turned to face Iannuk. Shifting his body faster than the eye could follow, Iannuk exploded, smashing a boot into Boris' crotch. It was a blow to cripple forever any man's mind no less than his body. Boris lay shattered, trembling uncontrollably, his body a shapeless, writhing heap. When Iannuk raised his eyes, he learned who the third man was.

Avrum saw the smoke and instantly shared the same knowledge. Then the blast resounded, and Iannuk — the invulnerable and fearsome giant — turned halfway around and doubled over. His face was awash with blood. Grigor moved again and aimed his pistol at Avrum, who weaved a mad zigzag back to the water. He heard the shot and the whistle of the lead, but his body was already suspended in the air, and an instant later, the water covered him.

He swam beneath the surface until there was no chance he might be seen. The cold air that then rushed into his lungs already belonged to a new chapter in his life. Hershel was somewhere in America, and it was time for Avrum to follow him. The boats were waiting at Odessa, he had his papers, and all the fare he would need was in his hands.

(15)

Even before the robberies had begun to plague the camp, Avrum had collected his papers and the fine watch he had bought in Odessa, and added the money he had saved over the years. All these he buried in a jar in the ground. The place was known only to him, though Iannuk had suggested at the time which area in the woods would be safest, an area they would not be working that year.

Now, when he unearthed the jar and found everything intact, his mind flooded with gratitude for his lost mentor. It would be hard to imagine a world that didn't include Iannuk's indomitable figure and giant shadow. With Iannuk dead, whatever had anchored Avrum's life to the forest was gone. All that remained was finding the strength of heart to turn his back on the lost bones of his mother and father. Those bones were now in the gray parcel of hard memories, and there they would remain until he breathed his final breath, but they were a parcel that belonged to the past. Ahead of him was a future that had to somehow include Hershel.

He doubted that Grigor would return to the camp. Still, Avrum decided against immediately sharing with the others what had happened. To do so would keep him at the camp, and this had to be his last hour there. He found half a dozen sheets of paper in Iannuk's cabin, surprised at how brazenly he had entered it. On each, he drew a map of where the clearing was, and below it, in a simple, almost childlike scrawl he set down what had happened. One sheet he left on Iannuk's table, and one he posted on each of the two tool sheds. The remaining three he scattered near the cabins. Thankfully, the darkness hid him and the papers would only be found in the morning. His problem now was to get away from the camp in as short a time as possible, and at as great a distance as possible.

There was a track behind the camp along which the horses would lug the trees. It traced most of the perimeter, and connected the camp to an old road kept up by the few farms that were still being worked. They were primitive operations, but a handful of *hryvnas* or a ruble or two was still respected there. He avoided the first because the farmer's son-in-law worked in their camp, and the farmer might find Avrum's movements in the night too suspicious to let pass without question. Likely, he also knew about the thefts, and Avrum might not be sufficiently convincing about the reasons for his awkward departure.

More than a mile farther on was the second farm, where Avrum was able to discern a horse tied to a wagon. Struggling not to surrender to exhaustion, he knocked at the door of the old house, which was built over the shed and stable. The horse stirred and got to its feet. Then a voice from inside the house asked who it was, and Avrum responded, injecting urgency into his words. The window opened above him, and a lantern emerged. Avrum begged the man's pardon and explained again that he was from the camp — that he was stricken with severe pains in the stomach and had been told at the camp that, for a price, the farmer would put him on the main road to Lvov.

"Why didn't you wait for the train in the morning?"

Avrum lied desperately. "The trains are cancelled for three days. Repairs — and I have to get to a doctor by morning."

"You don't look sick to me."

"The pains come and go. They think it is the appendix. I'll pay you whatever you ask."

* * *

It was close to three in the morning when Avrum stepped off the wagon. The night was at its blackest; clouds must have collected, but there he was on the main road. Everything he had in the world was at that moment either on his back or in his valise — the same old tattered and battered valise that he had first carried to Lvov, and later to Kiev and Odessa. It was past six when a carriage appeared, and another handful of coins changed hands. It carried Avrum half the distance to Lvov, stopping at a railway station where he could meet the next train. Later, as he watched the countryside rolling past him, he thought that every disappearing stone, house, tree, and post marked the distance between his present and his past. Despite everything, an extraordinary feeling of exhilaration flooded his body. He felt as light as a leaf and as unstoppable as the soot-covered engine chugging powerfully and clanking noisily ahead of him.

* * *

Avrum had expected to enlist the Kaplinskys' help in tracing the Flomens, who had taken Hershel with them to America, but the Kaplinskys were crossing the ocean those very same days. Leibel had indeed liquidated. Only a very few of the families that Avrum had known remained behind, but he was told that in America the Jews were organized, and that they had many societies that helped relatives trace each other. Often, one advertisement in a local Jewish paper sufficed.

Avrum left for Russia and Odessa the next day. For the three days and nights that followed, the cars shook and rattled loudly, but Avrum could not be stirred from the heavy melancholic trance that had settled over him. He had spoken to half a dozen people in Lvov; one or two recalled who he was, but none demonstrated interest or empathy, or wished him well for the future. Of all those on their way to America, he was perhaps the only one without an address in hand to give some sense of direction to the volcanic and convoluted transformations the days were thrusting upon him. Hershel and the Flomens were the only names and figures — as vague and uncertain as they were — that allowed him some notion of an ultimate goal.

In itself, the name "America" promised nothing. If there was one aspect of a man's life that all men were partner to, it could only be his inherent aloneness. Every last man at the camps — all those who worked the saws together, who laughed, drank, and gambled together — turned out to be as distant, as isolated, and as insulated from each other as Avrum had always been from them. Nothing marked this better than the events that culminated in Iannuk's murder, and he couldn't imagine what he might find in America that might change this.

Avrum looked down at his hands and feet. He imagined himself detached from them. In the end, he thought, everything was reduced to this: to dumb skin, meat, and bones . . . and luckier am I to be attached to them, than they to me. It occurred to him that he was cheating his own limbs. In his mind, he had no qualms about death — he would wish the inevitable sooner rather than later for himself — but his bones, packed in blood and sinew, were determined to take issue with such sentiments. They had taken a firm grip on life long before his mind could appreciate the futility, if not the tragedy, of his existence. When the shot was fired — perhaps even before then — his body had unceremoniously taken mastery over his mind. His will had not rebelled. He had done everything to remain alive.

On arrival at Odessa, exhausted and heavy with body odor, Avrum turned into the first small hotel that he found near the station. While still in the station, he had purchased a new kind of money belt to be worn under one's clothes; in the room, he fit it around himself and transferred his money to it. Moments later, he was asleep.

In the morning, he found that his clothes and valise had been stolen in the night. In a sweat, he felt under the bed for his shoes and found them. Inside were his papers, and they were untouched. He inspected his money belt, and then slipped his papers inside the pouch as well. "Let everything else burn and rot," he muttered aloud, still unsteady and shaken. Then he realized that his watch was gone, and he granted to himself that it, too, was a fixture of the old world that would stay behind. "Let everything burn and rot," he repeated. "*Oif kapurus*," as his mother would say in such instances. He thought perhaps there was a design to all this — that perhaps it was all predetermined. A child, about to be born, comes into the world naked. In like manner, he was to be delivered to a world external to everything that brought him to this frightening hour. It was as simple as that.

He also wanted to believe that locked in the stars was the pattern of everything he was, and everything that would be. Beyond the *why*s and *wherefore*s of all the trials that had etched their designs in his life, he felt with growing conviction that this grand design included his continued survival. He *would* find his way in America; even the Doctor had been certain of this, and said so often enough. Avrum clung to the echo of those words, which somehow seemed louder and clearer now than at any time when the man was alive.

The owner of the hotel was apologetic and greatly concerned that the lawlessness he described as being rampant in the city should have penetrated his door. "You didn't hear about the crime wave that has infested this city? People are leaving Odessa as if everyone was coming down again with the Black Death. No one is safe anymore — not inside, not outside."

Avrum complained that he was left without clothes, and the proprietor was more helpful than Avrum expected. He said that he probably had something downstairs that would fit him — nothing heavy of course, just a shirt and old trousers, but Avrum would at least be able to walk out respectably. A problem might be Avrum's continued stay there. The first night had been paid for in advance, but if he was robbed, how might he cover the coming nights?

"I still have my money."

The man seemed surprised and left. But then it was Avrum's turn to be surprised. The shirt that the man produced for him was the very one that had been on his back the day before.

"Impossible," frowned the owner. "It has been here for years."

"I know my own shirt."

"Are you accusing me of something?" A sinister edge crept into his voice. "To my ears, it sounds as though you are accusing me of something."

"I wore this shirt yesterday. It still has the grease marks where it rubbed against a door in the train. Look at that." Avrum stretched out the sleeve where the stain showed.

"I didn't have to give you the shirt, did I? I brought it to you as a kind favor. If I took your shirt, why should I give it back to you? Next you'll say that my trousers are yours, too."

"No, just the shirt."

"So keep it. I see that it will be impossible to talk to you."

"Maybe my pants and coat are downstairs, too?"

"I think what you're saying is that I stole them? Is that what you're saying? You're not from anywhere around here, are you? If you were, you'd think twice before even thinking the noises your tongue is making."

"A new coat will cost me more money than I can afford."

"And from this minute, you can't afford this room, either."

"All that I'm asking is for you to take another look near the place where you found the shirt. Maybe whoever took it threw my other things there, too."

"You are still insisting that it's your shirt? I can get someone to take it off you in a minute."

"There are police . . ."

"You want to throw police at me? That is supposed to make me shake?" The man erased any vestige of his earlier pretenses. "If you are not out of here in five seconds, you will remember this place as the last one where you were still able to move with your head above your feet. Test me if you want to, and don't think your size scares me." With that, he slapped his hand on the desk, showed Avrum his fist, and disappeared behind a curtain that probably led into his private quarters.

Avrum collected what was left of his belongings and left.

The steamship company's agent had an office in one of the elegant buildings in the port area. Avrum found it; it was crowded with people. When his turn at the desk finally came, he had already learned that the next ship leaving for the United States would be in no less than five weeks' time. It was possible, however, if he had no objection to sharing a room with at least another thirty men, that he might secure passage to a city called Montreal, which was in Canada. Everyone, it seemed, preferred New York, but a map was set before him that showed Montreal wasn't an impossible distance from New York. Nothing would prevent him from continuing to New York, but many immigrants had in fact settled in Montreal very successfully. The ship was scheduled to leave within the week, but word was that the ship was among the worst plying the oceans. Avrum was told that beyond Odessa, the ship would be calling at Naples and Barcelona, and that the steerage level of the ship adjacent to the engine room was where Avrum would find his cot.

Avrum opted for Montreal. With shaking hands, he showed his papers, delivered the money requested — money that he had counted over that day at least twenty times — and watched almost in terror as the clerk counted it twice again. After a flurry of stamping and tearing and signing, he was handed a bundle of papers, which, he was informed, was the ticket. He was told exactly where to be, exactly when to be there, and exactly what he was permitted to take along with him.

"And if for whatever reason you miss the boat, your ticket won't get you on any other boat. Also, you won't be getting your money back. This you understand, yes?"

"Yes."

Avrum felt himself becoming overtaken by a euphoria he had never before known. There was a magical order to the world, and his initiative was making him a part of that order. He felt at one then with everyone lined up in the office. They may have been strangers, but their lives were all linked, at least for a while, and maybe some of the links would persist. For no reason, he bought himself some flowers from a street vendor, and the vendor selected the freshest ones with special care. There was money left in his belt to last him a while. He'd keep from starving. He was young and he was strong.

Wait there, Hershel . . . I am coming for you. Don't look around. Don't interrupt for a moment the business of your day, and don't disturb the flow of your life. I will find you like the sun finds the land. I will trace a web through every city and ask for you at every door. From the instant I land, your ears will hear my steps and I will know yours, and the hand that will come to rest on your shoulder will be mine. I feel tomorrow lifting me like an eagle to the highest peaks.

(16)

The arrangements within the ship were predominantly for one class of passenger. The section where Avrum found his place had as many as twenty double-decker beds — and so crammed together that every man came to know intimately his neighbor's favorite liquor. The collection of valises, boxes, and sacks was piled almost precariously, one atop the other, against the wall next to the door, and an aging, unshaven steward had told the passengers in the sternest tones that these belongings weren't to be disturbed for the length of the trip. Whatever they might need, they were to store under their beds. Everyone agreed, everyone understood, and not ten minutes after he left them at least half a dozen passengers remembered things they urgently needed to retrieve from the pile.

The first one found his valise very close to the bottom, and to get it out, he had to free it from under a long, soft carton that was draped over it. Both were pretty much crushed under all the weight, and the man kept the box back with his foot while he tugged on his valise. Suddenly, one side of the handle broke off and he was thrown back with a jerk, which at least got the valise halfway out. More twisting and pulling freed the other half, and just at that instant, everything seemed suspended in the air. Earlier, someone had called the whole tenuously balanced arrangement "the eighth wonder of the world," and, much like the Colossus of Rhodes in the wake of an earthquake, this thing collapsed and disintegrated without due ceremony. Crashing down on five or six beds, some valises had their locks ripped away and some cracked open like watermelons. Sacking tore like thin paper bags.

In less than half an hour, the engines were to be fired, the ship would start out to sea, and already tempers flared dangerously. Some people were ready to terminate their odyssey right then and there. A fistfight broke out; then, someone noticed that one of the pipes behind the valises had ruptured, and the whole room was slowly being flooded.

The calamity was fed by an uproar that had spread from the other side of the ship where the women had their quarters. Some of the husbands had gone to help their wives, and had been asked to leave by other women, who were in the course of changing their clothes. Some of the men couldn't for the life of them understand what difference their presence made. An insult was hurled, and it spawned a dozen. Then someone threw something, and instantly, projectiles speared the air in every direction.

A mother stopped in the middle of breastfeeding, and — mindless of all she was advertising — raised her infant as if she were about to throw it at someone. A woman shouted that she was a whore, and that woman was slapped hard in turn by another who had charged at her from across the room. Women screamed and screeched, children hollered, and the men cursed.

One of the men actually spat on a woman, and this stunned everyone who had seen it. There was a sharp break in the din. The man turned on his best contemptuous glare and retreated toward his own room, but he wasn't alone: half the women and a few of the men were right on his heels in the passage — all of them anxious to get their fists and nails into his face. Their intentions were loud and undisguised, and the man shrank, scrapped his dignity, and broke into a run.

The luggage, mauled by the fall and absorbing water as fast as it left the pipe, almost caused him to pause, but he was running virtually for his life, and he rushed into the room, blindly sending his feet through everything in his way. The angry tide behind him then exploded into the room, and turned whatever valises, sacks, boxes, and sundry packages he managed to miss into a pulpy, splintery porridge. Pajamas, picture frames, odd shoes, candlesticks, trousers, shirts, books, bottles, underwear, and cutlery got strewn across the now-muddy floor, and from the pile of torn sacking, cardboard, and plywood, there slowly oozed an undistinguishable gel of more sopping garments.

Nothing, however, would stop the bloodletting, and the shouting drowned the first auspicious blasts of the ship's whistles. No one caught the first creaks and groans of the vessel — sounds that would be with them for the next month. But something had changed inalterably for all of them.

The arguments, the anger, and the personal accounts eventually gave way to seasickness when the ship began to pitch and roll heavily after passing the breakwater. Many passengers realized only then that they were free of the land — free of all the knots of the past, if only in exchange for the frightening uncertainties of the future. And with that, they began their endless parade to the rails. Some went for the view, others to meditate, but most went there to throw up.

* * *

High on the narrow platform around the smokestack, Avrum found a place where he could stretch out comfortably. The cool salt winds rushing at him were invigorating, and with his shoulders and head pressed against the warm steel he let himself become enveloped by the vibrations of the ship, the low rumble of the engines, and the temper of the waves. This was another of those rare moments that he would have chosen to carry on forever. The serenity of the endless ocean was so novel, so extraordinary and the tranquility so sublime, that Avrum almost had to struggle to accept that he was here on this ship, at this time, and feeling what he was feeling. The Doctor used to say that a man's fortune, like his mind, had more components than even the most expert dissection will ever expose.

The image of the Doctor surfaced repeatedly in his mind. Memories carried him back to the Potemkin steps and the coffeehouse in Odessa from where they looked out on the ships in the harbor. Even the taste of the cinnamon rolls they had eaten returned to his tongue — even to his nostrils. But there were also flashes of the Doctor's bloodied, twisted, and lifeless body wedged in the tree. And surfacing ever more frequently in his mind now were the heavy and haunting pictures of a bend in a distant road, where numberless other bloodied, twisted, and lifeless bodies were strewn everywhere.

There were so many times when he considered going back to that road. It wouldn't have been impossible. Yet in his heart, he knew it would never happen. Those were the moments when he would imagine himself still as the trembling nine year old searching for his own body, certain that in another fraction of an instant, he would come upon it. It was as though not a single hour had passed since then, and that not a single mile had ever separated him from that place. However long he lived, and to whatever distance this ship would carry him, he knew that he would forever be standing there with Hershel, both of them on failing legs, looking down at all the lives they had ever known, all the lives that were forever lost to them.

But the vistas, the pounding wind, the restless sea, and the creaking, groaning, and heavy rocking of the ship now challenged these thoughts. The images soon diminished and receded. Avrum shifted his body so that more of his back could absorb the heat of the metal. There would be no yesterdays to return to. Ghosts would linger, probably forever, but in the parcel of this hour was the promise of a very new and very different tomorrow. He delivered his trust blindly to the wisdom of the hands molding his fate. And what once he sensed only vaguely, he now experienced profoundly: that his life was somehow being carried by some distant design. His life was a beat in the pulse of the earth, the ocean, and the sky. Nothing would interrupt it.

Avrum elected to remain on the platform even as the sun dipped below the horizon. Under a gray sky, the ship lurched through the Bosporus, and would reach Constantinople before dawn. Avrum became absorbed by the distant lights on the mainland. He felt them strangely bewitching, but they belonged to strangers. Those lights would play no role in his life.

Avrum was abruptly shaken from his thoughts when hands from the deck below took a firm grip on the bar near his feet.

They strained, and the figure of a man heaved into view. He didn't climb onto the platform, but saluted grandly from the ladder, and let a rich and raucous laugh issue from his throat.

Impossible! The face should have been strange to him, and Avrum struggled to reject the image. The lights of the ship only made it eerier; coming from the deck below them, they turned his face into a virtual death mask.

The man lifted a hand in mock surrender and, still laughing, cried, "No gun — no gun."

"Grigor!"

"Ya, Grigor."

Avrum shot to his feet. Shaken and crazed with confusion at the sight of this man, he could only glare at him in disbelief. Panic followed quickly. His heart thumped loudly. "What? You? On this ship? Holy Jesus! On this ship?!"

Grigor broke his smile and assumed a serious confidential air. "You mind if I come up? I think we can talk like friends. After all, the forests are far behind us."

This just couldn't be happening. A wild rush of thoughts, questions, raw emotions and maddening images struggled to untangle themselves in his mind. Avrum could still hear the blast of the pistol, see the puff of white smoke, and Iannuk reeling backward before falling heavily to the ground. No words could reach his lips. Avrum got to his feet.

"You are surprised. I know."

"Criminal! Murderer! Thief!"

"I am not what you think, but I know how you feel. I saw you from the first day, but didn't want to push myself on you."

"Keep yourself away from me. We aren't friends."

Grigor wasn't a big man. There was the slightest evil curve fixed at the corners of his mouth, and this was matched to quizzical and somehow distrusting eyes set against the many folds of his forehead. He reminded Avrum of a merchant selling some marvelous elixir at the freak show in Kiev.

"I swear, climb up one more step — just one more step — and you'll get my foot in your face."

With every muscle as taut as a coiled spring, Avrum braced the length of his body against the hot metal of the stack. He half-expected Grigor to aim a pistol at him, but Grigor stayed where he was. He even seemed relaxed.

"Believe me, Avrum, I swear there was no chance in the world that I would have shot you. I fired only to keep you away from me and not to kill you. You would have broken my bones."

"Liar. You are a thief and a murderer."

"If I meant to shoot you, you'd be dead. I didn't want that."

"You shot Iannuk. You didn't shoot to miss then. And he trusted you."

"Did you see what he did to Boris? Do you remember what he did to Boris? He would have done the same to me."

"You were in with Boris all the time."

"All right. I confess to that, and Iannuk would have found out. But you don't know the whole story. There are reasons for everything. Look — maybe you'll come down and we'll find ourselves a quiet corner."

"It's quiet here," said Avrum, instantly regretting his words. Grigor had tripped him now as before. Surely he would again.

"Come down and we'll find ourselves a table and chairs. A glass of tea will relax both of us. If not that — perhaps this . . ." He withdrew a bottle from the inside of his jacket and offered it.

"I wouldn't drink with you."

"This isn't Urman, Avrum." Grigor looked down and shook his head. "Urman is behind us. Think that it never existed. Let's talk. Not like friends? So, like gentlemen. Not with me hanging on the ladder." He was silent a moment, collecting his thoughts. In a softer tone, he continued, "You and me . . . we're on our way to another world now . . . another life, in fact. The rules of the game change."

"Iannuk was my father. You shot him. Does that change, too?"

"I am sorry for a lot of things about me and my life. Believe me, I did not want Iannuk dead. I wanted no one dead."

"Why was Peter killed?"

"Well, may I come up at least before I tell you? I would prefer to talk to your face and not to your boots."

"If I had a gun with me, I'd use it on you now, Grigor. You are a murderer. Listen to the word, Grigor — a *murderer*. That's you. Just stay where I can't reach out and grab you."

"If that's the way you want it. But we are going to be almost three weeks in this bathtub. The only reason you didn't see me until now was because I saw you first — like I told you, on the very first day — and didn't want to risk your making difficulties while there was still a chance they could get me back to land. They *are* looking for me; that is true. Iannuk was as big a name as he was a man. But I have a story, too."

"What about Peter? Why was he killed — an old man, working with you. We knew that."

"That was Boris, not me. Remember that. I would have killed Boris myself for what he did to Peter. Peter caught Boris stealing, and Boris made him go along with him. It wasn't hard to do. The old man was frightened, and knew what Boris was capable of doing. But look — it's finished. It's all finished."

"Not for me. It will never be finished for me."

"Come, come my friend. This whole business belongs to a land and people you and me will never see again."

"You're a murderer, Grigor — and that isn't left behind. You weren't my friend then, and you're not my friend now."

Grigor stepped slowly down a rung and regarded Avrum with a theatrical sneer while shaking his head with pity. "I was not planning to push myself on you. Every day is a new story. If you can't finish with the old ones . . . if you can't shake them off, they get mixed up with the new ones, so that soon enough nothing makes sense any more. You'll still be fighting old stupid battles when everyone else has forgotten them."

Grigor disappeared down the rungs. A day or two passed without them meeting again, but each felt the presence of the other. There were instances when Avrum caught sight of him, often from a distance, but Grigor's narrow and cold eyes seemed always to have found him first. Then there was the morning when they brushed shoulders near the kitchen. A strained silence followed. Avrum still could not grasp that he was in such close physical proximity to the same man who only days earlier had aimed and fired a pistol at his back. Avrum pulled away, but Grigor took a firm grip on his elbow.

Grigor spoke. His tone was soft and low, almost apologetic.

"I killed Iannuk, and I live with what I did. I can't erase that. Don't think that I don't see Iannuk's face when I go to sleep at night. But it's done and I can't undo it. And how should I punish myself? By warping my mind and crippling any chance of building something up again? Iannuk won't come back to life; that's an ugly fact. If I killed myself, Iannuk still remains dead, and nothing at all changes for anyone. And in my heart, I know two things: that I had never shot anyone before Iannuk, and will never shoot anyone after him. I did what I did because he would have crippled me like he did Boris. Do you think he wouldn't have? Ask me why I stole. That's another story, but it's not murder, and there are explanations there, too."

"Keep them to yourself. I wouldn't believe them."

"Don't be a fool. America will bury you if you don't change."

Avrum was without reply.

"We have almost three more weeks together on this boat, and it is possible that we'll both be living in the same city. We will be seeing each other again." Then, with a half smile and a motion of salute, Grigor took a step to one side and let other people separate them. A moment later, he was gone.

It crushed Avrum to think that he was slowly succumbing to Grigor's words. Plainly, being partner to anything with Grigor, even conversation, meant violating the memory of the man to whom he owed his life and who had secured the earth beneath his feet. The heavens would never forgive him. It was Iannuk who had molded his body and fitted it with sinew. It was Iannuk who had taught him the wisdom in words that were best let to hang in the air, but never get spoken. It was Iannuk who delivered him to the promise of this ocean, this ship, this day, and this hour. And it was Iannuk whom Grigor had murdered. Avrum felt a gross emptiness . . . a void somewhere in his experience of life, where he might have set this encounter into a fathomable framework. Perhaps he was a fool. How frail were his convictions — how skewed his perceptions! Others always seemed to know better. His thoughts carried back to the Doctor. What would the Doctor have done in his place? Somehow, he knew the answer.

PART TWO

1911

(1)

If people heard of the town of Biranovici, it was invariably because the train from Warsaw to Minsk stopped there to allow the passengers to drain their bladders and to relieve their distended colons at that station's long double row of water closets. Not that the train didn't have its own toilets, but as surely as Monday follows Sunday, they would clog hopelessly long before the cars would roll into White Russia, though there were always people who would evacuate their bowels generously even onto the odorous and rising heaps. When the railroad authority first negotiated with the town council to set up these facilities, the minor wits in the town half-jokingly complained that this only proved that the cosmopolitans from Warsaw came to Biranovici *kak muhi na govno* (literally, "like flies to shit"). But when the stench around the station house began to filter into the town proper, sometimes to hang in the air for days, no one doubted that the Poles were having the last laugh.

The ritual bathhouse was the building closest to the station. The troubles in the Finegold family began when Falik, the youngest son of the venerable reb Leibel-Shimen, came home from St. Petersburg with a Christian education and a Christian woman, whom he was determined to marry. She was cream and pink and mild and soft-spoken, and it took either daring or stupidity, or a combination of both, to bring her to Biranovici. She said it had been entirely her idea to come, and it seemed she loved Falik enough to insist on going through the trying business of becoming a Jew herself, only when it came to the matter of having to dip into the waters of the ritual bath — the *mikveh* — she made an abrupt about-turn.

Nothing, she said, would make her cross the threshold of the bathhouse. If a pot of gold and all the tsar's jewels waited for her inside, it wouldn't move her to suffer the sickening smells that emanated from the other side of the door. True, they had taken her there on a particularly vile and stuffy day — the air just stayed where it was in front of their faces, and a man could almost suffocate from his own breath, as it were. But it seemed to her that if the smell could be so offensive and so oppressive, it surely wasn't in just water that they would have her submerge herself.

Manya was her name, and she could hardly have been more than seventeen or eighteen years old. Tongues in the town wagged about her from the start. What manner of parents would allow their daughter to set off openly on what was so plainly an illicit and not to mention so immoral an adventure? Love would be an excuse only for the dimwitted to swallow, and for all his worldly education, Falik had to be an utter ignoramus. Someone should tell him that if the girl had had it within her to take off with a man in so brazen a fashion, no great virtues should be expected of her as a wife, let alone as a mother. Such was the gist of the talk at this time, and it lent a dash of spice to the humdrum of the mornings at the marketplace.

There they were, then, in Biranovici, with their intentions for each other announced and the process of her conversion stalled. Not surprisingly, the same tongues were quick to come down on her, saying that never in the first place had it been her intention to convert — that Falik had let himself be duped by her candy lips, but no one doubted that the last delectable chapter in the story of Falik and Manya was still ahead of them. The gossips let their imaginations consume them, and overnight the Jews—and not a few of the town's Gentiles—became caught up in the sport of guessing how the situation would resolve itself.

Falik was not wholly oblivious to the stir he had caused, but he wouldn't let it touch him, except when his father would come home from the granary, tired and agitated, to confront his son with an updated account of the locals' talk. He would use this to reinforce his own opinions. Falik would tap his fingers impatiently and roll his eyes to the ceiling. "She is going to be my wife," was about all he would allow himself to say, but when the spittle would start to show at the corners of his father's mouth, and when his mother, Raizel, made certain that he could see her throwing herself from one corner of the room to the other, her hands clasping her head in impossible agony, he would storm across to his brother Max's house, where Manya had been given a bed.

Max was a full ten years older than Falik, and had married Bluma, the cabinetmaker's oldest daughter, when he was well into his thirties and she was well into despair. They were largely preoccupied with problems of their own, and these mostly centered around Bella, their infant daughter, who stayed in Bluma's womb for ten full months and who even then came out angry at the world. Did she want to stay in there for another ten? She would tear and bite at Bluma's breast for hours, and then scream and thrash about with colic pains until she'd throw up about half of what she'd taken in, at which time she'd roll herself into the rancid cheese and fall into a shallow sleep.

Falik would slam the door and pound on the table, though no one could make out the words under his breath. Then he bent over the basin and had Manya pour water over his neck so that it drained into his hair and across his face. Manya would feel the tension in his shoulders, and would have him remove his shirt, anticipating the warmth that would come over her when she'd trace her fingers over his smooth, unblemished skin.

Bluma would blush and turn away at such time, immediately finding something with which to busy herself; whenever these two came together, the air would become unbearably charged. She said as much to Max, but not in a way that would give Max the idea that she wanted the girl to leave. To herself, she said that the problems in the family were severe enough without her having to compound them, but behind the screen of whatever secrets she would confess (even to herself) were the reasons why her heart raced so whenever Falik came through the door.

Sometimes she'd catch the way their hands would skip over each other's bodies, and it wasn't lost on her the way when, in the company of others, their lips would speak one language and their eyes another. When, in heaven's name, were such bold fantasies ever invested with blood — at least here in Biranovici? Her own great romance came from the desk drawer of Fremish, the clubfooted matchmaker, and not once had she ever seen even a spark of yearning in watery eyes, or made to contend with the silent, hopeless plea of a youth to steal with her from the Book of Sins.

Manya's adamant objection to stepping into the bathhouse threatened to spiral the crisis. People were beginning to ask increasingly difficult questions of everyone in the Finegold family, and soon enough, Raizel came crying to Bluma that they were shunning her in the market. Bluma confessed the same, but warned that if Falik thought for a minute that his wasn't his home any longer, he would walk away from them forever. Meanwhile the rabbi had written a letter to the old rabbi of Slonim, who suggested that they use the bathhouse there. But since partaking of the *mikveh* could not be a one-time ritual, he wrote, and no river ran through the town of Biranovici, there were only two ways the problem could be permanently resolved: one was by having Falik and Manya make Slonim their home; the other was by moving the site of the railway station — that or the *mikveh.* The tone of the answer was less than hopeful, and the rabbi gave it to Falik to read.

The rabbi expected the worst from Falik, who had once called him "God's Cockroach" when the rabbi had a few things to say about the boy's exclusively secular interests. This was when Falik was only fourteen, and it earned him a stinging slap from the rabbi and more of the same from his father. But Falik was a wiry, bristling redhead, and his thin-skinned temper was an indelible part of the same package. This and the way his lips were chiseled thin and hard always made his words seem more cutting than he might have intended them to be, and people learned to be careful with him.

Only this time, Falik welcomed the rabbi with even a hint of excitement, and he applauded when he heard the Slonim rabbi's suggestions. From a box under his bed, he produced a roll of sketches and drawings full of crisscrossed lines and calculations that made no sense at all to the rabbi. But Falik quickly explained that he was an engineer, and that these were plans to move the whole railway station the way it was — toilets and all — to where the track bent around the far side of the town. From there, the winds would carry the smells past the town and not into it. It sounded impossible to the rabbi, but Falik already had an arrangement of boxes and sticks on the table, and showed how the whole thing could be lifted directly off the ground and rolled along the tracks for the whole distance to the new site. "Thirty, 35 people and six strong horses could do the job," he said, and the rabbi listened.

There were meetings and conferences, and heads shook at first, but slowly the idea took hold. It had the absolute backing of the women, and after a word here and there between them, they soon had more than a hundred men enlisted for the project. Falik was introduced to the people from the railway authority, and he told them right off that if the toilets on the trains would have had their trap doors removed so that the track could be permanently exposed, they would never have needed so many toilets in the station. To work the trap doors, one had to press down on a lever, and a man would naturally be reluctant to touch it — or even press down on it with his boot. Who knew what diseases would rub off? Besides, the excrement tended to stick to the trap doors anyways, so that even if they were opened, the holes had to clog.

On the morning of the third working day, they had the whole stationhouse raised and set intact on the tracks. The whole town showed up for the event and there was a good deal of cheering and drinking. Even the horses seemed taken with the spirit of the hour, and they snorted and put all the might of their backs into the rope. No one heard the distant rumble, and even the whistle seemed to belong elsewhere, but suddenly there it was, charging down on them with an unholy fury, and the people screamed and scattered like rabbits.

The toilets, purified with a hundred and fifty pounds of lime dust, wrapped themselves around the smoking black engine as if they were made of flypaper, and then the stationhouse just seemed to explode. Falik watched in horror as the engine and the coal car climbed the logs, turned on their sides, and plowed into the ground. Most of the cars behind them were also derailed.

It was a miracle that no one died, but more than sixty people were injured. Some would be crippled for life. There was an investigation, and Falik was arrested. He produced the notes given him by the men from the railway authority which listed the trains scheduled to pass through Biranovici. Every detail was there in their handwriting, and there was no mention of any train for the whole of the unfortunate day. At the trial, the same men insisted that Falik had only asked for the trains scheduled to *stop* at Biranovici and not for the expresses, which carried right through. Besides, the notes weren't officially stamped, and herein lay Falik's negligence, they claimed. He should have had the plan authorized either at Warsaw or at Minsk.

Falik was sentenced to the Vladimirsky Central Prison for five years. There was a lot of wailing and breast-beating, but shortly after that, the Finegolds seemed to retreat into themselves. Max, Bluma, and Manya, especially, seemed to close the door to everyone, until about a month later, when they announced that they were going to take up residence in Moscow for a while so as to be close to Falik.

Max and Bluma returned a year and a half later with a new baby — a girl they had named Fanya — and with the news that Falik had been released to work on military fortifications at some unheard of place called Lushunkou. This was all the way across on the Asian side of the continent and the constructions had something to do with a threat from the Japanese. Falik's working there was the condition of his release. As for Manya — well, she had never converted, and after a month or two in Moscow, had decided to find her life once again in St. Petersburg.

Now, this peculiar episode in the lives of the Finegold family might have ended right here, except that as the new baby girl grew, she showed a head of flaming red hair that many swore was a perfect copy of Falik's, and her temper developed into something which (the same people observed) was entirely familiar. So tongues were soon active again, and it was only a question of time before someone would ask, ". . . and don't her eyes and her forehead remind you of that slinky Christian girl — the one called Manya?"

Falik never returned, and his name came to be mentioned less and less until, suddenly, travelers reaching Biranovici brought with them the news that Russia was preparing to go to war against Japan in a land called Manchuria. Lushunkou was mentioned as the place where the Russians were building their fortifications, and the image of Falik came alive again. The year was 1885.

The Finegolds had letters posted to the highest agencies in the most distant capitals in the land asking for information of his whereabouts and circumstances, and almost a year later, they had their answer. It came from Moscow in an impressive envelope weighed under by a row of wax seals, and the letter itself had another seal made up of wax and green ribbon. It was written in the name of Tsar Nicolai himself, and a weakness came to the knees of those who crowded around the elder reb Leibel-Shimen when this was announced. No business the tsar could have with them directly could be healthy. This was about the first fact of life one learned. Still, when did the tsar ever send a Jew anything with ribbons?

It was a citation for Falik's contribution to the historic stand of the Russian forces that were preparing to defend against the Japanese armies in Port Arthur. The memory of this heroic son of the motherland would persist (they promised) in the hearts of all noble men and for as long as Russian history would be recorded.

Falik was dead. Reb Leibel-Shimen tore the sleeves from his coat and rubbed ashes into his hair. Raizel wailed loudly and Max and Bluma went to hold them. But around them everyone else slipped easily into a carnival spirit, and people started in to congratulate each other. Until then, the news that had reached them about Port Arthur and the fortunes of the Russian fleet in the China Sea had been decidedly dark. Port Arthur, they had learned, had been totally overrun by the Japanese, and the same news included the sinking of four of their largest battleships — the *Borodino*, the *Kniaz*, the *Souvaroff*, and the *Oslabia* — along with the abject surrender of the transports *Kamaschatka* and *Oural*. The critical wounding at this time of the sadistic, elitist, and rabidly anti-Semitic Admiral Rozhdestvensky, however, was spoken of as a sure sign that while God may have forsaken the tsar, He had not entirely forsaken the Jews.

Convinced that Biranovici had been marked out for an honor that lifted it from its supremely pale existence, the town council voted to commission a heroic statue of Falik and to set it directly in front of the building occupied by the council. There was a suggestion that it be set next to the railway station, but this evoked a bristling reaction and the idea never surfaced again.

The sculptor was a local man who had known Falik, and who, like him, had studied in St. Petersburg. It was said that at one time there had been a market for his works as far away as Paris, and, had he not allowed himself to become ensnared in the sticky intrigues of a disastrous romance and a very unfortunate political line, he would now have belonged not to Biranovici, but to the world. As a result of his behavior in those days, he had lost an eye and two fingers. The girl who had cost him the eye forgot him promptly at the duel's end, and the day after his fingers had been shot off while escaping the tsar's agents, the leaders of his cell in the Anarchist movement were themselves uncloaked as agents of the tsar.

No one in Biranovici knew him when he came there to live, and for years he lived a largely nocturnal existence. As time passed, however, he relaxed his guard. He was older and slower now, and no one seemed interested in him anyway. This work was the first that had come his way since those days, and so hungry was he for it that he would have done it for the promise of a bottle and a wedge of cheese alone.

The statue was done in bronze, and getting it cast took no small effort, let alone expense, but for the folk of Biranovici, it was the most impressive thing they had ever seen. Here and there, someone would mutter that it didn't much resemble Falik, but the figure was every inch the sort of man that the town wanted to be proud of. One arm was outstretched and pointed to the horizon, the other clutched rolls of paper and other tools of the engineering trade. A rifle was slung over his back, and the whole figure seemed to be emerging from a massive gate.

A photographer was paid to fix the work on film, and a copy was dispatched to the tsar with the greatest elegance and marked with just about every official stamp the council owned. Every detail of the venture was noted on a parchment entrusted to the town's most dedicated professional scribe. It was said that he invested an hour on each letter; for this, he had received a price that would have paid for ten such parchments by any other scribe, but the town council would not risk representing itself badly to the most august of men in the land. And the tsar's reaction was not long in coming: government men soon came to Biranovici and arrested the sculptor. They had asked a few questions, but otherwise made little noise and showed no interest in the town. Needless to say, the sculptor made no noise whatsoever from that day on.

(2)

From Grigor, Avrum learned that for some reason the ship would sail no farther than Quebec City. The passengers who planned to go on to Montreal, or through Montreal to the United States, would be obliged to continue by carriage or rail. Avrum was warned against falling victim to the surface charms of Quebec City and not to think of making it his permanent home; underneath lurked a powerful church-dominated French Catholic regime, which made little room for Jews. Far more open and outwardly liberal were the English Protestant regimes in Montreal, Toronto, and New York. The French preferred their Catholic and church-oriented lives, and the immigrants were smartest who linked their futures with the Protestants' culture and politics.

"And mind you, I am a believing Catholic through-and-through. I breathe my religion. The religion of the English Protestants is like a few drops of whiskey in a glass of warm milk — the whiskey is spoiled and the milk is smelly. But for myself, I'll still gamble on the English, and you are the last one in the world who needs the Pope hanging over your head."

Despite himself, Avrum was grateful for Grigor's persistence. Grigor was always there . . . always by seeming coincidence, always with soft words, always smiling . . . and always with observations that Avrum knew were critically important for whatever he had yet to encounter. At first, Avrum would turn away, communicating nothing except with his eyes and the tight press of his lips. The shots that felled Iannuk still echoed in his ears. But Grigor paid that no mind, and never relented. When he said that the intrigues of the land probably belonged to the land, and weren't their backs turned forever upon it, Avrum gestured with his hand that that changed nothing. But when Grigor whispered that most of the immigrants were doomed because of their ignorance and would never be allowed into the country, Avrum was anxious to hear more. Slowly, he relented. The next day, they made hot tea for themselves.

Of all those on the ship at that time, Grigor's was the only face familiar to Avrum. Perhaps Avrum had relented when he found no respite from the sense of loneliness and isolation that continued to weigh so heavily on his heart. Perhaps Grigor was right about the possibility of being turned away. As impossible as it was, he had only to close his eyes and listen to Grigor's voice to imagine them as friends.

It was Grigor who impressed upon him the importance of having the right answers pat in his mind when he stood before the immigration authorities. Avrum had never realized that there could be wrong answers — that for some, the doors to Canada could and would really be closed. Grigor seemed to have a ready store of knowledge about everything else that went on in the new world. The unwary risked tripping disastrously on their ignorance. There was an ocean of facts, all of which seemed terribly vital for the immigrant to know, like where to find temporary lodging and cheap but familiar food; how to manage with the new money until a job could be found; and, indeed, where jobs could be found.

One had to be especially wary of the "runners" who would be sure to infest the port. These were invariably old world countrymen who used the intimate dialects of home and an inviting thimble of whiskey to disarm the new immigrants of their suspicions before robbing them of their goods. Disorientated by the impossible strangeness of the language, the signs, the uniforms, and the documents, crushed with fears and on the precipice of despair, the immigrants would grasp at the seemingly altruistic gestures of these parasites. The moment when the immigrant trusted his luggage to them, however, perhaps because the immigrant needed his hands free to handle all his papers, was often the last the immigrant ever saw both of his "countryman" and of his belongings. And many were the immigrants whose lives had literally become crushed right then and there. It seemed that Grigor's uncle had been one of these unfortunates.

* * *

Grigor was leaving a Jewish wife behind.

"I am no blind stranger to the way you Jews think and live. It surprises you, but because of her, there was a time when I was half a Jew myself. Oh, she was something from another world, I tell you. I was prepared to shake off and forget my own blood for a chance to rub up against her private of privates. I even told her that if she would marry me I'd live any way she wanted me to. The first thing she made me promise to do was to cut the web off the end of my pump. Imagine! She said it reminded her of a dog, and for a long time she wouldn't let me touch her with it. I would have had the operation done, too, but something — something kept me back."

Grigor took his time searching for the words that would match the images that were surfacing in a rush behind his eyes.

"First, it was her ugly nagging. That little piece of skin was blinding her to everything else I was sacrificing for her sake. If her back was to me and I'd touch her with it — all this in bed, at night — she would tell me she was going to vomit. Then she'd make gagging noises that would even make my own throat catch." He took a deep breath and swallowed hard before continuing. Avrum's eyes never left him.

"On the other hand, there were times she would beg me to come on her like a dog. Begged me! She really wanted me to keep it. Her nagging was meant only to satisfy her own convoluted conscience. Anyways, we were only a few months together when she became pregnant. She let her teeth rot and her breath get foul. She put on so much weight and so quickly that I awoke one morning and thought that if I hadn't slept with her, I wouldn't have known who she was. Her once-smooth ivory neck, which used to do the craziest things to me, was, that morning, just a glob of rolling fat. And the stale sweat left on the sheets from her sleep had a rancid air about it — I still can't shake it out of my skull. But then she had nothing better to do than to rediscover her religion. I didn't mind the candles or her prayers. I also decided that it wouldn't be the end of the world if I'd live without a good piece of pork or speck in the house, but then . . . then . . . she comes into the house one afternoon and her hair is different — longer than I remembered and worked into the most perfect, unreal curls and waves. Then she lifts if off — just lifts it off — and underneath, she is entirely bald. BALD! I could have sworn that it was the head of a man."

Avrum struggled but failed to repress a smile. Despite himself, he laughed. Grigor continued.

"That day, I put the door of the house forever between her and me. I used to send her money from another city. She had my address and wrote that she gave birth to a boy, and that he would grow up a Jew. Well, she could force what she wanted on him. There was a time when the money I had wasn't enough for my own needs, so I stopped sending her any. I wrote that I'd carry on supporting them in a short while, but she had me chased, so I went to the forests and the sad end of the story you already know."

"But why the stealing?"

"Ah, the stealing — yes, well . . . there was just no way to avoid that. Believe me, my hands were tied. I was in debt to Boris up to my neck. Do you really want to hear?"

"You're good at making up stories, Grigor."

"Not such stories. If you want to hear, say yes. If not, just say no. I'm not built for games."

In his mind, Avrum loudly shouted, "No," but what he heard issuing from his lips was a weak, "Yes. I'm listening."

"I promise you every word is God's truth. You see, I know something about printing — my family's trade — and I tried to set up my own business in Zhitmoir. With a mountain of money I could have suffocated in, and very little of it mine, I bought the most advanced presses and the most modern lettering styles. The shop itself was in the most fantastic location imaginable, but it wasn't open a week when the most improbable disaster fell on me.

"Ask yourself if anyone could in his wildest imagination invent such a story — the horse that pulled the local vendor's barrel of coal oil suddenly went berserk and shook it off the wagon. But first, he shook the wagon right up against my window, and the barrel gets heaved right through it. If that wasn't bad enough . . ." Grigor seemed to wince. He half shut his eyes and shook his open hand at the sky. ". . . It fell right next to the stove where I'm melting the zinc. Before anyone had a change even to blink, the barrel split open like a nut and spilled all the coal oil onto the fire.

"It would have taken little for me to jump into the flames and die like everything else died. It was a fire like you could never imagine, and everything was lost. So, in a flash, the debtors were on my head, and Boris, who even had underworld connections then, got me to Szambor from where Iannuk took us to Urman. Boris was also running — and it seemed that eluding pursuers was a talent I had to learn from him. At Urman, I was penniless, and it was plain to me that the only way for me to salvage my life was to begin again in America. I didn't have a year to wait for my wages — even then, they would hardly have been sufficient, so, with Boris leading the way, we did what we did. Now Iannuk is dead, and for that, I really am sorry. Peter is dead. Boris with his balls gone wishes he was. I am here now and so are you."

Grigor paused, and his demeanor adjusted to the changing temper of his thoughts. "We're spectators at our own theater," he continued slowly in a low voice, as though he meant the words more for himself, "and no one, no one, no one, can guess what is behind the next curtain."

(3)

When the ship finally rubbed its side against the tires at the wharf, Avrum was inside answering the immigration authorities. They had boarded the ship when it was still almost a mile from the dock, and set up two tables just outside the steerage quarters, where they smelled the air and asked after those who had become sick. They seemed unconvinced when the passengers told them that no one among them had died. "Impossible," they said. "We get at least two to a boat."

Later, on the broad middle deck they arranged their tables again and covered them with an assortment of rubber stamps and colored forms. The lines formed automatically. Avrum had watched Grigor, ahead of him in another line, attack the questions and the papers with an assuredness that neutralized or deflated whatever traps lay couched in them. Then there was a handshake, a laugh at some confidence, the offer of a cigarette, and Grigor was through.

A number of families had stumbled, and were asked to wait until their circumstances could be better clarified. The wives became hysterical and the husbands twitched like rabbits. Caught between the hysterical panic of their women, their cowering children, and the icy, impregnable nerves of the inspectors, the men felt the grossness of their impotence and insufficiencies. They were crushed. Some whimpered and cried like lost children.

Avrum's turn came and somehow he was glad for his size when the immigration officer looked him over carefully.

"Your papers, please."

They were ready.

"Name." The man was addressing him in Russian and Avrum was anxious to show the inspector that he knew some English.

"My name is Avrum." He had practiced this line long enough.

"Ivan what?"

"What?"
The official looked at the papers.
"Wish . . . nitz . . . sky . . . A . . . brum, yes?"
"Yes." He would have said "yes" to any name.
"Know how to write?"
"What?"
"Never mind. These are your papers, yes?"
"What?"
They continued in Russian.
"These are all my papers." Avrum nodded.
"How did you get them?"
"My employer applied at the government office."
"You were with him?"
"What?" (What answer did the man want to hear?)
The question was repeated.
"Yes."
"Everything in here correct? Age . . . Mother . . . Father?"
"Yes."
"It says that they are dead."
"Yes."

The inspector was writing into a large white form over pink, blue, and yellow copies. He kept adjusting the carbon paper.

"Family? Wife? Children?"
"No."
"Alone? Unaccompanied?"
"Alone. Unaccompanied." (The page would soon be full.)
"Going where?"
"Montreal."
"Somebody there is waiting for you?"

The answers Grigor had helped him prepare were ready at his lips. "My brother."
"You have his address?"

Grigor had warned Avrum that of all the questions he would be asked this would be the most critical. He had written a letter to Avrum purporting to be from Hershel, which promised to house and support him financially *for as long as necessary* — deliberately underlining the last line. At the top of the page, in bold, spreading letters, he wrote an address. Grigor had told Avrum not to produce the letter immediately but when confronted by this question to answer "yes" that he was carrying a letter with the address in it — that it was a letter from his brother. ("Mention it, but wait until you are asked what work he does before talking more about him. And if he asks to see the envelope the letter came in, beg his forgiveness and say you didn't know it would be important.")

"It's written." Avrum felt a sudden terror overtake him. He was now in the uncharted territory of total lies. "I have a letter."

"Let me see it." The man sat back and stretched out his hand.

For an anxious, paralyzing moment, Avrum couldn't find it. But then he felt it tucked under his hanky, folded almost into a ball. Grigor said it had to look old.

"Where is the envelope?"

"The one who brought me the letter took the envelope. He said I didn't need it."

"Collected stamps probably. What does your brother do?" (How did Grigor know?)

"He is a furrier." Grigor had suggested the fur trade. The word "fur," he said, was translated instantly as honesty and money. ("And that's just what they want to hear.")

Amazingly, the officer nodded his head in approval and returned the letter without challenging it. Grigor had given him back his life.

But the inspector continued. "What money do you have?"

"Sixty-five American dollars."

"Where did you get them?"

"At the bank."

"What bank?"

"The bank at Odessa."

"What did you give for them?"

"Rubles."

"Where did you get those?"

"Worked for them."

"At what?"

"I'm a lumberman."
"A lumberman?"
"Yes."
"Well, that's good. There is a lot of work for you here."
"Yes. I want to work."

His passport and other papers were returned. There was a flurry of stamping and signing and tearing, but Avrum knew he was through. "Thank you," he kept saying, as much to himself and to Grigor as to this immigration officer. "Thank you and thank you."

"Welcome to Canada, Ivan. Downstairs you get your shots." He handed Avrum a yellow card. "They'll mark the vaccination and everything else on this. Make sure you keep it with you. And good luck."
"Thank you. Thank you."

Grigor was gone. He was nowhere to be seen in the clinic, neither was he on the wharf, nor in the vicinity of the exit gate. On leaving the ship, the passengers were directed to a long, low, windowless, red brick building. Inside they found a first-aid clinic, a money-changing booth, a post office, and a set of tables over which hung a sign saying "information" in five languages. Avrum wanted to get to the table, but there were hoards of people pressing tightly together with the very same intention. The noise was deafening. A thick ocean of unsettled people — lost children, screeching women, shouting men, a few stray dogs and frightened sparrows, all rushing from place to place — served as Avrum's first encounter with his new home. Where would they all be in another hour? Where would *he* be?

Within this multitude, Grigor alone knew his name, and suddenly that seemed terribly important, but Grigor didn't seem to be anywhere in the shed. It was as though he had been swallowed up by the earth. An unnerving anxiousness pressed heavily on Avrum's heart. In his mind, he found himself virtually clawing everything surrounding him for an anchor, and a cold dampness penetrated to his bones.

A rush of Yiddish conversation suddenly fell on his ears. It came from the far end of a nearby table, where he recognized the Jewish families with whom he had exchanged a few words at some time during the trip. Approaching them, he made out a sign on the table that read *The Jewish Alliance*. He overheard talk of trains, along with snatches of conversation relating to the work of "The Alliance." One asked about employment possibilities, another about language schools; most were concerned with lodging. One thin bespectacled man in an undersized fedora and oversized shirt, and two very stern looking women under identical flowerpot hats were the focus of these peoples' attention. Avrum eventually made it to them and asked the man, in tones that quite revealed his desperation, how he could get to Montreal, and where he might find a room there. An instant later, the man called out to a family whom he had spoken to a moment earlier, and who were starting on their way out. They returned to the desk looking worried, but the man bowed toward them and asked for a favor: Would they kindly take Avrum along with them to Montreal — just to the offices of the Alliance?

Outside the building was the street. Avrum caught his breath and let the sights flood his eyes and imagination. Buggies and carriages of every shape, size, and hue rolled everywhere. There were even a few elegant buggies with enormous wheels that rolled along without the benefit of horses. He remembered seeing a few of those before in Odessa. The fecal deposits of the horses may have entirely covered the roads, but in Avrum's nostrils, the air smelled of ambrosia.

On the sidewalk were a few youths, their caps angled menacingly over their eyes and their chins daring provocation. The girls and the mother moved closer to Avrum and the father walked ahead, studying a map sketched by the man from the Alliance. He looked right, then left, and back again at the map; finally, he elected for the right. "This way," he said. "From here, it's straight all the way to the station. Nobody let go of anything." He carried three valises, each of which was packed to bursting: one under an armpit, and one in each hand. The daughters carried bags, the mother coats and other pieces of apparel. Avrum had his own battered valise, and he offered to help the man. The offer was politely refused, but after another twenty difficult steps, and with his eyes threatening to hemorrhage, the man reconsidered. They reached the station to learn that they would have to wait almost ten hours for the train to Montreal. At least they wouldn't be stranded for the night. They would have all the next day to find "something temporarily permanent" (as the mother put it). Avrum thought of the distance that was quickly closing between himself and Hershel. The land under their feet was the same now.

The daughters were Bella and Fanya; the mother was Bluma and the father was Max. "We are the Finegolds," he told Avrum, "from the family of Biranovici's reb Leibel-Simcha. Maybe you have heard of us."

(4)

It was the kind of morning when one wakes up with a disquieting feeling in the bones that the day is already pregnant with strange and unpleasant surprises. Max stirred himself out of the pit in his mattress and listened for Bluma's thick snoring. When it came, he relaxed. He tried to satisfy himself that his intuitive senses were only plotting to confound him, and that the day would eventually pass much as every other.

Mentally, he made an accounting of where he stood. Passover was still a good month away, and the stock in the silos showed every sign that there would be enough grain to carry the demand through the holidays. There might even be enough to last until deliveries arrived following the first harvest in the south. The reports from there were encouraging. The yield was expected to be better than good, and the prices should be manageable, so what danger might possibly crop up from that quarter? A fire? It had happened before. Bluma, thank God, was in excellent health, and the girls . . . well, at least they were growing well. Bella, with her incessant whining and obsessive concern over her own personal comfort was something which they had long ago grown accustomed to. *In life,* he thought with a fatalistic shaking of his head, *such types invariably get their bread, along with the butter and honey to go with it.* Fanya was altogether another matter, and she lingered long in his thoughts. These carried him back fifteen years to Moscow and Vladimir province. Was it already fifteen years? It seemed like only yesterday that Falik had been taken away, and his mercurial girl Manya had confessed to them that Falik's baby was lodged in her womb. She wasn't lying. Then, when she had finally agreed to go to the *mikveh*, it was much too late, as Falik wasn't around to marry anyone anymore. Moreover, they had to hide the girl's hysteria as much from the family as from the townspeople.

This had not been a simple matter — every keyhole had an eye behind it, and removing themselves from everything familiar in Biranovici, especially with little Bella on their hands, would not be the stuff of vacations. But Manya was twice on the verge of driving a knife through her heart, and Bluma had to struggle mightily with her each time to wrestle the blade out of her hands. The only choice for all of them had to be the move to Moscow and to wait there for Manya to have her baby.

It had happened so long ago, yet suddenly it was all so fresh in his mind. Two weeks after she delivered, Manya disappeared. They had to find a wet nurse for the poor thing — an unnaturally quiet, hard-eyed little girl — and months went by while they waited in vain for Manya to reappear. They had expected that she would make an effort to visit Falik, but the prison authorities were entirely ignorant of her. Manya had known that Bluma and he were prepared to make the child theirs — that was, after all, what she had so tearfully beseeched of them, and largely why they had moved to Moscow in the first place. But her disappearance was eerie, to say the least. There had been something decidedly unnatural, if not unhealthy, about it.

But the years came and went. Fifteen of them. Manya had never once shown her face, and, except for Bluma and him, no one had ever come to know a single detail of Fanya's entry into the world; such details had long become meaningless, anyway. His blood was in the girl, and that seemed to be sufficient for

Bluma — especially when, in the first and second years after their return to Biranovici, she had delivered two stillborn children . . . two boys. The hurt still gnawed at him.

Within six months of each other, both his parents had crossed into the other world; finding himself alone with the prospering granary, he had taken on Haimeleh, Bluma's younger brother, as an equal partner. This was seven or eight years ago, and Haimeleh had shown himself to be an enterprising fellow. It had been a good decision, and he never for an instant regretted it. Was it just possible that after so long the fellow could change his colors? Not very likely. Haimeleh was neither a card player nor a womanizer, but a solid man with a strong back and a straight head — and a man, moreover, who was ambitious for the both of them.

Why then was he still so uncomfortable? Bluma gagged on a snore and Max knew that she'd be on her feet in less than a minute. He rose with her and they dressed, but she surprised him by asking what was on his mind and if he hadn't slept well. He told her of his undefined premonitions and she told him bluntly to chase them out of his head. Still, she took no chances herself, and went over to kiss the *mezuzot* even before washing her hands.

The day passed like every other, and so, too, the day after that. Max thought to himself that he should be feeling relieved, but somehow he felt even more anxious than ever almost as if someone's gaze had affixed itself to the back of his head — a gaze that was hindered neither by walls nor by the darkness of night. Then, on the third day, Fanya came home with a small oil painting. It showed a boy looking down at a bird with a broken wing, and Bluma, who was home alone, asked where she had gotten the money to buy such a thing. Fanya answered her almost curtly:

"I didn't have to buy it. It was given to me."

"By whom? Who wants something of you that they would give you an expensive painting?"

"A woman," she said softly, but with the ring of a challenge in the tone she used. "She said she was my mother — my *real* mother."

The blood drained from Bluma's face, and she felt the muscles in her legs too weak to support her. She dropped into a chair. "Who is this crazy animal? Who could say such an ugly thing to you?" she cried. Where was Max? Please God, let him walk through the door now. But the plea couldn't make it to her lips.

Fanya replied, "The woman said you would remember her name — *Manya*. And she is with a man called Viktor. Viktor is an artist and the painting is his. She made him give it to me, so, you see, I didn't have to pay for it. She also said that Uncle Falik was my true father."

"What? Falik! What insane — what kind of poison did this animal put in your mind?" But Bluma couldn't finish her words. And she had to escape the child's eyes. "Where is this — this — whatever her name is?"

"Her name, I told you, is Manya. And the two of them are staying at the Palace Hotel. Is it true, mama? I mean, she said that she came all the way from St. Petersburg just to tell me this."

"She came all the way from *Gehenom,* you mean. Can you swallow even for half a second that this animal — whoever she is — was speaking a word of truth? My God — where is your father?"

"She says I'm a *goya*, mama, like her."

Bluma spit a dozen times on the floor and stormed furiously out of the house. She was frightened of what she might say to the child. Every word that escaped her was a lie, and they would all be weighed against her on Judgment Day. Insane with fear and anguish, she rushed along the road to the granary, mindless of how she looked to the other travelers; she wasn't halfway there when she saw Max's carriage coming toward her. Somehow, he wasn't greatly surprised to find her here, but he had never expected to hear the story that poured like a storm from her lips.

At the church where the road forked to the north and south, Max had to use all his might to get the horse to turn right instead of left. It had turned left here every day for years, and now it couldn't be convinced that Max suddenly wanted to go the other way. They found Manya with a young boy in the restaurant of the hotel, and both Max and Bluma recognized her instantly.

She had changed totally, and then again, she had not changed at all. Her lips were getting the crevasses of age, and their lines may have been more deeply etched. Her eyes seemed grayer, but they were the same eyes. Maybe her nose was a touch puffier and her skin had its first faint wrinkles sagging slightly below her chin, but there was still an air of flower blossoms about her. Probably the way she let the curls of her hair cascade to her shoulders. Only what the picture of her included and what they could not recall was the hardness that seemed to have overtaken her voice. It was a hardness that spoke more of trials than of years — like a muscle overworked, like a bow pulled too heavily over the bridge of a fiddle.

"I was expecting you. Viktor here can tell you that we have been sitting here at this table all afternoon just waiting for you. Viktor — (What could she be up to with someone half her age?) please meet Mr. and Mrs. Finegold, the finest people."

Manya spoke easily to them — too easily perhaps. There was a lightness and openness to her gestures that would have given any stranger the idea that their encounter was meant for a chatter of little consequence. Max hadn't found his words yet. She went on.

"Do you remember if this hotel was up in my day? It seems too modern, yet the style of architecture and certainly the furnishings go back fifty years at least. Viktor says even more than fifty."

"You show your face here after so long to talk about architecture." Bluma hardly moved her lips saying this, and there was no suggestion of pleasantness in her voice.

"In a way, I suppose, at least as far as what concerns the new and the old. But why don't you sit down? Please, we're not strangers."

"No?" asked Max. "I think we are."

Manya frowned. "Oh, surely not strangers. Our lives have crossed in a very special way. You can't deny that. I don't even think you regret it. The child is one in a million. Please, again — sit down."

Max sat in the chair across from them, but Bluma remained defiant and distant. "Why did you have to tell her?" Max asked, shaking his head.

"I came from Petersburg all this way just to see her — to see what has become of her. We arrived two days ago, and the very same afternoon, by sheer coincidence, I picked her out on the street. Believe me, it was sheer coincidence. It was on Alexander Street, not far from the watchmaker's place. I was only looking at passing faces, not believing for an instant that even if she should cross my way, I would recognize her. I had planned to come to your home in the evening, but suddenly there she was. The blood of Falik cried out to me."

"The blood of Falik that you helped spill, you mean." Bluma punctuated her words with the sound and motion of spitting.

Viktor, a frail and wispy thing who grew what might one day develop into a moustache, stiffened, and Manya pouted and patted him on the arm.

"Falik is in my heart still. Yesterday, Fanya brought us to what is supposed to be a statue of him. You let them chisel a face that may resemble a thousand other people, but not Falik. Is that how you remember him? I can tell you even after all these years that that is not him. I can describe his face to you even now in such exact detail it would come alive."

"Why did you tell her?" Max's lips trembled.

"Don't you think that that was for you to have done long ago?"

Max tried with little success to mask his rage. "To tell her that she doesn't belong to us? That she isn't our own child? That her father wasn't married to her mother, and that her mother cared for her so much she just up and vanished in the night? Whose name should she have carried? You who threw a helpless child into the world expected us to tell her that she belongs to a night when you forgot who you were and where you were?"

"What remains is for you to add that I made her a bastard." Manya was as unmoving as a rock.

Bluma gasped and Max clenched and unclenched his fists, but he answered her evenly.

"Fanya is not a bastard, and you won't make her one. She is our daughter. If motherhood was your ambition, you would have shown an interest in her when your breasts were dripping with milk. At the very least, you might have said then that it was your intention to come back for her. But did you? No. You said the very opposite — that she *belonged* with us. Those weren't your words? Those weren't your very words? I hear them now as if you had said them only a moment ago."

"Blood is blood. We live by laws, not by lies."

"Lies!" Bluma could not restrain herself. "You — you despicable animal — you can sit there and talk to us of lies? All these years — fifteen years of love, of fevers and sicknesses, fifteen years of sleepless nights, of tears, of growing are a lie in your eyes? You think you can snap your fingers and tell me in that uppity accent that so many years can be forgotten because you are suddenly a champion of the truth? What are you going to teach us about nature? If nature really had laws, your eyes should have been inside worms long ago."

"You're being hysterical without reason."

"Max — without reason she can say. Did you hear? Without reason."

Max leaned across the table. "What exactly do you want of the child? And what do you want from us?"

"I wanted only to see her. I can't forget her."

"You succeeded for fifteen years."

"It was never easy, but things are different now."

"What, for instance?"

"We are thinking of moving to America. If not to the United States, then to Argentina."

"We? Who is *we* — you and this quarter chicken here? But never mind. It's not my business, and I don't care to know."

Manya's reserve was immaculate. "Yes . . . yes, of course — me and my devoted Viktor. But the point is this: I felt that by crossing the ocean, I would be cutting myself away entirely from my past. And a large part of my past is Fanya. I may not have seen her in all these years, but I knew exactly where she was, and that when I choose to, I could find her. Witness my presence here. But once I get on that ship, whatever I leave behind might just as well have never existed for me. It becomes cut away from me forever. Yet, say what you will, Fanya remains a living part of me and no one can deny that. This is my dilemma."

Bluma couldn't sympathize. "Somehow I'm sure you don't let your dilemma intrude upon your sleep. But, so that the heavens should hear — so that I won't stand without witnesses on the Day of Reckoning — tell me why you had to tell her that Falik, of whom nothing is left and who was robbed from her long before she was born, is her father and that I am not her mother. That instead of me, she has a part-time whore for a mother. If there is a God in heaven, you are already with a foot deep in the grave."

"Bluma . . . Bluma . . ." Manya closed her eyes.

"I don't want to hear my name come from your lips. Ever!"

"I just wanted to say that we are all born with our feet in our graves. And the God you speak of has a sure eye for justice even when it hurts."

"What are you trying to say?" asked Max.

"That in a thousand years, she won't be any less my flesh and blood, and that we must talk about the substance — the reality of this hour — more realistically, like civilized people."

"It takes more than nerve," shot Bluma, "for you to talk to us about flesh and blood and about being civilized."

Manya looked up at her but said nothing.

"Where does this leave us?" asked Max. "With a single stroke, you are bringing down my house and my family." He leaned forward. "If it was your intention to take her with you, then let me tell you right here and now that I will kill you first.

Let your friend Viktor here be a witness to my words — let him repeat them to every judge in the land: I will kill you with my own hands if you move to take her."

Bluma let a wail escape her and she brought her hands to her face.

"I know you don't mean it."

"Oh, but I do, Manya. I swear it. We took you into our house and we cared for you. Every one of your problems became ours. So that you could conveniently patch up your life and not leave a mark on an innocent infant, we stayed in Moscow a full year and a half, never moving out of the filthy, crumbling attic that I'm sure you still remember. You carried on with your own life wherever you were, so conveniently leaving your problems on our shoulders. Let me remind you that my brother would be alive today if your nose hadn't been so delicate. At least Fanya gives us something of my brother back, and we are not going to give her up to some sudden caprice of yours."

"You have no choice."

"Say it, then, in the simplest words — that you came here with the intention of taking her from us."

"My intention was to show myself to her."

"Well, having done that, nothing stops you now from taking the next train back to St. Petersburg, no?"

"I suppose we can and would. As you say, nothing is stopping us, except that we have no money. We thought we'd find something to occupy us here." Manya looked squarely into Max's eyes. Suddenly, everything was clear to him.

"And how did you expect to get to America? By swimming?"

"A plan is a plan."

"Oh, yes," repeated Max as he stood up and turned to his wife. "A plan is definitely a plan."

* * *

The same night, Max delivered not the hundred rubles that she had asked for, but two hundred, and for this, he had extracted from her a promise in writing to leave for America within a month. He saw the two of them to the train, and they had been effusive in their thanks and regrets.

Fanya was later told the story of Falik and Manya, but only up to the point of his imprisonment, and their subsequent departure for Moscow and Vladimir province. Bits and pieces of all this she had heard before, and Max went so far as to include Manya's pregnancy. But then he invented Bluma as being ripe with a child herself at the very same time, and he would have Fanya believe that Manya had lost her child, which had been delivered prematurely (because of her mental and physical deterioration). Then, when Manya, in her understandably wretched condition, saw Bluma's fine healthy baby, something must have snapped in her brain and made her believe that the child was hers. The poor woman must have suffered a breakdown, because she disappeared only days after Fanya was born, and there was no way of knowing where she had taken herself for these last fifteen years.

Fanya seemed to accept the explanation, but it was impossible to read her mind. The fact was that in some ways the girl was becoming almost a stranger to them. She had an appetite for the most unusual books, and was invariably secretive about how she acquired them. Indeed, she would be secretive about most everything that concerned herself. By last year, she had devoured everything that had once been Falik's collection — everything except for the engineering texts — and from the same books, she had brought herself to a level of proficiency in English, French, Latin, and Greek that allowed her to read comfortably in each of these languages. Yet at fifteen her dolls were still vitally important to her. She probably had a dozen of them, and though Max would grumble and say that there was something unhealthy about it, Bluma would assure him that the phase would pass. Neither dared recall aloud to the other that when Manya had come to their house, the first things she had unpacked were two dolls.

Three months later, a letter reached them from Manya. It originated from St. Petersburg, and not from America, and asked for another hundred rubles — nothing less — explaining that they still planned on leaving for the United States, but that certain embarrassments had in the meantime eaten into most of what Max had originally given them. A messenger, she wrote, would come for the money within a week, and if he should return to her empty-handed, she would be forced to come to Biranovici herself to collect either the money or her daughter.

When the messenger eventually did show up, he found another family living at the address Manya had given him. The Finegolds, he was told, had all left for America.

(5)

Avrum was given the address of a family on Clark Street and told that he would find a room there waiting for him. All the children of the elderly couple living there were married, and they were looking for a quiet boarder. The woman at the office of the Alliance assured Avrum that it was the perfect place for him. The house itself was over a factory owned by a Mr. Myer Goldenberg, and the woman thought that Avrum might even find work with him. "If you want, I can call him on the telephone and find out." Avrum thanked her, and thanked her again when she replaced the receiver. "You heard," she said. "You can go there even now."

* * *

Myer Goldenberg was more than the owner of the Sweet Mode Dress Manufacturing Company, Limited; he *was* the company. He did all the selling and all the buying. He reduced his cutter to the size of a microbe every time a marker had to be prepared. Not one to blunt or otherwise disguise his manifest distrust of the men's skills, he always made the first cut into the ply himself. "This is how I want every piece to look," he would say. If a finisher left a few threads or pinned a sleeve badly, he'd pull up a chair and do her work for an hour. Some felt so intimidated they upped and quit on the spot. It was the same with the pressers, one of whom actually scalded him when he told her that she belonged in a Chinese laundry. "Maybe she was sensitive about her buck teeth," Goldenberg later said.

His wife had dominion over the operators and the designing. Goldenberg never raised his voice to her — never dared. Her departments were the foundation of the entire operation. If for one reason or another she had to spend a day at home, Goldenberg would never make it to lunch without "rupturing an ulcer." "Shirley," he would gasp to his secretary, "my Milk of Magnesia." Shirley was also his niece — unmarried, but still family — so that in the arrangement of things, she could be intimate with his personal medicines.

He hired Avrum for two dollars and fifty cents a week. Avrum had walked into the factory and saw Shirley who was fixing a handful of long black pins into her hair. She was holding them tightly between pressed lips and her hands were working busily over her head. Her dress was almost sleeveless; it tried to get away with short, wide, and floppy pieces of material that draped from the top of her tight bodice back across her shoulder, and other things which he had never seen before — the lace of a brassiere exposed at the hole where the sleeve should have been. His eye also caught her shaved armpit, and it took him a moment to work out why it seemed so different from what he was used to seeing. He stood back, feeling awkward, very foreign, and somehow even ashamed.

"*Mmmphff?*" she asked. "*Gohzzzd unndd uhmm*," and she motioned with her head to the factory inside.

Avrum nodded, but stayed where he was. He smiled weakly and suddenly doubted that he had come to the right address. There was a clamor of machines back where the girl was pointing, and somehow Avrum couldn't picture himself fitting into this place. The noise was maddening and unnerving. He was preparing himself emotionally to turn and leave, when a man stormed in and seemed ready to devour the furniture. He brushed past Avrum, chest out and back straight; he was shorter than Avrum by at least two heads.

"They want to put me out of business," he fumed. "Do you see what they're doing to me, Shirley?" Shirley was still with her hair. "Chrissake! I'm talking to you, Shirley."

"*Ummlizzznnin.*"

"Lefarge put a hole through half a dozen of the *four oh twos*. Is she blind or something? They're ruined. Absolutely ruined. Not even good for seconds. What am I expected to do with her?"

"*Tcheezuhkaii*."

"What do you mean 'she's OK'? Jump over and see with your own eyes what she did. And those are the *four oh twos* that Cohen from Baby's World is waiting for." He slammed his fist on the table. "Ruined . . . ruined . . . Where's Florence?"

"Across at Wallinz's." The pins were gone now. Avrum was taken aback by the enormous size of her nose. He averted his gaze and studied the light fixture on the ceiling.

"Maybe you know why she keeps buying chickens from him? Everything that he has is double the price."

"But he gives them to her clean." She brought a hand nervously across her face, and Avrum felt guilty for having stared.

"Clean? You should see what they call clean!" He walked to the window and opened it. Then, framing his hands around his mouth, he shouted in the direction of a butcher shop across the street.

"FLORENCE!" A merchant selling handbags and hair wax was coming down Laurier Street ringing the bells on his cart.

Again. "FLORENCE!"

Across the street, a woman stepped out of a doorway. "What is it, Myer?"

"Would you come in? The minute I need you, you're out?"

"WHAT? I CAN'T HEAR YOU!"

"JUST WHEN I NEED YOU, YOU'RE OUT!"

"You also want to eat, don't you?"

"IN A MINUTE, YOU'LL HAVE NOTHING TO PAY THE BUTCHER WITH!"

"Okay, Myer. I'll be in in a minute."

The man turned away from the window. "Is this what they sent me from the Alliance?" he asked Shirley, looking almost pained.

"You're asking me?"

"You're the boy Mrs. Rosen sent me?"

Goldenberg was standing half-crouched now behind Shirley's chair; looking up at Avrum, his eyes were almost in one line with his eyebrows. An instant later, he straightened and walked around the desk to him. Avrum handed him a note that Mrs. Rosen had prepared. She had told him that it would introduce him. Goldenberg glanced at the note, but immediately crumpled it and gave it to Shirley to drop in the wastepaper basket.

"I see you. For what do I need a letter?"

Avrum smiled weakly.

In Yiddish, the man said, "Just off the boat?"

"Yes."

"Where are you staying?"

"Upstairs. I have a room. Mr. and Mrs. Kaplan." Avrum pointed to the ceiling.

"Right here upstairs? Good. I have my alarm switch there. I'll teach you what to do if it should go off when I'm not here." He pointed to the silver tape that lined the windows. "Anyway — tell me what you can do."

Avrum stared at him blankly.

"You have a head to learn?"

Avrum nodded.

"Well . . . I'll give you a chance to begin at the bottom — that's how I began — and if you have a head, I'll make you my manager and foreman. Maybe even my salesman. We could expand. All it needs is someone who is with me — someone who likes to work hard, not just one who from the minute he comes in in the morning watches the clock to see when he can leave. I don't need leeches."

Totally lost in Goldenberg's stream of words, body shifting, and flurry of hand and arm gestures, Avrum could only nod dumbly.

"Tell me — can you talk?"

"Sure."

"Anybody else, I'd start at one dollar a week. You make a good impression on me, so I'll pretend I'm not crazy and tell my Shirley to put you down for two dollars. Never mind — two dollars and fifty cents.

"Thank you."

"What's your name?"

"Avrum Vishinsky."

The door opened, and his wife walked through. She was taller than Goldenberg, elegant in her posture, and very pleasant to look at. Her hair was combed back, but a few strands escaped and fell across her cheek. Strings of beads, six or seven, draped her neck and fell low between her ample breasts.

"Florence, meet Mr. Vishinsky."

"Oh, how do you do, Mr. Vishinsky." She extended her hand and Avrum shook it happily. She was as warm as the sunshine.

"What's your first name again?" asked Goldenberg. "We can't keep calling you 'Mister.' Everyone here is family."

"Avrum . . . it's Avrum."

"Avrum . . . well no one is going to call you Avrum here, at least not if you want to get ahead in life. In Canadian English, Avrum is Abie. Get used to it — *Abie*. Then if you ever get to be important, people will call you Abe . . . like Abe Lincoln."

"Abie is nice," said Florence and Avrum thanked her. It made him feel good to hear his name pass through her perfect lips.

Shirley nodded her approval. "Abie is nice."

"I can give him something to do now," said Goldenberg to his wife. "He's going to be a boarder with the Kaplans." He arched his eyebrows to the ceiling.

"Oh, that's wonderful — but don't start like this, Myer. When did he get off the boat?"

"Today."

"You mean *today*?"

"Mrs. Rosen called in the morning. The boat came in yesterday, but he's just off the train from Quebec."

"Just a minute." She smiled at Avrum and pulled her husband aside. A frown crossed her face, and the man withered visibly. With her arms churning, she seemed to take another inch off his height. When she turned around, her smile was back.

"Finish your things today, Abie, and come in tomorrow morning. No, not tomorrow. You'll have things to do. The day after tomorrow."

"At seven sharp," added Goldenberg, glancing with evident annoyance at his wife.

"Eight." It was Shirley. "You only come at eight-thirty," she said to her uncle. "What is he going to do for an hour and a half?"

"Why don't you mind your own business? I'll have Charlie give him what to do."

"Let him come at eight," added Florence.

"Okay, okay," said Goldenberg. "A quarter to eight." Turning to Avrum, he added "Already all the women are on your side. Already they're letting you sleep in late."

"Thank you," said Avrum.

There was a ceremony of handshaking, which even Shirley joined. Avrum was very careful not to look at her nose.

(6)

Working with Myer and Florence Goldenberg meant becoming an extension of their lives, and Avrum felt little constraint to fight the role. He'd be told to sweep the floor, to spread the rat poison, and to fetch the coffee, and he was expected to feel that he was doing it for himself. He'd help them with their shopping before the holidays, with any plumbing that needed fixing, and when they moved from St. Urbain Street to Outremont, it was Avrum who carried most of their furniture.

Florence would cock her head, and with the suggestion of a pout on her lips, would say, "Abie, you wouldn't object to doing *(such and such)* for me . . . would you?" and Avrum, in his heart of hearts, really didn't mind. Sometimes she even called him "sweetie," and Avrum would have swum an ocean for her. Myer would say, "Abie, I need you," and Avrum made himself available. They became more family than employers to him, and it almost embarrassed him to go to Shirley on Friday afternoons to collect his pay envelope. He was glad for the money, but when Goldenberg would come back from the bank on Friday mornings, he'd ask Shirley for "the list," and to Avrum, his name on that list seemed to be a contradiction of the temper of his relationship with these people. When Shirley would pass him the slip to sign, he'd feel sharply that, in fact, he and the Goldenbergs belonged to very, very different camps.

He told them about Hershel, and Myer said that if he was in Montreal, they would find him. "Maybe even if he lives in New York, an ad in the *Forvertz* can do the trick. But how do you know he doesn't live in Texas — or Brazil? My cousin went from there to Brazil, the idiot."

Besides the *Forvertz*, they ran ads in the *Keneder Adler* and the *Montreal Herald* ("Maybe he goes for sports."), but no one responded to this except an Albert Fish, who said that he had never heard of any Hershel Vishinsky, but if they needed buttons or lace they should call him.

Avrum learned English quickly. For four nights of every week of his first year, he went to a night school for immigrants. There were classes from six to eight, and then from eight to ten. Tuition was covered by the Canadian government, and when the Goldenbergs let him off early, he would sit through both classes. He learned to write compositions, and became carried away by the drama of Ahab and *Moby Dick*. He was introduced to the strong, pummeling words of Bernard Shaw and wished urgently to learn more. "Help your minds to expand and develop," his teacher would say, and Avrum was convinced that she was speaking directly to him.

The Kaplans fretted without letup about him. When they learned of the salary Myer was paying him, Freidle Kaplan immediately charged downstairs and confronted Myer, who was sitting with a buyer from a new department store. Without why or wherefore, and ignoring the buyer, she told him in her loudest voice that if he didn't give Abie another two or three dollars immediately she wouldn't let him step into the factory in the morning. She might have been using a hammer with equal effect.

"You couldn't wait another ten minutes to tell me this?"

"No. And I didn't come down to ask you. I came to tell you."

"So you're telling me."

"So?"

"Freidle . . . what do you want from my life?"

"How could you do this to an orphan? He's a baby. And God bless you if it's a cent less than two dollars."

"You want to talk to Florence? She's in the back"

"How does she live with you?"

Meyer raised his hands. He had known it would cost him the moment he heard her voice asking Shirley where she could find him.

That was over a year ago. After deductions, Avrum now received a fixed wage of twelve dollars a week. With his first paycheck, Florence had taken him to the Park and Laurier branch of the City and District Savings Bank and opened an account for him there. He had since managed to accumulate forty-two dollars and forty-four cents. "Keep saving like this," said Florence with a wink after he showed her the latest entry in his bankbook, "and one day you'll be able to go into business for yourself." He adored her.

Goldenberg's shipper was a skeletal figure weighed down as much by dandruff and warts as by the triple-soled shoes on his oversized feet. When he first came to work, everyone pressed their own infallible cures on him, but his scalp and skin resisted everything. Singly and in combination, he tried vinegar, eggs, honey, butter, vodka, Ihles Paste, alcohol, hydrogen peroxide, tar, castile soap, kosher soap, and olive oil mixed with crushed garlic. But nothing held back the "snow" (even in July, as Shirley pointed out). Dr. Teitlebaum, whom Goldenberg credited with keeping his ulcer friendly, suggested that the man's physical problems were all rooted in "psycho-mentality diseases."

Goldenberg wanted to know, "What do you mean? Is he crazy? I got enough *meshugosim* around me without one that is also certified!"

"No, no — it is just that the man has his problems."

The shipper, Irving Strulevitch, would have agreed. Moreover, he would have pointed out that very nearly heading his list of problems was his boss. After one particularly violent encounter with him — when an order for Daisy Belle in Windsor was delivered to Lovely's in Ottawa, because, as it transpired, Goldenberg himself had fixed the address stickers on the wrong boxes — Strulevitch griped to Avrum that if Goldenberg didn't try so hard to be a cretin, he'd graduate one day to being just an idiot.

Myer Goldenberg saw things from a different perspective. "It's me or him," he confided to Avrum. "One day, one of us will end up either in the asylum or in Bordeaux Jail."

Just below Myer on Strulevitch's list of life's disorders were women; his obsessive preoccupation with them went past simple mental neurosis to verge on a pathology that only a castration might alleviate. Avrum's naivety, puritanical attitude, and plain dumbfounded innocence fired a calling in him to assume the role of personal educator. Incessantly, he talked about the way women were built, what they needed and expected from a man, and what their bodies could do to a man. He explained how it was possible to partially undress them without their being aware, where they most liked hands to move on their bodies, and how to touch what needed touching. He promised that it was possible to do it in a doorway — even with people walking by — and even in the back seat of a hired buggy without the driver knowing.

He advised Avrum to keep one of those new gut condoms and a straight pin in his wallet "even if you know you're only going to a funeral." With the first, he would be prepared for any opportunity when it comes. ("Suddenly, out of the blue, she wants it now, so what are you going to do?") The second, "to get it out if she suddenly locks up and freezes on you. You ever seen dogs? Same thing sometimes with women. What you gotta do is ram the pin hard and fast into her ass and pull out quickly. It's the only way to keep you outside a hospital."

Strulevitch lived his words. There were stretches when he could only work from a chair, and sometimes he would just put his head on the table and close his eyes — his thoughts light years removed from the factory. Avrum would never confess that the words also raised waves of confusion, not to mention heat, in his own insides — waves that became more forceful as story followed story. The fires which Strulevitch stoked may have first been kindled in the forests of Szambor and Urman by the crass and inarticulate accounts of the lumbermen. But these were as light on technical information as they were heavy on nuances and suggestion. At the time, they had raised only vague and ill-defined images in Avrum's mind of what marvelous adventures waited under the clothes of a woman. Strulevitch now went to great lengths to hone these images. He gave them volume and edges, and salted them with his own singular brand of lust.

Avrum sometimes wondered to himself how the man had come to be so expert despite his obvious handicaps, because, as if to poke an eye at all the rules, he also cultivated a kind of hunchbacked, foot-dragging walk and would smoke only the thickest and smelliest Havana cigars. Something crusty was always sticking to his eyelids, and an old matchstick cum toothpick was fixed permanently in the corner of his mouth. Surely, the smell of the brilliantine that he used couldn't, by itself, have worked enough magic to completely blind a woman to the sight of him.

Strulevitch admitted to having had four wives, two of whom had managed at the time to squeeze legal papers out of him. But they were all gone now. He said that from the start, he had had them understand that there would be no money and no children from him, ". . . so that when the axe had to fall, the cut would be clean." At the moment, he was living with a woman whom he allowed was ten years older and sixty pounds heavier than he. ("What she gets from me is all net profit, eh? She keeps me warm in the winter and gives me shade in the summer — do I need more?") But it seemed the answer was "yes." There was a girl called Frances who was an operator at the Bell Telephone Company, and who put up with more lewd conversation with Strulevitch in an hour than Avrum had heard in all his years with the lumbermen. And if such a thing as fornication by phone were possible, Strulevitch did it vigorously — with her and with another — a Jenny Belanger who made beds at the Ritz Carlton Hotel on Sherbrooke Street. Avrum had never met them, but Strulevitch would bring the receiver to his ear. Mostly, he heard giggles — but they were real girls' giggles.

* * *

Two doors up from the factory was a two-by-four coffee and donut shop run by a fellow everyone called Horse. Actually, Horse never learned to prepare anything more complicated than filter coffee. The soup was canned and his donuts were pre-packaged, but Horse was a one-man clearinghouse for anything that needed marketing. The shelf with his candlestick telephone served as Strulevitch's office, and Horse handled the incoming calls with the studied coolness of a personal and very private secretary. About a dozen other fellows also made this phone the heart of their operations, and Horse wrote all the messages on the wall. No one had ever missed anything meant for them, and for Horse, it was all part of the service.

One of Strulevitch's current (and longest running) operations was the act he constantly polished and refined as a secret Hollywoodland, nickel emporium, and picture palace talent scout. He showed Avrum his card. "I got at least a thousand of these." It read: *Irv Steel, Special Hollywoodland Picture Palace Talent Agent*. Underneath, in one corner was Horse's phone number; in the other corner was a post office box number.

"Notice there's no address. Eh? They're always asking for an address, but I tell them that in this business, I got to see the action in every city, and that I always got to move. I tell them that when I hear that there's another natural Lillian Gish or maybe a Mabel Normand in Toronto or Detroit that's got a future on the West Coast and the big time, I'm with my bags on the train in half an hour."

"You know who makes the moving pictures there?"

"You're still green, kid. I don't have to know anyone. Eh? Enough I know their first names. It's part of the operation. I tell you, Abie, this little white card that costs me nothing can get me into the pants of some broads so fast that sometimes I can't get my own pants past my knees before it's all over. Once, in a rush, I even rolled a skin down backwards and pulled out all my hairs."

"But why Steel?" Avrum guessed what a skin was.

"How far can I expect to get with a name like Strulevitch? Eh? One of the facts of life is that the right name is like money in the bank. Now y'see, *Steel* got the right sound. Y'hear it? Steel . . . it's strong — you can build on Steel, if you know what I mean. Eh? That's how it works in the mind. And Irv . . . how do you like the Irv? It got class."

Avrum tried to picture what images or impressions the name Vishinsky might evoke. Nothing very promising, he thought. He tried shortening it, to *Vish*, but found that even worse. He had had a chance to change his name legally and effortlessly when he first came into the country. Grigor had told him that he had only to suggest a new name to the immigration officer. Very often, these immigration officers couldn't manage with the old world names and changed them on their own initiative. He told of a distant cousin who got on the boat as Wladislav Radnetzkapov and stepped off as Dick Ratnet.

Strulevitch admitted that as useful as the card was, most of these women needed a show of loose money to get through to them. "And not the kind of money I'll ever see in this lifetime from Goldenberg."

That money came from Litwak. Litwak and Polanski were two abortionists to whom Horse directed some careless, if frightened, woman, and there would be one every month or two. They could be as young as seventeen, or even in their early forties with half a dozen kids already delivered to the world. Strulevitch was Litwak's "assistant." The Catholic regime in the province of Quebec outlawed abortions, and were absolutely unforgiving in their punishment of abortionists. This explained the sums Litwak and Polanski asked for and invariably received. For Strulevitch, that was good for a fat thirty-five dollars, ten of which went back to Horse. The remaining twenty-five was enough to cover a good table at one of the dancing clubs on and around Stanley Street. There were always class acts there, like May Irwin singing her "Bully Song," or Freddie Stone banging away his "Ma Rag-Time Baby." If Strulevitch thought his girl needed an extra nudge of convincing, he'd take her to the second show at the Gaiety Burlesque on St. Catherine Street.

Litwak, to be sure, was a fine, legitimate doctor, only he stuttered so badly that his only patients were those who found his name in the phone book at four in the morning. And these, if they remained alive, rarely consulted him a second time. Strulevitch would be the one to rent the room if Litwak couldn't do it in his clinic, and would watch out for unexpected and unwelcome visitors. If the patient became hysterical (as some did), Strulevitch would help keep her from climbing off the bed and dashing — screaming and half-naked — out of the room. Otherwise, he would stand behind Litwak's shoulder and look professionally concerned. For good form, Litwak would sometimes ask Strulevitch for his "expert" opinion, and Strulevitch would take a couple of long, slow puffs on his cigar before saying, "Yes . . . yes . . . it's the only way." As often as not, it was at this point that the terrified girl's hysteria would set in.

It was Horse who first saw the possibility of setting up an operation around Avrum. He called Strulevitch over to a corner of the counter one afternoon and broached the idea of turning Avrum into a wrestler.

"We could manage it together — you the handling, and me the promotion."

Strulevitch crushed the last inch of his cigar between his molars before delivering it to the ashtray. He snorted sharply and sucked air between his teeth. From this, Horse knew that his idea had found fertile ground.

"He's a natural — absolutely a natural, eh?" Strulevitch stuck a new matchstick between his teeth and continued with a studied self-importance. "And he's built as good if not better than any of the *shmuks* around today. I've seen him with his shirt off."

"Keep in mind he's a Yid," added Horse. "No one will miss that."

"It's gold in the bank," agreed Strulevitch, now replacing the matchstick with a fresh cigar. "Money in the bank. The only thing is he got to agree first."

"So work on him, Irv."

"Yeah."

"I can get him into the Arena with no sweat. Those bums owe me."

"Who's there that you know?"

"Minny Laplante. You see him here sometimes. It's OK, I got a button on him. When he got caught with a couple of bad IOUs a while back, he came to Horse to fix them — and, no problem, Horse fixed them."

"It's an idea, eh?" Strulevitch sifted the possibilities in his mind.

"With the right connections, it's a goldmine," said Horse, wiping away some of the ash from Strulevitch's cigar that had fallen onto the counter.

"Hey, not on my pants. Willya? Eh?"

"An accident. Sorry." But Horse didn't sound sorry.

(7)

Avrum had been watching one of those new modern motion pictures at the Regent Picture Palace, and when the lights turned on and he rose to leave, the two girls who had been sitting in front of him saw him and recognized him.

"Avrum?" they turned to each other and giggled.

Avrum didn't recognize them at first and there was reason for that: the lipstick, the earrings, and the blush painted on their cheeks were not there when they shared the same compartment on the train from Quebec City to Montreal.

"That's Bella — remember? And I'm Fanny — from the boat and the train. It was Fanya then, but it's Fanny now."

"God! You look . . . like real women."

They laughed. Bella introduced a frail fellow who seemed to be hiding behind her. "This is Sam — Sam Moskowitz." She turned around to him. "Say hello, Sam."

"Hello." He extended his hand and Avrum shook it. It had all the consistency of a fish long dead.

To Sam, Fanny said, "We spent the whole night on the train to Montreal."

Bella pretended to be embarrassed. "Well, it was not as if we were alone, you know. And there were lights on."

"I don't remember any lights," said Fanny, trying to sound as wicked as Theda Bara, the terrible vamp she had just seen who, with the flutter of an eyelash, could ruin any man. Still echoing in her ears (as read from the cards) was Theda Bara saying, "Kiss me, my fool." What madness! How her heart had pounded! Bella went along with her. She'd get Sam to lose sleep that night. And why chance having Sam suspect that men would find her any less desirable than her sister?

She said admonishingly, "Fanny! *Must* you?" But then she looked dreamily at the ceiling as though lost in some pleasant and secret recollection.

Later, they had coffee and apple pie together. When the waitress asked how many bills to prepare, Bella said to put everything down on one and to give it to Sam. It was about the only time they noticed him since the introductions were made. Sam slouched deeper into his chair.

Fanny wanted to be a painter, and she had found a job in an art shop on Fairmount Street just below Park Avenue that specialized in picture frames. She was consumed by the wish to preserve on canvas anything that could retain its innocence in a world that was determined to "pollute, defile, distort, derange, and otherwise contaminate and destroy whatever it touched." So mostly, she painted weeds and wild flowers. Bella had mastered the new double-needle machine and made collars and fronts eight hours a day for a shirt manufacturer. They agreed to meet again the following week, this time as a foursome, for another movie. Bella had hesitated at first when Fanny made the suggestion, and Sam silently pawed the ground with the heel of his shoe. But when Bella shrugged and said, "Well . . . maybe, OK," Sam straightened up and nodded his agreement, too.

They went to the Rialto, where the film tore a dozen times and the piano player knew little about playing a piano. While they waited for the film to be taped together after another tear, Avrum mentioned that some people at his place of work thought that he should try out as a wrestler. Fanny cried out "YEEECHHH!" which she accompanied with an appropriate facial expression, and Bella looked as though she had just cracked open an egg and found it had a blood-spot. Avrum defended himself, saying that he'd tell them in the morning that wrestling wasn't for him. It wasn't his idea anyway.

* * *

"Don't be a shmuck," said Strulevitch.

"Let's forget it, Irving. I'm not a wrestler."

"Look, you've never been to the Arena. You don't even know what we're talking about. It's not what you think. Eh? Come with me once — just once — you'll be my guest, eh? Give me a chance to point out to you all the fine points of the game . . . whaddaya got to lose? Eh? Tell me."

"No."

"Jesus! What's the matter? Just come once. No skin off your back. It won't cost you a cent, and you'll have a good time — a great time."

"I've seen the pictures in *The Herald*, so I know what goes on there. There was a picture with a guy who had his ear torn off."

"So what? It's an act. Eh? You're afraid you're gonna have an ear torn off? You want a written guarantee that that won't happen? I'll give it to you. Me personally."

"I don't want no guarantee."

"So what do you want?"

"Just what I'm doing now."

"I won't let you make a shmuckster of yourself, eh? Look — I'm gonna bring you to Horse and he'll have a talk with you. OK? He'll tell you what future you got here with the Goldenbergs. OK? Ten bucks a week now, and in ten years maybe twenty bucks. By the time you'll be ready for your pension, with a foot in the grave, maybe — with good luck — maybe it'll be up to forty. Eh? You're getting starvation wages. Don'cha wanna live a little? And what's it gonna be when you get married and have a dozen mouths to feed?"

"What Jew wrestles?" asked Avrum, now in a tone that suggested he might be bending.

"Aha! Aha! Aha!" Strulevitch bounced his head from side to side. "That's just it. Eh? OK, there was Big Bernie Melamed — ever hear of him? And Maxi Shapiro the boxer? And Max Konforti? All of them Yids, and all of them just muscles and crap that folded every time some tough Frog blew his nose at them. Eh? But look at them today. Melamed's Steak House was put up with his wrestling money. Maxi Shapiro has five taxis last I heard. Double M taxis — that's him. And Konforti now runs a gym somewhere in the States — first class and legitimate. Y'see what I mean? Eh? OK? The fact that they're Jews only made the gates bigger. Now even the Frogs who run the Arena have an interest in making a Yid look good. They know good money."

"Wrestling is trouble, and that's the last thing I need. I've got almost another three years for my citizenship papers, and I'm not going to take a chance with that. From the papers, I know that wrestlers are half-and-half underworld."

"But you'll have a handler and a manager. I promise you you'll be looked after. And hey — no one's telling you you got to quit you job here. Eh? No one's telling you you got to risk something. OK? Everything is on your off hours and you can probably begin putting away at least twenty extra a week from the word 'go.' We begin you slow, y'see, but in a year, if we get you to the main events, you'll be making a hunnert — a hunnert'n fifty for a half-hour sweat."

"I don't know. I said something about wrestling to my friends last night—"

Strulevitch wouldn't let him finish. "And they told you it wasn't for a good Jewish *boyehle*."

"Something like that. They almost threw up."

"Abie . . . Abie . . . you and me, we're friends, no? Eh? OK? So listen to a friend. Who in this whole world has your best interests in his heart more than me? If you know, tell me. OK? Eh? If you were already a wrestler when you told them, they'd pat you on the back and ask for free tickets. If they were broads, they'd already have had you screwing them 'til your *baitzes* fell off. All this I'm telling you 'cause I know. Trust me — I know all the ins and outs of this game." He nodded in perfect agreement with himself.

"I still don't know."

"But you'll have a talk with Horse?"

"Just a talk?"

"Just a talk."

The talk had to wait until Horse could have his appendix removed. Strulevitch was afraid that if the momentum of his argument wouldn't be maintained, Avrum would get derailed by the advice of his friends who would surely get to him before Horse came out of the hospital. He wracked his mind for some way to give Avrum the feeling that there are things in this world he would want that his friends couldn't give him.

"So, what — you're gonna go back and listen to what your friends are gonna tell you?"

"They're not really my friends. I just know them."

Strulevitch was suddenly hopeful. "I knew that from the first minute. Eh? Listen . . . how would you like a broad?"

"What?"

"Yah, y'know, a broad — box, boobies, and all," Strulevitch frowned to show how serious and how much a man of the world he was. He blew a cloud of smoke at Avrum's face. Avrum waved it away.

"From where? From your talent scout business?"

"Nah. Just something that's drifting around if you feel like slipping in half a bang. Eh? I know you got your mind on other things, but if you ever have a free five minutes and feel like tossing off a load, I'll give you a number — I'll even fix it up for you."

"No, thanks."

"Whattsa matter? So you got a *yiddineh* and she lets you cop a tit from the outside. OK I'm talking about a real twang. You go in there and forget yourself. Eh? Y'know what I mean?"

"I know what you mean." Avrum secretly felt glad that Strulevitch believed that he at least had had some physical intimacy with a woman. But the aching truth was that in spite of Strulevitch's "education," he had never once been alone with a woman — never once "copped a tit (even) from the outside," let alone seen a woman undressed. If not for Strulevitch's French postcards, he wouldn't even know what to expect to find under a woman's clothing. He could hear his heart pounding and he knew that blood was rushing into his face. "I know what you mean, but," he shrugged, "I don't really need it." Avrum thought ruefully that for him, losing and lying were probably parts of the same package.

"Y'know what? Try it first. Eh? Just try it. Eh? Then if you don't like it, you go for another fish. Waddaya got to lose? OK? I'll leave it up to you. It's not a heebee broad you got to worry about knocking up. And, by the way — if you do get into trouble with a heebee, it's no problem to fix it, you know. Don't even think it would cost you. I mean, me'n Horse wouldn't touch a cent — not if the three of us is in business together." Strulevitch waited.

"Well, if you have a number," said Avrum, trying to sound bored, "maybe I'll keep it on me."

(8)

While the girls were finishing their last pieces for the day and getting ready to close down the machines, Shirley stepped out of the office and called to Avrum to pick up the telephone's receiver.

"Right this minute?" shouted an annoyed Goldenberg from the cutting table. "Whoever it is can't wait a few more minutes?"

Walking hastily past him, Avrum said, "I don't know who it could be."

"But the girls are going now. You're going to let them leave me everything on the floor? They're going to oil the machines and drip over all the work."

Avrum turned and he was blushing. "Soon, soon, Mr. Goldenberg. This is the first telephone call I ever had in my life." Before speaking into the mouthpiece, he felt the weight of the receiver in his hand and lifted it to where he thought it felt most comfortable against his ear.

It was Bella.

"Bella? How are you, Bella?" He felt his heart suddenly begin to race.

"I'm disturbing you?" she asked.

"No, no. I'm free. How are you?"

"You already asked me that. Don't you want to know why I called?"

"Sure."

"I called because . . . umm . . . because . . . oh — just never mind." There was a pause. "It was a mistake, I think. I've changed my mind. I'm sorry."

"What's the matter? Something happened?"

Silence.

"Bella? Tell me."

"Tell you what?"

"What you wanted to tell me."

"I told you, I changed my mind."

"Why? What did I say?"

"It's nothing, Avrum . . . really nothing . . . never mind."

Goldberg shouted from somewhere in the back. "ABIE, YOU WANT THEM TO RUIN EVERYTHING? THIS IS JUST THE MINUTE YOU HAD TO PICK TO GO TO THE PHONE?"

Avrum put his hand over the mouthpiece and called back, "One more minute."

"You have to go," said Bella, "so go."

"Yeah . . . but tell me Bella. What's the matter?"

"The matter? Who said anything was the matter?"

"I didn't say—" but then he remembered he did. "You want to call me later?"

"I should call you?" There was repulsion in her voice.

"You want me to call you?"

"If you want."

"What's your number?"

"Talon one, six, five, two. But in twenty minutes, you won't find me here."

"OK, Bella. Goodbye."

"Goodbye."

Fifteen minutes later, Goldenberg was pacified, and Avrum used the telephone in the shipping quarters to return the call. Strulevitch was in the toilet.

"Brighter Brother Shirts," answered a girl's voice.

"Can I speak to miss, uh . . . miss, uh . . ."

"Bella?" she cut in.

"Yes, to Bella." For a moment, the sound was muted at the other end; then the same voice came through.

"Bella just left. Any message?"

"Just left?"

"Yes, a minute ago. Shall I tell her anything?"

"But you said she left, how can you tell her?"

"She can get the message tomorrow. Or I can even call her personally, if you want."

"Uh, no."

"Abie?" it was Bella.

"Bella?" Avrum was mystified.

"Yes, it's me. I remembered I forgot my umbrella, so I accidentally came back."

"Oh, well, I called."

"Yes."

"You want to talk?"

"I said I changed my mind — it was just something."

"Something what?" Avrum felt at a terrible loss.

"Oh, I can't talk about it on the telephone."

"Do you want we should meet?"

"If *you* really want to."

"Sure. Where?"

"Look. I'll come up to the mountains from Villeneuve. Take a streetcar and meet me at the corner of Park and Mount Royal — on the side of the bakery. If you get there first, walk toward Villeneuve."

"When are you leaving — now?"

"Well, I'll finish here in ten minutes."

"So in half an hour on the corner?"

"Half an hour. Goodbye, Abie. But remember to walk up to meet me if you get there first."

Myer Goldenberg's scowl and grumbling was no match for the urgency that had overtaken Avrum to make it to the mountains. Between Esplanade and Park Avenue was Fletcher's Field, and Villeneuve carried past Esplanade across the field to Park Avenue as a pedestrian crossing. Avrum had long since reached the corner and was trying to ward off doubts that Bella had changed her mind again, when he recognized her in a party of girls walking toward him. Bella was a heavy girl with generous breasts and massive hips, and Avrum noticed how, as she walked, everything moved at once. It was as though every part of her had a life which was independent of every other part. The calves that showed under her dress seemed to be angled outwards — but they were also solid enough to carry her bulk with certain lightness.

"Hello, Abie. I'm sorry it took me soooooo long. You were probably waiting an hour for me."

"How are you?" He was about to shake her hand and Bella must have seen it coming because she turned half aside to discourage it and said to her friends: "This is Abie. Abie meet my friends Malka, Phyllis, Esther, Sonia — and another Sonia." They smiled. Bella asked them if they wanted to keep walking along Park, but they said no — they'd take the number 29 streetcar. Avrum shook hands with them, and when he walked away with Bella, they heard the girls tittering.

"You didn't have to shake Phyllis' hand so long, you know. It was almost embarrassing. She may look like God-knows-what with all that lipstick and makeup, but underneath it she is the biggest fake you ever saw in your life."

"Which one was Phyllis?"

"As if you don't know."

"I was shaking hands with all of them."

"Don't pretend." Plainly annoyed, Bella tossed her head and refused to talk about it any more. She changed the subject.

"I wanted to talk to you about you and Fanny."

"Me and *Fanny*?"

"Yes — now you see why I couldn't talk about it on the telephone?" Avrum couldn't guess what he would hear next.

"I wanted to know your honest feelings."

"What honest feelings?"

"Just your honest, sincerest, and truest feelings about her. She's my sister, y'know, and we're very, very close — almost like one person."

"But I don't know what feelings—"

"Abie, promise me . . . swear two fingers up to God that this is secret between you and me."

"I swear."

"And I swear, too, so tell me."

"Tell you what?"

"If you really love her. You can trust me. If there is something, maybe I can help the two of you."

"Well . . . I think she's nice. You're also nice."

"But do you love her? That's what I want to know."

"I saw her once, twice. I know her just like I know you. How can I know what I feel yet? Does she like me?"

"Why don't you ask her yourself?"

"Well . . . I think she's very nice. But maybe she knows somebody else who—"

"Abie," Bella sighed resignedly, taking a hold of his arm at the same time, "just know that I am your special friend. You can trust me with everything that you feel, and I'm ready to help the two of you the minute you need me. And Abie . . . ?"

"Yes?"

"If I say so myself, no woman in the whole wide world is more honest and sincere than me," she said sincerely.

"Oh, okay" Her grip on his arm was strong and determined.

Overtaking all his senses, his mind exploded with excitement. He could almost count each of the fingers which were pressing above his elbow, though he didn't have the courage to look at them. And until she would withdraw her hand, he would keep his arm fixed and frozen in the position it was in.

He felt suddenly committed to her for her boldness and for her daring to be so openly intimate with him. She had fixed a very real and very physical bridge between their bodies. This unleashed thoughts and emotions that swirled madly behind his eyes. In his entire life, this was the most intimate he had ever been with any woman. Bella filled his mind completely.

"Abie? What do you think of Sam?"

"Sam?"

"Yes, Sam. The Sam you saw me with."

"Oh, *that* Sam." Avrum felt his throat catch, and he swallowed hard. He prayed she didn't notice.

"He's after me from morning to night, you know, and I don't know what to do." She gripped his arm even tighter.

"What does he want?"

"Oh . . . I don't have to tell you — you know . . . *that*!"

"Oh."

"And I don't know what to do. I just don't feel the same way about him, you know, and I want to be . . . fair. I'm the fairest person you will ever meet in your life, Abie. That's the honest truth."

"So say no."

"That would destroy him — he would have a nervous breakdown in a second; he would go totally crazy. It wouldn't even surprise me if he tried to commit suicide. You don't know him. He would really commit suicide. He wants to marry me. But Abie — you swore — this is strictly a secret between you and me. I would die if somebody else knew what I just told you."

"A secret. One hundred percent."

“I’m telling you life is not easy.” She shook her head tragically.

Later, they confessed to each other that they enjoyed the walk and the talk together, and they agreed to meet secretly again in one week’s time. “Take a week to think of all the things you want to tell me,” she implored. Avrum smiled and nodded, hoping she would go away believing he understood.

* * *

“. . . kin to the tender and quiet deer . . . chased by the rustling of leaves . . .”

That evening, Avrum stared through the thick, clear pools of fat — the floating windows to the bottom of the bowl — and let the rich smell of the chicken soup draw into his nostrils. Freidle Kaplan had started to plow one of her heavy suppers into him, and she had already taken up her usual position, which was about an inch away from the hand in which he held the spoon and half a step away from the stove. From there, one eye could measure his appetite while the other could measure the fire.

A mountain of grouts, stuffed neckskins, boiled chicken, small unhatched eggs, and a wedge or two of *kugel* — a noodle pie baked with raisins and *griven*, crisp squares of chicken skin deep fried in chicken fat — still waited for him. Normally, this table delighted him enormously — Freidle Kaplan’s culinary skills could send master chefs back to first grade — but early that afternoon, his mind had been given food of another sort to digest, and its taste was the taste of gall.

Florence had received word from the Flatbush address of the American Association of Jewish Immigrants from Lvov to the effect that Hershel would be impossible to trace. They said that Aren and Malka Flomen, the people who had brought Hershel across from the old country with them, had moved to Cuba, and that they had moved there without him. The other Flomen, Pinyeh, who was making a name for himself in textiles in Manhattan, was able to tell the people at the Association that this Hershel Vishinsky had become impossibly deranged not long after reaching America, and had simply vanished into thin air. The word was that at night, he used to wet his bed, and during the day, he would be found hiding crouched in the closets, until the last day, when he walked out of the door and never returned. They said that he couldn't have had more than fifty cents or a dollar in his pocket at the time, and the message hinted darkly that the boy had probably put an end to his life. All this had happened more than a year ago, and not a word had been heard from (or about) him to this very day.

"Don't you go around believing in maybes and could-bes and probablys." Mrs. Kaplan had scolded him. "Not for a minute! Only a person who is alive and breathing can vanish into thin air. These days, the minute a man dies — it doesn't even matter where he dies — somebody finds out his name and it gets written down in a hundred different places. You can ask anyone — it's a fact of death."

But this couldn't hold back the numbness, the crushing emptiness, and the agonizing feeling of loss and abandonment that now overcame Avrum. And rising in the wake of those emotions were some old and familiar ghosts who waited for the night to take liberties with his mind.

* * *

He was in the ring again, but this time nervous and fearful of the man who was in there with him. They circled each other, but Avrum could do no more than drag his feet heavily. They might have been sacks of lead. Opposite him was Iannuk, who wouldn't acknowledge that he knew him, but for the strangest reason, he only feinted with his shoulders, never once lifting his boots. Avrum laughed and asked, unsure, "In the end, must it be you or me?" Only it wasn't Iannuk any longer, but Hershel.

He was standing outside the ring, seemingly bored and disinterested, but there was just no mistaking him; it was Hershel. "I searched for you under every stone . . . every stone . . . every stone . . ." God only knew why, but Hershel seemed preoccupied with something else and felt no constraint to react. But an instant later, he was in the ring, and with unforgiving fury and lightning suddenness brought his boot down to crush Avrum's foot — never once looking him in the eye. Prostrate on the ground, Avrum watched Hershel walk quickly away seeing only his back.

Avrum thought he caught the Doctor throwing stones at him, but then he looked again and saw that the stones came from Hershel's hand. They stung and brought blood, but Hershel asked him to pay no attention to the wounds. "I myself have trouble with my joints . . . my elbows . . . my knees . . . and if I'd think about them, I'd never move at all."

Apparently knowing exactly where he was and what he was doing, Hershel slipped into a dark and curtained doorway and disappeared. Wanting to follow him, Avrum got himself infernally tangled up in the curtain, and he felt a great fear well up in him. Suddenly, and as if from a depth of a mile, he heard a splashing and coughing. Fanny Finegold seemed to be minding the doorway, and she said almost absently, "The curtain is locked now. I can't untangle you."

"But I can't lose him again." Avrum wasn't able to swallow his tears, and he thought he would choke to death on them. The curtain was at his neck now and almost across his mouth.

"Everything collects at the bottom of the river. Then I raise them and dry them. It's a dredge, I tell you. And for myself, there is nothing. But there is room in the river for you, too, I suppose. If that's really where you want to go."

"I can't get the curtain off me. Can't you keep it open?"

"Why? Whatever for? Nothing ever comes through from the other side." Then, from somewhere behind the curtain, he heard the gurgling and thrashing sound of a river rushing quickly to the surface, but what suddenly burst through the curtain with lashing tongues on either side of him were the hottest flames. Then he saw the rats swarming around his feet. He recognized them and they recognized him.

Freidle Kaplan opened the light in his room, and Mr. Kaplan stepped over and shook him lightly.

"Abie, are you all right? Don't scream, Abie. Don't scream. It's OK, *zunneleh*. We're here. It's just a bad dream."

Avrum heard them, but he cowered under his blanket, and there was no way he could hold himself back from urinating.

(9)

"*. . . the tree shall be resurrected . . .*"

Freidle Kaplan convinced Avrum to have a few words with an old world countryman of hers — a reb Melamed Kapitolnik, a magician. "It would cost a dollar."

"What do you mean, a *magician*?" Avrum felt himself blushing. Just that morning, Strulevitch had described to him the act of a magician at the Gaiety. ("From a distance of two-three feet, he blows out a candle with a fart.")

"If I were to tell you that he is a Kabbalist, it would mean something to you? If I'd tell you that the eyes in his head can see into another world, you would know what I'm talking about? Would you believe me if I told you that he can make things happen? That there are those who swear that he's brought people back from the grave? Oh, he's no ordinary man, this Kapitolnik — to this day, he fasts at least one day a week, lives mostly on onions and radishes the other days, and he still walks, I'm sure, with stones in his shoes."

"And you want me to believe that he would know more about my brother than the people from the Association?"

"Look, these Associationists can only know what is in front of their noses. Kapitolnik sees into the ground and over mountains. He can see from what's behind yesterday to what's planned for after tomorrow."

Avrum hesitated.

"Abie, this man has a million tricks. You listen to what he says and you do what he tells you. If you trust him — things happen. More than this, I can't tell you. But you'll go if I pay him the dollar myself. You're still young and healthy, and I don't want any more funny business with you at night."

* * *

After Florence had told him of his brother's emotional deterioration and then of his disappearance, Avrum had her get Shirley to write to every clinic for the mentally disturbed in the states of New York and New Jersey. She got their addresses from the American consulate, and their list included both states' insane asylums as well. Their replies had been prompt. Some had asked for more details, but it was plainly evident that Hershel was unknown to them. The director of one clinic, on his own initiative, had forwarded Hershel's particulars to a local radio station that often located missing relations through one of their programs, but two mentions brought no reaction.

"Don't take it too badly, Abie," Florence had said. "You're not really alone in the world. Everyone here loves you, so c'mon, give Florence a smile."

And Mrs. Kaplan wanted no more funny business.

Funny business . . .

Weird, punishing dreams, repeating themselves night after night, carried him mercilessly to the edge of madness. At times, his jarring screams would puncture the still nights and terrify everyone — even neighbors. He'd awake in a bath of sweat, terror exploding in his chest, and until the harrowing nocturnal images receded, his eyes would cling desperately to the figures of the Kaplans standing in helpless distress over him.

He would be alone in a room at the end of a long corridor — one vacant and narrow, and Hershel would be knocking at the front door. Hershel's clothes were in the room, and propped in a corner was that violin he'd once assembled as a child. Some premonition in his heart makes him call out, "Are you coming from the dead?" Only no reply would be forthcoming.

Despite himself, he'd turn the key and lift the catch from the trap. At that instant, he'd hear violent scratching and the door would be forced against him. He'd see it opening wider and wider, though he'd be pressing with all his strength to close it again. The door opens wide enough for him to discern a monster of a dog — ferocious and raging with hatred, mucous and blood streaming thickly from his nostrils.

"Your brother waits for you behind its teeth. Don't you recognize what you see?"

It would be Krimmer, who would be standing next to him working his terrible fingers into his own and wresting them away from the door. Now he could see bits of flesh and tissue mixed with the mucous and blood. It was a complete finger.

At first, the acrid fumes were so out of place in the room, and dreams so embraced him, that Avrum didn't react to them. But they thickened and filled the room. The smell became so pungent that Avrum suddenly bolted upright, the lining in his nose stinging. Something somewhere was burning. He pushed into his slippers and bathrobe, lifted open his window and quietly rushed to inspect the kitchen. The smoke and smell was as thick everywhere in the house as it was in his room, but the stove was out and the electricity was off. He woke the Kaplans. On other occasions, they could be the lightest of sleepers, but now it took some pounding on the door.

Freidle Kaplan cried out in a piercing voice, "A fire! Where is it coming from, Abie?"

"It must be from outside. I checked the house."

"You think from outside?" This was Mr. Kaplan.

"Yeah — I'm going to take a look. Could be it's in the building, so maybe you should get dressed."

"What do you think — that I don't sleep dressed? In this life, I'm ready for every emergency." This Freidle Kaplan.

He found the fire in Horse's place. Shorty had probably neglected the kerosene stove when he closed up. He'd keep it on all day under the oil for the French fries, and Avrum himself had heard Cy tell him that very morning that he was asking for trouble if he wouldn't move it from under the shelf. He had pointed to the stack of toilet paper up there, and said that Horse always moved it to the table by the sink whenever he'd use it. Shorty said not to worry — that he had everything organized.

Some of the neighbors were outside trying to look through the shop's windows. Two of them had run to the corner to the fire alarm post, but instead of setting it off, they started to fight — fists, teeth, feet, and all. It seemed that each wanted to be the one to break the glass window in order to set off the alarm at the fire department. One of them was heard to shout that he had waited all his life to work the alarm, and no one was going to cheat him out of his chance. But someone had already called them on the telephone, and a truck from the Laurier and St. Lawrence station was on its way.

The pressure of the water in the pipes was at its peak at that hour of the night, so that when the hoses were connected to the hydrant, it took a while to control them. Two men were holding the spouts at the time, but the pipes lashed violently out of their grips to slap around crazily on the cars, the carriages, and the sidewalk until they could finally be managed. Though the fire raged in Horse's eatery, the first windows to be smashed and the first rooms to be flooded were those of Meyer's Sweet Mode Dress factory.

A small crowd had collected. Avrum estimated that at least a dozen cars and buggies had been attracted by the clanging of the fire truck, and the men in black rubber had a grand audience. The door and windows of Horse's place were cleaned of every inch of glass in about a minute flat and the men armed themselves with picks and axes in readiness for the order to charge. The fire had totally surrendered by this time, but the firemen were not about to be cheated out of their sport. The fire initiated the game and the men would decide when to finish it — which, as it turned out, would be more than half an hour later.

The use Horse might now have had for his new cash register would perhaps be to use it as its own ashtray; a fireman had sent his pick through it a number of times, and then did the same to the enamel sink — through the stack of dirty dishes that Shorty had left for the morning. The sediment on the floor was all the coffee that Horse had carefully stored away, and mixed into it was just about the same amount of sugar. Mysteriously, all the cigarettes had disappeared, except for a couple of crumpled and soggy Craven A's, which had fallen to the floor. The place reeked of smoke tar, raw hamburger, and vegetable oil. The door to the icebox was open, but it lay flat on its face. Most of it was charred. Plaster began to fall from the walls and ceiling. The telephone, apparently with a life of its own, remained untouched. When it was over, the chief walked out and showed the crowd the small kerosene cooker, shaking his head admonishing the carelessness of some people.

Avrum wasn't there to see him. His attention had been alternating between the damage done to the factory and the antics of the firemen at Horse's, when he thought he saw the reflection of a flash of light coming from inside the factory. He walked up to one of the broken windows for a closer look and recalled that the alarm should have sounded from the Kaplan's house, but hadn't. He made a mental note to remember to tell Goldenberg about it in the morning. There was no imagining the light, however, when it flashed a second time. Someone *was* inside. He had been suspicious of the characters that milled around the factory when the windows were first broken; they had poked their heads through the gaping holes and into the office and showroom. Some of them may have slipped inside when everyone's attention shifted to Horse's door. A trashcan had been set there before. Avrum climbed onto the lid and found that it would take no effort to step from there onto Shirley's desk. He bent under the slivers of glass that were still fast in the frame, and, agile as a cat despite his size, let himself inside.

From the reflection of the moonlight coming through, Avrum knew that the back door of the factory had been opened. Then he made out at least three figures that darted between the door and the stockroom. One of them held a flashlight, but his head was over the lamp so that only a dull red glow showed through. A moment later all three seemed to have moved back to the stockroom and instinctively Avrum raced between the cutting table and the row of sewing machines to slam shut and lower the bar on the door — he had trapped them all — including himself.

The first to turn out of the stockroom saw him and bolted for the office. He had managed only a few yards, having chosen to make his way behind the cutting table, under which Charlie had left a few bolts of cloth sticking halfway out. They were one of two very similar patterns, and since Goldenberg had wanted only one to make up the table in the morning, he'd had Charlie pull these halfway out before he left so there would be no mistake. The fellow's chin struck the edge of the table as he fell, and somehow caught his tongue between his teeth, which sliced right through it. The other two tried to overpower Avrum or at least to get past him to the door. A fist crashed into his stomach, another landed knuckle-edged and hard directly below his eye.

Avrum brought his hands to his face to protect himself when he felt a foot plow into his shin, and the hands that grabbed the collar of his bathrobe tried to pull him down from behind. Avrum worked his left hand around and got a secure grip on the chest of whoever was at his back. With his other hand, he was able to half slap, half punch the face of the assailant who had kicked him and who had moved to strike again. This one reeled and fell next to the toilet door. With both hands now on the attacker who was behind him, Avrum swung him like a rag doll and threw him against his partner, who was getting to his feet. Using his fists like sledgehammers, Avrum pounded the two of them across their faces, stomachs, ribs, and kidneys until they lay crumpled and senseless on the floor. From Strulevitch's table he took the cone of cord that was used to tie the cartons, and after setting the two back to back in something of a sitting position, he wrapped about twenty yards around them before he was satisfied that he could knot it. Then, remembering the one who had tripped behind the cutting table, Avrum went to look for him but he was gone. Using the thieves' flashlight, Avrum checked the stockroom and designing quarters. Spots of blood on the floor caught his eye, and he followed them. Not surprisingly, they led to Shirley's desk and the window.

Outside the window was Mrs. Kaplan. The firemen were returning the hoses to the truck.

"Abie, is that you inside?
"Yeah, it's me — there was a robbery. Almost a robbery."
"Oh my God! Oh my God! Are you alright!"
"I'm fine. We have to call the police."

"Abie, Myer has to know. It can't wait 'til he'll show up in the morning, 'cause he'll get an attack. Take a taxi and go wake him up because they don't have a phone yet in the new house."

"What? I should go to his house? Now?"

"This minute! The windows are broken — anybody can break in. When the police get here, I'll keep them here, and in the meantime I'll watch. Do you know the address where he lives?"

"Yeah. I know. I've been there."

Avrum ran up Laurier to Park Avenue, where there was an all-night taxi service. Only when the drivers stared at him did he realize that he was still in his pajamas and bathrobe. "I'm from the fire," he told them and they asked about it. It was almost 2:30 in the morning. He tried to think what his first words to Goldenberg should be when the taxi pulled up at the house and the driver pressed on the horn. Lights turned on everywhere, it seemed, except at the Goldenberg's, and Avrum raced up the walk thinking how he must look to Goldenberg's neighbors. He rang the bell, and a moment later, he heard Florence behind the door.

"Who is it?"

"It's Abie — there was a fire!"

"At the factory? Oh my God! I don't know how much we're insured. Just a minute, I'll open the door."

Avrum heard her call Myer, whose voice replaced hers. The door opened and Myer came out, ashen and anxious.

"I forgot to bring money to pay for the taxi," said Avrum, embarrassed.

"What happened?"

"There was a fire at Horse's and a robbery at the factory after the water broke the windows and flooded the place. So I came to tell you while it's still happening. I didn't even change my clothes, and I didn't take any money."

Goldenberg called to the driver. "You know where the factory is? Come in tomorrow and I'll pay you."

"You won't know me tomorrow, and you can find half a buck to pay me now."

"Criminal," muttered Goldenberg, but then he called to Florence to bring money down to the driver. "I'll put my pants on and we'll leave," he told Avrum, "and next time, keep change on you wherever you go."

On the way, Avrum related the events in their sequence.

"So you mean to say they are in there tied up right now—and that you did it all by yourself?"

"Yeah."

"Well, I hope you didn't kill them." Suddenly, Goldenberg found it all very funny, and his initial fright gave way to an attack of laughter. "You mean to say that he ran with his tongue out, and when he tripped, his teeth chopped right through it? How could you see? I mean, how could you be sure?"

"There was enough light coming . . . and he screamed like you wouldn't believe. He's at some hospital now for sure."

The picture of it happening rocked Myer with another wave of laughter, and he wasn't listening for the answer. But his mood changed when he pulled up at the curb and saw the soot, the shattered glass, the unprotected windows, the water, and the policemen. These were holding the two whom Avrum instantly recognized as those he had fought with, only their cords were removed, and Goldenberg and Avrum saw that they were locked together with handcuffs. Goldenberg stared at them and murmured to Mrs. Kaplan, who had waited for them, that he couldn't believe that a Jewish kid — even if he was as big as Abie — could single-handedly overpower two such monster *zjlobs*.

"I can't believe it. There were three of them inside to begin with, and here is a *yiddeleh* who doesn't know enough to be afraid."

"You the boss?" asked one of the policemen walking up to them.

"Yes, officer. Isn't this just terrible —just terrible."

"Happens every day. Do you want to go in and inspect if they stole anything? They said they took nothing. Your boy probably didn't give them a chance."

The shorter and stockier of the two who were caught shouted angrily. "We only wanted to protect de dresses from de fire. Dat's de troot." His nose was bleeding without letup, and one eye was hugely swollen. He spoke with a heavy French accent and his partner carried on in French. "What would you have preferred — having us save your stock, or having it burned?"

"We know these angels," said a second policeman dully, "and both of them are just out of Bordeaux. Maybe a week. They'd steal from their own mothers, so don't believe them."

"What difference does it make if I believe them or not?" asked Goldenberg.

"You got to make a complaint. Otherwise, we have to let them go."

"Catching them in the factory isn't enough?"

"It's not enough — we need a signed complaint."

Mrs. Kaplan pulled Goldenberg's arm. "Myer," she said sternly, "this you really don't need. They'll come back for you one day."

Goldenberg approached the handcuffed men, who looked hurting and altogether defeated. They remained sullen and avoided his eyes.

"The police don't believe you, and maybe I don't believe you," he said carefully, "but I can't decide to make the complaint or not. I'm not looking to make you any trouble. It doesn't give me no special pleasure."

"We took nuttin'," said the shorter one. "Nuttin'. Go see for yourself."

"Well, would you promise never to do it again? Would you swear?"

"Sure." Again the shorter one, this time shaking his arm out of the policeman's grip.

"Can I believe you? Or else it's ten years in jail, y'know."

"You got our words."

The policeman scowled but released them. "You just gave them a chance to rob another factory tomorrow."

"As long as it's not mine," muttered Goldenberg to Mrs. Kaplan in Yiddish. But to the policemen, he said (loud enough for the two to overhear), "They look like they could be decent boys to me. It's not wrong sometimes to give guys like this another chance." Then Goldenberg took Avrum aside and told him that had he signed a complaint it would have given all the crooks in the city a score to settle with him. "And don't think that the cops are there when you need them. They're in cahoots with the crooks themselves."

Avrum fingered the swelling under his eye and tried to understand how it got there. Goldenberg patted him on the shoulder. "They'll remember the beating you gave them for the rest of their lives."

"The alarm upstairs isn't working," muttered Avrum. A feeling of resentment just short of anger stirred in him. He had beaten only himself.

(10)

"Eh? Y'mean he just let them go?" The episode had given Strulevitch tremendous capital. At once, his accounts with his boss had perceptibly fattened, and it brought all his old and tired grievances to blossom anew.

"I suppose he thanked you, eh? But your boss says to himself, 'Lucky for me, I got this big *shmuck* who will go break his neck for me if I tell him to.' Did you think for a minute that maybe one of them might have packed a rod? Eh? Did you think that anybody would have given a damn if you got killed? Eh? The dumb generous guys like you are always the first to get pasted — and all for what? For nothing! All you get is that he says to himself that if he ever needs a *zjlob* to do a job, he's got you. Believe me, it's the truth. If those guys would have sent you to the hospital for the rest of your life, Myer would have called the florist to send you half a dozen American Beauties, and that would have wiped his conscience clean. That would have been the end of that. You'd never have seen or heard from him again. And for this, you came to America? Eh?"

"So what — I shouldn't have gone in there?"

"Not for a parasite like Myer. He's out for himself, and everybody else is just there for him to use and step on. Do you see him stepping on me? Eh? No, 'cause he knows I don't take his crap. But boy, you have on your ass a printed gold invitation. I'm telling you, Abie, you got to see the picture for what it is. You went in there, took on three gorillas and came out with a fat eye. Eh? For Myer you saved a couple thousand dollars — like you put it with your own hand into his pocket. But what did he put into yours? Eh? And when I tell you to think about wrestling as a good honest racket — where all you got to do is go through a song and dance for a bag of greens that stays with you — to this you say no. Well, I say you gotta think again, and that's what you're going to do." Strulevitch's finger must have traveled a mile under Avrum's nose.

* * *

While they were talking, Shorty was down at the Dorchester Station buying a one-way train ticket for Syracuse. There he had an aunt — his mother's older sister — who lived by herself. She had buried his uncle years ago. Shorty considered his options, and even at 100 to 1, Syracuse had far and away the edge over every other possibility.

* * *

Avrum was seated on a low stool, and he felt Melamed Kapitolnik's long hard and boney fingers twisting in his hair. Kapitolnik was a tall, emaciated, jagged-limbed old man who took to shaving his head and caking it with white talc. Except for his eyes, which seemed black, sunken as they were in their cavernous sockets, his face was pallid and almost the same color as the talc. Thin streaking gray creases flowed from the corners of his mouth — a strange mouth that seemed to have sucked in its own lips.

While the fingers were going about their business, Avrum allowed his eyes to scan the room. Piles of books were massed against the walls, which were lined with diplomas and dozens of mysterious documents, each in a separate frame. Next to him was an ancient desk cluttered with brass hands, exotic feathers, pieces of coal, charcoal, and peat, strange beads, and chinks of blue-green glass. Over the window was a dusty, yellowing curtain, a corner of which was draped over a birdcage on a box. Two canaries were inside.

"I will give you five hairs," said the old man finally. "You take them. Each will be a different length, and each will come from a different part of your head. Tonight, you will half fill a cup with your spit, and you will soak the hairs in it. Cover them with five pinches of kosher salt and read aloud five times the fifth word on the fifth line of the fifth verse in the fifth chapter of *DVARIM* — the fifth book of the Torah. You understand? Maybe you should write all this down."

"Yes. OK, you'll tell me again and I'll write it down."

"Then, while you sleep, one of the hairs will climb up the side of the cup. This one you will bring to me. Discuss this with no one. Ask no questions. The instructions are simple enough."

The next day, Avrum delivered the hair.

"You did exactly as I said — to the letter?"

"Exactly," said Avrum. "It climbed higher than all the others. I don't even think the others climbed at all. How could you know?"

"I didn't. If your brother was dead, none of the hairs — not a single one of them — would have moved. Like this, I can tell you that he is alive this very minute and living in America. Another hair would have meant another continent."

"But where? Can you say where exactly?"

"That takes time — but tell me, it rose how? From the tip or from the root?"

"From the middle."

"Closer to the tip or closer to the root?"

"I . . . I can't remember."

"Think."

"I can't remember — closer to the tip, maybe. If you would have asked me, I would have been careful to look. Both sides look exactly the same to me."

"Think. Are you sure? Closer to the tip?"

"I dunno. Maybe. I think so. When I lifted it, the tip was closest to my fingers."

"Then let me tell you this: your brother is not in the best of health, but the worst is past him. The worst is definitely past him and he has survived. In fact, his health is improving daily."

"But if he is here in America, how can I find him?"

"I know — I know. It's not going to be simple. I need more information . . . let me think."

Melamed Kapitolnik sifted through some books and concentrated on various passages. Then he approached Avrum and reached for his hand. There was a blur of motion and Avrum saw a spot of blood rise at the tip of his middle finger, yet he'd felt nothing. The old man told him to press out a drop, and as Avrum did so, the man went and fetched one of the canaries. The drop was applied just above the canary's bill, and then it was released.

"NOW, SAY AFTER ME, QUICKLY — *YUD!*"

"Yud."

"HEI!"

"Hei."

"VAV!"

"Vav."

"HEI!"

"Hei."

"ADONAI, HASHEM ELOKIM!"

"Adonai, Hashem Elokim."

"BASAR V'DAM! HAI V'KAYYAM!"

"Basar v'dam. Hai v'kayyam."

"AVIR MAYYIM ESH V'ADOMAH!"

"Avir mayyim esh v'adomah."

The canary had lodged itself securely in the curtain a few inches from the ceiling, and Kapitolnik recited something in a rush under his breath. Both of them were as tense as whistles.

Avrum was to read to himself a verse from the *Tehillim* (the place was underlined), and Kapitolnik would light a candle. The smoke would have something to say.

"From the instant I light the match, you don't stop reading. If you finish before I stop, you begin again from the beginning, immediately. This you understand?"

“I understand.” Avrum looked at the passages. They were written in the first language he had learned to read and write.

“So from . . .” The match was struck and Kapitolnik signaled with his head. Avrum glued his eyes to the lines on the page and Kapitolnik held a sheet of clean white paper flat about a foot above the flame. He seemed to be waiting for something — which somehow didn’t happen, until finally he whispered to Avrum not to stop reading, but while reading, to walk over to the curtain and shake it. Avrum obeyed, and it caused the canary to desert it for a ledge on one of the framed documents hanging on the wall behind them. The instant the bird made its move, Kapitolnik snuffed the candle.

“That’s it,” shot Kapitolnik. “It’s done.” He showed Avrum the pattern the soot had made on the paper. “You see — it’s all here now.”

Avrum said nothing, and he watched as the old man sank heavily into his chair. His mouth began to twitch and move again. “Still . . . it’s curious that the bird should have chosen the north wall and that page specifically . . . yes . . . curious and strange. Makes me think.”

“Mr. Kapitolnik . . .”

“Don’t ask me a thing now. Not a thing. It will take me time to read the signs — to get everything untangled. Don’t think these things can be done with the snap of a finger. They just can’t.”

“Am I supposed to go now?”

“Yes. Leave my money on the table. Come back next Thursday. In the meantime, don’t eat any eggs — not a single egg. Eat one egg and it’s finished. Do you understand everything I’m telling you? Eat one egg and everything gets spoiled.”

“No eggs.”

“Goodbye.”

(11)

Her name was Lucille, and Avrum was to meet her during his lunch hour. They had agreed that their assignation would be outside the shoe store on the corner of St. Lawrence and Sherbrooke Streets.

Goldenberg could go to hell. Avrum was overcome with bitterness. If America had its lessons to teach him, and if these lessons had to be delivered to his face, well fine! At least he was still on his feet. For days after the attempted robbery at the factory he tried to give some solid definition to the sense of injustice done him, which increasingly gnawed on his sensibilities. Goldenberg, after all, had done only what was right for Goldenberg. Finished! Everything right or wrong, good or bad stopped here. Neither was it lost on Avrum under just whose umbrella of enterprise he enjoyed his new economic security. Getting the bitterness off his chest might do wonders for this chest, but it wouldn't pay for the bread and milk.

So the first lesson an immigrant like him had to learn was to avoid colliding head-on with Canada's way of life. America, where all the prizes went to the man whose grip was firmest on his profit and loss statement. Goldenberg had the knack of measuring his profits and losses in the wink of an eye, no small thing, so why hold it against him? And America did compensate its standard-bearers. Was there another country in the world that offered the same delicious diversions? Ah, the marvelous diversions — the prizes. Avrum got it into his head that if he'd get a taste of these diversions, he'd become a standard-bearer himself, and what epitomized these diversions if not the pleasures of an agreeable woman? Also, his body had long been begging his mind — begging incessantly — so perhaps the time really had come.

The number that Strulevitch had given him belonged to a girl named Denise, but Denise said that she couldn't work for a while; later, Strulevitch said that that meant either the curse or the clap. She had a friend, she said, one Lucille, who looked after her customers very nicely in the meantime. Lucille was supposed to be charming and clean, and open to everything. Strulevitch said that it was probably alright to take on this Lucille though he had no idea who she was. "What do you have to lose?" he said with a shrug. "But you should at least have asked how old she was, 'cause for the price she's asking, you get only the oldest *drek* and ugliest *shmattes* on the street. Eh? And if they're young, either they got no teeth or no hair, or else something else is wrong. But like I say — for a buck, what can you lose? You see her anyways before you go to the room, so if she turns out to be a cripple or something, you can always walk away."

Avrum was sure that that would be unlikely. The thought played on his mind that somewhere in this city of almost a million people was a wonderful girl who had willingly agreed to share a secret illicit hour of passion with him. (Actually, half an hour: he'd have to leave time for the ride there and back.) They would be locked together on a bed, the two of them, alone, behind a closed door, in a secret, forbidden room. And she would remove all her clothes. He would see her breasts in a brassiere, and she wouldn't stop him from looking. Then the brassiere would come off and he'd see. His gratitude even now was so profound that he loved her just for having agreed to take the dollar from him.

Strulevitch was being rushed by Goldenberg to get on with a few urgent orders that the Canadian National man would be coming round to collect in the early afternoon. Four styles were still at the finishers, and Strulevitch complained that he could only pack them as fast as they were being supplied. Avrum told Strulevitch that he planned to slip out the back door at least fifteen minutes before the lunch break to get a head start in case the streetcar would be slow, and Strulevitch warned him that Goldenberg was already frothing at the mouth, and that he wasn't too happy himself about having to stop the packing to run and look for the missing numbers.

"It's only for fifteen minutes," argued Avrum impatiently.

"The truth is, I'm more worried that you'll get lost in her hole and forget that there's such a thing as one o'clock."

The hands of the clock seemed to have frozen where they were. Avrum moved like a mechanical toy between the pressers, the finishers, and the stock room. A sudden lascivious thought or mental image would send blood rushing in a fury to his head, and at times elsewhere, so that he hesitated to relax and dally at any station. Goldenberg thought he had cramps judging from the way Avrum walked, and later, when he looked for him and Strulevitch said that he had gone ten minutes early to lie down because he wasn't feeling well, Goldenberg shook his head, but didn't press to know more.

Meanwhile, Strulevitch fumed with anger and frustration. On their racks, Avrum had mixed not only the styles but also the sizes. There were six-thirteens on the one-thirteen rack, and there were four-oh-fours mixed in with the three-oh-sixes. He was packing the size twelves of the three-oh-three and found four size sixteens among them. Among the size sixteens of the same style were at least a dozen size fourteens.

Myer Goldenberg, shifting the hangers, missed nothing. "Is it my eyes, or am I really going crazy?" he asked incredulously, his voice rising an octave. "That's the thanks I get? This is just sabotage — a knife in my back. Now, go unpack everything Irving — all the tied boxes. Everything! I'm not going to make a fool of myself. And if you ask for overtime (swiftly crossing his fisted left forearm with his right), I'll give you overtime!"

Avrum found the corner, but he was early. It was a warm mid-June day, the sun was in the middle of the sky, and he stood there shaking nervously. He shifted his weight from one foot to the other, shooting sidelong glances at the passersby, hoping to God that none of them could read his mind or guess what he was doing there. He strained to show a nonchalant demeanor and an interest only in the shoes in the store window. But from the way he arched his eyebrows, fixed his lips, jutted his chin, and hunched his back, he succeeded only in getting most of the strollers to keep a careful distance from him. On three separate occasions, he noticed a woman, still at some distance but walking directly toward him, and each time he felt his knees turn to putty.

He granted himself that Lucille might be less than a flaming beauty, at least on the surface, but that hers had definitely to be a beauty of the soul. A truly physically beautiful woman would likely paralyze him with fear. He was certain of this. Such a woman even for his single dollar would be beyond his reach. Many of the women as happened by he mentally cancelled for himself, whereas the three had impressed him as being the sort of women to whom he might relate in some comfort — women whose faces somehow projected terrible weaknesses of their own. These seemed to be women who might not recoil in the face of his ignorance and would perhaps even welcome his sincere interest in their lives. As each woman approached he turned to the window and then half turned back to face her when she came to within a few steps of him. But none had stopped.

Then from his blind side, he heard a woman ask, "George?" That was for him. Strulevitch had warned him against using his real name for a host of reasons — beginning with paternity suits and ending with anti-Semitism — and said that a name like George or Dick or Mike would assure him anonymity. "Y'gotta think about the possible problems in advance," he had said. "Like, suppose you're walking on the street with a respectable *yiddineh.* Eh? And up she comes, recognizes you, and says, 'Oh, Abie, how are you, it's been so long . . .' or something like that. Y'see what I mean?" so he opted for George.

"Oh, hello." Avrum turned and looked at her.

Depending on how he trained his thoughts, his heart dropped or climbed like a yo-yo. Mostly it dropped. She was considerably older than he had expected and vastly more repulsive than even Strulevitch had feared, but there was a thick sweet perfume in the air around her and she was smiling warmly at him. She was also very fat, and there were a number of black and blue welts on her arms. Her dress was straining against her bulk. It was frayed around the sleeves, and there were dark spreading sweat marks at her armpits. But her breasts . . . her breasts were absolutely enormous, and pressed dangerously against the buttons that only by a miracle held them back. These could be for his voluptuous pleasures in a moment or two. Her hair was stringy and uneven, and the patches of shadows over her lip and under her chin cried out for a sharp razor. A button from the lower part of her dress was undone and because she was standing with one leg forward, Avrum could see something pink and satiny and very intimate behind it. If he'd go with her, he thought, he would likely get to see all of it.

Still, his mood soured terribly. The woman was of an ugliness that verged on the positively grotesque. A tooth was missing near the middle of her mouth, and she fit a cigarette into the space keeping it there with her tongue. He avoided her eyes and thought it may just be best if he turned and walked away. What kept him there was a sudden surfacing of conscience. To leave her would be tantamount to a slap in the face. And she was standing there, waiting only for him.

"You wanna come wid me?"

On the other hand, what did he have to lose if he would go with her? He wouldn't have to answer to anyone's jibes or snide remarks for putting up with her gross disfigurement. Who would know? And it would be just as well perhaps to break into this new world of experience with so supremely forgettable a creature. The half hour ahead of him would come and go.

"Okay," he said. "Where do we go?"

They walked to Sherbrooke Street and turned east where house after house had a "Rooms to Let/*Chambres à Louer*" sign in a window. It was into one of these houses that she led him. A woman clad in black came to the door. For a moment, Avrum was back in Lvov, alone, standing with his suitcase in front of that woman who laughed when she sent him up the stairs. They walked down a narrow passage and stopped at a door. Here Lucille asked Avrum for fifty cents, which he instantly produced and which was handed over to the woman. A moment later, they were through the door and Lucille checked the lock.

The room was long and narrow. Against the wall near the door was the bed — an arrangement of iron pipes on which the paint was flaking. Over the sheets was a dusty, faded rose bedcover. Across on the other side was a window covered by a roll-up blind, and alongside the window was a small sink; above that was a small light that had a short string hanging from its switch. Otherwise, the room was bare. For its purpose, a picture, a chair, or a table were superfluous. Surely, no customer ever complained about their not being there. Some customers did comment on the absence of a wastebasket. Where were they expected to deposit their used skins? They wouldn't fit through the grill in the sink so for lack of recourse, they invariably threw them under the bed.

"*Je t'aime*," she said, drawing heavily on her cigarette. "*Vous êtes três joli*." Avrum just nodded.

"Wan' a cigarette?" she offered him the crumpled package.

"No, thanks. I don't smoke."

"Hey — y'know, I trus' you," she began, "but maybe you give me d'cash 'afore we start? Maybe I jus' forget, y'know." Avrum gave it to her immediately. It struck him suddenly how wet his hands were.

Lucille proceeded to undress. Watching her, Avrum was struck with the gruesome and unsettling fascination of a young high school boy dissecting a frog. His stare was fixed as though in a trance, his eyes glazed, and his nostrils flared. She had worked her shoes off, and Avrum caught a whiff of their fetid air. The first rush of their intimacy was upon him. Then she rolled down her flesh colored stockings to reveal sagging puffy thighs stained by spreading yellow/purple blotches. They jiggled like water bags. Black curly hairs covered her legs, and on the side of one calf was a long, bloated scar — a violent red growth that refused to let time still its shrieks. The cosmetic paint on her gnarled and grubby toenails was more pitiful than comic.

She undid the buttons of her dress, slipped out of its sleeves, and let it drop to the floor. Avrum watched dumbfounded as she went on with even movements to rid herself of the frilly pink slip that she had on underneath. It had a tear along the hem and glossy fat stains between her breasts and her tops. He wished mightily that he could be elsewhere at that moment, but there was no breaking the macabre momentum that had locked him to this woman. At that moment, it seemed that every demon in the entire tumultuous universe was with them in the room. Nature could not have created a creature more hellish than the one he was sharing this moment with.

She stopped to inhale again on her cigarette. Then, after the smoke had left her, she tucked it up into the space between her teeth and held it there with the tip of her tongue. This freed her hands to work on her corset. Her hands tugged and pressed and pulled and pinched at the clips and knots at her back, but her eyes were blank and bored. Suddenly, it released her, and Avrum found himself choking in the grip of his newest agony. Her belly might have been a mass of aspic — a boneless, muscle-less, amoeboid suspension that pitched forward in waves to bounce and roll loosely in the air. But it was not over.

Avrum was still struggling to manage with the sight of this gross mountain of shapeless protoplasm, when again there was a blur of movement, and lo, she stood there minus her brassiere. His tongue glued to the roof of his mouth. They reminded him of nothing so much as baseball bats with their massive, bloated heads stretching away from narrow, wasted handles. The area of skin that kept the breasts attached to her chest seemed to him no larger than half dollars, and he tried to think why they didn't just tear away entirely. They were now draped across her belly, and he fought to overcome a choking in his throat when his eyes fell on the inverted nipples surrounded by their great, round, dusky brown areolas. These were marked off at their edges by a few pimples and long, shiny black hairs.

A white belt around her waist now occupied her hands. Sewn into it were short elastic straps which hung to her legs and which had interlocking clips at their ends. Then, when these came undone, she tucked her thumbs into the baggy elastic drawers she wore, and pulled them down and away. Under this was another silky undergarment, which discreetly covered what had to be the most secret place of all. But before Avrum could think much about it, it was on its way to crown the pile of her discarded clothes. These she then lifted from the floor and dropped them in a heap on the far side of the mattress near the foot of the bed.

Avrum studied the black cavernous fold that draped her belly button, and noticed that falling from it was a thick furry line, which lost itself somewhere under the lowest billowy bulge of her belly. Peeping out from under there were the tips of a few curls, which were pinched together between her massive, shapeless, dimpled thighs.

"*Alors*," she said softly, "*vous aussi*."

She pointed to his clothes and motioned for him to remove them. Avrum remained fixed to his place. His face showed much the same color as an ice sculpture, and radiated much the same temperature. She stepped up to him and slid the suspenders off his shoulders. Then she touched his shirt and pants, and started into make an animated charade of undressing. Avrum stood, and not daring to think about whether he really wanted to do what he was doing, removed his clothes until he stood before her in only his drawers and stockings. But she continued to stand there waiting, so the drawers came away, too — but not before he first turned his back to her. He shook as though it was the middle of winter, and the sweat was cold and heavy on his face and hands.

Lucille reached into the pile of her clothes and retrieved her purse. From it, she removed a small washcloth and turned to the sink. Avrum studied the pudgy, spreading, jelly-like mountains of sickly white flesh that bounced behind her — yet another horrific perspective of her body that violated his eyes. Yet, for all this, his feelings were tinged with sadness and pity for this woman. She was prepared to give herself to him in a way that no other woman ever had, and nothing about her cruelly grotesque body could obscure this truth. Her intentions demanded his gratitude. Yet he wished for the both of them that she had been less revolting. He wouldn't leave her, therefore, until what had to happen happened, then he'd be severed from her without any stubborn tentacles of guilt clinging to him. She, on the other hand, was doomed to live with herself for the whole of her life, and despite himself, he felt in his heart the heavy burden of her fate.

Lucille soaked the washcloth and wrung it. Then she walked over and handed it to Avrum, cocking her head as if to say that it was a necessary nuisance. Avrum looked at it in his hand and wondered what he was expected to do with it. But she only stood there, about a yard and a half away, watching him and waiting and smiling. Then, almost impatiently, she said, "*Et bien, mon cherie*," and pushed a few hairs from her brow.

Then it struck him — the dampness on his own brow; she had apparently seen his discomfort and anticipated his need. He pressed the cloth firmly against his forehead and rubbed briskly. Then he did the same to the back of his neck, and that done he went on to rub the sweat away from between his fingers. Seemingly confused, she refused the cloth when he handed it back to her, and Avrum began to feel faintly embarrassed.

"You not *finis*," she said with a hint of impatience, and she pointed directly at his penis, which had retreated into itself like a frightened worm. He turned his back to her and put the cloth to its intended purpose. When she took it from him to carry back to the sink, she held it by a few threads at one corner as if the rest of it was contaminated. Avrum suddenly felt that his conscience wouldn't have any claims on him were he to leave her at this moment. But all the initiatives now were hers.

Climbing onto the bed on all fours, she resembled nothing so much as a mammoth marsupial that had already delivered a dozen pups, but had forgotten another dozen still inside. Avrum lay on his back rigid as a board.

She let her long paps flop about on his chest and belly. At first, Avrum experienced a certain detachment from himself, and the only stirring he was conscious of was the slight but uneasy movement in his stomach. But then, he didn't feel quite as detached when, a moment later, he realized that more was stirring than the chime in his belly.

She asked him, "You like firs' d'French way?"

"Whatever is OK with you," he answered, trying for an air of bravado. He hoped that meant doing it the *real* way.

So she worked herself down to where the heavy heads of her breasts fell in softly between his legs, and the friction which she caused by gently swaying them from side to side there was out of all proportion to the sudden rise in his body temperature.

But even as he witnessed his own impossibly charging and altogether involuntary chemistry, a fresh current of curdling disgust arose within him when she maneuvered her body so that her head lay where her breasts had been only an instant ago. Now the full frontal aspect of her backside was flush in his line of view — so close as to make him aware of its unhealthy dankness. He closed his eyes and held his breath.

Then he felt her tongue on the inside of his thigh, licking its way to his crotch. It climbed from there over his testicles until it reached its station, and then, suddenly, it left him. Avrum took a furtive look to see what else she might be up to, and was aghast to see her mouth agape coming down on him like a carp in the Kaplan's icebox. Her lips worked around the head and then slid over it and down as far as they could. She started in to work her own head up and down until a wonderful tension grew to the edge of a waiting explosion.

"It's — it's going to come out," he managed to blurt. But Lucille only turned an eye to him and, without stopping, seemed to nod that that would be okay.

Not a muscle twitched during her entire feeding. It left him so hard that it might have torn through a bedsheet halfway across the room, and spasm followed spasm. Her tongue worked inside like a shovel and didn't stop until it had cleared away the last drop. Then, when he relaxed, breathless and drained, she straightened up, her job done.

Vividly imagining how the warm and sticky formula must feel and taste in her mouth, Avrum felt himself suddenly overcome by a nauseous raking at the catch between his throat and his stomach. The chemical balance in his gut rapidly deteriorated and he struggled against its foul function. Just at that moment, Lucille tried twice to clear her throat, and Avrum could hear the thick, frothy gurgling of what his discharge had lodged there. His stomach heaved slightly and tightened. Then, with one long and loud rumbling effort, she again tried to clear her throat. And again, he heard the deep sound of the gurgling froth. Then, whatever had risen to her mouth she swallowed in a single hollow gulp. It was the hammer crashing down on the pin, and a calamity rocked the room.

A hot, sour, pulpy, semi-liquid mass jetted in a long stream from Avrum's stricken throat to splatter across Lucille's arm belly and thigh. Startled, she jumped from the bed and watched in disbelief as a good portion of the contents of his stomach dropped slowly down her legs. Before he finally made it to the sink, he had discharged another two streams of the same sour matter — once across the bedcover, the other on the floor when hurtling himself to the sink. Even here, however, his throat constricted repeatedly, and each time he would choke and gag miserably. His mouth reeked like a cesspool, and he could not recall ever having felt sicker in his life.

* * *

It was fifteen minutes short of two o'clock when Avrum stepped back into the factory. He might have been back at one or only a very few minutes past that, but he needed desperately to walk. It wasn't even a conscious decision. Before he realized where he had to be, he found himself on Bleury walking toward Pine Avenue. This put him almost a mile from the wretched room, but set him almost two miles distant from the factory. After a time, he waited for a streetcar and rode it to Laurier. He bought some lemon drops to clean his mouth of the persistent aftertaste, but he was bedeviled by the catching of his throat and the retching sensation that came over him every time his mind started in to replay any of the earlier scenes.

He imagined that if he would slip into the factory from around the lane at the back, his absence might pass unnoticed. But between Myer Goldenberg and Strulevitch that would do no more than delay the inevitable confrontations. At this moment, Avrum had neither the heart nor the mind, let alone the energy, for subterfuge; he went in through the front door.

"Look at this that just walked in. The Prince! Taking all the time in the world. Mind telling me where the dickens you were?

You broke a leg or something? There was a revolution somewhere? Tell me — you came to punch in or punch out? Are you coming or going?

Avrum understood that he would have to wait patiently until his boss could build up an appropriate storm. Until that rose and subsided, time would stand still.

"So where in heaven's name were you? This is the only time you could pick to stick a knife in my back? For a whole week it's quiet and everybody *shleps* like it's a graveyard, then out of the blue comes something urgent and I ask for a special effort — an effort for a customer who pays all our wages, if you want to know. So what do you do? It's like taking a gun and shooting me in the back. You want to sabotage the business? Tell me!"

"Myer, you're going just a little too far," said Florence. "And he doesn't look too well."

"Actually he looks like somebody pissed on him, eh?" said Strulevitch, who was bringing packed shipping boxes to the front door. He avoided looking in Avrum's direction.

"Maybe you'll shut your filthy mouth, Irving? In front of Florence? She has to hear this kind of talk?" Goldenberg was livid.

"It's alright, Myer," said Florence sweetly. "I wasn't born a lily of the valley, you know."

"So? You want to give him license to talk like a hooligan in front of you?"

"Sorry, Florence." Strulevitch dropped the boxes.

"So, where in God's name were you?" Goldenberg was back at Avrum. "First, you disappear half an hour early; then you forget to come back. I thought myself maybe you were sick, so I went up personally to see if you needed something, and what does Mrs. Kaplan tell me? That you were never up there in the first place! So where were you — you went out looking for another job?"

"No."

"You think for a minute there is someone else in the world who will give you a penny more than you are already getting? Forget it, mister!"

"I wasn't looking for another job."

"You're not satisfied — talk to *me* first. You think you'll find a better place than this? This isn't your home? Everything you invest here goes back to you ten times ten. If a dollar makes all that difference, you talk first to me about it."

"Myer, he just looks sick," said Florence, "I think he should go lie down."

"Anything else?" asked Myer, turning to his wife. "*You* have to stand over the boxes checking the orders? I have a million and one things to do, but if he's not here, the boxes will get tied themselves? So *I'm* tying the boxes. He's getting the wages, and *I'm* tying the boxes."

Strulevitch brought in another two boxes from the back and slapped the invoices down on the table. He chewed on his cigar, but said nothing. It was a silence that, for some reason, Goldenberg found unsettling. This wasn't Strulevitch's style. Did he know something that he was keeping to himself?

"Well," said Goldenberg finally, "go take a drink of water and get to those boxes. The CN man is going to be here in five minutes."

"Abie, maybe I'll give you some of Myer's Milk of Magnesia?" Florence walked up to Avrum and mothered him. "It'll do you good you know. If it was something that you ate, it will stop the food poison. I know what's good for you."

"I'll be all right, Florence."

"An aspirin maybe?"

"Give him a two-twenty-two," called Myer. "Give him a two-twenty-two and let him go." This was Goldenberg's great cure-all. It made little difference if one had a broken leg, a nose bleed, or lead poisoning — if it had to do with a violation of the body, this aspirin-cum-codeine was his universal remedy. One pill, however, was enough to give him heartburn for the better part of a day, but he invited the pain and insisted on suffering. With Myer, the more it hurt, the more he was sure it was helping him. As the pain mounted, he would cry out "Oy-oy, oy-oy, oy-oy," until, of course, it got so bad that Florence or Shirley would be rushed upstairs to prepare some boiled milk with honey.

“I’ll be all right,” insisted Avrum. “Don’t worry about me.”

When Avrum appeared, Strulevitch hissed through lips which hardly moved. “You look like somebody really pissed on you. And I really hope that that’s what she did. Eh?” Then he picked up a hanger and waved it under Avrum’s nose. “You got it coming, the way you so royally screwed me up today.”

“And what exactly did I do to you?”

“Nothing. Just that your *putz* got to your head. But what, for Chrissake, had to take so long? Y’had to go make it a double header? Eh? Myer was sitting on my head from twelve thirty, and nothing went right. Everything you hung up was in the wrong place, and instead of *you* looking for the numbers, I had to. Then he found mistakes in my addition, so I figure one o’clock, you’ll show up and take the pressure offa me. But one o’clock and you’re still with your nose up her ass. Anyways, was she any good?”

“I threw up.”

“You threw up?”

“I threw up.”

“You’re not queer, eh?” Strulevitch looked at him strangely.

“Queer?”

“Nah,” Strulevitch shook his head in disbelief. “I can’t believe it. Queer, maybe, but not that way, eh? Please God!”

(12)

Horse was back. Cy Green and a couple of the other regulars had boarded up the entire front the day after the fire. It was Cy who broke the news of the fire to Horse that afternoon at the Montreal General Hospital. Horse had had his operation, but the effects of the ether still lingered. Horse asked about Shorty, but there was nothing to tell except that Shorty made no appearance during or after the fire. Cy offered to send his younger brother over to see if the door could still be salvaged, and he would see about getting a new frame for the window himself.

Horse knew Cy's brother had been a carpenter at one time, but he was only a month out of the can. The man had gotten a local council in some Laurentian town to give him his first project as an independent contractor. They wanted a new reservoir. He gave them his hand on his heart along with the very lowest estimate. But cement wasn't wood; it turned out that his iron rod reinforcements were half the diameter the engineer's plans called for — and spaced two where four should have been. A couple of C-notes and a bottle of Seagram's got the engineer to suffer a spell of blindness until after the cement got poured. The iron mesh might still have held had he not tried the same trick with the cement. Instead of one part cement to three parts sand and gravel, he pushed it one to five, and when it dried, no one could really tell the difference. But then the reservoir had to be filled.

The head of the council was there, the treasurer, and the council's project manager. Some farmers showed up, and a table was prepared with salted tam-tams, herring, cream cheese, olives, cakes, and whiskey. There was a speech and the pump was started. Half the reservoir had been filled earlier to save time at the ceremony, but now when the water was only about a foot short of its intended level, the walls collapsed on two sides and flooded three properties. Some of the visitors were up to their knees in the rushing water and still couldn't grasp what had gone wrong.

The council demanded that its money be returned, though they knew even while they asked that they'd never see a penny of it again. Still, form had to be followed. Lawyers came in the wake of letters, inspectors followed the lawyers, and police followed the inspectors. Then the whole abortive enterprise was recounted before a judge, who, unfortunately for Cy's brother, happened to be a Jew. A French judge might have called for a stiff fine, a financial settlement, and a suspended sentence. The Jewish judge, however, was unsettled by his chair and was determined with a vengeance that no one should doubt his impartiality. Over a crippling fine, he slapped on two years in jail. And he did it with such enthusiasm and conviction that

Cy's brother considered himself fortunate that the law books didn't let the guy hang him.

"How's he managing these days?" asked Horse.

"Trying to pick up the pieces, if you know what I mean."

"I can imagine."

"He'll give you a good price. I mean, I'll see to this."

"Oh, I'm not worried. OK, have him take a look. Just tell him to keep it clean and cheap — no cream."

"You're all right, Horse. I'll get Silver to fix the glass so that by the time you're out of here, you'll be ready to open for business."

"You're a pal, Cy. I think this time I'm going to see that Shorty gets himself removed once and for all."

"He's not showing."

"Nah — he's probably up in Syracuse. Every time he blows something, he shacks up at his aunt's there for a week. He always crawls back, but this time I'm gonna break his gonads."

"He's got it coming big, but he's just a dumb punk, demented with certificates — what'll it give you?"

"Mark my words. Everything this costs me I'll get back from him with interest. It won't come in a day, but it'll come."

"Maybe . . . say — about your new cash register. You'll need a new one. If you want a good deal I got just the thing."

* * *

Thursday came at last. Avrum felt that he had lived through years that had passed faster than the last few days. It took every last ounce of restraint to keep from jumping up to Kapitolnik's on Monday, Tuesday, or Wednesday. But now it was Thursday, and Kapitolnik was surely at the top of the stairs waiting for him. The question was, with what? Was Hershel any closer? How much of what this strange man would promise could he believe?

As intensely as Avrum questioned his own mind and good sense about how far to let Kapitolnik's hocus-pocus take him, the exercise was futile. The moment the door opened, he found himself the prisoner of every gesture and work Kapitolnik delivered. The first of these exploded in his face.

"Both of you — you and your brother together — have been caught up in a bond of blood and have risen from a sea of blood. Both of you are the pearls through which has been threaded a most mysterious fate . . . a fate somehow in the weave of an ancient prophecy. You see? Nothing of this escapes me. And more than this — I can tell you that the bond, long strained, has never been severed, but waits for the spilling of yet more blood. I'm sorry, but yes — more blood. Only I can promise you this, that before it loses its heat, before this blood cakes and goes the way of dust, the thread will have swung the pearls together, and this shall be the hour of your reunion."

"Is he still alive?"

"You're not listening."

"So whose blood, Mr. Kapitolnik? Do you know this, too?"

"Whose blood? Whose blood? Whose blood if not your blood! But I don't see you dying yet, so don't stop me now with your foolish questions. Your brother Hershel is a philosopher, a thinker, a searcher — but mostly a worrier. Oh yes, a great worrier! His nerves are in trouble. A terrible, terrible restlessness is what I see. It is a restlessness that is carrying him many distances. It is also a search for you — unless maybe there is another brother somewhere. But his mind is shaking."

"There is no other brother. Where is he now?"

"Right now he is everywhere. In his body, he could even be here, or around here. The bird chose the north wall. Also, if you noticed, it chose the *ZEREI AKHIM* scriptures, which foretell the reunion of brothers. And it is definite that the reunion will be here and nowhere else. This is a one hundred percent guarantee."

"But when? How do I find him? He won't look for me; he thinks I'm dead."

"He thinks you're dead, you say? Well . . . maybe, but it doesn't matter. The prophecy is still vivid and alive, Avrum. I don't see this every day. It comes from the very tongue of *DEVORA*. And the spirits of *BARAK* and *MIKHEIMUS* have been invested unto you. You are invincible."

"Mr. Kapitolnik . . . I will find him, you say?"

"No. It is for him to find you. But I can speed the coming of that day for you fivefold."

"Why can't I find him?"

"For the same reason that you can't fit the Cassiopeia over the Big Dipper — the patterns are fixed."

"Mrs. Kaplan said that you can change patterns."

"Never patterns like these."

"But when the day comes — you said it will be my death?"

"I said only that blood will spill. Did I say how much? Did you hear the word 'death' come from my lips? No!"

"Well, how can you speed up the coming of that day?"

Kapitolnik was focusing on something deep within himself. He nodded in silence and then looked squarely into Avrum's eyes.

"There are ways," he said softly. "You have another dollar?"

* * *

It was the day before Passover. The house had been thoroughly scoured, the hometz *removed to the shed except for a last dish or two, and in the large basin outside, some of the pots and pans were about done with their week's soaking.*

Avrum watched his mother chase down Heftzibah, their brown chicken, and then go after Zilche, its sister. As she tied their legs together, she spoke to them through their frightened cackling, and when she pressed them into her basket, they were quite pacified. Strange. If it was him in there, he thought, he'd be screaming to the heavens.

"Where are you taking them, Mama?"

"To the rabbi. And it's late — they still have to be koshered."

"Why the rabbi?"

"Dear child — he's also the shochet. *I'm not allowed to do it myself."*

Avrum sensed something distinctly unpleasant and darkly dramatic about her intentions. At five years of age, it was sill a mystery to him how the slips of soft meat which his mother would deliver from the stove could go by the same name as the fowls in the yard.

"I want to go with you, Mama. I want to see what he does."

"Well, we can't leave Hersheleh on his own. Fetch him and we'll be off. Maybe it's a good hour to have the rabbi give you both his blessing."

Heftzibah was plucked first from the basket. The old rabbi, under a black cylinder skullcap and in a stained apron over his vest and trousers, turned the bird over and secured it between his waist and forearm. The same hand gripped the head and bent it backwards, presenting its neck to the terrible instrument he wielded in his other hand. Then the rabbi half closed his eyes, and through his beard, delivered a rush of mumbled words. He'd hardly done with them when the knife moved sharply where it had rested. A tongue of blood whipped instantly into the air. The bird squawked and the rabbi threw it across the yard. There was a short flurry of wings and a weak, dizzy charge, and Heftzibah collapsed on her side, her head at a terribly unnatural angle.

Zilche was already secure in the rabbi's grip when Avrum lunged at the man and snaked his arm around the bird.

"Not Zilche!" he cried angrily. "Let her go!"

Doubtful if with amusement, doubtful if with annoyance, the rabbi looked down at him and squinted. "Away with you, boy," he said. "I'm not playing."

But Avrum struggled for the bird.

"She's not yours. Give her to me."

His mother, flustered and blushing, stepped up to them and pressed her fingers gently on Avrum's cheek. "Avremeleh, move away. It has to be."

"No! One is enough." Tears began streaming from his eyes.

"Zilche has been waiting a long time for this moment, and now she's quiet in her heart. Come — let me explain something to you."

"No!"

But the rabbi yanked Avrum's arm away without ceremony and lifted the bird beyond his reach. The blessing was jumbled and muted, but Avrum, with sinking heart, knew the instant he saw the man's lips in motion that Zilche was lost. Meanwhile, Hershel, unable to wrest his hand from his mother's grip so that he might attack the fringed garment that hung loosely at the rabbi's waist, also wailed loudly. But when Zilche began her terrible dance, his tongue froze and he tried desperately to understand.

Later, when Avrum spurned the rabbi's blessing, Hershel would have none of it, either. Avrum flatly rejected his mother's first attempts at explaining the ritual slaughter. Hadn't he seen with his own eyes that the blessing didn't check the spurting of blood?

"And I saw how it hurt them. It hurt them a lot."

"The blessing is one thing, the pain is another," his mother said evenly. "The blood that leaves the bird's neck is difficult to watch, but it's a sign that God has blessed us. If the blood was not there, we would not be here. This is the way of the world."

If Avrum allowed himself to be reassured, it was less by her words than by her oddly aloof amusement. She was so utterly certain of the truth of her words. Then she went on:

"Still, even a chicken's blood is significant, and must not be spilled recklessly. Blood is God's own making. He uses it to chain all life together, and the blessing, my dear children, is to make certain that when the blood goes into the creation of another living thing, it will not have been defiled. For this is how evil gets into the world. Do you think you can understand?"

Avrum tried to sort out all the questions in his mind. "What happens, Mama, when I bleed? Like yesterday, when I cut my foot on the fence, or when Saltche scratched my arm — what did God do with the blood?"

"Well, first He patched you up, didn't He? And . . . oh, Avremeleh, I can't have all the answers. But remember this, if nothing else: when blood spills, God is at work. Yes. The

reason may be clear or not clear, but God is definitely at work."

One question still waited to be asked.

"Why Zilche, too? Couldn't Heftzibah have been enough?"

His mother gave long thought before she answered. "Yes, she could have been. But they were sisters, no? God couldn't have the blood of Zilche in one world and leave Heftzibah's in another. There would be a great restlessness in the heavens until their blood again came together. It is always that way."

* * *

There were flowers, chocolates, and whiskey when Horse opened his doors again, and the atmosphere was as charged with revivalist fervor as might rival a baptism at the local fundamentalist church.

Cy's brother never did a finer piece of carpentry in his life. When Horse saw how he was putting together the storefront, he gave him the whole counter to repair and extend, and had him reinforce the back wall. The man had worked like a relentless machine from six in the morning straight to ten in the evening for over a week and a half, and when Horse asked for the bill, he gave him a price that barely covered the cost of the materials. Horse had added an extra fifty, but it was handed back. "The job itself is all the profit I need now." It was a well-calculated gesture; Horse's patronage was worth the investment, and now Horse kept asking everybody if his eatery wasn't in a class with the best.

An attraction in itself was the new wallpaper — a garish red-and-gold pattern that might have been inspired by the interior of a Neapolitan bordello. Cy's brother wouldn't hear of anyone putting it up but himself, and Horse defied anyone to find the seams.

When the store couldn't hold any more people, the crowd spread to the sidewalk and a couple Johnny Walkers were sent out there. Avrum was standing outside with Strulevitch and the bottle was passed to them. Strulevitch took two hard swallows.

Avrum let the spirit catch him and forced one great mouthful past his throat. He gagged, but recovered quickly, and in good cheer, handed the bottle to someone else. Strulevitch began to try to squeeze his way in and Avrum was pressing behind him. He saw Willy Button, the midget bookie, dancing on a table. He was snapping his fingers and banging his heels rapid-fire in what was supposed to come across as something Spanish. Everyone around him was clapping in unison. Then Martha, one of Goldenberg's pressers, was hoisted onto another table, and with two ashtrays for castanets, she took the female lead opposite Willy. People began to throw pennies at them, and she swiped the air reaching for them. Those she caught, she dropped into her brassiere. Soon pennies rained from everywhere. Those that had fallen to the floor were picked up and thrown again.

Horse had a bottle handed up to Willy, who took a swig and passed it to Martha, shouting that she was a darling and that he loved her. She also took a swig, and then another. The clapping didn't let up, and her feet didn't stop pounding and turning. Then Willy tried to recapture some attention by driving the mouth of the bottle halfway down his throat and swallowing so that everyone could see the bubbles of air coming into the bottle. That lasted the shortest second; then he let some whisky spill over his shirt when he handed the bottle down. With his hands free and trying to keep to the rhythm of the clapping, he tried a handstand. Loose change spilled from his pockets and the table tipped, sending him crashing to the floor. Hands hauled him to his feet and he said he thought he was going to vomit. That got him pushed to the toilet in the back. Meanwhile, Martha had opened a button on her blouse and pulled the cups of her bra out a bit to catch the pennies directly. Soon, nickels and even odd dimes were in the air.

Strulevitch and Avrum were through the door when Martha suddenly stopped her dancing and opened her arms as if to embrace everyone there. The applause and the kisses made her smile stretch another inch toward her ears. Then, in a final, ultimate gesture of camaraderie, she removed her false teeth and pretended to throw them to the crowd. Her mouth seemed to have suddenly caved in, and someone called out that it looked like Benny's ass. Benny was suspected of being something of a *feigeleh* to the boys, and the place rocked with laughter. Benny who was in the crowd, somehow found it in himself to laugh as well.

Horse then noticed Avrum with Strulevitch. Stretching his arms, he called them over. Strulevitch clasped his hands together over his head, did something of a pirouette, and shook them like a winning fighter. Horse called out for quiet. He said he had an announcement that was going to be for the sports pages — something they would always remember, which was said here first today.

"Y'all see that man mountain there?" He pointed at Avrum. "That's the big 'A' — y'all know Abie, Abie Vishinsky — and us in this camp here are gonna build him up to be one of the class wrestlers of all time. I want all of you to let him know we're with him, and that we'll make a lot of noise for him. So let's hear it for Abie!"

There was a burst of applause and shouts of approval. Avrum, waving them down, tried to react as though nothing of this was to be taken seriously. But his shoulders and back were slapped, and people shook his hand and said that they were a hundred percent sure that he'd be the champion soon. Behind Avrum, Strulevitch was pulling everyone he could get a hand on to go up to Avrum and congratulate him.

"You'll all remember this day, and you'll all remember who told you," continued Horse, "and if I see any one of you buggers don't show up to root when he's on the card — you're sure as hell finished with me and this joint. So — where in sweet fuck's name are the bottles? Let's drink to Abie here, and tell him we're all his boys. Let 'im know he's already got a crowd with his name on it. Whadday'all say?" Again, applause and cheers and pushing and backslapping.

Avrum felt his embarrassment vanish. A feeling of rich, unmitigated pleasure came over him now. He loved these people. In a way, he felt they were all one family there, bonded in a moment that would last forever, and he thought that if he really would become a wrestler, it might somehow keep them all together, and keep them feeling good about everything. Yet he reminded himself that he had never even once seen a professional wrestling match, and that his future in the sport was entirely the invention of people who, despite all the noises they were making, were still strangers to him.

(13)

The telephone shook the house when it rang. Avrum looked at his watch in the gray light that the street lamp managed to force through the slanted shutters. It was nearing eleven, and in the quiet of the hour, every ring sounded rude and threatening. Mrs. Kaplan had the earpiece off the hook after the second ring, but she was so terrified that it took an effort for her to manage an audible voice. Then Avrum heard her footsteps approaching him, and she knocked at his door.

"Abie? Are you up? It's the telephone for you."

"For me? Who could be calling me?" But he was already in his bathrobe and at the door.

"I don't know, but it's a girl — a girl for you. She said she's sorry it's so late, but it's an emergency."

"My God — I'm sorry it had to wake you up." He rushed to the phone, and Mrs. Kaplan was right behind him.

"Hello?"

"Abie? Abie, is that you?"

"Who is this? Bella?"

"It's Fanny. If I sound like Bella, then you're still sleeping. Abie — I know it's the middle of the night, but you were the only one I could call. Abie, I have to leave the house right now, and I have nowhere to go." She spoke in a rushing whisper, which seemed to be tempered less by despair or desperation than by a presumptuous confidence — and even anger.

"Nowhere to go? What happened?"

"It's a long story, but it's not a story for this minute or for the telephone. I'll tell you when I'll see you. But I'm going tomorrow to New York, and I have to leave the house right now

— this very minute — and if you can't help me, I'll sleep in the street."

"You can't sleep in the street."

"I'll have to."

"I would bring you here, but I just have a rented room."

"Oh, Abie . . ." Her disappointment was heavy and urgent. "Do you suppose if you asked? Just for this one night?"

Avrum put his hand across the mouthpiece and turned to Mrs. Kaplan. He seemed helpless, staring blankly at her and saying nothing.

"Who is she?" asked Mrs. Kaplan, frowning angrily.

"A Jewish girl who was on the boat with me. She hasn't got a place to sleep, and she has to take the train to New York tomorrow morning. Could you let her sleep in the parlor?"

"What's a Jewish girl doing without a house in the middle of the night? An hour before she couldn't call? What's wrong with a hotel?"

Avrum waited.

"Abie — maybe you shouldn't get mixed up—"

"I know her . . . she's alright. Something just happened, and she can't tell me on the telephone."

"Nu—" Mrs. Kaplan grimaced. "There's a choice?"

Avrum turned to the phone again. "It's OK Can you get here? Mrs. Kaplan says you can have the parlor."

"Just for tonight," prompted Mrs. Kaplan. "Tell her."

But Avrum was listening to Fanny. "Thanks, Abie, really, thanks . . . I just have a small valise and I can walk. Give me the address."

"You can't be on the street by yourself at this hour. Especially not with a valise. Where are you calling from?"

"My house — actually, from the pay phone next to the soda shop near my house."

"You know what — wait near the door. I'll walk over and bring you. It's only about ten minutes from here."

"Abie, you're saving my life. Tell your landlady that I won't be trouble. It's just for a few hours and I don't need blankets."

"It's OK I'm leaving in two minutes. Goodbye."

"Thanks a lot, Abie. I'm waiting."

He was about half a block from her house when he saw her running toward him.

"Thanks, Abie. I knew you were the only one I could trust, even if we are not special friends." She intoned the *not special* as if to underline it. He took the valise from her.

"What happened in your house that you had to leave in such a rush?"

"It's a long, stupid story."

"Because of New York?"

"New York is partly because of the story. Tell me . . . are you sure Mrs. . . . whatever her name is — your landlady — won't mind?" They were walking quickly and Fanny seemed to be out of breath.

"She said it's OK for tonight. But say, what happened?"

"It's something with some stupid police. Two of them came to the house, and in front of everybody, they said they have questions to ask me."

"Police?"

"Can you imagine? Making me like some criminal?"

"What did you do?"

"Did I have to do anything? But listen to this — you won't believe it. They said there were complaints by some parents that I — I tried to do some sick things to their children. They came with these crazy idiot stories, and they told them in front of Bella and my mother and father. So, you know, I just laughed at these stupid things, but Bella looked at me — my mother began to cry, and my father slapped me. Right there in front of those two *goyim*, he stands up and gives me a slap in the face. I still feel it. But he'll never see me again. I'll never forgive any of them for believing those stories — even for a second."

"But they didn't come to arrest you." It was a statement and a question at once.

"Of course not! Then can only arrest you if there is something to arrest you for. Go explain why anyone should make up a story that isn't from this world and stick my name on it. And these police knew that it had to be a whole fake thing. Only they didn't have the brains to tell the people who brought these stories to them that they belonged in the crazy house. So I said if they think that I could do such things, they should take me to jail. If I were guilty, I'd have to go to jail, right? But they said no, no, just that because a complaint was signed — *signed*, can you *imagine* — they had to ask their ridiculous questions. It could have all passed you know, except that my own family believed *them*. My father will never see me to put a hand on me again."

"It's just a mistake, you know. They'll forget it."

"Maybe they will, but I won't. I hate them — despise them."

"Where will you go in New York?"

"I have a friend there — a man." Fanny looked at Avrum as if daring him to think a critical thought. "I don't care what anybody will say or think. I'm going to go and stay with him…maybe even *live* with him."

Avrum was speechless. Her blatant, vulgar boldness fed on a vengeful and spiteful rebelliousness that would be deaf to mediation.

"He isn't your regular man-in-the-street. You can take my word for it. If I had more nerve then when I met him the first time, instead of worrying about being a good Jewish girl, if you know what I mean, I would have gone with him straight away. Instead, I said no. Also, he's not Jewish, and I don't care."

"Maybe it's still not such a good idea."

"I'm going to live my life the way I want to — not the way anybody else says I should. The fact that I'm a girl only makes the whole thing less fair to me, but I'm going to die anyways, and I'm not going to miss anything because of other people's stupid ideas."

"What about getting married and children?"

"OK, what about getting married and children? What's the big thing here? Believe me, they're just strings that guarantee we should live our lives like puppets."

"Still . . ."

"Still, what? Let me tell you something, Abie. They teach you in school that man ate from the tree of knowledge — you remember, the story about the apple — well, that's the biggest lie ever in the whole world. It's a lie, made up to make people think that they know everything there is to know. But if they really did have knowledge, real knowledge, it would be the end of the world, because everybody would have committed suicide a long time ago. Like, explain to me what my mother and father had to be born for. He gets up at six every morning, goes to the store, comes back at seven, sometimes eight in the evening aggravated and angry, and goes to sleep to wake up to do it all over again. Who will remember that he was ever alive a minute after he dies? With my mother, it's even worse. All God gave her were two holes, you'll excuse me please, and a talent to make trouble with both of them. Like all of us, she's just a space with something empty filling it — only with her, it's more obvious. All the rest of us think we are something more special."

Avrum felt like a copper penny set on the railway tracks, with the train charging over it and the wheels pounding it flatter and flatter.

"There are good things, too."

"So fool yourself if you want to." There was a numbing finality to her words.

They walked in silence until they reached the house. Avrum wished that he hadn't alienated himself from her, but suspected strongly that unwittingly he already had. She wasn't beautiful, but she was alert and alive. Her long, unkempt steel-wool hair seemed electrically charged, but, very unlike Bella, her frame was sharp and angular. Her thin lips were aptly fitted to the hard biting remarks that came easily to her, and her chin jutted determinedly downward and to a point. It was her forehead, though, that dominated her face and seemed to stretch for half its length. For Avrum that reasonably well accounted for all the restless, unrelenting, and pressured activity that went on behind her eyes.

Mrs. Kaplan inspected her at the door. "I don't want to stick my nose into anybody's personal business you know. What you do is not *my* business." Stubby and graceless in her flowing nightgown under her husband's heavy jacket, which had at least a dozen pencils sticking out from the vest pocket, she looked like some impossible, androgynous curiosity. "But I see right away, miss, that you're making a bad mistake. Don't think I say this because I don't want you here — see inside, I have the chesterfield already made into a bed for you — but a Jewish girl doesn't solve her problems by going out in the middle of the night and sleeping in a strange house."

Avrum stood there embarrassed for both women.

"You're one hundred percent right," said Fanny with disarming softness and humility. "And it's only a family tragedy that makes me have to go to the States. A tragedy doesn't know what time to come. It could have come at two in the morning, too — like it could have come at two in the afternoon."

Freidle Kaplan nodded in sympathetic agreement. A sigh escaped her. Tragedies, at least, she could understand. Just being alive was itself the stuff of tragedies. For her, it's what gave life meaning.

"I know Abie from the ship — we came here together, we began together — and I need to talk to him a little before I leave."

"What about a mother and a father?"

Fanny stood there looking at the woman. Her lips trembled and a tear moved down her cheek, but she said nothing.

"Okay, okay, never mind," said Freidle Kaplan. "Like I said, I don't want to stick my nose in anybody's private business. You two have to finish talking — so finish." She pointed to the kitchen. "Then, Abie, you go back to your room."

"We're almost finished talking," said Fanny quickly. "And thank you.

"What I didn't tell you, Abie," she said a moment later, "to show you how crazy everything is, is that my friend in New York is a monk — a painter and a monk. He lives in a monastery."

In the morning, Fanny was perfunctorily polite and awkwardly distant. She agreed to have some orange juice, but refused anything else. By forcing her mood, she seemed to be trying to graft the truth of the night before onto the innocent new day. Finally, she said that she had to rush if she hoped to make the train, and she turned down Avrum's offer to accompany her to the station.

When Shirley called Avrum to the telephone at noon and whispered to him that there was a girl at the other end of the line, his face registered almost as much annoyance as surprise. But this changed abruptly when he identified the caller. It wasn't Fanny, stranded at the station or having a change of heart and wanting another night on the chesterfield; it was Bella.

"I saw you meet Fanny last night — near the corner," she said. "It was you, wasn't it?"

"She called me, so I came. It's nothing secret."

"Where did you take her?"

"Take her? Who took her? She said she had nowhere to sleep last night — that she was going to sleep on the street . . ." Avrum noticed that Shirley was sinking into a glazed trance, filling like a sponge on his words. "But listen — listen. We don't have to talk about this on the telephone. There are a hundred people around me. Do you want to meet where we did last time?" Shirley blushed and plunged back into her work.

"Alright — at Park and Mount Royal. Five o'clock?"

"Yeah," said Avrum. "That's a lot better for me, too."

"Be there."

"Me? Sure, I'll be there. What do you think?"

Bella clucked her tongue. "Goodbye."

"Goodbye," he answered, but the line was already dead.

* * *

Fanny lent her body to the lurching and rolling of the train while her mind darted between two severed worlds. On her lap was a yellowed, weathered book that she had rescued from Falik's diminishing collection, and just having it there and being able to feel it was a comfort to her. It was a copy of Pascal's *Pensées*, and she had originally found it wedged between some impossible texts on mathematics and hydraulics written apparently by the very same author. Only what had caught her eye at the time was that her father had preserved the book in a thin leather sleeve, and had taken to underlining great lengths of passages beginning from the very first page.

She remembered letting the pages slip evenly from her fingers — French was still strange to her — when it stopped where he had inserted a small drawing of a girl's face. It was of a young girl with beautiful eyes, long, fair hair and a high forehead. Angled across the bottom of it and written with fine, rich hand were the words: "*Le Cœur a ses raisons que la raison ne connait point.*" And there, underlined in the text at the bottom of the page, were the very same words. The strangest exhilaration had come over her, and a dictionary quickly explained what she had already guessed. And if the distances separating her from her uncle and this girl were more ethereal than physical, what did it matter? These were dimensions in the mind alone, and she knew that there was a very real and solid bridge between her and them.

Then, in her mind, she replayed the morning when Harry first came into the store. He seemed a customer like every other, but what had caught her eye was the odd, almost unnatural way he'd move his head and neck ahead before the rest of his body followed underneath. She thought with some amusement that it resembled nothing so much as the walk of a chicken or duck. Then he had surprised her by asking directly if she happened to be Fanny Finegold, and it struck her instantly who he had to be. It wasn't at all what she had expected. At most, she thought she would be getting a letter — certainly not the man's actual physical presence.

A woman had been to the store many days before with a picture to be framed. It was a daring and strange piece of work. The lines were as bold as the colors were dramatic, and though she had never seen the likes of this style before, something about it teased her with a distant familiarity. "It's a lovely bird. Sad, though, isn't it…that its wing should be broken?" she had said.

"Yes," replied the woman, "you wonder what the artist was trying to say. And it's not even a wing. Where it's broken are trees in flames and broken eggs."

"And next to it — or behind it?"

"Well, it's a boy, obviously," she had said. "And doesn't he look as sad as the bird! Also, you can see that the way he painted the eye of the bird is exactly the way he painted the eye of the boy. This couldn't be by accident, and I don't think it's my imagination."

Fanny agreed with her. She had tried to make out the artists name, but it was just a swish of lines. The image of Viktor, the sympathetic creature who had hung in Manya's shadow, sprung to her mind, and she had asked the woman if she knew who the artist was. The woman had studied the signature and said that she couldn't be sure of the name. It was a wild scrawl and might have been "Weitz" or "Zeitz." She did recall, however, that he was a very intense young man, balding a little too early for his age. He was with a dozen other painters at an exhibition of works of immigrant artists at some Jewish center in Newark, New Jersey. She had bought the painting almost out of charity.

"I thought his paintings might mean something fifty years from now, but . . . that he'd be needing something to eat until then."

The names had meant nothing to Fanny, but the description had closed in on the dim figure in her memory. She remembered what his strange patron Manya had had to say about him — and herself: That she had taken it as her role in life to protect "the purity of his genius and the distilled clarity of his soul." These had been her exact words . . . and that if left exposed to all the vile pollutants in life, her "Virgin Flower," as she called him, would "swell with rot and cake with mold between one sunset and the next."

By that evening, Fanny had a letter posted to the same Jewish center asking about an artist by the name of Weitz, or Zeitz, who had sold a painting to a woman from Montreal. She wished to know if the artist had ever had a patron by the name of Manya, and whether they weren't both originally from St. Petersburg. She closed with her very complimentary opinion about his talent as an artist.

The man who had walked into the store that afternoon was Harry Weiss. He had known very well, he told her, that he wasn't the man she had hoped to find, but after reading such rare words as she had chosen to describe his artistic talent in general, and this painting in particular, he felt powerfully moved to frame this woman, living and breathing, in his own eyes. It was worth the expense of the trip, he said.

She had brought him home, but the encounter with her parents and Bella was a horrendous experience, and exposed deep rifts in the family matrix. They were set on edge the instant she mentioned who and what the painting of the bird and the boy had her recall, and right under their noses, her guest had put away half a bottle of shnapps. They had set up a couch for him in the kitchen only to hear a howl and a clatter in the middle of the night when he rolled off it. Instinctively, he had reached out for something to break his fall, only to grab the cutlery drawer in the table, pulling the table and all the contents of the drawer down on top of him.

The next day he offered the Finegolds a small painting of his, but Bella took one look at it and, grabbing her neck and sticking out her tongue, made as if she was choking; the sounds which accompanied her actions left little doubt as to her sentiments. "Dada Art?" she asked. "What's Dada Art? Maybe you meant Kaka Art."

Bluma had said that if, instead, he could sell it, he would at least see some money. Max added that he thought that a frame for it would be more than they could presently afford. With hurt, anger, and considerable embarrassment overtaking her,

Fanny had felt Harry take an uncertain grip on her wrist and say for all of them to hear, "You have my address." Later, he seemed to advance on her and retreat at once. "Would you — I mean, you wouldn't come back with me now, could you? Maybe? No, that's impossible. Even crazy."

But Fanny could only shake her head. Not that the invitation hadn't teased her, and not that she wasn't curious about him, but his nose was still red from the alcohol, and somehow, at that moment, she didn't expect she could ever get to think of him as *her* Virgin Flower.

Only now, she wanted to think that she could inspire him to greatness.

* * *

"You didn't have to make a *kourveh* out of her, y'know. Even if she made it easy for you." Bella started right in with hard and bitter accusations. "Even if she says she wants to meet you, but you see it's after eleven, ELEVEN! So you tell her you'll talk to her in the morning. Now there is a stain on her and on us for the rest of our lives."

"If you were in my place and she tells you that she's going to sleep on the street, you wouldn't say OK? Mrs. Kaplan gave her the chesterfield, and nobody touched her. We didn't even shake hands."

"You don't understand a thing. It's not important what you know you did or didn't do. It's enough people know that she spent the night in the same house with you."

"Only Mr. and Mrs. Kaplan know that — and now you, but they also know that we were in different rooms. Really, Bella, you're making a big thing out of nothing. Why did you let her go? You knew she had this artist friend in New York."

Bella froze. "What artist friend in New York? She went to New York — to that dumb, stupid clown Harry?"

"I think that's what she said. She didn't tell me everything."

"The only one she knows in New York is Harry Weiss, who thinks in his dreams that he's an artist. Did she say Harry Weiss?"

"She mentioned no names. Just New York."

"HARRY WEISS!" Bella struggled with this possibility, which seemed incredulous to her. "An artist? He couldn't even paint a wall."

Avrum remained silent.

Bella couldn't contain her confusion and panic. "Oh my God! OH MY GOD! You mean to tell me she took the train herself to New York? I'm going to die."

"She ca—"

"YOU! You couldn't stop her? A Jewish girl and you couldn't stop her? Better to call the police to put her in jail than to let her go herself to New York. Now she's finished, finished, finished, FINISHED!"

"I spoke to her . . . Mrs. Kaplan spoke to her . . ."

Bella wasn't listening. "Oh my God . . . Oh, Mama! I'm going to faint. What am I going to say to Mama and Papa?"

"Why didn't you stop her when she was still in the house? She said there were police and that your father slapped her, so it wasn't a surprise that she walked out."

"Why? I'll tell you why. Do you know what she did?" Bella was blinding herself with her rage. "She let these little boys from the public school near her art store come and touch her all over. Yes! Just imagine! Their parents had to go complain to the police because she kept buying them presents, and when their parents found out what they were doing at the back of the store, they were sure she was some kind of sex maniac and would hurt the kids or kidnap them or something. Yes, that's what she did, and that's why Papa had to slap her. Imagine — can you imagine *goyim* police in our home?"

"I didn't know — Jesus!"

"How could you know such a thing? But you should have used your brains and talked to her."

"Nothing would have stopped her."

"And of all people, why Harry Weiss? He's an idiot drunk — a real, original Jewish drunk — probably the one and only Jewish drunk in the whole world. He says he's an artist, but he never has a cent on him. And once I saw his painting. A painting? *Smish, smash, smotch* . . . a whole *plotchkeh*. He calls it a painting and expects someone will come and put it on a wall."

Avrum could add nothing. Bella was in terrible distress.

"It finishes her reputation," she said in a low voice — almost to herself. "And because she's my sister, it finishes my own reputation. Think about it."

Avrum tried thinking about it but got nowhere.

(14)

"I'd like a little quiet word with you, Mr. A.," called Horse from the sink when Avrum stepped in for a coffee. The clipped manner of his speech seemed more accented now. The tone was curt but Avrum didn't miss the wink that accompanied his words. Then the telephone began to ring, and Cy Green rose from one of the back tables and said that he'd get it. As he passed behind Avrum, he patted him on the shoulder and muttered under his breath that Horse was worth a listen. Avrum reacted with a smile and shrug of resignation.

"Horse," called Cy a moment later. "It's Litwak for you."

"Christ! Something screwed? Ask him what's the gas. Never mind. It'll take him half an hour to get it out." He dried his hands and went to the phone. "Chrissake, Litwak! I got a sink full of dishes and a big man here waiting for his filly minion. What's up? . . . Slowly . . . take your time . . . slowly — slo-o-o-o-wly, Litwak. Listen, Doc, by the time you'll get it all out, I'll have to shave again. Yeah . . . uh-huh, uh-huh." Horse turned around and showed everyone the receiver, his jaw working silently up and down like a puppet. He listened for a long while before managing to get in a word of his own. "Yeah, what? We'll keep it for nine at the same place." He lowered his voice. "I'll come up with someone."

Horse dropped the receiver on the hook and tried to work something out in his mind. He stepped up to Avrum, but still waited to arrange his thoughts before saying anything. In a whisper, he asked if Strulevitch was still in the factory, and

Avrum told him that he'd be there until six because they were putting in an hour of overtime that day.

"Well, look . . . I really wanted to talk to you — how much time you got now?"

"It's three . . . 'til three-fifteen, three-twenty. What can't wait?"

"Whaddayasay, kid, we find a table in the back? I'll bring you a coffee there."

"Sure."

They went over to Cy's table. He had it covered with cards, having just set them up for a game of solitaire. Horse scrambled them, and when Cy made a face, Horse said that he wanted to talk undisturbed to Abie, and asked if Cy would take the counter for ten minutes. His answer was taken for granted.

"This is a talk we had to have a long time ago," began Horse, "but like you know, I had to go donate my appendix to medical science, and I got the feeling that they cut me up with an old used razor. Or that or they took out my appendix and gave me back someone else's, 'cause shit, I can still feel it."

"Y' don't look to me like you're suffering."

Horse brought his chair closer to the table. "Like you seen yourself, we all kind of got something going here. You saw the crowd we had a few days ago — and we're all kind of one family."

"And I kind of know what you want to say."

"Don't be so sure, and don't be too brilliant with me. The thing is that when a guy is altogether on his own, he drowns, sooner or later. Because if he ever needs anything, nobody got any good reason to be there for him. And sometimes there are things that are important to have, but that you can't buy with money. Y'follow me?"

"A piece here. A piece there."

"Like right now . . . just 'cause I happen to know you and you're alright with the guys — and with me — I'm going to throw you thirty-five greens for nothing more than a half-hour appearance somewhere tonight."

"For doing what?"

"What's it matter? Figure how much you make a week against thirty-five smash for a half hour of doing nothing but being somewhere."

"It sounds too easy for my mind."

"Yeah, well, that's what I wanted to hear. Because Abie — Mr. A. — from this minute, you're on your way to making your own fortune with all of us behind you. And when I say all of us, it includes guys up to the mayor. Anything needs pulling — we got the guys who pull the strings."

Avrum seemed unconvinced. He rolled his eyes skyward. "And when am I supposed to wake up?"

"It's time, Abie, that you stopped being green. The way these things work, while you stash a bundle, some of us make something from you on the side — fair's fair — but nothing comes from your own pocket, only from overall profits. Look, I'm getting ahead of myself, but the idea is this — try to see why Canada is so great. Canada gives you a chance. You came here in the first place for the chance to do something with your life that was impossible in Minsk, Shminsk, or Pinsk. Am I right or wrong? So you're a dumb *shmuck* if you let it pass when the chance comes up to you on a silver platter."

"Even in Canada, you don't get something for nothing."

"Go now!" said Horse in mock exasperation. "I'm beginning to think maybe your body is a ton of muscle, but it got a brain that weighs maybe half an ounce. Now, just shut up and listen to me. No one says you do nothing. But there is easy money — brain money — there is also sweat money. For every buck you make the second way, you can make a hundred and even a thousand times more the first way. Like tonight. There is this contract. I need you to show up at an address on Fairmount Street. Litwak is going to be stuffed up to his elbows in some teenage kid — actually, he's going to be saving a girl from killing herself. She got pregnant and no hospital or regular doctor will give her an abortion. Litwak's gonna do it, and for that, he will go to heaven one day.

"But he called up just now — that was him I was talking to on the phone — and he tells me that there's a chance the girl will know Strulevitch, and he doesn't want him to show. He wants someone else in his place. Now, he just wants an honest guy with him in case something goes wrong — like someone to help her home. Otherwise, there is absolutely nothing to do. Nothing. Once there, you get fifty greens. My cut from that is fifteen *smootch*, which leaves you with a fat thirty-five in your pocket. So, you see, I get money and I'm happy. You get a bundle for a breeze, and you're happy. Litwak puts away a full fifty, and it's coming to him. But the happiest of all is the girl who doesn't have to throw herself under a truck. And y'see — all this comes to us 'cause we're all part of the same crowd, 'cause I know you and you know me."

"But an abortion is against the law, isn't it? I don't need trouble."

"If she kills herself, that's legal? And where do you see trouble here?"

"You think she'd really kill herself?"

"Look, I don't know who she is. But she's a heebee broad — a kid — that's not married. And of all people, the one that knocked her up is Norm Zellinger, the druggist. You'd think he didn't know they invented skins. Maybe the bugger thought he'd save himself a nickel. Now he's putting down a C-note to save her reputation." The word *reputation* stung Avrum's ears. "He'd even put down double that and more. He's as desperate as that. Read the papers about broads who close the windows and turn the gas on. Ninety-nine percent of them got something growing in their bellies. Y'wanna guess how many die rupturing themselves with knitting needles? Anyways, Litwak is very careful about these things. Like how many would insist on talking to the girl first just to calm the girl down?"

"How can a talk with Litwak calm a girl down? By the time he gets a word out . . ."

"So he stutters. So what? It's enough they see his license that he's a real doctor and not a butcher. And like now — he knows who this kid is, and it came out somehow that she knows Irving. I don't know how he found out, but he did, and it's a good thing. That's why you got this chance, and you're not taking nothing away from nobody."

"OK, Horse. I'll do it." Avrum smiled, almost surprised himself at how swiftly he had made his decision.

"Now you're on the same track with me. I'll give you the time and the address. Tell Irving that tonight is off for him. Tell him to come to me for a second, and I'll explain him why. This is not everything I wanted to talk to you about, only that will have to wait for later. I think you better go back now." They rose and shook hands.

Avrum went to Horse again after work.

"Get yourself a bite to eat and have a rest before you take off," said Horse. "I left a message with Litwak's mother that I'm sending up a new man, so he'll be expecting you."

"Listen, Horse, I haven't a clue what to do up there. Am I going to be in the room when he's doing it to her?"

"That's the point. Ninety-nine times there's nothing to do but watch the show. But then there is always that one time when he needs you, and Litwak wouldn't do it if he wasn't sure that he had every corner covered. So if she faints or begins to scream her head off, he's not going to pull out his scraper and take half her box out with it, y'know what I mean? So he says to you what to do — to keep her down and quiet. And the whole business takes only a couple of minutes anyway. I tell you, it's an education. After you've seen a dozen of these things . . . when you see that a guy breaks his balls just to see what surprise she got under her dress, y'realize how it makes dumb shmucks out of all of us. Y'see that a hole is just a hole. The difference, I tell you, is that some of them stink more than others, and Irv tells me that he never goes in there without his fly swatter."

Avrum just knew this couldn't be true. The image of his mother flashed behind his eyes. Impossible was too weak a word.

Horse chuckled and reached down the counter for the ashtray, where he had earlier discarded an empty package of cigarettes. He tore open the wrapper, spread it out flat in front of him, and removed a pencil from his pocket, the tip of which he wet with his tongue. "Now I'm giving you the address. It's not far from here, but be there at eight sharp, remember." He wrote out the number and folded the paper carefully before handing it to him. "You'll find it just above St. Lawrence — no problem."

Avrum tucked it into his billfold behind two car tickets, and went again for Horse's hand. He shook it gratefully, and Horse smiled and said, "You're alright, kid, and this is just the beginning."

From the back of Avrum's mind, some old and dusty words began to surface in his memory. They were Grigor's. "Grab whatever you can . . . what a man can hold onto is his . . . the unspoken rule . . . every law in America says that what is in your hands, you keep." Avrum even recalled standing in the ship's washroom and looking at his hands. He had wondered then if they could ever learn to "grab" and now, thanks to his friends, they were being offered that chance; he wasn't about to deny them. He had a good feeling about himself and Horse's parting words were almost superfluous. The moment he had agreed to replace Strulevitch, he sensed with a lightness in his heart that at last he had severed himself from the grip the old world had had on his mind. Now his brain belonged with his body, and both were finding a home in America. Together they would yet discover its promises and enjoy its prizes.

He first suspected that he had a problem when the address he was given began to pull him too far to the east of St. Lawrence. Then, when he found it and rang the bell, the door was opened by three messy children, and the noises and smells from inside were all French. Still, he asked if Doctor Litwak was there, and, as he somehow expected, they said no. He checked and rechecked the address on the paper against the number over the door, when the children's father came and asked what he wanted. Avrum showed him the address Horse had written, and said that a Doctor Litwak should have been living here. But the man, who had on only sagging trousers and long underwear, rattled off a stream of French and pointed repeatedly at the paper and in the direction back to St. Lawrence. Avrum didn't understand a word, but gathered nevertheless that the house he was looking for was somewhere back there.

He had left a generous margin of time to find the house, but eight o'clock was rapidly approaching. When the hour came, every second that ticked past it violated and bruised his conscience. Litwak, Horse, possibly even the girl, were depending on him to show, and here he was walking aimlessly on an unfamiliar street. He was no closer to his destination than when he started out to look for it.

At 8:15, unsettled and confounded, he stopped a policeman and showed him the address. It was only a moment later, however, that Avrum connected the implications of what was on the paper to the man in uniform studying it. With his heart sinking rapidly, he saw himself being deported. Thankfully, the policeman seemed bored, and Avrum thought to grab the paper from his hands.

"You okay?" asked the policeman, puzzled.

"Oh, sure, officer. I think it's a mistake, anyways."

"Cause it's right here — just two doors down." He pointed.

"What? That house over there?" Avrum asked incredulously.

"Yes. It's Doctor Litwak's address."

"That's right. Doctor Litwak . . ." Avrum desperately tried to explain his interest in the Doctor. "My landlady — y'know old people — her stomach . . ." He almost blurted out that she was pregnant. "She needs pills for the pressure."

The policeman nodded and walked on. Avrum looked at the number over the door, and saw that he had read an eleven for a seventy-seven. He'll have to get used to their not crossing the sevens here. Why hadn't he untangled the error himself, he thought as he bounded up the stairs, taking three at a time. He was twenty minutes late.

"They waited and waited," said the elderly woman who came to the door and showed him inside. "My Solly said that when you come, you should put this on first before you go in. But just a minute, let me tell him first that you're here. He decided maybe to do it himself." She handed him a white cotton smock and walked over to a door made up of two frosted glass panes. There was a strong white light behind it. "Doctor," she said, tapping lightly on the glass, "your assistant finally came."

"S . . . s . . . s . . . s . . . sen . . . sen . . . send . . . send . . ."

"You can go in," said the woman to Avrum, while behind the door her son was still trying to overpower the other words in his way.

As Avrum cautiously let himself through the door, feeling at one totally beyond his milieu in the smock yet somehow also terribly important, he noticed first the tray connected to the electrical outlet and the silver instruments inside, under water that was being brought to a boil. Then his eyes moved to the girl, who was still adjusting herself on the table. When Litwak saw who it was, his jaw dropped, and his eyes seemed to pop from his head. He began to flay the air wildly with his hands, but could manage to say no more than "Guh . . . guh . . . guh . . . guh—"

Something was very wrong. Avrum's attention quickly returned to the figure on the table. Her bare legs were raised, resting on supports, and parted widely. A great shadow of hair was sunk there between them. At first, her head was turned to the wall, but now she, too, had absorbed the doctor's sudden anxiety, and she looked to him in desperation. Then he saw the woman and she saw him. Of course something was wrong. The woman was Shirley.

There was no abortion performed in the house that night. Shirley became hysterical, vomited, and fainted in that order. Avrum turned on his heels and stepped out of the room. He felt he had to say something to her, that he would drive everything he had seen from his mind — but the situation left him numbed and dumb. Litwak stayed where he was, raising and lowering his hands like a mechanical toy. His jaw was working furiously and white froth appeared at the corners of his mouth, but not a sound left him. Then Litwak's mother came from the kitchen and asked if they wanted her to find some music on the radio. After a glance into the room, she went back for the mop.

* * *

Horse blamed Litwak for not telling him who the woman was. Litwak managed somehow to get across to Horse that when he called up to cancel Strulevitch, he implied that the girl had something to do with Goldenberg's factory, and that Horse should have understood as much. Avrum blamed himself for no reason except that Shirley was so brutally shamed because of him. And Shirley was committed, in her own mind, to giving her family an early surprise funeral.

What postponed this event from one hour to the next was the reaction of Norman Zellinger. He was as anxious and as in despair about what had happened as she. But then it entered her mind that if the momentum of his reaction could be sustained, she might just translate this disaster into an accomplishment that had otherwise eluded her for the longest time. She refused to return to the factory, and instead, played a tragic figure in his pharmacy from the minute he opened it in the morning until he pulled down the screen in the evening. Her "*I couldn't sleep all night. I'm a finished woman, Norm — ruined! Tell me, Norm. Tell me. Tell me, please. What am I going to do*?" or, "*Norm, I'm finished. You know this, don't you? You ruined me. Norm, this is absolutely the end of the world for me. Life is over for me, Norm. You put me in the grave,*" repeated like a broken record a hundred times a day, quite ossified his mind.

Except for the two hours at noon when she napped in his stockroom, he enjoyed no letup. He had never seen eyes so red and so terrified. Too many things were happening that Norman couldn't contend with at the same time. He began to make mistakes in filling the prescriptions — a few of which he even read wrongly. Shirley took to looking through his drug cabinets and asking him what would happen if she were to swallow a teaspoon of whatever might be on the shelves that was marked with a skull and crossbones. So his eyes had to be glued on her every minute. He couldn't tell her he didn't want her there, because he was — well, because he was Norman Zellinger who had been trained to feel guilty from the day his mother introduced him to the toilet.

He pleaded with her to go a second time — he'd find another doctor . . . he'd send her for a weekend to the Laurentians, even to the Catskills, but he was scraping futilely at the sides of the pit he had dug for himself. Shirley sensed it and pressed even harder. She would find over what to trip, and when he would help her to the couch in the back room, she would start in to improvise a deathbed scene that was every inch the equal of Sarah Bernhardt's *Camille*. Norman lasted six days.

Then he told her that he had this great idea: they could get married. Milking the situation for everything it was worth, Shirley said, "*No, not in a million years.*" She would never marry a man, she said, because he thought he *had* to marry her — marriage had to come from love. (At the same time, she would put a hand over her heart and sigh a pitiful and hanging sigh of sacrifice.) So Norman said that he had always loved her, and she said she had always loved him — adding (even if she was a year older than him) that they were made for each other. That evening, she told her mother that with the money he was probably making, their wedding could be catered and they could move right-off-the-bat to a house in Outremont.

(15)

Horse had taken thirty-five dollars from his own pocket and given it to Avrum. A contract is a contract, he said, and if it didn't work out, it wasn't for Avrum to sweat. He also said that the time had come to get into something heavier and they settled on an evening when Avrum, Strulevitch, and he could meet after closing time to talk seriously. When that hour came, Horse got Hank to drive them downtown to some club near the corner of Bleury and St. Catherine Streets.

Hank was invited to join them, and perhaps he would have liked to, but the instant he hesitated, Horse had said, "Well, maybe another time when you're not so busy." Hank got the message and said "Yeah, maybe another time." Gunning the engine hard, and even before they were all out of the car, he held down the clutch and threw the gear into first. When he finally pulled away on screeching tires, Strulevitch said that he had the impression that Hank really wanted to stay. Horse said "could be" but that Hank had a wife, mother, and three kids to feed, and it was enough he spent his days with the boys. Were he to do the same with his nights, his whole family would starve to death.

Strulevitch's mood darkened when the bouncer at the door to the club ignored him, but had an effusive and lengthy exchange with Horse. Inside, it worsened when the cigarette girl pressed her hips against Horse as she held out the brand of cigarettes she knew he smoked. He hadn't even made the effort to ask for them. To let her know that they were part of the same family, Strulevitch struck a sharp I've-seen-it-all pose and said to Horse (for her to overhear), "Take the kid to a good table, eh? I'll be right witcha." Then he asked her for a certain Havana cigar, which had to be the most expensive thing in her tray. She handed him one and he said he had room in his pocket for six. He added slickly that somewhere else he had a room for two, but she was fixing her smile at someone by the door, and completely ignored him. In a dry tone, almost as an afterthought, she said, "That'll be six dollars and sixty cents."

He fished for the money in his wallet and found he was short a dollar twenty. He handed her what he had, and said that actually he only wanted four cigars. She said, "Well, make up your mind, willya," and walked past him as though he wasn't there. Strulevitch figured that forty cents was still coming back to him, and if she thought it was her tip, she might at least have thanked him. He knew that if he let this episode pass without his reacting to it, it would riot in his mind for years — what he said . . . what he should have said . . . — he'd replay the scene *ad nauseum* until it devoured him. This was painfully familiar territory, as he was already weighed under by a long history of similar incidents. Had she only thanked him and manufactured a kind of smile . . . He stole up behind her and tried for an authoritative I'm-in-charge tone, saying, "I think I got a box of matches coming to me, doll." She didn't even turn around, but picked one out of her tray and handed it to him.

"That'll be twenty cents." She said.

"Twenty cents? But it's coming to me. My change from the cigars, eh?" Forgetting himself, his voice rose an octave.

"That'll be twenty cents, or give it back."

"What about my change from before? Eh?" People were beginning to turn around and fix their eyes on him. Some eyes were hugely amused. Others delivered daggers.

"That's the service, sir," she said, raising her voice in a way that made Strulevitch wish the floor would open up to swallow him. "Either you give me the twenty cents, or give me the matches back if you can't afford them." And even while she half shouted at him, she stubbornly looked elsewhere. The people around them were definitely taking in this scene. He demonstrated his contempt by tossing the matches back on the tray.

"For four bucks of cigars, matches are on the house, eh?" (At least let them know he smokes expensive stuff.) She put the matches carefully back with the rest and walked away. Horse, plainly annoyed, had come back to fish him out of the quagmire. He led him away and said that they were there for more important things.

"But hey, don't cry, Irv. I'll let you have all *my* matches," he added as if addressing a child.

Couples were dancing and Strulevitch asked the waiter who came for their order when the show would begin. "Half hour, maybe," mumbled the waiter. Horse ordered beers for all of them, and when Strulevitch leaned over and told him he didn't have any money — that he'd given the cigarette girl his last green — Horse sneered and said he'd mark it on the ice. Avrum was absorbed by the goings-on on the floor. He had never seen social dancing before, but glancing at Horse, he knew somehow that there would come a day when he, too, would get to that dance floor. Canada would soon show him all its magic and promise.

"We come to talk about you tonight, Abie," began Horse, "and if you want to listen to me, you'll mark this day on the calendar, because it is going to be the start of some of the best things that will ever happen to you in your life."

Avrum had heard this earlier during the ride over, and his eyes stayed with the dancers. Strulevitch was watching a young girl with enormous breasts and small, straight hips dancing with a man whom he guessed had to be at least fifty years her senior. Every time the man pulled her to him, Strulevitch imagined her breasts flattening themselves against his own chest, and a yearning filled him. If she would just turn toward him, he'd rush out and split her off from this museum piece. But his designs dampened hopelessly when it became obvious that the man was not so much pulling her to him as she was pressing herself against him. Maybe he'd find a way to pass her one of his Irv Steel cards . . . maybe.

The three beers were set on the table and Horse said quietly that if they didn't have a head for business, to say so — that it had been his impression they didn't come here only for the entertainment. There was enough threat in the tone he used to get their eyes focused sharply on him.

"Nah, nah! We're here for business," said Strulevitch. "Who's going to begin, me or you? I think for starters—"

"Just shut your trap, Irv. I'll run this thing, and if there's something I say that you don't like, just tell me, and I'll give you carfare home, OK?"

"Hey, for Chrissake! Why the damn hell are you getting so hot under the collar? If you remember, all this was all my idea in the first place. Eh?" Strulevitch struggled to regain some honor.

Very slowly and very deliberately, Horse took a dollar from his pocket and set it in the middle of the table.

"Pick it up anytime you want and take a swift powder. One more 'remember' from you, and I freeze the picture completely. One investment more or less makes no difference to me. But if I'm in it, I run it, so sit there and button your lip." Strulevitch, plainly soured and grim, returned his attention to the dance floor. Horse pulled his chair closer to Avrum.

"Now look, Abie," began Horse, "let's forget everything you've heard 'til now, and let's build the picture from scratch. Let's get this picture right. You with me?

Avrum nodded weakly.

"We begin with who you are and exactly what you can do that makes you special. Then we're gonna take a look at the three of us and get a picture of what we can do as a team, all of us doing this piece together. Y'follow me?"

Avrum said nothing, but carefully poured himself some beer.

"Now, just to put some color in the picture, you have to know that we're talking about money — a lot of money — mostly for you, but some for me and him. But like we were talking the other day — no one gets anything for doing nothing. Here we can put together an operation that uses the talents of the three of us — and that *depends* on the talents of the three of us. Still, you're quickly going to see that this operation is built mainly around you, so that most of the money gets to stay with you. And we divide the rest. Like for every dollar the operation makes, you get sixty cents, I get twenty-five, and Irv gets ten." Strulevitch glowered, but kept his tongue. "The five cents from the dollar left over goes for other expenses — operating expenses, equipment, things like that. Y'get the picture of an operation so far? And I'll just tell you that, the way I see it, it should bring you at least an extra thousand — a full grand a month after six months — ten months. Otherwise, Mr. A., it's not worth it for me, so after a year I say, boys — boys, we tried . . . it was an honest do . . . but it just ain't for me."

"We don't settle no percents here yet, eh?" muttered Strulevitch.

Horse leaned over and said nothing, but tapped the dollar. But when he spoke, it was to Avrum. Strulevitch took his beer, pushed the glass away, and guzzled from the bottle. "The fact is none of us knows what you can really do as a wrestler." continued Horse. "You never did sports, but you got a build and a body that a good trainer can shape into something serious. You also got a baby face all the girls will go for. Then I heard how you plastered the frogs who busted into Myer's place when I had the fire. Nothing surprised me. I figure they were lucky you didn't kill them. But never mind. I got a good guy — the best in the business, if I say so myself — who I'm going to get to take a look at you. If he likes what he sees — and he'll say right away yes or no — we'll take it from there."

"Who is this guy?" asked Avrum.

"You never seen him. His name is Zed Chicago, a *shvartzer*. He runs a little gym off Bleury — not the fanciest, but he's the only one in the racket who got an honest eye for talent. There's nothing in this business he doesn't know." Horse turned his attention to his beer and drained half the glass.

Slowly and deliberately, as though in deep thought, he wiped the foam from his lips. Then, jabbing his finger in Avrum's chest, he continued, "It's for protecting you and being able to make these kinds of arrangements that I'm getting my cut. It's protection and direction for you at one and the same time. And I don't have to tell you, it's nothing you could do on your lonesome. Do you understand?"

"Horse, I never even saw one wrestling match in my life. I don't even know if it's something I *can* do — never mind if I *want* to."

"There's nothing to know that you can't pick up in ten minutes. Irv will take you to the Arena next Wednesday and you'll come out an expert."

"And how do you figure about Goldenberg?"

"Yeah, well, we got to talk about that, too," said Horse, "just to clear the air. Now, say we don't know for a year how you're gonna make out, so it's stupid for you to go and quit your job. That means you stick with your job no matter what — see what I mean? You practice say from six, six-thirty after work, and all the matches begin after eight anyway. So whatever you can make as a wrestler, it's all cream — and that's the beauty of this whole business — nobody's got nothing to lose."

"And if I break a leg?"

"That doesn't happen. Look, what guarantee do you have that when you cross the street you'll make it to the other side? It's the same thing. If you don't plan on breaking a leg, don't think about it. And there's something else besides. Y'know I had a little talk with Cy Green." Horse refilled his glass and sucked in some of the head that was about to spill over the rim. Avrum tasted his beer. Earlier, he decided he didn't much like it. Now he was sure.

"I had a talk with Cy, and I like to listen to him because he's got a head. And he's been through a lot, believe me. Anyway, he told me he really liked talking to you, and he also told me what he thought about you. He says you're a natural . . . that you're a natural for anything that needs strength, size and speed. That's what he said, his exact words."

"Thanks."

"Mr. A, I'm telling you. This is just the start . . . the beginning of the beginning. From this minute, everything is going to open up for you." With that, Horse leaned over and slapped Avrum once on the shoulder and once on the back of his head. He made a grab for his ear, but Avrum, smiling broadly and enjoying the warmth of Horse's attentions, slipped away in time.

Strulevitch silently drank to his ten percent. He lifted a cigar from his vest, but then recalled the matchbox denied him. He pushed the cigar back into his pocket, not sure whether to feel disgusted with himself or angry at the girl.

(16)

Avrum sat on the edge of his bed and removed his shoes. He was especially careful with his right foot, because taped between his big toe and the one next to it was a pea-sized chunk of blue-green stone. Almost immediately, blisters had developed where it rubbed into the skin, but Kapitolnik insisted that it had to stay where it was. By weeks' end, the blisters had developed into running sores, and bearing down on the foot now was as painful as putting a hand into a fire.

Kapitolnik had relented, but he allowed for the stone to be removed only at midnight that night. It would be the start of *IYYAR*, he said, the month of rejuvenation, and the stone had then to be set in a window, or wherever else the full moon could get its magnetic light directly upon it. The stone moreover, had to be coated with a fine film of Avrum's semen, into which would be mixed the ashes of four of his hairs — one from each armpit, one from his pubic mound, and one from his head. All this would then be set on a bed of fingernail and toenail clippings, from his own hands and feet, of course.

Kapitolnik explained, "The stone is the vibration of your life; the semen is the cry to whatever living generation has your blood mixed into theirs. The hairs direct your cry and your vibrations to the north, south, east, and west of you, while the nails, under which the life force is naturally drawn into the body, pull to themselves the vibrations of every living thing that beats in harmony with you.

"Bang a musician's tuning fork and bring it near another fork. Without them even touching, the second fork will start to vibrate like the first. Without any physical connection between them, the second fork receives a message from the first, and want to or not, it is forced to react. The stone, prepared the way I've instructed, will work the same way on your brother."

In the morning, Avrum saw that the stone was buried under a mountain of ants. He wondered if this meant that his vibrations and theirs were the same.

* * *

At eight that evening, Avrum was at the corner of St. Urbain Street and Mount Royal waiting for Strulevitch. He saw the lights of the restaurants below on Mount Royal, but behind him, near Clark Street, was the entrance to the Mount Royal Arena where Marcel Duval was soon to meet Doug "Tigerman" McDougal in what the papers played up as the grudge match of the year. Strulevitch said that these two promised a show which guaranteed a packed house. And, in fact, people were already converging on the place, streaming from all directions with excitement and anticipation evident on their faces.

Posters along the walls showed the combatants in their most aggressive poses, and alongside each was a list of the championships they claimed for themselves. It was all very impressive, even frightening, when Avrum considered that it was expected that he find a place in the company of these intimidating fighters. Farther along the wall were other posters that listed the lesser bouts scheduled for the same evening; it seemed that the customers were truly assured their money's worth of brawling. The clang of a bell came from inside, and the crowd's roar filled the street. Avrum felt increasingly nervous and was anxious to get inside. Latecomers were now running to the entrance, and behind one such group that had come from the other side of St. Urbain Street, Avrum picked out Strulevitch.

"Hey, Abie," he shouted, waving his cigar. "C'mon."

Avrum met him at the entrance, and Strulevitch, puffing heavily, said he had been delayed. He showed two tickets to the doorman who tore off the stubs and they were let inside. They rushed through the narrow, dimly lit lobby, which reeked of sawdust and stale tobacco. Old faded and peeling billboards of boxing, wrestling, and equestrian events decorated the walls; from there, they made their way into the arena itself. Avrum was struck by the hard, worn, dusty, altogether gray look of the place.

Cigarette smoke was already thick in the air, and hung heavily with the dust below the lights over the ring. The ring itself was a platform raised about a yard off the ground; a few wooden steps led up to it. Inside it, the sweating, reddened fighters and an emaciated, white-shirted and bow-tied referee stood out sharply against the grim surroundings. The customers sat on chairs and benches — when they sat at all, which was seldom — and there were those who lived the fight with every ounce of themselves. Raising their fists, they shouted advice, yelled threats, and hurled insults. Sometimes a crumpled pack of cigarettes was thrown into the ring. A customer would leave his place and rush right up to the ring, as if he intended to climb inside. There were burly, heavy-limbed ushers, however, who would turn these people back — often in such a manner that the latter inspected their bodies for marks and bruises afterwards.

Strulevitch hardly looked in the direction of the ring for most of the first fight. He pointed out a short, balding figure in the first row and told Avrum that that was none other than Smitty of the *Montreal Herald*. Next to him was Lippy Lou, also from the *Herald*, and right behind them was Axelrod from the *Star*. The fight would make the headlines tomorrow, he said. "Y'see how important they make these things? Eh? I mean these guys, especially those in the same league with Tigerman McDougal, are famous. Duval already owns a tavern on what he made from his first couple fights alone with this McDougal. Smitty wrote a whole page on the money floating around in this game. Wait 'til you see the action. Eh? You'll see that it's absolutely nothing you can't already do yourself — and even better." But Avrum listened with only half an ear.

The fighters seemed well into middle age. Both of them wore black stocking pants with a wide strap across one shoulder, but that couldn't cover their bloated paunches. They grunted a lot and seemed to take turns on the floor, which they slapped loudly with their forearms as if to give the impression that something cataclysmic was happening to them. Sometimes the referee dropped to the floor, too, to slip his hand under a shoulder and begin a dramatic and ominous count, "One . . . two . . ." but then the fellow on the floor would suddenly twist away, and a moment later, the other fellow would be with his back on the floor. The exchanges seemed almost calculated, with the way they seemed to be taking turns being on top. Boos began to erupt from some pockets in the crowd, then the bell rang and the referee called both wrestlers to the middle of the ring. It was a draw, and he lifted their hands together. Jeers greeted the decision, and more boos followed the wrestlers to their dressing rooms.

"It's an expected thing," Strulevitch said unmoved. "They always use a couple of old horses to warm up the ropes. The second match will also be a nothing; it's just to kill time before the semi and the main. But keep an eye on the things they do. Eh? The last bums got twenty-five bucks apiece, just for going in there. Was it so bad? Eh?"

Flanked by an attendant, the next wrestler came down the aisle and passed within two yards of Avrum. He wore a soft green robe, and someone was rubbing his shoulders and back as he walked. He seemed younger and harder than the others, but when he got into the ring and removed his robe, the actual picture was mildly disappointing. He had a slim waist with clean lines flowing from high, straight shoulders, and even a fleeting, cursory comparison convinced Avrum that his own dimensions were rather more impressive. On the far side, the second wrestler was making his way into the ring; he was a bigger, heavier fellow. When the announcer introduced them, it was evident that the crowd knew both of them well; they cheered and encouraged the first fellow and hollered blistering insults at the second, then a restless tension settled over the crowd in anticipation of the bell.

The heavier fellow, who was introduced as Shamrock Mulligan, walked out slowly to the middle of the ring and fixed himself into a pose that recalled the posters outside. His opponent, the crowd's favorite, was Yvon Leduc. At the sound of the bell, Shamrock Mulligan bounced off the ropes in his corner and circled the ring in a catlike half-crouch while his arms flayed the air windmill-fashion. Suddenly they were facing each other. Mulligan lunged, but Leduc moved swiftly to one side. The momentum of the lunge carried Mulligan to the ropes and halfway through them. He struck at them in angry frustration and turned around to face Leduc again. A mean scowl crossed his face as Leduc bounced from one foot to the other on the other side of the ring and invited Mulligan to rush him again. The pattern repeated itself, and Mullligan came off the ropes snorting like a bull. The crowd laughed at him, and Leduc confidently invited a third charge.

"Now, watch how Mulligan catches him, eh," muttered Strulevitch, bending closer to Avrum's ear.

An instant later, the crowd groaned along with Leduc when Mulligan only feinted a lunge, but drove his fist into Leduc's stomach instead. The crowd hollered, and the referee shouted at Mulligan, who, showing his open hand to the crowd, swore that his hand had been open when he struck. Leduc lay in agony, contorted with pain, when Mulligan turned to resume his attack; he threw himself like a massive bear over the prostrate body, but Leduc had seen him coming and rolled away with a sudden, unexpected surge of life. Mulligan crashed heavily to the floor and seemed stunned. Leduc rolled him over and threw himself across his shoulders, trying for a quick press. The referee dropped to the floor and checked Mulligan's shoulders. "One…" he shouted. "Two…" but Leduc might have been a feather the way Mulligan threw him off. Both men rose quickly to their feet and, settling back into their attack poses, they again squared off against each other. The crowd seemed let down by Leduc.

Strulevitch put his hand on Avrum's arm. "Let me explain to you what's going on. Forget those shits, eh? I'll tell you right now that Mulligan is going to win."

"How can you be so sure?" asked Avrum.

"It's just the way it has to be. Everyone here knows it — even when they scream their heads off for Leduc. Eh? Leduc is young, he looks clean, he's fast, and he's French. But he's got no weight, eh? And between you and me, speed is just for show. So the promoter has this ape Shamrock Mulligan, a *zjlob* hasbeen Irish drunk come-on, like that friggin giant Jack Johnson, as if all he's got on his mind is to tear the other guy apart — rules or no rules. He knows the crowd will come hoping to see someone knock the crap out of him. Eh? Y'understand! So for this, the promoter needs a good clean guy who can *almost* do it."

"Why almost?"

"That's the way it's got to be. Look, they can see that this Leduc is soft; the only thing he can beat is a roll of toilet paper. Eh? Y'see, Mulligan beats him, but he beats him dirty, so the crowd says 'Just wait 'til another guy gets you who can be dirty, too.' Eh? So, like this, the promoter can bring both of them back. Leduc lost, y'see, not because he wasn't good, but because the other guy used every dirty trick in the book. Mulligan then comes back to give another guy a chance to give him what he got coming to him. Y'see how it works out?"

"And all this Mulligan and Leduc know?"

"Sure. At least for these grade-C dump fights, eh? Look, for these guys, it's a quick green. Mulligan knows he can't afford to lose to a spring chicken like Leduc, and Leduc knows it's alright to lose if the other guy fights *shmutzik*. They're not up there to get themselves crippled — not for the thirty-five bucks they're collecting, eh? They want to make sure they make the same roll again next week — if not here, then somewhere else."

Strulevitch had to stop talking. The crowd was in an uproar. Mulligan had Leduc on the floor and was choking him. Whenever the referee would look away, his hands would drop from Leduc's chin and encircle his neck. Leduc would kick out and keep pointing to his neck, but whenever the referee turned to look, Mulligan would twist both their bodies — by pulling

Leduc's hair — and the neck would be blocked from his view again. The crowd hollered at the referee, who seemed to have trouble understanding what they wanted of him. Finally, Leduc stopped resisting and Mulligan let him fall before dropping across his chest. The referee counted to three and the bell rang. Mulligan was the winner.

The crowd cursed and shouted expletives in a dozen languages. Meanwhile, Mulligan strutted around the ring as if he were king of the world. Leduc had recovered with miraculous speed and was protesting loudly to the referee. The crowd backed him, but it was plain that the verdict was final. A minute later, the ring was empty and a low murmur dropped over the crowd. What had happened a moment ago was forgotten. Only the next contest interested them now.

The next contest — the semi-final — was a freakish attraction. It featured one Gerry "Giant" Gowan, against three nondescripts. The announcer introduced "Giant" Gowan, saying that he weighed 448 pounds, and there wasn't a soul in the crowd who doubted him. "Giant" Gowan didn't climb the few stairs up to the ring; from where he was standing on the floor, he just rolled his massive bulk onto the canvas. Inside, he had to be helped onto his feet, and it was plain to see that if he could be gotten onto his back again, the win would go to the other side. But standing there in his corner, he looked fearsome indeed.

"This is also wrestling?" asked Avrum.

"Nah." Strulevitch ground his cigar into the floor. "But it's what's called a crowd-pleaser. Eh? Watch the way they eat it up. It's good for a laugh before the main event."

Avrum watched. The bell had rung, but no one in the ring seemed to know exactly what to do. "Giant" Gowan stood a yard out of his corner and waited, while the other three flitted around like butterflies and kept a respectful distance from him. The referee made sweeping motions with his hands signaling them to make contact, but none of the three wanted to be the first to experiment with the idea. The crowd hissed and laughed and some of the customers began to shake their fists.

Finally, one wrestler pushed another into "Giant" Gowan's clutches, and everyone, in and out of the ring, watched with gruesome fascination as the massive, ponderous arms wrapped themselves around the unfortunate fellow like a voracious Venus flytrap closing over a helpless insect. A moment later, the grip was relaxed and the body dropped in a heap to the floor. Attendants rushed in with a stretcher which had conveniently been brought to the ring before the fight began and they carried the moaning figure back to his dressing room.

The two that remained withdrew hastily to a corner and tried to plan a strategy. Finally, they seemed to agree on something and the crowd was anxious to see what that might be. For a minute or two, they circled Gowan as if what they had in mind was to attack simultaneously from opposite sides. Unfortunately, the fellow in the front moved in too close too soon, and the attendants were soon back in the ring to retrieve him, as well. That left one against one, and it seemed only a question of time before "Giant" Gowan would put away the third pest. But this one displayed more cunning and he kept to the back of Gowan; this seemed to confuse the latter, who had to keep turning and taking backward steps to find him. This must have been the smaller man's intention, because he suddenly dropped to the floor behind "Giant" Gowan's feet, and the big man tripped.

The fight was declared a draw. "Giant" Gowan was down, so he lost, but he had fallen so heavily over his opponent that the crowd moaned in pain. The motionless body looked crushed, and this time, the attendants flew into the ring with the stretcher, rolled him on almost piece-by-piece, and rushed him away. "Giant" Gowan was rolled to the side, and he was helped to his feet on the floor. The gong sounded a number of times, the ring emptied, and the fans sat back to relax and light up another cigarette. There would be a ten-minute intermission before the main event.

Strulevitch pulled out another cigar from his vest pocket and delicately removed the wrapper. He bit a piece off one end and tasted it before spitting it out. A man standing opposite him offered a light and Strulevitch nodded his thanks. While he was puffing at the match, the other man asked what he thought would happen in the next fight. Strulevitch, letting out a cloud of smoke, said importantly that it was wide open, because each had already won once and the promoter couldn't carry them more than three fights. Still, he said he was leaning on Duval because Duval was the local boy, and McDougal didn't have to worry too much about his reputation here, since the papers said he was going to be at least six months on the road in the States, anyways. Duval, on the other hand, had to keep the Frenchies happy, so winning was more important to him. "Yeah," said the other guy, impressed. "I see it that way, too. I got a fiver running on him."

Strulevitch turned to Avrum. "So? What do you say?"

"What's to say?"

"Well, how are you liking it? The lights . . . the ring . . . eh? And whatta crowd! Y'see what people dish out good money for? For a program like this, the promoter rakes in a fortune. Eh? But everybody goes away happy. I tell you Abie—" Strulevitch spit some tobacco on the floor and Avrum couldn't help noticing the litter thickening around them. "You just picture yourself in there for the next fight. It don't matter that you don't know the holds, just watch the tricks. It will look like one guy is clobbering the other with his fists, for instance, but all the punches are choked. They couldn't take the air out of a paper bag. Y'see, if one guy's gonna hit seriously, he's gonna *get* hit, and his living depends on getting out of that ring in one piece so he can show up clean tomorrow night in another ring."

"So why does he pretend to hit him in the first place?"

"Eh? It's the show, for Chrissake; didn't you figure that out yet? It's one thing to know how to wrestle, eh, and the fact is you also gotta know how to make it look like you're taking punishment. If you don't give a good show you're no good to the promoters."

"It doesn't sound like a sport."

"Whoever said it was a sport? For you and me, Abie, it's a business, and we just gotta learn to be good at it. Eh? We figure in a couple months, after Chicago works you over, we can have you in some main events. We can work you up an image. You're a Yid, so that's easy, eh? And you'll be packing them in like the way you see here."

"Maybe," said Avrum, but there was nothing hopeful in his voice.

Avrum looked around at the flushed faces. The smoke in the place was thick and hung fixed and heavy like a mountain fog. It burned his eyes. He thought sadly that if he became a wrestler then these strange faces — along with the grime, which really was everywhere around him — would somehow be a fixture of his lifestyle. His body might have been there in the Mount Royal Arena, but not so his heart.

The roar of the crowd signaled the entrance of "Tigerman" McDougal and Marcel Duval. Duval appeared through the entrance on Avrum's side, and a crowd immediately blocked his way. People fought to get close enough to touch him. They slapped him on the back and told him to kick Mcdougal's balls off. He half acknowledged them, and it seemed to Avrum that the wrestler's mind was preoccupied with something else. His handler pressed ahead, and Duval finally made it to the ring. When he bounced over the ropes and waved his hands to the crowd, their cheers seemed to lift the place right off the ground.

Boos and jeers drowned McDougal when he did the same. In retaliation, he waved his fist at the crowd and invited any among them who dared to climb into the ring with him right then and there. Not surprisingly, no one tried, and he called them all yellow and chicken and ratshits. They hated him. They depended on Duval to take up the challenge for all of them. Their wildest hope was to see Duval rip McDougal's guts out and maybe hang him from the lights with them.

Fights broke out in the crowd and benches were overturned. Ushers and police had to run back and forth to keep the place from rioting, while at ringside, the bell clamored for the crowd's attention. The referee climbed into the ring and called the fighters to him; he had begun to inspect their hands when McDougal slammed his forearm into Duval's breadbasket and Duval instantly returned a forearm against McDougal's mouth. The latter dropped like a brick and scurried on fours to a corner. The referee held Duval back from going after him and signaled the man at the table to sound the gong. The fight was on, and everyone in the place was standing on tiptoes on their chairs or benches screaming furiously at the ring.

Until Duval caught McDougal in his backbreaker fifteen minutes later, the two mauled each other in a free-for-all that spread from the ring to the first rows of chairs. McDougal pulled Duval's hair and drove a sharp chop at his Adam's apple. Another man would have been crippled for life, but Duval just turned around and poked his finger into McDougal's eyes. McDougal was surely blinded forever, but no, he just shook his head and charged, and the two collided again. Then Duval trapped McDougal backwards on his back, and McDougal screamed his surrender. The crowd exploded with joy.

But the winner was the one who would win two falls or two submissions, and Duval would have to repeat his success before the match could be behind him. "McDougal is going to take the next one," Strulevitch said to Avrum.

"How can you be so sure? This McDougal looks like he can't move anymore."

But Strulevitch just rolled his eyes. "McDougal's as fresh as if he just got up in the morning," he said.

But when the gong called the fighters together again, McDougal still seemed to be in serious distress after Duval's backbreaker. He retreated and Duval punished him with hip throws and leg locks. "McDougal's finished," said Avrum.

Strulevitch continued chewing on his cigar. "Can't you see they're just resting? Eh?" he said. "They're eating up time, but McDougal's gonna take this one or else it's just half a show." And it was then that McDougal seemed to regain his footing. He caught Duval coming off the ropes and smashed his knee into his groin, then three successive wrist jerks somersaulted a stunned Duval across the ring and back again. Duval seemed helpless. McDougal worked a complicated arm lock on him that seemed to cut off the blood supply to half of Duval's body. The crowd expected Duval to kick his way free, but McDougal pressed harder and got in some eye gouging and hair pulling when it seemed that the referee was looking elsewhere. Shouts went up. Bits of paper and more empty cigarette packs were thrown into the ring. Duval still seemed to resist, but then McDougal caught him in a chokehold with his knees, and Duval raised a hand in submission. The referee broke them up, the bell was sounded, and McDougal strutted around the ring acting terribly proud of himself. Duval remained on his back until an attendant brought him water and a towel and helped him to a corner.

"Duval can act good," said Strulevitch. "I told you it would go one–one, eh? Now the crowd's all nervous, y'see? But I tell you, Abie, it has to go to Duval. I know for a fact that he's lined up to take on the Michigan Butcher here next week, so it don't pay the promoter if he loses now."

"Maybe," said Avrum, shaking his head, "but Duval looked like he was really hurt."

"Hurt? *Bobehmysehs!* Don't tell me that if it was you, you couldn't get out of that hold. Eh? What was McDougal doing to him that was so impossible to break?"

"So, the whole thing is an act . . . if everything is fixed . . ."

"Y'know something, Abie? It's a business. It's fixed, and it's not fixed. Eh? It's an act, and it's not an act. Eh? The funny thing is that the guy that *has* to win is the one who almost always does — excepting if there's an accident, which sometimes happens. And when the two guys are in the ring, they both know which of them needs to win and which of them can live without it. It's practically decided when they sign up for the fight with the promoter. I mean, the guy who is gonna be on the road for half a year can afford to lose. He's not gonna break his back over one stupid fight when it's more important that the local give a good show. Eh?"

"Well, you can't call it a sport."

"If it was a sport, you could be doing it by yourself. We talked about it. Eh? But it's ninety percent business, and that's why you need Horse and me. Maybe the other ten percent you can call sport, because you can't go into the ring altogether a cripple. Eh? There are things you got to be able to do in a sharp, flashy style. Eh? And it needs a lot of muscle. I mean, I could be dying to be a wrestler, but who would I convince?"

"Ninety percent is business?"

"You'll live and learn, Abie. Y'can make a mint out of this racket, eh, but only if you do it the right way."

The fighters were back to pushing each other around. The advantage moved from one to the other and Duval was being encouraged by the crowd to fight dirty. Suddenly, McDougal seemed to stun Duval with a forearm smash to the heart and a knee to his kidneys. Duval reeled, and McDougal lifted and locked him in his dreaded airplane spin. This had to be the end, but as Duval was on his way to the floor, he somehow caught McDougal under his shoulder and around his neck, so that it was McDougal who got crushed under Duval's fall. Duval then got up and maneuvered McDougal again backwards across his own back, and McDougal, screaming in agony, gave up.

"Let's get out of here fast," said Strulevitch, rushing for the aisle. Bedlam was spreading in the hall and the police and ushers had to fight with the crowd to keep them away from McDougal. Duval basked in their cheers. The smoke was still stinging painfully in Avrum's eyes and he pressed hard behind Strulevitch, even pushing him until they got out to the street.

"That's it," said Strulevitch. "That's what it looks like, and there was nothing there that you couldn't have handled yourself, eh? After Chicago works you out, we'll bring you up to the top money. And I guarantee, after the first time, you won't see or hear or feel — not the noise, not the smoke, not the dirt, not the shouting, not *nothing!* You'll be in business for yourself, eh? Your own honest, legit business."

"I could have done everything they did," said Avrum on reflection. "I think I could even have done it better."

Strulevitch lit another cigar. "Yeah, and each guy pulled in at least two hundred smootch tonight, easy."

"More than I ever made chopping down trees," muttered Avrum. "You're not joking? Really? Two hundred?" That was more than showed in his bankbook after almost three years of working for Goldenberg.

He walked alone along St. Urbain Street after Strulevitch cut west for Park Avenue, and Avrum let the vivid images of the last hour and a half float through his mind. A cold, damp air descended on the city and he felt a sudden rush of wind at his back. His mood broke. Then the first drops of rain began to fall.

When he turned into Clark Street, it rained harder. The colors, smells, and sounds that were still with him from the arena were punctuated by the patter of drops falling on the street. The trashcans were lined up at the curb for the garbage collectors, and the cats were at them. Sometimes his steps would surprise them, and they would leap out and scatter in fright. Avrum had three blocks yet to cover, but he wasn't in a rush to close the day. He turned up his collar and settled into a hunch, and saw that he was alone on the street. Alone, the street was his. He felt strangely that he was damned as its king and doomed as its prisoner. Flashes of the pogrom came back to him, and he could still feel the thorns of the bushes cutting into his face. He could still feel Hershel half-covered by his own body, and he could feel the earth move under the horses' hooves.

Hershel . . . where was Hershel now? Who else remembered the screaming and the shrieks and the guns and the smoke and knives and the blood? Hershel's existence was the only thing he could cling to that might keep the past real. What was Avrum Vishinsky who belonged with his dead mother and father, both long in the earth at the side of an old forgotten road, uncertain now if it was in Poland or the Ukraine — what was this same Avrum Vishinsky doing now, here on Clark Street in Montreal, in the rain with cats and garbage cans, coming from a wrestling match? Avrum looked down at the wet sidewalk. The city had planted saplings along the street, and the wet leaves glistened. Someone had planted them; someone had fixed iron grating around them to protect them. But what did these trees have to do with him? The water was moving slowly in the gutter, and a desperate cutting loneliness bit into his chest. He opened himself to a sadness that quickly enveloped him.

(17)

The next day, Avrum was back at Kapitolnik's flat. The man was asking a dollar and a half now, but for this, he had prepared

Hershel's mystic number. He said it had required hours of endless calculations, with checks and rechecks, but Avrum now had only to use it properly for his brother to be induced to show himself.

The number, he said was eight — at once, the most tragic and the most spiritual of numbers. It is the number of justice and the number of sacrifice. It is the number of rebirth, of dedication, and of commitment. It is the number of secrets and mysteries. Eight prophets had the blood of Rahab, on the eighth day is the Jewish child circumcised, and eight candles mark the Festival of Lights. He went on to say that the dreaded *SHABBTAI* is the planet of the number eight, and its day is none other than *SHABBES-KOIDESH.* On this day, which commences every Friday at sunset and lasts until the sunset of the following day, Avrum was to get eight small pieces of lead ("Go to the shop on Esplanade near St. Viateur where they make stained glass windows."), which, he was told, is the metal of *SHABBTAI*, and he was to set them around a vial of mercury ("Break a thermometer."). Into this vial, Avrum was to deposit the Hebrew letters that made up his brother's name, and these letters would have to be cut from the parchment removed from the back of a *mezuzah*. The vial itself had to be set where the rays of moonlight could get to it.

"But beware," warned Kapitolnik, "not to so much as shave the *SHADDAI* on the reverse side of the parchment. Also, with the letters removed, the same parchment is now an evil to you because it is a world from which your brother has been removed. What you must do then is this . . ."

Avrum had to stain the *SHADDAI* with a drop of iodine and then cut up the already-torn parchment into fifty-three pieces. That, plus the eleven letters that were removed earlier, gave a total of sixty-four pieces, which was a multiple of eight by eight, yet the six and the four came to a one, which stands for the sun, the planet of discoveries and new beginnings. Each of these fifty-three pieces had to be set in its own small crumb of dough and baked, and these had then to be taken to a river known to have fish and there thrown to them with the left hand alone.

The bits of dough, each with their slip of parchment, were ready. And when he caught Mrs. Kaplan leaving with her bags for Rachel Market, Avrum jumped upstairs, buttered a frying pan, and set the dough on the fire.

On Friday, with the sun beginning to darken, Avrum made his way to the water's edge across from Longueuil and there, with his left hand, threw the contents of his paper bag into the river.

* * *

Horse told him to put twenty on Slipper Sue in the third at Blue Bonnets and another twenty on Green Grass in the fifth. Avrum said that he had no clue at all about horse racing — that forty dollars was a lot more than he could afford to gamble away — and that he wouldn't even know how to go about making the bet. Patiently, Horse heard him out and called to Cy Green at the phone to get these bets down for him. Cy saluted and a moment later got them across. At the counter, Horse counted off four bills from the fat bundle that he carried loosely in his pocket and slapped them down in front of Avrum. "You'll pay me back when you can afford it, Mr. A.," he said. But his eyes were laughing.

The next day, Willy Button called to Avrum from one of the back tables and handed him two hundred and eighty dollars. "Congrats," he said dully. Avrum only realized they were his when Horse asked for his forty back.

(18)

Avrum called Bella at work and asked if she would like to meet him after work. Bella said that he should call her again at five because she would know only then if she had the time. He called at five. She hemmed and hawed and finally agreed. She hinted that something important awaited her in the evening and she needed enough time to ready herself properly. Avrum said that that was OK

He told her in a general way about his recent financial gains — how in a matter of days he had accumulated a sum that matched years of savings. She was suddenly very pleased for him and asked immediately for details, but Avrum found no way to explain an aborted abortion and a forty-dollar gamble on horses he had never seen or heard of in his life. However, to show her that his fortunes were indeed on a steep rise, he produced his wallet, which was thick with bills. This impressed her. She closed the distance between them, hoping that the Arliquinade she had earlier splashed on her cheeks and breasts would reach his nostrils.

"But how did you do it, Abie? I think it's just wonderful, and I'm absolutely the happiest person in the world for you. You can believe me when I say this."

Avrum just said that he was working with some important people ". . . in a kind of organization that had people inside different businesses arranging things together."

Bella turned her nose, saying it might be illegal. "Did you ever think of that?" Avrum blushed and swore he would never involve himself in anything that was not completely on the up-and-up. Bella said that it was wonderful to be so rich — that she herself always thought that it was natural for her one day to be rich. Avrum said that if his interests with this organization of people continued, he would soon have more money than he dreamed one man could spend in a lifetime. Bella wasn't about to ask any more questions.

She steered him along Park Avenue and then to a path that led behind a cluster of trees on the mountains. It was a crisp, late afternoon summer day; a wonderful freshness was in the air, and Bella reached for his hand. He felt his teeth almost freeze over and he could say nothing. She walked quietly next to him as if they had been this way for years. At that moment, the rich feeling he had in his heart outweighed even what he had in his wallet, and he played with the thought that Bella Finegold might be happy to be his girl. Finally, he asked about Sam, but she didn't want to "discuss" him. She just wanted a quiet walk with "someone I can just absolutely trust with my whole heart."

She squeezed his hand reassuringly. But soon she had to go. He walked her home; on the street, she wouldn't hold his hand, but their bodies touched many times.

That evening, Sam called at her house but they couldn't agree on what to do. Sam said he wouldn't mind seeing the pictures at the Rialto, but Bella said that the flickering of the camera always gave her headaches, and if she never complained about it to him before, "it was only because I just didn't want to spoil your pleasure." Sam tried to make a quick calculation of all the movies they had seen that Bella had said she would die if she missed, and multiplied the number by thirty-six cents, which was what two tickets cost. It came to a respectable investment. He choked back the remarks that now surfaced in his mind.

"We can go to Stein's for a milkshake," said Bella. "There is something I think now is the time to talk about, anyways."

"Like what?" asked Sam, feeling a familiar nervousness creep into his words.

"Like what, like what . . ." she mocked. "You just have to know everything this very second? We'll sit down with a milkshake or maybe an ice cream and we'll have the talk we had to have a long time ago."

"Bella, we talked about that already."

"Maybe you think we did, but *I* don't think so." Her words snapped at him, and resignedly he shuffled to the front door and waited until Bella finished readying herself. Eventually she followed him and he saw her parents poke their heads out from the kitchen and steal a look their way.

"Bella," he said while they were still on the stairs, "I hope it's not . . . I just hope . . ."

"Since when did you have a monopoly on hopes? Just maybe I have some myself? Maybe you're just thinking of yourself a little too much? A person doesn't live by himself, you know. You have to take into consideration those around you and maybe that is something you don't do enough."

Their talk had exhausted itself a long way before they reached Stein's. Bella insisted that she wanted to marry, and rattled off an arm's length of reasons why it was coming to her. Sam was determined to earn his degree in medicine, and the odd jobs he managed to find barely paid for his books and tuition, let alone his grocery bill. His uncle helped him out some, he admitted, but if he couldn't keep a pauper's discipline on his finances and stick to his books uninterrupted for at least another four years, his chances of ever making something of himself "would be washed down the drain."

"So marrying is like getting washed down the drain, eh?"

"You don't have to say it like that, Bella. I just can't do anything for at least four years. Once I'm a doctor, I'll be able to do what I want. I mean, even if I should decide that I want to go on and specialize, it wouldn't necessarily bother my career if I got married."

"You don't expect me to wait a whole four years?"

"What can I do, Bella? Really, what can I do? Y'know how hard it was to get accepted at McGill in the first place? Y'know the university's quota on Jews. It was a miracle that they looked at my name. Guys — brilliant guys — with an average just a point or two below mine got rejected because they were over their quota, but *Goyim* with 15, 20 points lower got accepted without a second thought. When I got their OK, I swore, I swore, I swore that I'd turn over buildings, but I'd make it. I'd starve, but I'd make it. I'd even steal, but I'd make it. What is four years against a lifetime? But these four years will make or break my whole life. Try to understand."

"I'll understand what I want to understand. Your story isn't mine. Let me tell you, you're just stubborn and selfish! You just don't want to see the things I need, and the way I feel. A girl my age just has to have a house and children, and I tell you Sam, it can't and won't wait four years. You think I don't want you to be a doctor? I should die on the spot if I thought that. But what's wrong if you do it maybe a little slower? Aren't there night classes or something that could let you hold a good job during the day? You got a head, and it's you that should figure these things out — not me. But I just know there must be a way. You want the truth? I'm beginning to feel in my heart that all this time you were just using me. And when I think of all the men who asked me out, and I told them that I was busy — so what am I sacrificing myself for? On whom am I depending?"

At Stein's, Bella ordered a triple ice cream on a waffle, but said she'd have to force herself to eat it because he had taken her appetite away. Sam lost himself in the bubbles in his glass of soda water.

(19)

Horse got one of Goldenberg's girls to tell Avrum that he had to have a word with him as soon as possible. But it was only nine-thirty, and Strulevitch was still scratching his way though the first orders of the morning, complaining as usual that Avrum wasn't organizing the styles and the sizes fast enough. One presser didn't show up, and the finishers began to sit at empty tables. When Goldenberg saw one of them filing her fingernails on his time, he took the iron himself so that Avrum couldn't for a moment evade his sight.

Unfortunately, Goldenberg used the iron with more enthusiasm than skill, and when he burned a collar while fighting a stubborn crease, he got one of the finishers to take over from him until enough work accumulated to keep her busy again at the finishing table. Then Strulevitch called his boss over to the half-empty boxes and asked how he could get them ready when he was waiting for the four-eighteen, and they were giving him everything else. Ninety-nine percent of the time, *they* meant Avrum, and Avrum complained that the last of the four-eighteen — a full five dozen — went out the day before. Another four dozen was stuck at the buttonhole maker because Goldenberg himself told Mme. Bouchard, who worked the machine, not to touch anything until she finished with the size fourteens of the six-oh-sixes. "And she mixed up the buttons on them because the factory sent her too many off-colored ones all in the same box. So she stopped production."

"Soooooo?" asked Goldenberg between clenched teeth. "What's she doing now — getting ready for her two weeks' vacation? Until she gets the right buttons, she can't give you the four-eighteens?"

"She won't touch anything until the six-oh-sixes are done — on purpose. She says you shouted at her. So she's ripping out all the bad buttons."

"How many could she have ripped?"

"Almost ten dozen."

"TEN DOZEN! THAT'S A WHOLE DAY'S WORK — DO YOU KNOW THAT?" There the conversation ended. Goldenberg would gain nothing arguing with Avrum, and he rushed away to his operators. Avrum figured that that would give him up to ten minutes' breathing space, and, pretending to get some sacks of odd cuttings out into the lane for Menasche the mattress maker, he slipped over to Horse's.

"You're going to handle a card game for me tonight, Abie. Y'up to it?" Horse was leading Avrum to the little stockroom in the back.

"What do I know about cards?" said Avrum as much to himself as to Horse.

"You don't got to know nothing about cards. Look, I got a game set up with four class millionaires — or practically millionaires. There's going to be Plotkin from the stock exchange, Millman and Pirelli the builders, and Jackson from the lumberyard. Four top calibers, but I know them, and they're all kinda nervous types. With you there standing over them, and them knowing you're my man, they won't worry about any funny monkey business — because the pots are going to be the fattest things you ever saw in your life."

"But what do I do, just stand there?"

"Nah, nah — you'll be there to see that everything runs smoothly. You'll get there early and set up the room nice. You'll make them coffee and sandwiches, as much as they want, and you'll have beer and a couple bottles of whiskey if they ask for it. Y'see here, I got everything — the folding table, the chairs, the box for the ice, the electric stove to make the coffee. Hank'll take you up with the stuff at five-thirty, and they'll start to roll in at about seven-thirty. I'm giving you this hotel key and you got the room number marked on it — *204*. I used it before and it's nice. Hank'll show up again between ten and eleven with more ice — you'll also need some of that to keep the butter hard. If you'll need more tomatoes and lettuce, he'll bring you them, and he'll be waiting to pick you up beginning at three in the morning."

"It won't finish until three?"

"He'll be waiting from three. It could finish at six, too."

There were more instructions, but Avrum had to rush back to the factory. "It's a platinum contract," said Horse, and Avrum thanked him and said that he'd handle it well, and that he'd be back at twelve to get down all the other details.

Pirelli was the first to come. Avrum answered his knock and was mildly taken aback by the tall, angular, elegantly dressed gentlemen who introduced himself. The man had a slow, intimate smile, but his eyes, small and deep under thick and wild eyebrows that stretched uninterrupted over the bridge of his nose, were coldly domineering and untrusting. They shook hands at the door, and Avrum asked him in.

The bridge table was set up in the middle of the floor and it was covered with a green felt cloth. Four chairs were set tightly around it, and next to two of them were floor-mounted ashtrays. Another cloth was stretched across the dresser, and on it, Avrum had arranged plates of sandwiches and a couple of bottles of Seagrams behind half a dozen whiskey glasses. Two boxes of ice were on the floor: one had cubes for the drinks, and the other was loaded with soft drinks, beer, vegetables, an extra pack of butter, mustard, and a wrapping of salami and cold salted beef. At the window, the drapes were drawn and another table was set up to one side, with the electric stove and coffee maker on it. Shiny spoons, a bowl of sugar cubes, a small jug of cream, and half a dozen of Horse's cups and saucers were arranged neatly around them. Also on the table, stacked one over the other, were five fresh packs of playing cards.

"Can I offer you anything?" This was a line Horse had made Avrum practice. "It's got to be class from beginning to end," he insisted, "and I trust you 'cause you're naturally respectful." *Naturally respectful* — Avrum had wondered ruefully if this wasn't more the reflection of a weakness than of strength. There was a soft knock at the door just then, and Pirelli said that he would help himself to some whiskey.

Millman was there with Jackson and Avrum recognized them. They would come to Horse's from time to time, never staying long, but Horse would always leave the counter to one of the regulars and sit with them until they left. There would always be smiles, pats on the shoulders, and long, firm handshakes. Millman wore a loose-fitting cream-colored jacket and a shirt with an open collar. No tie. No vest. Nothing stiff or formal. Jackson, the taller of the two, balding and with a heavy spreading waist, carried his jacket over his shoulder, and the delicate gold chain across the front of his vest stood out against the dark gray of the worsted cloth. Avrum also remembered him from Horse's, and Millman smiled at him, patted his arm, and asked how things were.

They noticed Pirelli, who Millman knew, and they walked over to have a drink with him. Avrum started to introduce them, but Millman cut him off and said that they were old friends. They shook hands after Millman introduced Jackson to Pirelli, and each silently evaluated the other. Their talk then turned to business and to the troubles in Europe.

It was almost eight when Plotkin showed up. He was a small man with quick eyes behind rimless glasses and tight, bluish lips. He couldn't have been much older than Avrum, but his manner bespoke a carelessness that only the monumentally self-assured could allow themselves. He wore a tired black vest, his trousers seemed oversized, his shirt undersized, and his tie — an arrangement of gaudy green and red patterns — fell too low. Altogether, he seemed very much outside the pale of the other three. He apologized for making them wait, hinted that a scandal was brewing at the bourse, and asked Avrum for a cup of black coffee to help him catch his breath. Horse had said that Avrum would recognize Solly Plotkin in an instant. "Imagine a stiff as a scarecrow and you got Solly."

They arranged themselves around the table and Avrum brought them a pack of cards. Millman tore off the wrapping, opened the package, and spread the cards evenly in a semi-circle.

“Gentlemen,” he said, and they each picked out a card. Jackson won the deal, but Pirelli took the first hand; he asked Avrum for a plate, into which he dropped two bills. Horse had told Avrum that a percent of every pot went to the house, but to let every winner do the figuring for himself. “And never, never let them see you count what they give you.” He also warned Avrum to stand where they could all see him, the point being that no one should have reason to suspect that he might be reacting to their cards — even in innocence.

Half an hour later, the plate had to be emptied. Avrum dumped the bills into the bag he brought for the bread, and replaced the plate on the table. By ten o’clock he was looking around for another bag, and when Hank showed up at a quarter to eleven with more ice, he remembered that Hank had an empty shoebox in the trunk of the car. Hank went to get it. At the same time, Plotkin had run out of cigarettes, and Avrum got Hank to buy a couple of flat fifties of Export A, Plotkin’s brand. Avrum asked the others if they needed anything, but they said no.

The windows had to be opened at ten o’clock to let the smoke out. By midnight, Avrum had prepared and served six rounds of sandwiches apparently to everyone’s liking, and only coffee was asked for now. Jackson was the big drinker, having put away almost a quarter of the Seagrams and following it with two beers, but one couldn’t tell it by looking at him. Plotkin, who started out badly, seemed to have straightened himself out by winning what so far had been the fattest pot of the evening. He was sitting with a flush while Pirelli and Jackson were banking on full houses. From where he stood, Avrum caught the forty dollars which Plotkin later dropped into the plate.

He also caught the remark that escaped Plotkin when he made his win. In the wake of a sigh, he muttered: “Like I say . . . the sky is always turning.” Avrum suddenly became as rigid as though an electrical charge had ripped through his body. When they’d done with the next hand, Avrum turned to him.

“Mr. Plotkin?”

“Yeah, Abie.”

"What you said — the sky is always turning. My mother used to say this to me." Instantly he regretted having opened his mouth. What answer could he have hoped to elicit?

"If I was you, I'd believe it. Me? I had to learn it on my bones the hard way." But then he scooped up the cards dealt him and another game got underway.

Avrum retreated.

After two a.m., he had only warm olives to offer them. The ice had melted and garbage had accumulated. Instead of messing with the toilet, which was in constant use, he deposited the garbage in one of the dresser's drawers. At three, Hank knocked discreetly at the door, but when he saw them still stuck fast at the table, he waited downstairs in the lobby for another hour and some until he saw the four of them leave. Avrum had set the table and chairs by the door, and by the light of a new day, they carried everything to the car and drove home.

He hadn't counted what he had in the shoebox, but at eight thirty, the box was in Horse's hands. When he came in again at his ten o'clock break, Horse slipped him a hundred and fifty dollars. "There are poker games and there are poker games, Mr. A.," he said smiling, "and I already got the word that this one went smooth as cream. I knew you were my man."

Avrum counted the money almost in disbelief. It wouldn't even fit comfortably into his pocket. But he was rich, and by the drift of things, he'd be getting even richer. "Another thing, Abie," added Horse. "I think you can use a good suit — something with a little class — maybe a gray stripe. And I also think you can afford to go to a class tailor now? You think about it. If you want an address, I'll give you the best."

* * *

Just before noon, Goldenberg handed him an envelope. It was an invitation to Shirley's wedding. Charlie, Strulevitch, and a couple of the operators also received invitations. Since the episode, she hadn't shown her face at work and Goldenberg had hired another girl — a Mrs. Bell, who owned and drove her own car — to take her place for a month or two. "Shirley will be back after the honeymoon," he promised.

Strulevitch confessed to Avrum that if he lived to be a hundred and twenty, he'd never understand what Norm saw in Shirley that would make him want to marry her. "Personally — and just between you and me — it would kill me to have to look at that face first thing every morning. Eh? But I got a feeling, Abie, that it's all a little stinky. Look at the date — it just squeezes a month. And how long could they have known each other? Eh? When a girl has a serious boyfriend, y'feel it, and with Shirley, I didn't feel it." He drew heavily on his cigar, grimaced and shook his head. Avrum decided to take Horse's suggestion and have a proper suit made up. He'd wear it to the wedding.

At noon, Avrum went upstairs to lie down. When he didn't come down by two o'clock, Goldenberg went up to see what was keeping him. Avrum needed hard shaking to wake up.

When he stepped into Horse's just before closing time, Avrum saw Solly Plotkin standing at the far end of the counter talking animatedly with Cy and Horse. He had barely stepped through the door when all three turned in his direction and almost as one called him over to them.

"Neat timing," said Cy through a half smile.

"Waddaya say, Mr. A.," Horse was shaking his head in mock resignation. "My establishment finally gets the honor of his royal ass," he nodded in Plotkin's direction, "and it turns out he comes just to see you. Me? I'm not worth it anymore?" Saying this, he followed up with a noise that was something between a jeer and a bark. Then he delivered a theatrical right cross at Plotkin's shoulder and went back behind the counter.

"Something to do with the game?" asked Avrum.

Plotkin made clucking noises with his tongue. "Nah, Abie. But I hear you made yourself a nice bundle. Next time, we go partners."

Horse, again from the sink where he started in washing dishes, "Yeah, n'he's buying me an oil well for my birthday. Fix you all a coffee? Hey — take a table, bums."

Plotkin turned his eyes very strangely on Avrum and studied him carefully. "Whereya from, Abie? I'm asking 'cause I got to clear up something in my mind."

"That's not an easy question. Until I came over, I worked in the forests around Szambor — Szambor, Lvov, Urman . . . was in Kiev . . . that part of the world"

"But where exactly were you born? I mean, where were you all the time as a kid?"

Avrum wondered how he could explain a village whose name, if it ever had one, he couldn't remember. Who had ever called it anything except *the Village*?

Plotkin didn't wait.

"Look, ninety-nine percent I'm climbing up the wrong tree, 'cause these things just don't happen these days. But at least I'll sleep better tonight. Listen. About a day's ride from Lvov, there used to be this village — a nothing *shteitle* — that got burned down. There was this pogrom — frigg'n Cossacks — y'know maybe something about it? All this goes back . . . oh, maybe fifteen, sixteen years, maybe more." Plotkin took a deep breath. "Had a little pisshole of a river in it."

Avrum felt his face grow hot, yet icy chills raked his body. He felt his mouth dry and his tongue thicken in his throat. His words came from somewhere deep within him. It wasn't his voice. "Yes. A little river."

No one moved.

"And could it be — could it be that you're Avremeleh? Hassia and Menachem's boy? You had — have — a brother . . . Hersheleh? Crissake, don't tell me no."

Studying Avrum, who sat frozen in his chair, Sol Plotkin's eyes burned with an unnatural intensity. There was the first glistening of tears appearing in their corners.

"Yeah . . . I'm Hassia's boy." Avrum nodded. He felt his lips trembling. "But Solly? Solly Plotkin?"

"Try Shloimke. D'you remember a kid who once tried to drown himself?"

"Shloimke? Shloimke Plotkin!" Yes, he remembered everything. But how . . . ? How . . . ? In Avrum's head, there were as many questions as there were stars in the sky. His heart raced madly. His eyes watered, and thick humors suddenly drained from his nostrils. He turned away and blew his nose in a napkin.

The two looked at each other almost in disbelief. The longest moment passed, and in that moment, the world stood still for both of them. The moment after that found them locked tightly in each other's arms. Solly Plotkin wailed like an infant. Avrum, his eyes shut tightly and his head pressing against *Shloimke*'s, was back in the village.

Solly Plotkin, his face beet red now, shifted restlessly in his chair. He related to the small crowd that had gathered around them about his attempted suicide on his Bar Mitzvah day. But soon, he shifted to an encounter that followed it. "This boy had a mother . . . had — I mean, the pogrom got her too, no?" His eyes never left Avrum's face.

Avrum nodded. *Could all this be real? Could all this be happening?* he wondered.

"Well, like you see him . . . this boy — this Mr. Hercules here — had a mother like it would be impossible to describe. The closest thing to a saint — a woman smarter and holier than anyone you will meet in a lifetime. She put all your great *mayvinim* in her back pocket. Y'see, here I am wishing the end of the world to come when she walks into the house, takes me aside, and has this talk with me. I'll remember it 'til I die. 'Shloimke,' she says, 'the world changes from one day to the next. Today, something is black — tomorrow, it's white. *The sky is always turning*.' That's what she kept saying over and over . . . the sky is always turning. 'Whoever is up today can be down tomorrow. And the opposite. I promise things will change for you and your turn will come. *I promise*. It's as sure as summer comes after winter.' I remember every word and the sound of every word.

"So here is your Abie stopping me when I said 'The sky is always turning,' telling me his mother used to say the same thing — and I didn't put two and two together until I got home. Then I think, nah, it can't be. But her kid's name was Avrum, *Avremeleh* they called him, and he was five or six years younger than me. Coincidence? Should I believe in coincidence? So sleep was out of the question until I got this straightened out. And now . . . here I am from the dead, and here he is from the dead."

"I thought just me and my brother, Hershel, got out."

But Solly Plotkin couldn't veer from his own mind's tracks. "Why do you think I remember your mother? My father couldn't stand my guts, so he sends me to his brother, who was a lumber agent in Minsk, and through him, I pick up about banking and stock markets besides lumber. Meanwhile, the village gets erased, all my father's money helps him now like *bankis* help the dead, and I'm the only one from there who stayed alive. At least, I thought I was the only one. What about your brother?"

"He's alive, too, somewhere."

"Where?"

And Avrum told his story.

Horse had them all put down a shnapps. There was a lot of vigorous handshaking and talk of the future, but when Plotkin later walked out to his car, Avrum was suddenly overcome with the feeling that somehow he'd been cheated. As though Shloimke had stolen from him. What was there to steal? What came to take shape in his mind was that Shloimke had occupied Hershel's space, and had violated the only true reunion that mattered in his life.

Until his arm would link with Hershel's, his life would be half a shadow. Even two fingers can make a hand work, but a hand with only one finger is a hand with no fingers. It only mocks its owner.

Solly Plotkin would never know his crime.

(20)

Strulevitch led Avrum through an alley off lower Dorchester Boulevard, past Saint Hubert and across a scrap iron yard to the back of a row of black and red buildings. At one of these, he turned into some stairs, which climbed to a splintering gray door on the second landing. There was a lot of scrawling on the bricks, in chalk, crayon, and maybe pencil, but there was nothing that might have given a clue as to what went on behind the door. Strulevitch tried the handle and it turned. The heavy, almost noxious smell of old sweat and stale air hit them right there at the threshold, and when they crossed it, they found themselves virtually in another world.

They heard thuds and thumping, a lot of wheezing, and a lot of grunting. Thin mats covered about half the floor space, and ten or fifteen wet bodies were exercising strenuously on them. Most were working in pairs, pushing and pulling with their arms locked and their heads pressing into each others' shoulders. Benches had been set near the walls, and lying on a couple of them were men heaving barbells off their chests. Behind the benches running up the walls were wooden exercise racks; a few boys were working out on these. With them was a short, stocky black man whose head was so bald and polished it reflected the ceiling lights. He was barrel-chested and powerfully built, with thick rippling biceps, which explained why the sleeves of his shirt were torn off.

"That there's Zed Chicago," said Strulevitch, pointing. They walked over to him, and Chicago, who had seen them come in, had a last word with the boys before he stepped away to meet them.

"Let me guess hard which one of you is supposed to be the wrestler," he said by way of greeting. But he wasn't smiling. They shook hands and Strulevitch introduced Avrum.

"Yeah," pouted Zed Chicago, rocking his body from side to side, as though not having quite given up on his exercising. "I had a couple words with Horse. He says the kid should be good material, and I tol' him I'll look'im over." There was a pause while Chicago seemed to be trying to straighten something out in his mind. They waited, and Chicago looked at the floor. "Y'ever in your life done any wrestling, fella?" he asked, his head still down.

"No." A fleeting image of himself squared off against the lumbermen of Zhitomir and Urman came to him — but that was hardly wrestling.

"Yeah, got'ya." Chicago shook his head. "But y'know I got to tell y'fellas what seems to me Horse don' wanna hear." He looked up at them now and Strulevitch began to chew hard on his cigar. "I mean, I can see even through the clothes that the body's got the dimensions, n' if y'stick to a minimum trainin' schedjul, y'can probably in a month or two take on most of the bums and punks awready in the game. Yeah, but Horse tells me no farts — that what he got in mind is f'me to bring his Mr. A. up to the main events. So I try t'tell 'im that some of the boys are hard pokers up there — that it ain't a class for a part time this and a part time that, if y'get my drift. Y'unnerstand, it's the money class, and the joes in there are damn hungry. When they're that way, they're mean shits, and when they're mean shits, y'need more than just a good body t'keep up wid'em."

"Yeah, but there are other things, eh?" said Strulevitch, who had a need to spit, but swallowed it instead. "Like being serious. A guy with no brains can be mean and rough. But Abie here is as hungry as the rest of them — just a few years off the boat, no mother, no father, no uncles, lives by himself in a room, works ten hours a day just to pay for the rent and groceries. What more does he need to be hungry like them, eh? Fact is, he's hungrier than all of them together. And he can be bloody rough — three bum punks broke into his boss's place in the middle of the night and the kid y'see here in fron' of you went in there alone and broke their *cojones*. He ties them all up together and the police came just to collect the package. So I know he's rough enough. Eh? But when y'add that he got a head and that you're working with someone serious, then y'got someone who's made for the top class. That's a fact!"

"Well, that's what you say. What does he say?" Chicago angled his head toward Avrum.

Avrum hesitated and shrugged. "I think I can learn."

"Y'think," repeated Chicago, insinuating some doubt.

"What more do you want? Eh? He wants to learn, he's ready to learn, he's got the head to learn, he's got the weight, he's got the size, he's got you, and he's got us." Strulevitch marveled at his own eloquence and Chicago seemed to bend.

"I never said no. But I figure — when was Horse the last time at the Arena? What does he really know about the business that he can tell me his boy is top shit material?"

"Yeah," said Strulevitch, his face lost in a cloud of his cigar smoke, "but y'still won't be disappointed."

Chicago wasn't finished. "I was thinking if Horse ever saw a guy like Tigerman McDougal working someone over — or this Gerry Alaska. They got the muscle, and they're where they are because they come on like butchers."

"We've seen McDougal. And Abie here — the way he's standing here right now, eh? He could have taken him."

"Maybe . . . maybe . . . at least y'built for the racket," he said to Avrum, jabbing a finger into Avrum's board-like belly. "C'mon after me t'the lockers and we'll see what's available there."

Chicago took ten dollars as a month's advance, and fixed Mondays, Wednesdays, and Thursdays between seven to nine as Avrum's time with him. "Start missing days, start comin' late n'I wash my hands."

"It'll work out," said Strulevitch. "Y'got a real serious boy here in your stable."

"Yeah? Well, we'll see. Anyways, I gotta move now." He backed away.

"Thanks for your trouble, Zed," said Strulevitch. Avrum mumbled his own thanks. Outside, Strulevitch had to stop every yard or two to spit. "It was killing me inside, but from the way I know him, he'd make me lick it up if I spit on his floor."

Avrum wasn't listening. Chicago was the first black man he had ever had words with, and his peculiar strangeness mildly unnerved him. Somewhere, he felt sorry for Chicago being black. At the same time, he tried to accommodate the fact that this man and his uninviting place would be the focus of his steps along another blind road in his life. He kept silent for most of the way home.

* * *

Avrum complained to Kapitolnik that the spells did not seem to be working.

"If that's the case, then we can take it as a fact that your brother doesn't go now by the name you gave me. He's changed his first name or his last name, or both. It happens every day. The newcomer steps off the boat, but he leaves his name behind in the old world — thinks a new name and a new suit will bring new luck. Sometimes they're right."

"So what's next? Is it hopeless?"

"Nothing is hopeless. Nothing! And nothing is wasted." Kapitolnik frowned and pressed his lips tightly together, showing his annoyance and impatience. "For instance, your own mystic number happens also to be eight, so that the lead and the mercury must definitely have gotten their vibrations into you. If you did everything I told you, then they fixed your own spirit so that it is in perfect harmony with the stars. Tell me the truth — things have been working out well for you lately or not? In a word, say yes or no."

"Better than well. Money is falling on me from everywhere."

"So it's yes . . . so it's yes. Today, you can leave me two dollars." But then Kapitolnik sighed and shook his head. "Only *SHABBTAI* will see that you don't enjoy it. That's the way this planet is made."

"Why? I'm enjoying it."

"Oh, yes? We'll see! *SHABBTAI* is the great stone hanging an inch over your head."

Kapitolnik ran his long and bony fingers through his hair and fixed his black box-shaped skullcap carefully over it. This seemed to reassure him about who he was and how certain he could be about the knowledge he was partner to. Speaking with absolute conviction, he continued. "It never likes to see anybody happy or silly. The men born to *SHABBTAI* are the world's greatest survivors and they live to old age, but they live with gloom like a second skin except for one period of seven years every twenty-eight years. If the people prepare themselves for these seven years by working hard for the twenty-one years before them, well, I can tell you that they are promised the best from heaven. But it means hard work, very hard work and no playing — no monkey business."

Avrum waited, not sure he was making sense of what Kapitolnik was telling him.

"The trick — the whole trick — is not to fight your fate, not to fight the reason you were brought into the world. And this could be cleaning garbage or writing books."

"Wrestling, too, maybe?"

"Wrestling? I don't know what wrestling is. But if it brings you higher up in the world — that's your sign. It should feel like a key in the keyhole made for it. If you know it is your purpose in this lifetime you will do it well and everything that belongs to you will come to you. But if you try to force your fate — to rush it, to take a different direction — *SHABBTAI* will crush you like a cockroach. This way, your brother will only run from you."

"How can I know if *SHABBTAI* meant for me to be a wrestler?"

"*SHABBTAI* always makes his will very, very clear. You will be sucked into his dark world one way or another. But face this world with your chest out, not with your back bent." Kapitolnik touched his forehead and shook his finger as if to brush away what they were talking about.

"What about the seven years?"

"Yes. To work out exactly when these seven years begin takes complicated and twisting calculations. It has to account for the north-south alignment of the bed you were born on. And the difference between this and the North Pole gets converted from a measure of degrees to a measure of time."

"I understand nothing."

"I'm not telling you this so you should understand. I'm telling you this so you should hear." Kapitolnik's impatience was reflected as much in his eyes as in his voice. "And there is still a lot more, because over this pattern are two more — the time of your conception backwards to the true middle of summer, and the day of your birth forward to the true middle of winter."

"This is not a language I understand. Can you just tell me if you know when those seven years are supposed to begin?"

"What I have to work out is nothing less than a geometric progression of space and time on three dimensions and then work out the same for *SHABBTAI, ZEDEK*, and the sun. This will cost three dollars. Did I say two before? It should be three."

"You're asking for another three dollars to give me this answer?"

"If you didn't have for bread, I would make it five cents, but now if you have money, maybe it's thanks to me."

Avrum was trying to collect his thoughts and offered no reply. Kapitolnik continued.

"I have a special wheel — my own invention," he said. "I work it with one of my canaries and it gives me all the details which are lost to you — like the alignment of the bed, the date of your conception . . . everything."

With that, he reached under the desk and produced a narrow bamboo cage that had a wheel in it. Around the wheel were cup-shaped strips of leather, and the whole arrangement was able to turn freely. Kapitolnik cleared room on his desk for it and then fetched a canary from another room, which he slipped inside. There was no room anywhere for the canary except on the wheel, which it caused to turn. Avrum was made to spread his fingers over the cage, and Kapitolnik poured sand through them from a jar. The sand — some of it, at least — landed on the leather pieces, and the new weight affected the turning of the wheel. When the last of the sand was poured and the frightened bird calmed down, the wheel stopped turning and Kapitolnik checked its position.

"Now, go for a smoked meat sandwich," he said, "and come back in an hour."

An hour later — an hour to the minute — Avrum was back. Kapitolnik started right in.

"*SHABBTAI* is cruel and unforgiving, but *ZEDEK* is being very generous with you. In fact, another man would give his right arm to have *ZEDEK* over him the way you have. But what *ZEDEK* gives, *SHABBTAI* takes away. Until . . ." Kapitolnik cleared his throat, "until *MADIM* finally pushes *SHABBTAI* out of the picture. Never for very long, mind you, but sometimes it's just long enough."

"So, that's good?"

"Except that *MADIM* is your strength and your health. In neutralizing *SHABBTAI*, it weakens itself dangerously. Black *SHABBTAI* literally drains it of everything."

"Does that mean that I will die? I have no chance?"

"Ordinarily, yes. For anybody else, it would be the end. But this is the point — it just happens that it is also the mark of your entrance into the seven good years, so there is a very good chance that you come out of this dangerous time in one piece. Personally, I think you will live to a hundred and twenty."

"Do I find Hershel by then?"

"Definitely! I was never more sure of anything in my whole life."

"Only one simple question. Can you tell me when?"

"When? I'll tell you when. You have a simple question, so I give you a simple answer. When you have climbed to your lowest and fallen to your highest. This is your sign. You will recognize it when it happens. I can tell you nothing more. I can know nothing more. Now go. You have no more business with me."

Kapitolnik seemed to have withered.

(21)

In the morning, a letter from Fanny arrived. Avrum felt his heart race. He pulled up a chair at the shipping table and took it out to read, but when Strulevitch positioned himself where he, too, could see it, Avrum angled the chair back against the radiator and balanced himself on its two back legs. The handwriting was small and tight, but easy to read.

"Dear Abie,

"I am surprising you, I know. I hope you are well, but I'll get right to the reasons for writing this letter.

"It's not a secret that I'm living with my friend Harry Weiss — that is his address at the top of the letter. (Avrum couldn't stop himself from blushing, and Strulevitch made some comment about a law against sending dirty things in the mail.) "*But I imagine that you can't understand why I am telling you this, and it is possible that I don't entirely understand why, myself. Still, I'll open my thoughts to you, if only because I feel that you won't judge me or think bad of me, whatever I may say or do. Am I wrong?*

"There is something in me which says that a lie is just that — no matter what reasons, excuses, facts, and what-have-you dress it up to make it look like the best thing in the world. The list of such lies stretches from today to every tomorrow, and when I think of them — when I think of how they invade every minute and every move in my life — I feel choked . . . suffocated. And I don't have to tell you that a drowning man is dangerous to anyone who goes out to save him.

"But what are these lies? In a word, they are all the lies against nature. The first one comes when the mother slaps at her baby's hand when she finds it playing with his pee-pee. She tells him that if he'll keep playing with himself, it will be cut off, or that it will fall off and that his body will rot. ROT!! Did you know that some mothers actually paint spots of iodine on their boys' bellies at night as a sign of the rot, as 'proof' to show their kids that they were secretly playing with themselves? I tell you Abie, the iodine fades away in a day or two, but the child's mind is stained for the rest of its life. And only in smallest details is the story different with girls. Imagine how insanely criminal it is to poison the most sensitive and delicate minds on the lie that anything having to do with their sex is filthy, evil, dangerous, dirty, and, maybe worst of all, against God. Against God! Sex is probably the only gift he blessed us with.

"And from here, the lies spread in every direction. So it is honest and respectable to wear the uniform of the post office and spend forty years delivering other people's mail. It is respectable to wear a police uniform and put people who can't

pay their bills in jail. And observe how uniforms are the tools that control our lives. Do you know of two people who are made the same — who feel the same way about the same things? So in the schools, the uniforms are in the form of clothes. But the lessons are uniforms, too. Outside the schools, they take the form of the newspapers and the radio. Everything is dictated from some 'greater' superior authority that has no connection, real connection, with the individual; and the poor individual, to keep a grip on what he calls his sanity, to keep out of the insane asylum, he bends and keeps rebending his brain until even his own personal signature becomes a forgery!

"Would you believe me if I told you that as different as you are, many of the things I see in Harry are somehow there in you, too? Maybe this is the reason I am writing you. And I know this with a sense that often tells me more than my eyes and ears."

Avrum felt helpless in the face of her language and convictions, and suspected that the tools to answer her at her level were well beyond him. He looked up from the letter and wondered if her true intention was to confront him with his own intellectual limitations. Shame and regret touched him. He had never felt driven to exercise with a richer English vocabulary, nor with any esoteric ideas that were divorced from any immediate bearing on his physical existence, and all this seemed to matter terribly now. It mattered that his back had so totally overtaken his mind in their race for his attentions. Now someone like Fanny might regard him with honest contempt for being little more than a machine that others had made and that others would order about.

Bella had once complained that Fanny read too many books for her own good. "I can't call them dumb books," she had granted grudgingly, "but they are turning her brains into a wishy-washy *plotchkeh*. And not only won't they wash the dishes for her, but they won't even buy her dishes." Avrum suspected that on Fanny's list of essentials, dishes, if they'd be included at all, would be squeezed in very near the bottom — possibly ahead of hats.

Strulevitch broke into his thoughts, asking him to collect some styles and sizes from the finishers and to staple together another few boxes. Avrum saw Goldenberg closing in on Charlie, and expected that the shipping table would be his next station. He busied himself for half an hour until Strulevitch was appeased and Goldenberg had taken Florence and a salesman from one of the textile mills into the showroom. Then he returned to Fanny's letter; there was a page and a half left.

"Harry says that because his own life began as an unfortunate eviction from death (his exact words) — read again the word 'unfortunate' — and if that is so, he sees no obligation to lend his soul to the scalpel of any social order. At the end, he says, he'll go back to his death (like everyone else), only his days will have been entirely his own.

"Like you, I think, and like thousands of others who managed to get across from Europe, Harry lost his family when he was a child. Eventually, he went to live in a monastery somewhere in New Jersey. But he lives waiting for death to come and collect him a second time. And this act of waiting is an act of devotion to the inevitable. Everything about his life is given to devotion, which so perfectly explains why he likes the monastery.

"How are you like Harry then, when he has a different religion, lives alone, paints alone, writes alone, drinks heavily (also alone), and you do none of these? You are also more than five times his size, but in both of you, there is the same sadness. In your own ways, you have preserved an honesty and innocence, even a purity, which is so precious to me — and, yes, I confess, this attracts me.

"When Harry came to see me, he came from the monastery. When we are together, it is sometimes in the room he rents in Newark. At this moment, I am alone in a flat in Flatbush, (sounds funny — a flat in Flatbush) waiting for him. I can only chance a guess as to whether he'll return — maybe in an hour, maybe in a year. But I am sure that you are well, and though it bothers me to admit it, I am curious to know if there is anything between you and Bella. I can't tell you why I think there might be, but I'm asking all the same. For now, I'll put my pen down and walk over to the post office."

Hugging the last line was her small tight signature, and under the weight of everything above it, it was easy to miss.

* * *

In the afternoon, Bella called Avrum at work, ostensibly to apologize for having cut short their last "wonderful" walk. She said she couldn't say how sorry she was, and Avrum said that it was alright. Unable to contain himself, he added that since that walk, he had practically doubled the amount of money he had shown her, and she let out a sharp squeal of joy. She was proud of him, she said; now he was more than rich — he was wealthy. And when there was nothing more to say, Avrum asked if she wouldn't like meeting him again after work for another walk. She agreed at once.

It was Friday, and they both felt the exquisite lightness that came with the shedding of another week of work. They met somewhere on Fletcher's field, instinctively reaching out for the other's hand even before a word had passed between them, and they turned west toward the two great stone lions at the foot of Mount Royal. Behind the statues, they found a road leading into the mountain, and which probably led up to Beaver Lake. Afterwards, they turned into a soft path that branched away from the road and weaved between the light forest of maple trees.

Bella began to talk about her boss and how much everyone depended on her in the factory. By her own accounting, the place would long have closed without her. She gossiped about some of the girls who worked with her, and embellished the stories with her instant judgments. At times, she seemed to blush — mostly when the stories supposedly touched on intimate details, for she evaded being explicit about anything by letting suggestive nuances, like her blushes, fill the blank spaces. But without words that would bind the actual accounts, Avrum's imagination carried her hints like a hurricane would a balloon. Silent waves of heat crossed between them, and a mood of closeness pressed them subtly to the earth.

Bella put a hand over her breast and pretended to be exhausted. "Oh, Abie, I'm all out of breath. I think that from Park Avenue, we have been climbing all the time."

Avrum was understanding. He faced her, smiled, and suggested that he carry her, and Bella wasn't sure that he wasn't serious. She held back a doubting reply, possibly suspecting that as strong as he was, she was too heavy for anyone to lift.

"Maybe," she said, looking away, "I'll give you a chance some day. But let's sit somewhere. No one is rushing us today."

She broke away from him and walked a few yards to a tree, where she tried as gracefully as possible to sit down. A long, aching sigh escaped her, and when that was over, she arranged her dress so that nothing under it was exposed. Avrum hesitated only the smallest fraction of a moment before he stepped onto the grass to join her. They were quite alone where they were. Despite the climb, they could still see down between the trees to the traffic moving along Park Avenue, but the noise didn't reach them. In their minds, they were comfortable with the feeling that eyes wouldn't reach them, either.

"I have a surprise," said Bella. "You won't think I'm terrible if I show you?"

"I would think the opposite."

"How could you be so sure if you don't know what it is?"

"I just know."

"And what if you change your mind?"

"I promise I won't."

Bella blushed, half smiled, and looked at Avrum uncertainly. Then she opened her purse, inspected its insides for a second, and fished out a cigarette and a small box of matches.

"One of the girls gave it to me — Sonia, the one whom I told you changes into a pleated scotch skirt whenever she wants to be with her boyfriend."

"I remember." And Avrum blushed, recalling how Bella explained how the skirt opened up. "But you know how to smoke?"

"Let's try it, Abie."

"Oh, I smoked before."

"I never saw you."

"Well, I didn't like it very much."

"Do you think I'm terrible? A Jewish girl smoking like a *shiksa*?"

"Just the opposite. If you want, we can have a smoke together."

"I'm a little afraid. What if it's going to make me want to smoke all the time?"

"Bella," said Avrum with authority, "it can't happen from one cigarette. Not from one, and not from two."

"I hope so. Do you want to go first? Come on, Abie, you go first."

Bella struck a match and he lit the cigarette much like Strulevitch would light his cigars. He tried to swallow some of the smoke, but it choked him at once, and he coughed out a cloud. It was a loud, racking cough. Bella said that maybe the brand was too strong and she reached out gingerly to try one herself. "You hold it like this?" she asked, fitting it between her index and middle fingers. Avrum nodded, feeling disappointed at his own failure. To his amazement, he watched her inhale easily and throw her head back as she let the smoke out in a long, smooth flow. For an instant, the cigarette seemed the most natural thing in her hand.

"Hey, that was very good," he exclaimed, applauding.

"Really? It burned my throat a little."

"Did you like it?"

"It was marvelous and fantastically relaxing."

Saying this, she absently dropped a hand onto his lap and a tremor passed through him. He couldn't move, and to his horror, he felt himself fast growing hard only inches away from her fingers. But Bella seemed absorbed only in her cigarette and she wasn't looking at him.

"I'm going to try it again," she said.

This time, she inhaled deeply and kept the smoke in her lungs for a long time. Finally, she let it out, sending a faint stream though her nostrils. She looked quietly down at her shoes for a moment, and then squirmed into a prone position with only her head now against the tree. For this, she had to press into Abie's thigh.

"Oh, this is really sooo, soooo relaxing. No wonder it can get to be a habit."

Avrum looked down at her and saw that she had closed her eyes. He reached over and took the cigarette from her fingers, and quietly practiced inhaling. It choked him again at first, and he didn't enjoy the taste much, but finally he worked it down and exhaled. The coughing persisted. Then he felt his head spin, and, trying not to disturb her hand, which was still on his thigh, he dropped more onto his back. But he felt her take her hand away anyway, and his heart sank.

Suddenly she began to murmur, as though to herself. "Oh, Abie…Abie." Her lips continued to move as though she were in some kind of delirium. The blood rushed to his face, and he turned closer to her and touched her waist. At the same time, she reached for his head and pressed it between her neck and her shoulder. Avrum thought that this was how the wrestlers usually squared off against each other, but the sweet and delicate perfume that rose to his nostrils carried him back to her body. His own body was contorted and twisted awkwardly as though different parts of it disagreed stubbornly on what position to settle on. He needed his hands to support himself, but however he dared move, they would rub against her breasts, which now seemed to have spread everywhere.

"Oh, Abie," she moaned hotly. "I can feel something happening."

"Yeah," he muttered, still trying to find where to put his hands.

"You really feel it too?"

"Yeah." He kissed her neck and it struck him that this was the first time he had ever kissed a girl. He liked it enough to want more.

Likely, with all the pressing and rubbing at her neck, she hadn't felt his lips, but they had smacked loud enough for her to hear, and she sighed and seemed to sink deeper into the grass. From far below came the faintest sounds of traffic, but at that moment, the two belonged to another planet.

Avrum shifted his lips to her chin, not yet daring to move higher, and he kissed her again feeling a hair slip out from between his teeth.

"What do you feel, Abie? Tell me." Now she kissed him on his temple.

"What do *you* feel, Bella?" he asked under his breath as he kissed her again — this time near the corner of her mouth.

"I asked you first." She had her hand in his hair, pressing, pressing, and when he found her lips, she waited for him.

They kissed until they were out of breath, and only then did Avrum realize that his hand had found a place at the side of her left breast. It felt soft and impossibly holy in its secrets. The excitement proved more potent to his senses than his will could endure, and his passion spilled in pulsing waves — with everything discharging into his underwear. He stiffened uncomfortably, and she wrapped her arms around him tightly.

"Oh, you *do* — don't you, Abie?"

"Bella . . ."

"Oh, tell me, Abie . . . tell me . . . tell me." They were embracing fully now and half rolling in the grass.

"I like you, Bella."

"Just *like*?"

"More than like . . . I . . . I . . ."

"Oh, I know you do . . . I know. Because I do."

"You do?"

"Oh, Abie . . . tell me what you say in your heart."

"I say . . . I *love* you."

It came out in a breathless whimper, but the words exploded in his ears. Dimly, he remembered Strulevitch warning him about telling a girl you love her. "Most of the time," he said, "it's your pecker doing the talking while your head is on vacation." Nevertheless, the words flooded his mind, and now he couldn't say them often enough.

"Bella, oh, Bella, I love you . . . I really love you." He kissed her wherever his lips found her. "I love you, Bella."

"Oh, Abie, I think I *always* loved you."

"And I love you."

"Did you always love me, Abie? I mean secretly . . . from the very beginning?"

"From the train, you mean? Or from when we first bumped into each other in the pictures?"

Bella grimaced slightly. "With me," she said, "it began with our first walk. I knew in my heart it would come to this."

"I think it was the same with me, too." A cold wetness started spreading down his legs and Avrum suddenly became terrified that it would show through his pants. He looked at himself, but there was no stain yet.

"Will we always love each other, you think?" she asked. "I feel — I feel so helpless with you. I feel you could do with me anything you want to." Her *anything* began to play havoc with his mind. "Everything and anything — I just trust you, Abie . . . I just trust you."

Avrum wondered if *everything and anything* really meant everything and anything. He felt himself getting excited again. Self-consciously, he set his hand again on her breast, and she moaned and covered his hand with hers. Then she opened a few buttons, and he was touching her brassiere under her slip. Bella worked her hand in next to his and lifted a cup away from one breast.

"Kiss it," she whispered throatily.

It was too much. When his eyes caught the massive pinkish brown nipple and his lips touched the soft, warm skin, a second powerful discharge blasted into his underwear. He felt it down to his toes.

On Saturday night, they went to the movies, and on Sunday afternoon, they joined the young couples strolling along Park Avenue. Avrum felt the street was theirs.

(22)

On his way to the gym, Avrum stopped at a few stores and outfitted himself with a pair of high black sport shoes, woolen stockings, red-and-white sport shorts, and a soft gray sweatshirt. He found it too embarrassing to ask outright for the contraption Strulevitch called a jock strap, and he decided to let that wait for another time. From home, he had brought a towel, a comb, some brilliantine, and a bar of castile soap, so that when Zed Chicago opened a locker and told him that the key to it was his, and when minutes later, he saw all his own things filling it, he felt attached almost organically to the place — the smells notwithstanding. The sights and the sounds surrounding him were all still very foreign experiences for him, yet inwardly he knew — without satisfaction, yet also without regrets — that he would soon get to wear them like his skin.

When Chicago saw Avrum come out dressed and ready to begin, he kidded him for looking like an advertisement "for anything you want — from milk to toothpaste." Avrum felt strong and healthy in the outfit. He said so, and said also that he missed feeling his muscles strain hard against something like they once did with lumber. Chicago said that he wanted first to see how he breathed, and told him to circle the room fifty times in an easy run. Fifteen minutes of light calisthenics followed that, and Avrum felt a comfortable elasticity working into his joints. Then Chicago asked if he was up to running another fifty without a rest, and Avrum took off without answering.

After ten or fifteen times around, however, his lungs had to struggle hard for air, his legs began to weigh heavier with every stride, and near his twentieth turn, Chicago shouted to him to break to twenty-five walking and twenty-five sprinting. When the sprints dragged, Chicago changed it to thirty walking, ten sprinting, and the fifty rounds were finally done. Avrum dropped onto one of the mats and Chicago came over immediately and reached for his wrist. A minute or two later, he counted his pulse again, and a smile cracked into his cheeks.

"Well, kid," he said, "maybe — just maybe — I'll be able to work with you."

Later, Chicago led him to the weights; from there, he called over a bushy and burly fellow named Leon, who was having someone throw medicine balls at his stomach. Leon explained and demonstrated how the weights were supposed to be lifted, and he moved them in an easy, polished style, which Avrum would copy. Avrum handled them awkwardly at first, but when Leon pointed out a fault in his timing and Chicago forcibly straightened his back a few times, his motions smoothened out and became more fluid with every try. Soon, he was asking to handle the heavier, "professional" weights, but Chicago said that if he ever caught him using anything heavier than what he personally allowed, he'd have him out on his ass.

"I know you Jews think you cornered the market on brains, but muscles are still my territory. Work the wrong way with even half a pound too much, and you'll be walking crooked the rest of your life. I'm not going to be the one responsible for that."

Avrum was stung. "I wasn't going to touch more than what you gave me. But when did you hear me say that Jews have all the brains?"

"All the brains and all the money," came a loud, hard voice behind them.

They spun around; seeing who it was, a mean look crossed Chicago's face. For Avrum, the figure was somehow too well dressed and too formal to have any business in a gym.

"You don't understand the King's English, Freddie?" Chicago said acidly. "I told you, I got an allergy to your shadow in here, and this is my place, so scram. Find the door, OK? I don't want no trouble from you right now."

The man had ice in his unmoving eyes, and there was nothing warm in the hard smile turning at the corners of his mouth.

"Hey, hey, Mr. Zed. This is the example you're giving this nice gentleman of a nigger's hospitality? Georgie himself will be up in a minute, and I promised him you'll even invite us for a cup of coffee. Now you're not going to make a liar out of me, are you?"

"Get the goddamn hell out of here, Freddie. Someone is going to piss on you one day."

"You think maybe it'll be from a bum punk like you, Mr. Zed?"

Freddie never broke his smile, and he half turned his back to them — like a matador taunting a wounded bull.

Avrum wondered what great advantage Chicago enjoyed in all his thick rolls of muscles if he could let a flea like this Freddie make him out to be so impotent. Leon walked away and Freddie laughed at his back. Avrum became agitated and impatient.

"Look, Mister . . . ummmm, Freddie," he began. "You're breaking up my lesson."

"Did I hear you talking to me, fella?" Freddie turned to Avrum and seemed concerned. He looked around the hall in mock innocence, pointing a finger at himself.

"I was," said Avrum, "and I asked you why you're not leaving. Mister Chicago runs the place, and he asked you to go. So why don't you go?"

"*Mister* Chicago — OK, you know what? I'll be real nice to you. I'll give you 'til ten to get out of here yourself. I'm going to count till ten, and then, if I still see you anywhere in here," he pulled a small snub-nosed pistol out from under his jacket, "I'll let this continue the nice discussion we're having, OK? I'm fair, or not fair?"

Avrum froze and looked at Chicago. Now he understood.

"Can it, Freddie — I don't want these games here," said Chicago, starting forward nervously. But Freddie motioned with his hand for him to stay away. He began to count. Avrum faced him less than a yard away, and at "five" he still hadn't moved. His eyes were locked on the gun, as though he couldn't understand what was happening. With fear clinging to his words, Chicago urged him to break for the door.

". . . six . . . seven . . ." Freddie's knuckles were whitening. ". . . eight . . ."

He never got to nine. Unseen and unexpected, Avrum's fist lifted like a cannonball from his side and seemed to explode in Freddie's face. The gun flew from his hands, and Freddie was on the floor in a pool of blood. He brought his hands to his face, and soon they, too, were awash with blood. Leon was the first to react, and he laughed. But then the door opened and no one moved. Two equally formal and dark-suited figures stepped in, and, on seeing Freddie writhing on the floor, drew guns. That same moment, Avrum had reached down for Freddie's pistol, grabbed it, and raced with it back to the lockers. The first one who walked in was about to shoot at Avrum's back, but the second man told him to hold off and pulled his arm back.

"Now, now," said the second man to Chicago. "How do you let a thing like this happen in such a respectable establishment? I thought you ran a square place?"

"I try to, but your bum Freddie? He farts from his yap. He pulled a gun on the kid there. He knows from nothing — it's his first time here — and there is your Freddie sticking a gun in his face. So the kid is fast and lets him have it. He don't know you, and he never saw Freddie before in his life, so what does Freddie have to pull a gun for?"

"Alright, alright . . . go in to him there and tell him that no one is going to do anything to him. Freddie always had this blood pressure problem, y'know, so this bleeding a little is actually going to do him some good. Go in there and get the gun back from him. I'm a quiet man, Zed, you know that, and my business is too serious for a stupid circus like this. Tell the kid there that I apologize, and that you and him have my word that he can walk out of here quiet."

"Georgie, that's your word."

"You got it, and everybody heard it."

"Yeah, but how do I convince the kid you'll keep it?"

"He knows and you know that if we were going to shoot, we'd have done it before he got to the gun. But I tell you, all this is bad business. It just gets in my way."

"'I'll talk to him."

Chicago turned to the locker room, and a moment later, he came back and told Georgie to get himself and the other fellow across to the other side of the room — that Abie would hold on to the gun until he got to the door, then he'd give it up to him.

Georgie nodded and said fair enough. Chicago called to Avrum, and Avrum stepped out slowly, keeping the pistol well ahead of him. He was as white as a sheet. Then Avrum and Georgie saw each other. The color came back to Avrum's face, and he seemed uncertain, flustered, but not scared. Then Georgie approached him and Avrum waited, but he had already handed the gun to Chicago.

Georgie was Grigor.

* * *

They stood wordlessly facing each other. Then they embraced for a long time. No one quite understood exactly what was happening — least of all Freddie, who, while still on the floor, watched Grigor approach him after separating himself from Avrum. An instant later, he felt Grigor's hard polished shoe dig swiftly and heavily into his mouth and nose. Freddie pulled the covers over his agony and surrendered his consciousness to the blackest night. A few teeth spilled to the floor. These quickly got lost in the pool of blood that had been collecting around Freddie's face.

Grigor invited Avrum to a quiet club-restaurant off Pie IX Boulevard and ordered two of the thickest and juiciest T-bone steaks the house had to offer. The waiter was very respectful and bowed constantly, and when he produced the steaks, they were everything he promised they would be. Red wine came with them, and the waiter poured some into one of the sparkling glasses on the table. Grigor sipped it, nodded, and the waiter filled his glass almost to the rim, then he filled Avrum's glass. Avrum tried to understand the intricacies of the napkin, the dishes over dishes, the regimented cutlery, and realized that he'd be smart to follow Grigor's lead. He mentioned to Grigor that his clothes weren't up to the class of the place, but Grigor told him to forget it. "You're with me," he smiled, "and they kind of know me here. For them, it's like you're in a tux."

But Grigor shook his head in shame every time the scene of the last hour played out in his mind. He had sworn to Avrum while they were still in the gym that nothing was really what it appeared to be — not that shit Freddie, not the guns — and he wanted very much to explain, only in a calmer atmosphere, so he began:

"You would think that guns are something natural to me. I take a shot at you in the old country, and one of my men pulls another gun on you on this side of the ocean. I hope you broke his face so that it shows on him for the rest of his life — and don't worry, he won't ever put a finger on you. But I have to carry a gun for my own protection. When I explain, you'll see — and it's not because I'm doing anything bad. It's not even illegal, this business. Not here, at least. And in the end it is for the good of a lot of other people."

Grigor spoke about the Anti-Saloon League, the Prohibition Party, and others who were pushing for new laws in the United States that would make the sale of liquor illegal everywhere in the country. Right now, it was illegal only in the South, but it was only a question of time. He said that he and his men were interested in nothing more than stockpiling cases of good Canadian whiskey in warehouses there, and seeing as how it was all going to be illegal soon, anyway, there was no point in paying the high taxes the Americans were asking to get them into the country now.

Avrum was listening intently. At the same time, his mind tried to fathom the scene he was partner to. It was all so unreal, with the old world and the temper of the distant forests suddenly so thick in the weave of everything describing his life today on the concrete streets of Montreal. How was it possible to grasp that the same Grigor who worked lumber with him in the thick forests of Urman — the same man who shot and killed Iannuk before his very eyes, and who would have done the same to him — was now sitting in front of him in this fancy restaurant, dressed like a Rockefeller, with gold and silver designer rings on his fingers, all inlayed with heavy gems, cutting into a thick, juicy steak and sipping wine?

“So the picture is this, Avrum.” Of course, for Grigor it would still be *Avrum*, which he would continue to pronounce *Abrim*. “I put together an operation on the up-and-up that gets the whiskey in the States. Not only that, but I own the warehouses there that store them. The only sticky part is getting it there, and even that is now a well-oiled operation.”

Avrum nodded. He studied his immaculately dressed and well-mannered countryman, and admired how swiftly and how adept he had been at adapting to the new world. Grigor’s easy air of authority and his grasp of the trinity of money, people, and situations had Avrum feeling not a little fortunate to have Grigor relate to him in this way. At that moment, the taste in his mouth as he devoured the steak was the taste of all the marvelous developments his adopted land was so generously delivering to him. At the same time, it crossed his mind that something in Kapitolnik’s communication with the heavens must have short-circuited. First Shloimke Plotkin, and now Grigor. Why couldn’t the man just focus on Hershel, and get to the address that really mattered?

Grigor explained that he had worked out a route from a short way past Kingston in the province of Ontario, across a small stretch of Lake Ontario, over to some point near Buffalo, New York. “We shove off with a full load say around ten, and by five in the morning, it’s all over and we’re on our way back. Nobody sees nothing, nobody knows nothing, no one gets hurt, and altogether it’s like a fishing trip — one hundred percent vacation.”

Avrum agreed that it all sounded like the perfect setup. Still, he was curious about what interest Grigor had in Zed Chicago’s gym — that needed sending a character like Freddie there, a thug who plainly identified with the underworld.

“I’ll tell you so that all the cards will be on the table,” began Grigor, spreading his hands. “The Americans have to go through the motions of pretending to watch the border. They know that the best whiskey comes from Canada and that they’re losing millions in taxes. But sometimes, and believe me, by accident, the Americans bump into my boys, and if they run for it like some of them do, the Americans will shoot. Instead of paying a stupid fine, they get themselves buried. So, not everyone rushes to do this work. But these are all your nickel-and-dime punks. My setup is something in an altogether another league. It is clean, smooth, safe, and easy, and it comes with good thinking."

Avrum could hardly he believe was hearing all this. A man could live all his life, he thought, and never know of such things. He wasn't quite as certain, however, whether what was transpiring at this time between Grigor and himself was good or not good for him.

"Now about Zed. The operation simply needs guys who can lift a case of whiskey, who can be free in the middle of the week, who don't have to show up to their wives after work, who feel that the money is worth a minimal risk — y'see? And these guys, I mostly find at the gyms. A boxer or a wrestler temporarily out of work and maybe down on his luck is almost always a good bet for us. And besides the fact that they get a couple of bottles to take home with them, they make enough cash to pay their rent for half a year. But Mr. Chicago — a real nice guy . . . personally, I like him — somehow got it into his head that my interest gives his place a bad reputation. I can't see it that way, y'see. A guy who is down and out comes on with us and a couple days later he brings home enough to give his wife to pay all the bills and even some to put away in the bank. Believe me, Avrum, that's what's gonna get me through those pearly gates into heaven when my time comes."

Avrum was still trying, somehow, to fit himself into Grigor's stream of talk.

"So I just wanted a quiet talk with him — actually with some of the boys working out at his place. What was so terrible?"

"Freddie?"

"Don't remind me. The punk talks from his rear end. The only reason he goes with me — now I can say *went* with me — is for my protection. Like I said, sometimes in my business I need it. But he makes even me nervous, and what happened today was coming to him. He shoots too fast, but it's mostly with his mouth, and then he thinks that if he has a gun, he doesn't need brains. But I got to say, now that I think of it, you are something special yourself. It's one thing to be big. Lots of guys are big lugs. But guts you don't eat for breakfast and you don't pick off trees. A hundred other guys in your place would've run like chickens."

Grigor removed a silver cigarette case from his vest pocket and pressed a clip. It sprang open. "Smoke?" Avrum shook his head — though at the same time, the thought of Bella lighting up on the mountain came back to him. Grigor tapped the end of a cigarette on the table and fit it snugly into the corner of his mouth. A waiter sprang at him with a lit match. Avrum was impressed no end.

Behind the smoke he exhaled, Grigor continued. "Y'know, between the two of us, with the things we got going for us, we can lift all the cream off this business. I know you, you know me — I mean, we're an old team. And I got the feeling I want to make you a millionaire. Do you remember what I once told you about learning how to grab? You remember — there on the boat?" Avrum smiled and nodded. "Well, I think I am going to teach you personally. And this is one thing I think I can teach pretty good."

Avrum was still smiling, but he said he wasn't sure.

Later, when they rose from the table, Avrum swore that never in his life had he eaten anything as good as what was served them that evening. Grigor slapped him on the back and said that if Avrum stuck with him he'd soon be eating things that would make those steaks seem like straw. They laughed together and Avrum saw Grigor leave a tip for the waiter that was as much as the bill itself.

"Oh. And by the way, I knew there was something I should tell you." Grigor took a firm grip on Avrum's shoulder and pressed his lips into a wry smile. "You remember Iannuk?"

"Iannuk is not someone you can forget, Grigor. Me, he gave me my life."

"Yes, maybe . . . well . . ." Grigor winked, and his smile suddenly stretched the width of his face, "that bum son-of-a-gun is still alive and kicking. He's a millionaire today and owns two freighters — two cargo ships. I'm not surprised. My shot took his ear off — his ear and a piece of his scalp, but that's all. He never died. I also thought he died, but he never died. I left the camp as quickly as you did, and didn't stay around to ask questions."

Avrum froze. "How do you know this?"

"I make it my business to know. I keep in touch. Things like this don't get past me. If you want to write to him, I'll give you his address. Send him a postcard." But then Grigor paused and reflected. "Sure — and if the bugger ever got my address, he'd come over here just to break my bones." Again, he dug his fingers into Avrum's shoulder and smiled, "Still, if you'll ever want to get in touch with him — he really is a big man these days — just come to me."

Grigor wrote down Avrum's address and phone number and handed him a card that had his name and address (under a company label) embossed in a modern lettering style. Everything about the man was class, as Horse would say. Grigor drove him back to his house, and when they finally parted, they shook hands vigorously with both hands.

Later that same day, Chicago got hold of Horse over the phone and told him of the peculiar encounter.

"He's one right bastard," Chicago said admiringly. "He got in one shot at this turkey — the guy never saw it coming — and now they're going to need a zipper to keep the pieces of his face together. If he sticks with me here and doesn't fall for Georgie's lip — and there is something old country between them that could give Georgie some leverage — then I got the feeling he'll work well with the promoters. He'll learn the wrestling all right — all the style and heart he needs is already in his blood. Y'saw right, Horse. I tip my hat."

Horse stopped Avrum during his ten o'clock coffee break the following morning. When Avrum got back to the factory, Grigor was no longer a factor in his plans. When, two weeks later, Grigor called to ask Avrum if he was prepared to make the weekend a long one, Avrum said that that was impossible. Grigor didn't ask why, but said that he would call again another time. Avrum said that they should keep in touch and Grigor reminded him that he had his card, and that if he'd ever need anything — "*Makes no difference what,*" — he'd have a good chance of finding it at his number. Avrum thanked him and said he would remember.

(23)

A landsman passed away and Bella's parents had gone to visit the bereaved family. Bella wouldn't join them because, as she told her father, she didn't like these things. "Mendel didn't like dying either," admonished her father, "but you think that helped him?" Still, she was adamant and they left without her.

Later, Avrum came to take her out for an ice cream, but she said she didn't want to miss *Radio Theater*, so they stayed at home. Bella warmed up some leftover chicken for him, which she also helped him finish, and a few minutes before the program was to begin, they went into the parlor, where Bella switched on the Atwater Kent. "It takes almost a half an hour to warm up," she complained in a voice that underlined her annoyance. "If I miss a word, I'll just die." But somehow Avrum was affected less by the temper of the radio than by the temper of their situation. An intangible air of contrivance had penetrated the locked front door, and it hung heavily in the room. It worried as much as excited him.

The play was about a young orphaned girl who was taken in and cared for by her father's secret and adoring mistress. This lady looked upon her as the child that might have been hers, and, to her mind, rightfully should have been. Its true mother, killed along with her father in a car accident, had been a spiteful and selfish woman, and it was insinuated that she more than flirted with the strange men with whom she secretly consorted. But the mother's mother wanted the child with her, saying that she loved her as only a grandmother could. The listeners knew in their bones that what she really wanted was someone to serve her — to wait on her, to run errands for her, to prepare her meals, to do the laundry and the housecleaning. Everyone knew now why her daughter had been as unpleasant as she was.

Unfortunately, however, the law books were filled with the coldest, driest, and most heartless words, and the grandmother had a cruel lawyer get a judgment that gave her legal rights to the child. Lacking the financial means to fight back, the child's father's mistress took the only course she saw open to her. She ran off with the child.

Through stockyards, under bridges, sleeping at hobo camps, with dangers lurking behind every strange sound and shadow, they constantly had to outmaneuver the police, who were always at their heels and seemed always to have them surrounded. Forced to steal food, their offenses only multiplied, but worse, the robbed merchants would notify the police, who were thus able to track them closely.

With about three minutes left to the end of the program, one of the police dogs finally trapped them under some trees in the midst of what sounded like a typhoon in a tropical jungle. Earlier, the same dog was always heard barking and growling ferociously, but now, perhaps seeing the sadness in the eyes of his captives and sensing the beastly injustice of it all, he began to whimper piteously. Then, when his master saw the dog's reaction, he realized how much he too had been mistaken in letting his duty determine his judgment, and how much the orders he had been given had undermined the true temper of his heart. At this point, the entire mood of the program changed. Love seemed to come into the picture, and the only wind that was heard now came from a forty-piece orchestra that must have been out there in the rain with them all this time.

Bella blew her nose violently into her third handkerchief. Her eyes were bloodshot and kind of raw-looking and still bathed in a pool of tears. "Oh, that poor, poor woman," she cried. "Will that policeman marry her, do you think?" Avrum's impression was that it was probably the dog that wanted to marry her, but the truth was that the heavy pathos got to him as well. When he blew his own nose and dabbed at a spot of wetness at the corner of an eye, Bella said to him triumphantly, "You see? You too!"

The story faded quickly for Avrum, but not so for Bella. He had been sitting with his arm around her shoulders for a long time, careful to keep his hand a respectful distance from her generous and overripe breasts. But now he itched to discover more of her and have her surrender more of the "everything and anything" she had promised. His fingers crept downwards and along the side of her breast, and at first Bella seemed not to notice. But when this encouraged him to put a finger or two lightly over where he expected her nipple might be, she pushed his hand away and shifted away from him. "How can you — at a time like this?"

Avrum apologized, suddenly hurt and shamed, and Bella, to underline how she still felt, again brought the handkerchief to her eyes and nose. Avrum rose and said that maybe he should go. The locked door bothered him now, and he went to look through the glass down at the street. It was deserted. She walked up behind him and put her arms on his chest, pressing herself into his back. "Wasn't it a good program?" she asked. Dutifully Avrum said it was. Rubbing her nose against his shirt, she added, "It teaches us what problems in life really are. We just don't know how lucky we are." Avrum wondered if Fanny would have had the same opinion. "How many times can it happen," he asked dully, "that a beautiful mistress will steal her lover's little girl from a bad grandmother, especially when she has no money and nowhere to take her?"

"That's the point," said Bella. Avrum wondered what point exactly she had in mind, but he let it pass.

Bella brought them tea and apple cake, but Avrum remained uneasy. The radio played soft romantic music, and Bella said she wanted to dance. Avrum told her that he didn't know how to dance, that he never danced in his life. But Bella only laughed and said that dancing was the easiest thing in the world, and that she would teach him. So she positioned them in the middle of the floor and arranged his hands on her. It excited him. Then, when she looked down to tell him how to move his feet, she couldn't help noticing the unusual way something behind his fly was pushing against the front of his trousers. She blushed and broke away saying that she didn't want to dance with him anymore.

Later, however, she took him into the kitchen and closed the door so that they were doubly isolated from the outside world. Shyly she undid her blouse and showed him her breasts in their brassiere. "Now turn around," she said, and Avrum turned around. When she called him to face her again, she was naked to the waist. Avrum was overwhelmed by the treasures that his eyes were taking in, and when he walked over and hugged her, she pressed herself hotly to him. Then he brought his hands to cover them and she whispered, "Put it in your mouth," so he bent over and quickly slipped a nipple into his mouth, touching it first with his tongue before starting in to suck it. "My baby, my baby," she cooed. "They're just for you — only for you. I hope you know that."

Then she broke away and Avrum wondered if he somehow offended, or worse, disappointed her. But she only walked over to the light switch and closed it, and he watched, wide-eyed, as her breasts bounced ahead of her. They quickly found each other in the dark and embraced passionately. Then Avrum felt her hand slip into his pants — he held his breath — and she touched him with the tips of her fingers. Then she dared enough to hold him hard in her palm, but only for the briefest dizzying moment. He felt his steaming seed pressing to be released, and when she withdrew her hand, he was just able to hold it back. He wouldn't have wanted her to think he'd dirtied her on purpose.

Later, they made a date for another evening. Avrum mumbled something about his training schedule at Zed Chicago's, hinting what it might be for, but Bella didn't react. Walking down the stairs to the street, he suddenly felt a painful heaviness in the pit of his stomach, and it quickly got worse. Soon, he couldn't close his legs. His testicles were frighteningly tender and hurting terribly. The pain was so acute he considered going to the local emergency medical clinic on the corner of Esplanade and St. Joseph Boulevard, which was a short walk from the Kaplans'.

At the last moment, he opted for his bed, but it took him the longest time to manage the stairs. On his bed, he had to lie on his back with his legs bent and spread apart. His face was drenched with cold sweat. He had no idea what was happening to him, but thankfully, and quicker than he had hoped for, sleep released him from the pain. In the morning, he touched himself warily there, even before opening his eyes. Miraculously, the pain was gone.

(24)

However he positioned the fedora on his head, he couldn't get it to feel right. He tried to ape the professional way the salesman had broken in the top of the hat (with a sharp slicing motion of his palm), and it seemed to work. But in the store, the salesman had also set it just so on his head, not too high and not too low and at a perfect slant, and this Avrum couldn't duplicate alone in the front of his mirror. After twenty minutes, he had to be satisfied with the best he could manage, and, again at the mirror, he stood back to study himself. His thoughts carried him back to the terrified nine-year-old boy tied up in ropes and in the murderous clutches of that deranged woman with the elephantine legs; if in the forests of Urman and Zitomir someone would have told him that ahead of him was a day when he would see himself this way in the mirror, he would have thought that that person surely belonged in one of those dark dungeons where the insane were kept chained to the walls.

He felt proud and terribly impressed at the image of himself in his grand attire. He was in his new suit, an immaculate fit, tailoring at its best — a rich three-piece, pinstriped brown, double-breasted tweed, with the lapels cut in the latest fashion, and with creases as straight as a ruler and as sharp as a razor. How could he ever thank Horse? Were the words he needed even invented? He had bought a dark maroon-and-gold paisley tie from the peddler who came to the factory once every week or two. Florence had picked it out for him, and had taken the time to teach him how to knot it. He was grateful to her for always being ready with such minor attentions, and the moments when he could be near her, to study her magical lips and breathe the mysterious, sensual, otherworldly perfume that always surrounded her, were moments that extended to delightful hours in his memory.

Shirley's wedding was being held in the small hall that adjoined Rabbi Levinger's synagogue on Hutchison near St. Joseph Boulevard. It was only a few blocks away, and Avrum was one of the first guests to arrive. Shirley, all in white, was sitting in a corner attended to by women relatives and friends. She was crying bitterly. Minutes later, resplendent in their own shiny new clothes and polished shoes, two families with about a dozen sticky children between them joined him.

He watched for the arrival of others, and when they came, he compared his suit to theirs. He admired the women in their delicate veils and flowing finery, and thought how fortunate it was that there were such occasions when people had the perfect excuse to step out of their real selves and real lives, if only for an hour. He began to feel not a little self-conscious when each of the women, without a single exception, set their eyes on him and kept them locked on him for the longest time. None seemed the least embarrassed, even when their eyes would meet. The same was just as true for the men who accompanied them. But until Charlie the cutter came, he had no one to talk with. When Strulevitch showed up, they kidded each other about their fancy duds, though Strulevitch soon admitted that Avrum looked like a million dollars. "Fact is," he said, "you look like a champ already. Eh?"

From the window, they saw the Goldenbergs drive up in their new Packard. "*Ask the man who owns one*," smirked Charlie, echoing the Packard jingle, and they all kind of smiled and half nodded. The Packard, with its whitewall tires, really was a class car. But if Charlie intended that line as a joke, they missed it. Charlie was always saying things the point of which only he could understand. Still, they sort of snickered to please him and to make sure they didn't appear dimwitted in the unlikely event that there really was something funny buried there somewhere.

Shirley looked like nothing more than a heap of snow. "If she'd promise to keep the veil over her face for the rest of her life, eh, it would be Norman's best wedding present," said Strulevitch behind his hand and out of the corner of his mouth. They were standing in the passage to the parlor, which at other times served as the prayer hall, and Shirley had to walk past them. She must have seen Avrum, who tried to hide himself behind Charlie and Strulevitch, because she seemed confused and rushed ahead too quickly after a flash of hesitation first made her break her stride. But Strulevitch blocked her way to offer his effusive congratulations. Charlie's hand ploughed in after his, and that left Avrum, who from a distance extended his on hand and managed a garbled "*Mazeltov.*" Shirley clucked another dry and distant "Thank you" that might have been intended for anyone and quickly continued ahead.

Myer and Florence Goldenberg, following in her wake, stopped long enough to exchange blessings with their employees. Avrum still thought that Florence was the most beautiful woman he had ever seen in his life. She whispered in his ear that the suit turned him into the most handsome man she had seen in the last thirty years, "but don't dare tell this to Myer, or he'll divorce me." Avrum radiated his pleasure. In his heart, he loved her for giving him even this little conspiracy to share with her.

They sat Shirley in a fine hand-carved chair, with a tall, richly worked leather back. Standing over her, crying as though it was the worst day of her life, was her mother. Thanks to her nose, even guests from the groom's side didn't have to ask how she was related to the bride.

The guests had all stepped up to wish her a *mazeltov*. They had already handed over their presents, and they soon found themselves milling about with nothing to do. The children started playing games of tag. Some of the girls wailed loudly that the boys were pulling their hair, and then they ran off to throw hard candies at the boys. Parents started running after them, shouting threats, and one of the ladies tripped and sprained an ankle. Everyone kept asking when the ceremony would begin. It was hot in the hall, and sweat was ruining the ladies' faces. They would dab at their eyes and smear the mascara, and their rouge caked. Seeing what was happening to the other women, they each checked their own faces in their purse mirrors. In a veritable orgy of facial contortions, they started in desperately to reconstruct what they could.

Rabbi Levinger was sitting in the half room off the hall with the *Ktuba*, which the groom and the witnesses had yet to sign, and he was becoming increasingly impatient. The *latkes* would be cold and the guests would soon begin to think of their stomachs.

Norman was late. Most of his family was already there, including his mother and father, but he was supposed to come in his brother Louie's car. A rumor spread that the car had had an accident, but then those close to those-in-the-know said that it was nothing more serious than a flat tire. Kalman Finiffter, the upholsterer who was a self-proclaimed expert on cars because he did their seats, said with a loud authority that a flat tire at sixty miles an hour was instant suicide. The word *suicide* made three or four turns around the room, and though they tried to keep it from Shirley, it landed on her ears. A horse coming from nowhere kicking her face with its hind legs would have shocked her less. To her thinking, suicide was a distinct possibility as far as Norman was concerned, and she wondered if in any final message he might have left he'd say anything that would reflect badly on her.

But then the car pulled up; Louie and another fellow got out, only Norman stayed where he was. Louie opened the back door and got in next to his brother, but Norman shrank, sinking even deeper into the seat. They were arguing loudly, and Norman sounded a little drunk. Louie tried pulling him out, but Norman fought him off with his top hat, so Louie got the other fellow to help him. When it seemed that Norman would let himself get dragged across the gutter only by force and ruin both their rented tuxedos, Louie pushed him back in and got in again behind the wheel. He told the people who came to see what was the matter that he was only going to take Norman for another turn around the block to get him over his nervous jitters. Five minutes later, they were back, but this time Shirley's mother was out there waiting for him, and her eyes did all the talking for her. Norman edged himself out, cowering. Holding him securely at the elbow, Louie rushed him up the stairs. He looked like he had just seen the world from the trenches of World War I.

The rabbi married them, but Norman's mood never changed. Shirley cried to her mother, "If I live the rest of my life, I'll never forgive him." But the guests were less concerned with the groom than with the tables of food along the walls. Florence approached Avrum and introduced him to a mother and her redheaded daughter. "Myrna is studying typing," she said about the daughter, "and I sewed her first baby dress. Mrs. Polansky is my friend for the last forty years — isn't that so, Sarah?" Sarah found something to say to Florence, and Avrum felt he was expected to be polite to the daughter.

"Typing is hard?" He ventured.

"Just at the beginning," said Myrna.

"And where are you now?"

"At the beginning."

"Oh!" Sarah suddenly turned and gushed at them. "It's nice to see that you two *children* have so much to talk about." She squeezed Avrum's arm and affected her most gracious smile.

This caused a flake of powder to drop off the black wart that grew at the corner of her lip. "But, I'll leave the two of you to get better acquainted. The world these days is for *young* people." With that, she sighed, giggled, and headed for the food. After standing wordlessly next to each other for a few minutes, the girl broke away to join her mother, whose expression turned ugly when she saw her alone. Avrum walked to the other side of the hall, and as he looked around him, it struck him that no one was really very happy there that evening. Even the violinist was picking the saddest tunes to play.

(25)

The nights continued to bring mind-wrenching phantom terrors upon Avrum. He would approach his bed, wary of the hours that had yet to be crossed before his eyes would again find a safe anchor on the distractions that came with the light. Sleep generally overtook him effortlessly, but reaching under the blanket of that sleep, a hand would seize his heart and he would awake breathing hard. Struggling to contain the thumping in his chest, he would lie in the stillness of the dark room, certain that his death was only moments away. This might happen at three or four in the morning, and like waves, the fears would have their crests and undertows before subsiding. What hours there were left 'til the morning were spent in a state of shallow half sleep wherein his mind would deliver a train of images to pass behind his eyes. He would think that he hadn't slept at all, but these hours always passed seemingly in minutes and for this, he was grateful.

At the same time, unnerving premonitions and anxieties intruded alarmingly into his days. They came upon him unawares, snakelike, but these he could generally ward off by occupying himself with the hundred and one things in the theater of his surface life. They plagued him nevertheless, if only because the forms within them became increasingly distinct and recognizable. He was still alone in the world, and he felt his aloneness as a heavy and festering sore that seemed inured against time.

He would be drowning and a voice would ask, "Who is that out there? He seems to be in trouble." Another voice would say, "His name is Avrum Vishinsky, but he doesn't really belong here. Does anyone know this bum?" Some voices would say that they could recall someone by that name having passed fleetingly through an hour of their lives, but that otherwise he played no role that might concern them. "Well, does he belong to anyone? Where does he live?" And no answer would be forthcoming — no answer and no rescuing arm. The waters would swell over him. Fanny had written about her friend —

how he felt expelled from death. Well, Avrum might tell her that a man truly alone is a man who feels expelled from life — living only in a vacant nether world.

Fired by his sudden riches, he had spent freely on his made-to-measure suit, but it hadn't ended with just that tie and the fedora. He allowed himself a new Tavannes wristwatch, an extra pair of shoes, and another two white shirts along with the high, detached collars in the style of the Arrow Collar Man. Then there was the gift of a delicate stone brooch for Bella, initialed handkerchiefs and a fine ultramodern Louis Waterman fountain pen — not to mention the extra towels, shirts, shorts, and shoes that he needed for his training. He had encouraged Bella to think that every Sunday night he would take her out for a fine meal. They had done this three times, and each time Bella had allowed herself to order from higher up on the menu. The first time they went, she had been agog with excitement and in a frenzy about what to wear. It so pleased Avrum that he had told her then that she had better get used to such evenings. She was still a little giggly the second time, and the third time she had stern complaints about the way the silverware was cleaned and about the surliness of the waiter. The third time, the bill came to almost double what it had been the first time. Avrum thought that there was a lesson for him somewhere in all this.

Before long, his spending was cutting into his original savings. For himself, he needed nothing more. But Bella had come to expect things from him, and he *needed* her. Avrum had hinted repeatedly to Horse that he could use another tip on the horses, or even another card game. But Horse would only laugh and say that once Avrum would start in on his own career, he wouldn't need these things, "not if the facts live up to the promise."

But would the facts live up to the promise, he wondered. At least once a day, Avrum would check that he still had Grigor's card, and once or twice, he had even set it in front of him at the telephone. But he worried that the call might be premature. Then again, Grigor himself had said that he would call another time, so perhaps it was better to wait. Would the facts live up to the promise? Horse had a promoter in the town of Dorval put

Avrum on a card set for two weeks away. Chicago thought that Avrum was ripe for his first go, but he advised Horse to set it up outside the city "just in case we miscalculated." He was scheduled for the second fight of the evening against someone called Roy Lebois Cardinal.

Perhaps it was Roy Lebois Cardinal who spurred the phantoms that plagued Avrum's nights. In a very real way, he would have to fight this man for his life.

* * *

Chicago had to warn him against overtraining. "There *is* such a thing, y'know, and if it happens, you're in deep trouble," he said. "Y'gotta get in there loose — relaxed. The muscles got to give, and overtraining, especially with the weights, can pull them too tight. Y'don' need them to tear, fella."

In the days left, Chicago worked Avrum hard on speed and techniques. He took Leon off the weights, and had him harden Avrum's mid-section with the medicine ball. He taught him two of the fancier submission holds that had recently been introduced from the States, and had him perfect the timing that made their execution both potent and grand crowd pleasers. The first was a reverse leg lock, which made a man feel that his stomach was about to tear away from his chest, and the second was a particularly vicious reverse back throw, which invited a dislocated neck if the victim tried to resist it. He showed Avrum how to rest when a hold was applied on him, and how to slip into just such a hold if he needed the rest himself. Strulevitch came to watch the last few workouts, and Chicago instructed him on how to get Avrum to time his fight. He got word that Cardinal was a local fireman who had a following made up mostly of the boys from his station. But he was a straight wrestler — and he generally wrestled to win.

The ring was set up in a small converted warehouse on the road that connected the town to the water's edge. Hank had a problem finding it because Strulevitch, who had told him that he knew exactly where the place was, had him turn left at a crossroad when they should have turned right. The road led into desolate farmland, but Strulevitch insisted that he knew just where he was. Finally, the pavement forked into two smaller dirt roads and Strulevitch admitted that they might have shifted the place. When he tried to turn the car around, the right front wheel sank into the soft shoulder and Hank lost his temper when he felt the back wheel burning rubber while it drove the front wheel deeper into the mud. So Strulevitch and Avrum got out to push, and in less than a minute the car was free. When they started back, a rabbit dashed into the headlights and stayed in the beam while it raced inches ahead of the fender. Then it disappeared, and Hank said he probably ran over it. Avrum wondered if this wasn't an omen of sorts — but whether for good or bad, he couldn't know.

The far side of the warehouse was partitioned so that one of the rooms served as a makeshift dressing room. Oily sawdust was thick on the floor. There were three benches and a few old lockers set against the wall, but there were no showers and the smell of the place vaguely suggested that barn animals might have spent some time there. A small, yellowing sink under a single leaking faucet was on the wall across from the lockers. Over it, a tiny first-aid cabinet, the door of which hung crookedly from only one hinge, had a small bottle of iodine on one of its shelves. A bare light bulb hung from the ceiling. Otherwise, the place was empty except for another wrestler who sat sullen, huddled deep in his robe, alone with his cigarette. He introduced himself as Roy Lebois Cardinal, and said that it was a place like this that made the business such a shitty racket. Avrum agreed. They shook hands while silently measuring each other up. Fitting his things into a locker, Avrum whispered to Strulevitch that Cardinal seemed strong, but Strulevitch said no way — that the bum was missing a couple of teeth, that his nose was broken, and his eyes had been cut more than once, which meant that altogether he must be easy to get to and was probably a slow mover.

They listened to the noise of the small, tight crowd. A sustained burst of shouting and applause and the clanging of the bell told them that the first preliminary was over; within a minute, the wet, reddened, heavy-breathing battlers burst into the room to drop onto the benches. They ignored each other. A small porky man followed them and stepped quickly up to Avrum. "Abie Vishinsky?"

"Yeah."

"Glad to meet you. Y'look good. M'name's Bravender."

"The promoter," said Strulevitch to Avrum.

"Yeah, well, you're on now, boys." He smiled and nodded to Cardinal. "Give a nice show for the customers, will ya? I wan'em all t'want t'see y'back."

The bell was calling them, and Cardinal invited Avrum to go out first. They shook hands again. Avrum felt his stomach tense uneasily as Strulevitch pushed him ahead, saying, "Take everything slow — take everything slow. Show the bums you got all the time in the world, like you been doing this since you were born."

It was a peculiar feeling to step out there half-dressed in a robe and towel, and to feel the weight of hundreds of eyes. Avrum was deaf to the polite scattered applause that greeted him until he slipped through the ropes and saw that many faces in the crowd were encouraging him. Here and there, someone waved to him and he waved back. But the pitch of the noise rose sharply and suddenly when Roy Cardinal came through the rows, his hands raised in acknowledgement of their cheers, and it seemed to Avrum that the whole crowd was one behind his adversary.

"Well, he's a home boy and they don't know you yet," said Strulevitch from the floor at his corner. "Just take it slow and easy."

". . . AND ONE FALL OR ONE SUBMISSION DECIDES THE WINNER," cried Bravender at the top of his voice. He was doubling as the announcer, but either the information he had been fed was wrong or simply misspelled. He introduced Avrum as "Aay Bee Cee Whiskey — direct from the deepest forests in Russia where they wrestle bears."

Avrum was certain that in the dressing room, Bravender had addressed him as Vishinsky. He looked questioningly down at Strulevitch, who, with his thumb and index finger, gave him back an all-OK sign. Strulevitch then pointed to the third row behind him, and Avrum's eyes fell on Horse, who clasped his hands over his head in a victory sign, and around him were at least half a dozen other familiar faces. Some waved at him, and they all shouted their support.

The fight lasted twenty-eight seconds. Avrum had walked to the middle of the ring and Cardinal circled him menacingly in a catlike crouch. Then they locked and Cardinal, moving with surprising swiftness, threw him across his hip to somersault awkwardly to the floor. Stunned and ashamed, Avrum bolted to his feet and they locked again, and this time Cardinal let Avrum work a full Nelson on him. But instead of giving him time to test the hold, Avrum threw him backwards and sideways against the ropes. Cardinal was mildly surprised and annoyed. Amateurs were always a headache for him. Feigning grogginess, he got to his feet with his back turned unsuspectingly toward Avrum, whose instincts collected the scene faster than his mind could reason. Sensing the chance to replay the moves that Chicago had worked him hard on over and over again, he leapt at Cardinal and maneuvered him into the reverse back throw.

Had an express train come crashing through the walls, it would have surprised Cardinal less. His shriek of submission echoed off the ceiling and the referee rushed in to free him. The crowd was on their feet roaring, and the referee raised Avrum's hand. But rage was fast blinding Cardinal, who couldn't digest the low swindle he had just been made to swallow. Avrum's hand was still in the air when he felt Cardinal's fist smash against his jaw. Hurt and confused, Avrum felt himself being thrown back, and from the corner of his eye, he caught a maddened Cardinal breaking away from those who would restrain him. Charging again with his fist cocked, there was a sudden flurry — a blur of movement and Cardinal suddenly found himself doubled over on the floor, gasping for breath. Avrum had stepped into the charge, but veered sideways and exploded his fist just under Cardinal's heart. It moved faster than anyone could see, but no one doubted that Cardinal had good reason to stay where he was on the floor.

A policeman accompanied Avrum and Strulevitch back to the dressing room where the wrestlers who were to follow on the card were now rushing to undress. The promoter helped Cardinal to his feet and tried to calm him, but the man was plainly not inclined to try another round with Avrum or anyone else at that moment. When they were all in the dressing room, Bravender explained that the fighters generally used the first ten or fifteen minutes just to warm up. "I can't have every fight here finish in ten seconds. The crowd would take this place apart if I don't keep things alive for at least an hour and a half." Avrum said that no one had told him this and he tried to apologize to Cardinal, who refused even to turn to face him. Bravender tried to have them sign on the spot for a return match in a week's time. "I'll make it a semi-final," he said, and Cardinal made a show of bravado in his rush to agree. Strulevitch stepped in and said they'd give their answer in a day or two — that he would have to talk to Horse. Outside, the crowd was still roaring their pleasure.

As it turned out, Horse was for it, but when he called Bravender on the phone, he was told that Cardinal had backed down. The same day, there was a picture in the *Herald* of Avrum standing over the crumpled Cardinal in a ring crowded with at least another fifteen people. It was impressive.

* * *

Like a mother hen, Florence crowded Avrum all day, clucking her excitement. She knew that he exercised regularly, but to wrestle a tough *goy* in front of a crowd of *goyim* was almost unheard of for a Jew — even unthinkable. And even so, fighting the man was one thing — but winning belonged to another world. In the States, there was this Jewish boxing champion, Benny Leonard, and she had read in a newspaper that the experts were saying that either Benny Leonard or someone called Joe Gans was probably the finest boxer in the whole world, but that the two couldn't meet because this Gans had passed away years earlier. (She remembered the name Gans because she had called up her friend Mona Gans to ask if this

Joe might have been a relative.) Anyhow, what did she know of these things?

She also heard talk of another Jewish boxing champion — a Joe Choynski — who knocked out a terrible *shvartze* even though his mother wanted him to be a violinist or an actor. But her Abie was definitely a champion like them. *Her* Abie — now so important it seems that the newspapers have to take notice and make him famous. A storekeeper came with his son-in-law to buy some dresses and she introduced them to "*my* Abie." And Avrum, still flushed with his victory, jokingly introduced Florence as *his* Florence. Everyone laughed except Myer, who looked at his wife strangely.

At Horse's, they were talking of the twenty-eight seconds as being an all-time record. A dozen copies of the *Herald* were lying around, and Horse had cut out the picture and caption and tacked it on the wall next to the cigarettes. A few of the boys asked him to autograph the picture in their copies of the newspaper, and Avrum wouldn't even bother to turn to see who would be patting him on his back. He looked at the picture almost with disbelief. The caption read:

Bedlam At The Barn. In the record time of twenty-eight seconds, newcomer Aay Bee Cee Whiskey demolished Dorval's own Roy Lebois Cardinal with a crushing reverse back throw. Cardinal then tried his luck at boxing, but with one tremendous right uppercut, Whiskey brought Cardinal down for an unofficial count of two hundred.

These were Avrum's happiest days. Thankfully, they had taken the ghosts away from his nights.

* * *

Bravender had Avrum back on his card the following week — this time in the semi-final slot against a rough fellow named Colin Buck Brian. Horse said "A guy that goes through life with three first names is like a tree that got lots of branches but no roots: you sneeze and it falls over." But Bravender said that the boy was out to please the crowd and not the rulebooks, so someone should tell Avrum what to expect. He asked Horse if

Avrum had a photograph of himself in a fighting pose — "standard page shot for the albums" — and Horse said they would have some to deliver in another week. He made a mental note to get Avrum to go to Cashton's Park Avenue studio with his gear, and he'd have to get Strulevitch to go with him to pose him right.

The tension returned to Avrum's stomach on the morning of the fight, and stayed with him until he stepped into the ring. Colin Buck Brian looked cleaner and about thirty pounds heavier than Cardinal, and he kept to himself in the dressing room. Bravender told Strulevitch to get Avrum to coast for at least fifteen minutes before getting anything serious into his head. Strulevitch nodded, pleased that Bravender had recognized his authority with Avrum.

Brian was booed roundly on his way up to the ring, and then again when Bravender introduced him. Avrum began to understand why when they locked the first time and Brian broke with a sharp and wholly illegal forearm smash aimed at his neck. It landed high on his chest making noise but little damage, and Avrum didn't feel moved to react to it. Still, the rule was that when the ref told them to break and step back, that they had to break and step back clean. The second time they locked, Brian shouldered him hard into a corner and delivered another forearm smash after the referee had told them to break. Avrum hesitated and Brian caught him for a hip throw and tried a fast body press.

Avrum squirmed out at the count of one, but Brian caught him for another throw, this time by the shoulder and neck. Avrum landed heavily and from the corner of his eye, caught Brian's knee on its way down to his chest. The crowd started in to loudly boo both fighters, but as Brian was coming down, Avrum rolled away and Brian pretended that having missed the mark, he had dislocated his knee. He succumbed to a wrist throw and a leg lock and seemed to be in tremendous pain until he wrenched himself free by pulling hard on Avrum's hair. Again, the referee warned him, and the crowd was urging Avrum to react in kind.

They traded reverse elbow bends, full Nelsons, and chin locks, with Brian getting in head butts, hair pulling, and knee lifts off the breaks. All this seemed to stir the crowd more than it did Avrum, and the many who expected to see a flashy Aay Bee Cee Whiskey repeat the performance of a week ago were fast becoming annoyed. Some threw their empty cigarette packs into the ring. In one of the rest holds, which let Avrum lie on his stomach with his legs seemingly trapped in Brian's "Wisconsin Leg Lever," he had a chance to ask Strulevitch how much time had gone by. "Eight, nine minutes," said Strulevitch, looking worried. Avrum thought that was time enough.

He twisted out of the hold, and when the fighters rose, he landed his own forearm smash against Brian's ribs that made the man's eyes almost fly from their sockets. Leading blindly with his head, Brian tried to butt Avrum, who moved faster and used the force of Brian's charge to lift him for a high and long throw. The crowd had never seen anything like this before. He flung Brian so high and so far that the unfortunate wrestler might have been mistaken for a rag doll. Suddenly, they were all on their feet, shouting and stomping, and Avrum was their hero again.

Brian might have let himself get pressed for the three counts after that landing — he had felt something jar at the base of his spine and was reluctant to test it. But Avrum had him in the air again with a stylish hip throw that left the victim hanging in the air upside down. A press would have been certain, then; instead, Avrum lifted Brian a third time, this time backwards across his shoulders from where he spun round and round. A rolling explosion of lights caught this extraordinary sight, and reminded Avrum of the photographers and the newspapers. Brian was shouting that he couldn't take any more and the referee signaled Avrum that the fight was over. The crowd was delirious, and Avrum wondered if Bravender would again complain that he had made his moves too early.

Wrestling promoters from as far away as New York and Chicago got through to Horse and asked about the chances of getting "Whiskey Vishinsky" (Horse preferring this to "Aay Bee Cee Whiskey") on their cards. Ever since the *Herald* produced two sensational pictures of the Brian fight — one that caught Brian's massive bulk leaving Avrum's hands from almost two yards in the air, and the other showing Brian stretched backwards across Avrum's shoulders, Whiskey Vishinsky became the hottest name in the sport overnight.

His first appearance at the Arena was in the main event against the masked Gorilla Goran, and even standing room was sold out when the Jewish population had to see with their own eyes what was impossible for them to believe from the papers. A week later, again in the Arena, Avrum was pitted against Albert Bolag — the Mad Pole. And this time, there was a fair scattering of women which added a festive mood to the evening. The Herald had written about the earlier fight: *Whiskey Turns Gorilla Into Monkey*.

Avrum became inundated with fan mail. The letters were mostly from women who proposed marriage, or who promised their favors on far less binding terms. A few sent him their panties doused with perfume, and some wanted him to be their bodyguard. Young boys asked how he got his muscles. Others invited him to invest his winnings in their guaranteed moneymaking schemes, and even others asked to borrow from him. One called him over to Christ, and another (unsigned) wrote that he would follow Avrum's next fight through a gun sight with his finger itching at the trigger " . . . and I'm going to be aiming at your horsecock." Horse had the police look at this one.

But serious, legitimate proposals reached him too. One of these came from Lawrence Feldman, who was a habitué at Horse's and who invited Avrum to join him in investing in a new B-A gas station. He knew of a building project on the city's edge that would be ripe for such a concession in half a year. Horse agreed that it was the best thing he could do with his money. "Y'gotta think about an insurance policy for the future," he insisted. "You won't be wrestling for the rest of your life, y'know." Avrum liked the idea and figured it would take less than three months for him to save the amount needed. Feldman was a straight guy, and they shook on the deal.

(26)

Fanny was back in Montreal. She had found a flat in the small bohemian quarter downtown on Metcalf Street, and an art supply shop nearby gave her work. She wrote this in a short note to Avrum explaining that Harry never returned — that he probably returned to the monastery, and when the rent was two months in arrears, she was forced to leave.

Avrum had gone to see her and found her giving painting lessons to three neighborhood children. He remembered her red wiry hair, only now it was cut short and combed almost like a man's. She was also decidedly thinner. She wore a gray-striped and plainly oversized man's jacket over a long, loose-fitting white seersucker dress.

She received him coolly — even with some confusion — and he soon left. He asked her if she needed any help, help of any sort, and her reaction was to tear a poem out of some dusty yellowing newspaper and to insist that he read it aloud then and there. It was about a bird that never saw the sky. The children seemed hostile and impatient, and he could find no place where he might comfortably seat himself. It occurred to him that Fanny hadn't invited him to sit down. The house seemed to consist only of that room, with the toilet set in a niche behind a stained violet curtain. Altogether, the room was an impossible kaleidoscope of paints and newsprint and boards and boxes and cloth and pipes and dishes and bodies. As much seemed to be hanging from the ceiling as resting on the floor.

Fanny hadn't asked about Bella, and when Avrum said that he had to go, she simply said okay and let him walk alone to the door.

(27)

Bella was becoming increasingly wary of Avrum's new confidence. She refused to regard his wrestling as more than a reckless excuse for exercise and sport. His future was with Sweet Mode Dresses, and she would impress upon him that only there would he be sure of a regular, steady income.

Once, he showed her a day's fan mail, and the attraction that women seemed to find in him was not lost on her. Her temper quickly deteriorated to a point verging on apoplexy.

"So? You would let those filthy *shiksas* get near you? You better tell me now so I'll know who I'm in business with." But even before Bella finished her line, she suddenly thought better than to chance an honest reply. "Just remind me to keep a ten-foot pole between us — better, a twenty-foot pole. If you want the syphilis, mister, if you want your head to rot and grow worms in your eyes, it's OK by me. I don't have to tell you where to go. You got all the names and addresses." Plainly agitated, she puckered her nose and with the back of her own hand, waved away the envelopes he was holding. One might have though she was trying to escape some noxious odor. Her face twisted in disgust.

"Actually, I think most of the girls who wrote me *are* Jewish. At least a lot of them." Avrum's voice had dropped to the level of a whimper. "You saw the names: Shwartzman, Klein, Mend—"

"No difference," Bella cut sharply into his words. "Don't throw me names. Suddenly, everybody has to be so modern. Just don't come running to me when your you-know-what turns green and falls off. That's what happens, y'know."

(28)

Goldenberg would read about Avrum's latest triumphs and find it hard to believe that the same man might that very moment be shuffling in his gray apron between the sewing machines, distributing work to the operators. His wrestling no longer had the air of a passing adventure, and more than once, he said to his wife that if the papers were right, Avrum was making more money than they were. If that was so, then the wages they were paying him was a poor joke; no conceivable raise in his salary would make it any less of a joke. By coming to the factory every day, when, as the papers were saying, so many promoters in Canada and the States were clamoring for him, Avrum was losing a fortune. One didn't need the logic of a *yeshiva* rabbi to realize that he would soon be leaving them.

"So if you think he's going to go on the road anyway, why don't you make him a salesman for us?" Florence was cleaning fish over the sink when she suggested this, and her husband fell in love with her all over again. He clapped his hands.

"Such a simple idea, and I'm not capable of thinking of it myself? It's perfect! Abie — he's such a famous celebrity that the customers will fill the order pages just to keep him in the store a little longer. He could be a gold mine. Do you think he'll go with it?"

"If I ask him, he'll go."

"How can you be so sure? Horse will have something to say about what he does, even that sick idiot Irving — every time I see that cigar and that dandruff, I picture everything falling into the boxes when he makes the orders. I swear, just for my ulcer, I keep away from him. But even he has something to do with Abie's wrestling."

"The difference between you and me, Myer, is that I know how to talk to both of them."

"Y'think so, eh? Let me tell you, Florence, if I had *tzitzes* like yours and walked around all day showing my legs and smelling like I took a bath in Chanel No. 5, they would also listen to me."

Florence laughed, but she wasn't altogether ignorant of that truth. She was also a step ahead of Myer. She had spoken to Horse to get a drift of the plans they had for Avrum, and Horse didn't hide the fact that he was pressing Avrum to take a month's vacation from Sweet Mode Dresses.

"Just for a month?"

"Look doll, I can show you telegrams from a hundred promoters across the country that are ready to promise him the moon. A month is enough to give him a good taste of working a circuit, and it's possible he won't like it. Being on the road is no fun thing. After that, I figure we'll all know better. If he can't take living on the road, he'll keep to the Montreal area, and in that case, it's no sweat to you. He's already been to Burlington and Plattsburg in the States, but four hours after the fight, he's home, and you always see him at work in the morning."

"Between you and me, Horse — is Abie really that good a wrestler? I mean, can it be a career that in the long run is better than working for us?"

"You kidding, Flo? If he works steady, your Abie can make in two or three weeks — that's five or six appearances — more than you pay him in two or three years. He's already put that much away just working around here. But I'll tell you, hon, he's in a class with the highest moneymakers. The promoters won't pay everyone what they're ready to pay him. And for his own good, this is the time he has to make his moves."

"Well, how would it be — and this is just between you and me — if Abie, when he goes on the road, takes a couple of our valises along with him? On his days off, he could show the line to the stores in the towns, and this way he makes his extra commission and doesn't have to leave us even if he stays on the road for years."

"That's up to him."

"Is it possible at all?"

"Well, he won't always be where your customers can get to him when they may need him."

"If he just shows the line and takes the first order, it's enough. He'd also get his commission on repeats."

"My honest opinion, Flo? Y'wanna know my honest opinion? The job would probably make it easier for him to stay on the road wrestling. He'd at least feel that he was keeping his connection to this place. This is the only home he really has, y'know."

In the end, Avrum went off on a two-month circuit that took him as far west as Niagara Falls and as far south as Delaware. In the New York area alone, he stayed a month appearing in different parts of the city, and from there, upstate as far as Albany. He worked towns from New Haven, where the crowd was mostly students, to Wilmington, where the smell of manure from the mushroom hills around the barn — which doubled as a sporting arena — stayed in his clothes seemingly for days after the fight.

On the road, the announcers would introduce him by one name or another, but always as "the Wrestler from Montreal." For Avrum, these words — delivered to the world as though carved in stone — always registered in his heart with a thump. They carried a message of belonging. Might he begin to believe that his life had really found an anchor — a genuine anchor in this land? A ripple of excitement tempered with happiness would overtake him for the few seconds it would take the angry behemoth across from him to once again command his attentions. But with the fight behind him, he would recall the announcer's introduction and the doubts would again surface in his mind. Could his life ever really find an anchor in any place in this world that did not include his brother?

The towns were all about an hour's ride by bus or on the Hudson and Delaware trains, and Horse had sent a chastened and repentant Shorty along as his bagman. Unfortunately, Shorty's euphoria at being resurrected dampened quickly. In the town of White Horse, he got himself arrested (and kicked in the face) when a woman climbed up to the ring to get Avrum's autograph and he ran his hand all the way up the inside of her leg — and this in front of almost 500 people. A few days earlier, Avrum had to intervene with a tobacconist in Toronto who called the police after he caught Shorty taking off with three packs of cigars. Shorty swore that he'd never let anything like that happen again, and when Avrum reminded him of his promise when the police came down on him because of the woman, he said, "What the hell, did you see me stealing any cigars from her?" Avrum mailed Horse the item that the local tabloid had printed about the incident; it came to two small paragraphs under the caption *Cops Feel — Feels Cops.*

Goldenberg didn't sell to the States, so Avrum sent the samples back after he finished his bouts in Canada. Along with the valises were three books crammed with orders — enough to keep every machine in the factory busy for the next six months.

(29)

The air was thick with the small of freshly buttered popcorn. Bella bought the large family-size box, but complained to the girl who took Avrum's nickel that the box she gave her could hold a lot more. She pointed to the boxes handed other customers, and the girl, visibly annoyed, added a few more kernels, pointedly avoiding Bella's eyes. After delivering the first handful to her mouth, Bella whispered to Avrum that if worse came to worst, she could live on popcorn for the rest of her life.

They went downtown to the new Loews cinema; Bella wanted to see Harry Haiselden in the movie *The Black Stork*. She'd seen it before — it was an old movie, but everyone was still talking about it. At least, that's what she told Avrum when she insisted he take her there. "You'll see it's for your own good. Maybe you'll even learn something. And, anyway, you should know what is really happening in this world."

The movie gave a dramatic account of the torments of a family that had to decide whether to keep alive their infant who had come into the world suffering severe multiple disabilities, including congenital syphilis, or to permit its demise. As though triggering a wake-up call, each time the word *syphilis* was mentioned, Bella would squeeze and shake Avrum's hand. The learned surgeons tried to convince the parents to keep the infant alive by permitting them to operate on it, but Dr. Harry Haiselden, who played himself, convinced the parents to let their child die. It died just as Bella scraped the last of the kernels from the bottom of the box.

Blood and Sand with Rudolph Valentino and Nita Naldi was the feature film, and followed *The Black Stork* after a fifteen-minute intermission. Bella used the time to get Avrum to bring her an Orange Crush and more popcorn — this time in the medium-size box.

They saw Valentino as a Spanish matador who wins fame and fortune, but who cheats on his adoring wife with Nita Naldi, who plays a seductive and very wealthy widow. Bella didn't much enjoy these scenes. Whenever Valentino would take to licking the length of Naldi's bejeweled neck, she would complain loudly about the piano playing. She especially didn't like the scene when Valentino set his hand directly on Naldi's breast, but her complaint got drowned in the hum of *oooohs*, *ahhhhs*, moans, and groans that instantly filled the hall. The end suited her better. His wife, played by the sweet and petite Lila Lee, learned of their affair (from Naldi, of all people, after Valentino spurns her), and Valentino wallowed in abject misery because Lila Lee wouldn't forgive him. In this state, he got gored by a bull, and there was an extended death scene where, a moment before he was delivered to the next world, she relented and tearfully forgave him.

"Did you see all those strings of pearls that floozie wore around her neck?" asked Bella as they left the cinema.

Avrum tried to unscramble the pictures that rushed to his mind. Was she referring to someone on the screen, or someone in the audience? But Bella never meant for him to answer.

"Wax — they were all made of wax. The cheapest wax, too. I know about these things. And she is so ugly I don't know how someone like Valentino could kiss her for real." Avrum had his answer, but he found refuge in silence. In his heart, he knew that granted the chance, he would have given years off his life to kiss Nita Naldi the way Valentino had.

There was a faint drizzle, but Bella had her umbrella. She wanted them to walk home. It was an ambitious decision considering the distance, but after fifteen minutes, they reached the corner of St. Catherine Street and Bleury and she thought the streetcar was a better idea.

Closing the umbrella at her door, Bella told Avrum that it was okay for him to come into the house — that at that hour, her parents were long asleep. They tiptoed into the parlor, and Bella told him to wait a moment while she changed. When she returned she was wearing a long, pleated, red-and-green tartan skirt, into which she tucked a bright yellow embroidered blouse with wide ruffled lapels and billowing sleeves. Somehow, it reminded Avrum of what Nita Naldi had worn in some of the more torrid scenes. He seemed also to recall something Bella had once described about a pleated Scotch skirt her girlfriend would wear when she wanted to be with her boyfriend.

"Can you guess why I'm wearing this blouse?" she asked him, turning her head away shyly.

"Because it's nice?"

"No, dumbbell. It's nice, but not *because* it's nice." With that, she opened it fully and exposed her bare breasts with their large dark areolas. But only for a moment. "Aren't they nice? Do you want to see them again?"

Avrum remembered their moments behind the trees on the mountain, and not that long ago in the kitchen. "Very nice. Really very nice," he replied in a quiet throaty voice, as though the words were meant for his ears alone. He also remembered the impossible tryst he had with Lucille, that sad prostitute, and he could say (thankfully) that at least Bella was definitely healthier. Still, he had to be careful not to come away a second time with what Strulevitch told him were *blue balls*.

"So? You didn't tell me that you want to see them again."

Under her tartan skirt, Bella wore nothing. She closed the light of the table lamp, and opened Avrum's trousers after slipping the suspenders off his shoulders. Later, she said that they made love and that it was wonderful, but Avrum could only remember discharging his seed barely an instant after feeling his penis try to find a path through the thick forest of her pubic hairs. He also remembered the towel Bella placed on the chesterfield before setting herself down on it. Now he knew its purpose.

(30)

Freidle Kaplan had just returned from her daily mile trek to Rachel Market on St. Lawrence Street laden with vegetables and freshly slaughtered chickens when the telephone rang. It was Kapitolnik. Freidle couldn't grasp that it really was this man at the other end. "Which Kapitolnik?" she wanted to know.

There were, after all, a number of Kapitolnik families in the city. Even when she heard him say, "Melamed Kapitolnik," it took a long moment to register. What, after all, could a man who knew God personally and who could make changes in the heavens want with someone as insignificant as herself? But in an instant, everything fell into place when she heard him ask for Avrum. Blood rushed to her face and her hands shook.

She heard him say, "I have another thing to tell him. Send him to me."

* * *

"Yes?" When Kapitolnik opened the door to Avrum, he looked at Avrum as though seeing him for the first time.

"Mrs. Kaplan told me you called and that you still had something to tell me."

"Yes — but only you. Nobody is with you? Nobody is waiting outside for you?

"Nobody. And only Mrs. Kaplan knows I'm here."

"So why did you tell her?"

Avrum could not understand where all this was leading. Kapitolnik's decided aggressiveness and critical demeanor before he'd hardly stepped foot in the house left him uneasy. Was he about to see ghosts? Would Hershel suddenly step out from behind one of the doors?

"I didn't tell her," he replied. "*You* told her. She said *you* called her."

"But you didn't have to tell her that you were coming to me *now*. If you wanted, you could come to me in the middle of next week — in the middle of next year."

Avrum kept his silence. There was nothing to gain searching for a reply. He wasn't sure Kapitolnik even expected a reply. The man had broken away from him and went to a bureau at the other side of the room. From the top drawer, he withdrew a prayer book and a small blue and gold bag. From the bag, he lifted a set of black leather phylacteries. These he proceeded to unfold.

"Now, what I'm going to do is dangerous. Do you hear what I'm saying? Dangerous!" Kapitolnik was setting a phylactery on Avrum's forehead. His hands were shaking. "It's playing with fire. Your brother — he's your blood brother, yes? From the same mother and father, yes?"

"Yes."

He then grabbed Avrum's right hand and stretched it out in front of him. "Roll your sleeve up to the top," he ordered. Avrum complied and watched Kapitolnik wrap the second phylactery tightly over the length of his arm and across his middle fingers.

"You see what I'm doing? I'm putting it on your *right* arm, not on the left. It's as much a sin as if I tied it around your leg. But now you do everything exactly, EXACTLY, as I tell you."

Avrum nodded. Kapitolnik was to read some verses from the book of Ezra and Nehemia, and when Kapitolnik would give him a sign with his eyes, Avrum was to immediately raise his left arm high above his head as though reaching for the heavens and shout — not just to say, but to shout — *"AMEN, AMEN — SHIMU SHAMAYIM — MI'BAVEL LE'YERUSHALAYIM!"* And while he would be reading the passages, Avrum was to clutch the wrist of his left hand with his right hand. After a few minutes of practice, they were ready.

When it was over, his eyes tired, his face ashen, Kapitolnik removed the phylacteries and told Avrum to go home. He hardly looked in his direction. But before Avrum let himself out, he reminded Avrum, now dazed and speechless, to leave a dollar on the table. "Maybe even a dollar and a half, if you have."

(31)

Bella was late. She called Avrum at the factory and told him matter-of-factly that her monthly should have come two weeks ago, and that she was starting to get worried. "I'm never late," she said. "Never." That left Avrum with a loud and rapid thumping in his chest.

He spoke with her every day after that hoping each time he'd hear that the threat of a pregnancy had passed. When he told her that he couldn't understand why because of him she should be late — that he wasn't even inside her when they had those few minutes of intimacy in her parlor — she progressed from being somewhat despondent to being positively insulted.

"And what makes you such an expert on these things? Did you know that it shoots out even before you feel it shooting out? Did you know that it takes only the tiniest tiniest tiniest part of a little drop to get inside and make a girl pregnant?"

Yes, he knew. It was something he had known since he was ten years old and in the company of lumbermen. But through the maze of his tension and confusion, what surfaced in his mind at this time was the question of how it came to be that Bella could be so knowledgeable about such matters.

"Maybe what you really want is to leave me having a baby while you say that you had nothing to do with it. So go pretend you're innocent. Tell people that you don't even know me. Who will believe you?" Then, after catching her breath, she added, "Maybe the best thing for me to do would be to throw myself under a train."

Bella never threw herself under a train. She never missed a day at work, and, as far as Avrum was concerned, her last period became a distant memory. There was one instance when Bella challenged him to give an honest answer, and this was when she asked him if, in his heart, he wanted her to get an abortion. Because if he did, she informed him with every word seemingly carved in stone, she would rip it out herself with knitting needles and probably bleed to death.

That line was enough for Avrum to suffer a mental replay of Shirley's botched abortion. Quietly, he surrendered to Bella's agenda.

(32)

Horse promised Avrum a bachelor's party. "But the fact is you're still a green, wet-behind-the-ears *shmuck*, Mr. A." he said. "Here you're getting up to twenty letters a day from women who tell you how big their tits are, and you have to be in a mad fool rush to get married. What for? If you want a glass of milk, you can have as much as you want. You don't have to buy the whole damn cow. I mean, even if your Bella is the second Clara Bow, what would happen if you'd wait a year or two? At least you'd squeeze in a couple of memories before taking the ride she's got planned for you."

Avrum said something about being tired of living in a room by himself, but Horse could only shake his head sadly. "Like hell it's the room. I know you, y'know. You're just a bugger gentleman, and *shmucks* like you always make it easy for someone to squeeze their balls. She wants to get married and you want to be nice. It all comes down to you needing to be nice. What happened to your goddamn *baitzes*, kid?" But Avrum just smiled and Horse slapped him on the back.

"Anyways," he went on. "We'll just have to make it a night you won't forget so fast. And besides the fact that it's coming to you, I think we all need it. This is the maddest year I can remember since the time my mother complained about a leaking pipe, and my father found out what pipe she had in mind when he caught her with the plumber." Avrum laughed. "I'll get some of the boys to bring down a piano and maybe we'll get juiced on some Dixieland. What d'ya'say?"

Avrum was high in the air. He had never known better days or better friends.

But Bella was furious when she heard of it. Avrum had come to the house while the seamstress was fitting her wedding dress, and she made him talk to her through the kitchen wall. It would bring bad luck, she insisted, if he would see her in the dress before the "final ceremony." Somehow, the way she intoned the word *final* left Avrum decidedly uneasy. Then, when she heard of Horse's plans and caught the too-enthusiastic tone in Avrum's voice, she found the scheme altogether suspect.

"You would really go out gallivanting like a *shaygitz* the night before our wedding? This you would do to me?"

Avrum's mood plummeted. Her worlds deflated and defeated him. "What's so wrong?" he asked. "I mean, tell me what harm it would be doing to you."

"You have to ask? If you have to ask — if you can't see the reasons for yourself, then go — go and enjoy yourself."

"C'mon, Bella . . . you know I'm not going to go if it's going to make you feel this way."

"Oh? Since when did you start to care?"

"Hey!" Avrum's face was almost pressing into the wall. "Why do you say that? You know it's not true."

"Oh — so now I don't know. OK, so I don't know. Go out and have all the fun in the world without me."

"Look it's only in another week. We don't have to talk about it through the wall. Believe me. I would have told him no right at the beginning if I had known it would make you feel like this."

"How do you know how I feel? How am I supposed to feel when you disappear for two months and I have to be by myself here?"

"But I wrote you almost every day, didn't I? I sent you clippings, didn't I? Where is the problem? What could be so wrong?" It pained Avrum that she should keep bringing up the problem of his absence time and again. Those two months, after all, had brought him in over six thousand dollars and alone had made the marriage possible. She knew this well. She had, after all, counted the receipts herself when he came home. And what did this have to do with the bachelor party? None of these thoughts, however, ever got translated into words.

"What could be so wrong? Everything! Just everything! But I don't expect you to understand — and I don't want to talk about it anymore."

"So I'll cancel it."

"Not because of me."

Avrum could think of nothing to say. If not because of her, then because of whom? What logic had he missed? Why was her evasiveness making the injustice she seemed to feel all the more profound?

Suddenly, Bella gave a loud shriek and Avrum heard the seamstress say that if she wouldn't move so much, the pins wouldn't stick her. "Well, I can't help it," said Bella for Avrum to hear. "I'm all nerves now." Mrs. Finegold asked him if he wanted a nice jello, but Avrum shook his head.

* * *

Horse reacted with impatience. There was nothing ambiguous about his opinion of Avrum's strength of character, "Even a fish fights back harder," he said. "Did you ever do anything in your life that was your decision?" His tone defined perfectly on which side of the line between pity and contempt his words stood.

"Actually, I'm surprised," he said. "Usually they wait 'til after the wedding before they start with their *shtick*. Y'know, the general rule is you gotta be dead before they can bury you."

Horse knew he was embarrassing Avrum. That was his intention. A somber Hank was sitting at the counter a yard from them. Willy was right behind them on the phone, and even Strulevitch, who was buried in a newspaper at the back table, could hear every word. It was the morning break; girls from the factory were walking in and out, and several other regulars were around.

"And I tell you this," he went on, "'cause I owe it to you. Let me give you a tip from my own experience. A week after I got the idea I could make a mint on the ponies because I knew some of the jockeys personally, I see I'm losing more every day. But I didn't have the brains to pull out — to quit with a little loss. I figured things would turn around with a couple good breaks. When I finally woke up, I was lucky I still had shoelaces. No shoes. No stockings. Just the laces and a dozen IOUs out there floating with my name on them. My pants I lost long ago. The point is that the difference between the winners and the losers in this world is that the first are wise — ready to pull out and cut their losses when they smell shit — while the second are all the *shmuck* heroes who go down with the ship. Y'get my message? You, Mr. A., still have the time to save your shoes *and* your laces."

Avrum hemmed and hawed until Horse raised his hands and said that he was going through with the party anyways.

Still, Avrum's heart sank when he saw Horse close up early and cover the front window with a bedsheet. He had told everyone to come in through the back, and had gotten some of the boys to bring Solomon's piano down from his place across the street. Solomon had arranged for his drummer, trombonist, and bass-man to mix it with him that night, and all it took was a word that the whole place would be swimming in liquor. The four of them used to be names even in Chicago and St. Louis, but they had this problem with the liquid refreshments, and getting arrested three times a week cut into their careers there. Roland McNeil — the best comedian they'd ever had at the Gaiety Burlesque — said he'd come with some of the girls, and it didn't take much convincing to get Lippy Lou to promise to leave his desk at the *Herald*. Zed Chicago wouldn't miss it, either. They were all there that night — the chief from the station, Willy the dancing bookie, Hank, Cy, and all the regulars; it was impossible to count them all.

They set the piano against the phone and, helped by crates and tables, balanced the drums on top of the counter. In front of the drummer on a chair stood the trombonist, and below him on the floor was the bass-man.

The crowd was too much for the place and spilled back into the lane. The noise got to all the neighbors and some of the men came down to see what the ruckus was all about. When they didn't return home, their wives went down to fetch them, and in the end, they all stayed for the fun. When they started dancing the rag in the lane, Horse brought out a couple of tables and set some crates of cold beer and sandwiches on top of them. It was everybody's party.

Avrum heard it all from his room — at least until nine-thirty, when he broke and went down to show his face. The crowd swallowed him up and Horse made a little speech about the first real beating that the great Whiskey Vishinsky was going to be getting since his illustrious career began. He extended his right arm directly ahead of him and slapped his biceps with his left hand. "And you all know exactly where he's gonna get the end of her umbrella." Then, a doused Roland McNeil said that if speeches were in order, there was a little passage from Shakespeare that fit the moment, and hands helped him climb to the top of the counter. The drummer gave him a loud and fast roll, and McNeil doffed an imaginary hat in Avrum's direction and then swung it unsteadily to take in the whole crowd. They cheered him. Then he began his hand solemnly across his heart.

"It's from *A Midsummer's Night's Cream*, and I hope our guest of honor will listen well." The clinking of the glasses and the snickers became a shade softer. "Maestro!" he shouted, pointing to the drummer, who took the cue and started another roll. Then with both hands pressed against his chest, he burst into song:

"There was magic in the air . . ." His full-toothed smile commandeered his face.

"And there was magic in her hair . . ." Now throwing his arms in the air, he tried a pirouette. He might have been a duck in a tree, but his effort was applauded. The drummer did his thing again, and fingers tapped the piano keys.

"There was magic over here, there was magic over there"

"But the magic that was best . . ." His voice climbed to a tremoring falsetto.

"Oh, yes, the magic that was beeeeeeeeeeeest . . ."

". . . was the magic in her underwear."

An instant later, an explosion of laughter, applause, stomping on the floor, and shouts of glee filled the air. But Roland McNeil wasn't done yet. Again, with both hands pressed against his chest and arching slightly forward, he began to recite. It was as though he meant his voice to reach distant bleachers.

"I TURNED AND BENT ABOVE HER THING . . ."

(Then, aside, with his hand screening the side of his mouth . . .)

"THE SMELL WAS OVERPOWERING."

The waves of shock and incredulous laughter lasted almost five minutes. Everyone looked to see the women's reactions.

He continued, showing the palms of his hands as though apologizing.

"LOOK, I SAID, WE EACH HAVE FLAWS." The howls and whoops of laughter just continued.

Again, aside, with his hand at the side of his mouth:

"MINE OF WHICH WERE 'TWEEN HER JAWS."

Another wave of loud raucous laughter followed this line and stretched as though forever. One woman shouted that she was pissing in her pants. More howls. Tears were streaming from the drummer's eyes. McNeil raised his hand for quiet.

"OH LORD, I SAID, I SWEAR THAT'S NICE." Everyone waited expectantly for the line to follow. McNeil paused. His timing was perfect, and the crowd was his.

"SHE WINKED AT ME AND SWALLOWED TWICE."

A crescendo of mad, hysterical laughter now rocked the place and it seemed as though the entire building was shaking on its foundations. The drummer fell off the counter, and here and there, people doubled up on the floor holding their stomachs. Solomon, his head on the keys, was crying like a baby. This on top of the liquor was too much.

* * *

Bella said that there were too many last minute details to look after for them to get together before the wedding. "Anyways, it's not allowed. I'm not so old-fashioned, you know, but every custom has a reason, and on the night before the *chupeh*, the bride isn't supposed to see the groom. I don't want my children born blind or without fingers. Is that what you want? Anyways, you'll live one night without me. We have the rest of our lives to be together." To Avrum's ears that sounded more like a threat than a promise.

But at ten o'clock, she needed desperately to take a walk. Dragging her mother with her, she headed for Horse's place. At first, she stayed across the street, but then she saw it was safe to look inside. Where the bedsheet left a space in a corner of the window, she studied the faces inside, and next to the fat man standing on the counter, she spotted Abie.

(33)

"Their grapes are grapes of gall,
Their clusters are bitter."
[Deuteronomy XXXII:32]

Avrum and Bella were married in Rabbi Unterman's little synagogue on St. Urbain Street near Fairmount Street. It was as though a heavy black cloud had rested over the place, because no one — perhaps with the exception of Strulevitch, who probably felt that the field of available ladies was now clear for himself — found reason to smile. Under his breath, he whispered to Cy Green that Abie could have had any broad he wanted — that they were all getting their pants wet for him. "I mean, it should only happen to me, eh? And he goes and picks this piece of *drek*."

"Yeah," replied Cy. "Go figure. She'll make mincemeat out of him before no time."

Bella, for her part, cried as though getting married was the very worst tragedy that could have befallen her. The one moment her tears stopped was when Fanny appeared dressed all in black. Bella asked her mother how Fanny could do such a thing to her — coming to her wedding as though dressed for a funeral. "Is she trying to show how uppity modern she is? Would you believe she's my sister?" Bluma's reply would never reach her lips; she sufficed by patting Bella's eyes with her handkerchief. "Be careful you don't let the mascara run. You don't want to look silly."

With the ceremony done and the glasses of *shnapps* emptied, along with the small table of cakes, breads, *kugels*, and *shmaltz* herring, Avrum and Bella took a fine horse-drawn carriage to the train station for their honeymoon in New York. It was there, in the new, ultra-modern Pennsylvania Hotel, that Bella told Avrum that God was with them and that she just got her period.

"Why couldn't it have come just a little earlier?" she asked in mock complaint.

Avrum was sure he knew the answer to that. He registered no surprise.

* * *

After three months in the house that they had rented from her uncle's cousin on his wife's side, Bella decided that from that moment, it was absolutely impossible for her to continue living there. She admitted, without anyone having to point out, that it was she who had only suggested that they move in there — though at the time, Avrum had the distinct impression that she was insisting. "And why not," she said. It was an upper St. Joseph's Street address. It was away from the *Frantzoizen*. And because it belonged to family, the rent would be more reasonable there than anywhere else. But how was she to know that the whole district would immediately become "bombarded" with so many primitive and filthy immigrants — even if they were all Jews.

"I walk into their houses, and everything I see there came from the secondhand man. When he comes around with his wagon, they drag me out for my opinion about this or that. Am I supposed to tell them that I wouldn't touch any of the things there with a ten-foot pole? Every disease in the world gets into that wagon. And then they come to my house and put their hands on my curtains. They buy a bag of French fries from the street peddler and empty a bottle of vinegar in it. It leaks all over and then they come into my house to sit on the chesterfield. All the dirt from the streets, they wipe on my carpets. I feel like puking."

She wouldn't let up. "Their husbands are all wet *shmattes* scraping for every cent, and you should see them in the grocery store or at the butcher's. I buy like for a human being, and they ask for a small piece of this or a quarter of that while they look with their big eyes to see what I have in my bag. Sometimes I even feel ashamed that I can afford a dollar or two."

If it was only a dollar or two, it wouldn't have been so bad, Avrum had thought to himself. Bella allowed herself considerably more than that. She had convinced him that the house needed curtains "to show that people and not pigs live here." But why did the material she just had to have need to be the most expensive in the shop? When he said a word to that effect, she said sourly that he knew absolutely nothing about curtains.

"Buying the best now only means not having to buy again in a year from now. You leave the buying to me and don't stick your nose into what's not your business." Then she would hurl at him, "Go back to your bachelor party." This was a line she found reason to repeat at least once each day.

After the curtains came the carpets, and after that, a complete chesterfield set with two rich mahogany lamp tables; then Bella found it impossible to sleep on beds that weren't part of a complete bedroom set, and that meant a matching dresser as well.

It was then, when the house was finished and all the friends and relations had been called to inspect it, that Bella started in to complain about the neighborhood. Lawrence Feldman was sending him discreet feelers about their partnership in the gasoline station, but they always seemed to come after Bella had undertaken yet another massive expenditure. He had told her about this opportunity to make an investment for the future, but for her, a gasoline station meant only grease and the kind of smell that would never come out in the laundry. "If you have the money," she said, "find something *menshlichdik* so that people will look at you with respect."

She kept repeating that all her real friends lived in Outremont and Westmount, and that only she had to be married to someone who couldn't afford a house there. But one day, she heard of a place available on deVimy, which was Outremont and exactly the area she wanted. "Living on deVimy," she said, "will show people that we aren't living a hand-to-mouth existence." A month later, they moved there, and the curtains turned out to be too small for the living room, and they didn't suit the bedroom, which had its own curtains anyways. At the store where Bella had bought them, she was told that there was no more of that material, so she had new curtains made up and gave the old ones to her mother. The house on deVimy also had a coal shed and dining room leading from the kitchen. Bella got it through to Avrum that without a dining room table — and matching chairs — she'd be miserable for the rest of her life and ashamed to bring anyone into the house. "A fine dining room table you buy once in a lifetime," she said. "It costs you once, and then it's over with. I'm not going to have people come in and see a dining room and think that we can't afford a dining room table."

Avrum reminded her that, at first, she had said the room would be perfect for when the children come. But Bella was never without a ready answer.

"There's enough room in this house for children. I don't plan on having a dozen. Believe me."

To get the house, Avrum had to pay three months' rent in advance, and he told her as simply as he knew how to that they were very low on money then. The table would have to wait. For a week, Bella wouldn't let him touch her. It was also the week before her period when her temper didn't need much provocation to flare up, and Avrum made every effort to be understanding. Then she moaned and groaned through her menstruation until one night, by lying inches over on Avrum's side of the bed, she let him know that he could have her. But he also had to know that it was entirely a sacrifice on her part, and he was on top of her no more than a minute when she asked him to hurry up and finish. For all the life she let herself show, Avrum might just as well have been fornicating with a tree.

Bella got her table. Avrum was the biggest attraction and money-drawer the Mount Royal Arena had ever known. He had invented a kind of flying kick that sparked a long debate over whether it was legal or not, but that in the end was allowed. And the crowds came in hordes to see him do it. The promoter signed him up for an unprecedented six consecutive weeks, and Horse wrangled a five-hundred-dollar advance, which was another unprecedented arrangement. During these six weeks, Avrum also appeared in Dorval, L'Abord-à-Plouff, St. Jerome, Laval, and Val Morin so that even after the table was bought, the bank book showed almost enough to make the investment with Feldman; he'd borrow the rest from Horse. It was then that Bella found that she needed a fur coat. ("My friends should all have their mink coats and stoles, while I have to parade in this old imitation rabbit? You don't care what people should think of me, do you!")

After the coat, Bella set her eyes on a set of china for twelve places. Fine silverware followed that, and by the end of the year, Avrum also owned a shiny new DeSoto. The investment with Feldman that was always "just another couple of matches away" was forgotten. Feldman regretted that the project couldn't wait and he had another fellow who was prepared to go in with him. "But frankly, Abie, I was hoping to God it would be with a guy like you."

Bella's friends were the women who made up the local chapter of Hadassah, and she was forever talking about the marvelous work they were doing for *Eretz Yisrooel*. Their president was the very devoted Myra Tannenbaum, who spoke of herself as a personal friend of the Hadassah movement's founder, Henrietta Szold. Her husband was Tannenbaum, the ear, nose, and throat specialist. It was known that she could pick up the phone anytime to A.J. Freiman himself, who was the president of the Canadian Zionist Federation. Lillian Freiman, the woman who had gotten the Hadassah movement underway in Canada, was also an intimate of hers, and Myra never showed up for a meeting without being able to report details of another vital conversation that had passed between them.

The tea break was always a terrifying time for Bella. Until a meeting was called to order, the women would talk about the agenda and about past and future programs, but the tea break was the time they talked about their families. If their husbands weren't doctors, then they were lawyers. If not lawyers, then at least they were chartered accountants, or else they ran their own successful businesses. And under her mink coat and diamond ring, Bella would eat herself up imagining what the women were really saying to each other about her, even while they smiled in her direction. Her husband was none of these, and she suspected that the worst mistake in her life was not having waited for Sam, for another enervating embarrassment which she was forced to endure was Sam's courtship with Myra Tannenbaum's daughter Charlotte, who from time to time made an appearance at these meetings. She wondered what nerve Sam had reaching for someone above his level.

Charlotte was a slim, tallish girl studying at McGill on a scholarship, and she always looked smooth, serene, and demure. Bella tortured herself thinking how everyone must be comparing the two of them, and she worked hard at being smooth, serene, and demure herself. No one would have guessed about her own past with Sam, but his sudden appearance when he came the first time to collect Charlotte surprised her, and before anyone explained anything about their relationship, she had called out, "Sam, how did you know I was here?" Of course, he didn't know, and long and altogether confused explanations ensued.

Then, in one of his fights at the Arena, Avrum's face registered a look of such surprise when his opponent surprised him with a flying kick of his own that the editor of the *Star* saw fit to print it. Avrum won the match with two straight falls, the second of which had brought the doctor into the ring to check the fellow's spine when he seemed unable to straighten up after Avrum's double back lock had crushed him — but that Avrum won was noted only in a few words at the bottom. The caption suggested quite the reverse. It read: *When the Boot Is On The Other Foot: Whiskey Vishinsky gets a taste of his own medicine and finds it a crushing experience. Moose Moonie the Danish Dynamo gives the teacher a lesson in Aero Dramatics.*

At their next meeting, Myra Tannenbaum had opened the meeting but paused, suddenly remembering something that apparently concerned her. In front of all the women, she asked Bella if her husband was all right "after that terrible kick in the face that they showed in the newspaper." Bella blushed and shrugged the fight off as just an act. Myra carried on with the meeting, but Bella was frozen with shame. She couldn't even bring herself to say that in the end her Abie had won.

And she couldn't work the episode out of her system, no matter how often she repeated the story to Avrum and to her parents. Finally, she said that whatever the consequences, Avrum would have to stop his wrestling. The shame of it would kill her, and anyway, with his name and reputation, he could make as much money, if not more, as a salesman. Goldenberg could give him a territory and he could go on the road. Avrum said it was impossible, and if Bella would see how many of the city's finest Jews came to watch him, she would feel proud instead of ashamed. He was their hero — even the Jewish daily, the *Keneder Adler*, said as much. And the *Yiddisher Forvartz* wrote up all his fights.

Bella remained unconvinced. Until Avrum stopped his wrestling, she would "be only half a person and could never show her face at the meetings again." Her distress totally exhausted all her own sexual desires, and made her impatient with any that arose in Avrum. She wailed that she wouldn't sleep with him in the same bed. Taking a blanket, she carried it off to the chesterfield. Five minutes later, she was back saying that she didn't see why she had to be the one to sleep on the uncomfortable chesterfield. "You're the sick one. It's not me who is oversexed."

Avrum asked Bella to meet him halfway. He explained that they simply needed the money — that everything they owned came directly from his wrestling. He would agree to keep strictly to the Montreal area and cut down sharply even here on the number of matches he'd take on. "But if I stop completely, they will forget me," he said. "A lot of people depend on me, and I depend of them."

"But these people don't have to live with you," she retorted. And when Avrum came home hurting after his first defeat at the hands of a tough, young Irishman, he found that Bella had gone back to her parents. She left him this note:

"I'm just fed up being taken for granted. Find somebody else who will sweat and slave for you, cooking night and day, scrubbing floors and washing your stinky, dirty underwear. I have to do everything for you and you can spit in my face. My own worst enemy wouldn't do to me what you do. So see how it is to live with your own miserable self."

But then Avrum read a line that made him catch his breath. *"I'm going to Mama. Not that it should concern you, but I'm going to have a b—y. At least here somebody will take care of us."*

She left it unsigned, but her childlike scrabbled scrawl was signature enough. And she wrote "baby" like she would "God" — framing the word in its first and last letters. Did she think she was carrying the next messiah? Nothing about his wife could surprise him anymore.

Bella came home the next day. Avrum had assured her that all his wrestling days were behind him. He said he wanted a family and a fine home as much as she did, and if his wrestling had brought them what it had, perhaps that was more than he should have expected in the first place.

Horse reacted with a cool "If that's the way you want it." But Strulevitch stayed on his back for a week until it finally percolated through to his senses that Avrum was up against something that was impervious to everything in his own arsenal of insults and arguments. On the other hand, Goldenberg was pleased. True, he was paying Avrum more than he'd have liked to — after all, how long ago had it been since the boy stepped off the boat? — but a good deal of their business the last year, especially the new business, was in one way or another thanks to him. Now, when in spring and fall he'd have lines to show, he'd take Avrum with him around the city, and maybe he'd send him on his own to Ottawa. Perhaps even to Toronto and all the towns in between — everyone would remember him.

But in the most imperceptible way, perhaps in the liberties people would take with the tone of their voices if not with their choices of words, Avrum was regarded as a disappointment and as a failure. Where once the operators anticipated what he might need of them and have it ready before he'd get around to asking for it, now they needed coaxing, understanding, and favors. It surely didn't help that he had quit the ring on the heels of his first defeat. The papers rushed in as one to play up the poor loser angle in their stories, and the final letters that trickled in to him now had mostly unflattering words. He had let them down, they felt. One wrote that it wasn't fair that he had promised so much at the beginning only to disillusion every little Jew who needed a hero — a Samson. Avrum showed these letters to Bella, but she turned up her nose. "It's time someone told you that only idiots write such things. Anyways, only a dumb fool would do or not do something because some stranger wanted it. And if a stupid ignoramus tells you to go back to wrestling, you'd listen to him before you'd listen to me?"

Bella became devoted to her pregnancy. She wouldn't allow Avrum to lie heavily on her, and he had to promise that he wouldn't do more than rub the head of his "thing" on "the inside of the outside." And she would bear him silently while he'd be at it. When she wanted a woman in to do the laundry and the floors, Avrum mumbled something about what it would cost, but he didn't fight it.

Then the last of the money ran out. Goldenberg was paying him thirty dollars a week, and that about covered the rent and the groceries. Not a penny could be set aside for shoes or anything else, and Avrum had even to tell Bella once that they couldn't go to the picture she was desperate to see ". . . at least not until I get my wages on Friday." Bella demanded to know how he expected to support both her and the child when it was born. "It's going to need a crib, diapers, blankets, a carriage, a bath. It's going to need bottles and milk and toys . . ." Avrum was equally desperate for answers, but he hadn't any. He turned to

Horse for a chance to handle another poker game, but Horse told him that everything was dry. "If you're short, though, I'll loan you as much as you need," he had said, and Avrum thanked him but said he'd wait at least until the kid was born.

Then he remembered Grigor. It had been a long time since that last phone call, but he found the card in a drawer and called the number. A woman's voice at the other end insisted on knowing who wanted him. Avrum identified himself, and there was a pause until a man came on and said that Grigor had suffered an unfortunate accident and was killed. Shocked and crestfallen, Avrum asked what happened, but the man just apologized and hung up. Avrum mentioned this later to Strulevitch, who said, "Didn't you know? Georgie and two more were shot moving crates of whiskey across the border. Eh? And you once wanted to go with him, didn't you?"

Bills came for the car insurance and Bella needed new clothes. House repairs were put off and dishes that broke couldn't be replaced. Bella's anger and bitterness knew no bounds. She was unable to talk to him without shouting and her heavy sarcasm and insulting references to his sudden sexual impotence crushed him. Avrum would come home and sit with his paper on the balcony, like the old farmers did along the Laurentian highway where the road cut through their villages. They'd sit there dull and stupefied watching the cars stream by, and Avrum was beginning to do much the same thing. Once, she threw boiling water at him; luckily, only two or three drops touched his skin. She shrieked that she wanted him out of her life, and demanded from God that He put an end to her suffering.

Avrum slept two nights at the Drummond Y.M.C.A., but then he answered an ad for a night watchman at a large central bank, and with the promise of an additional salary, he went home. Bella heard him out and told him that he did the right thing. She translated "night watchman" into "special security officer," and attached to the name of the bank, it sounded impressive enough for her. But then she stopped going to her Hadassah meetings when she felt that it would be impossible for her to show her face in the same hat she wore the year before; and a new hat — at least one that would do her justice — would cost more than she could get her hands on. On those evenings, she would sit sullen and silent. Avrum knew she was blaming him. But he would be thinking of the night and of all the terrors he would again be alone with. They had come back — this time entrenched securely in all his glaring insufficiencies.

(34)

Horse told Avrum that a letter came in for him about a month ago. "It was addressed to *Whiskey Vishinsky, cee ohh Braverman* and had landed with him. He figured it was from another broad sending you her lipstick on a napkin that forgot you weren't wrestling no more. So seeing as you were out of the business, and that anyway you were hitched, he forgot all about it. A couple days ago, I seen him on some business, and he remembered the letter and gives it to me." Horse felt around in his vest pockets and then in his trouser pockets where he found it. "It's a little crumpled, but what the hell."

It was from an address in New York. There was no way to understand what the sender of the letter wanted to say. Attached to a note was a small brown photo of what seemed a piece of parchment. On the parchment could be seen the faintest printing of Hebrew scripture. Nothing more. The note itself was a large and almost wild scrawl. Horse tried to help Avrum fathom the letters. It was signed by someone named Larry, or Gerry, or Jimmy, and appeared to ask Avrum if he knew what was in the picture, ". . . because if you do—" the rest was almost illegible "—then you know I go on and on or I am a lie." Horse and Avrum concluded that they may be reading it wrong but that in any event the message was probably meant as a prayer by some religious dodo who promised eternal life. Letters from lunatics and religious crazies were always being received. At the bottom of the message under the signature and in the same impossible scrawl was a telephone number.

Avrum crumpled the letter and was about to deliver it to the wastepaper basket when he had second thoughts. If that photograph of the paper or parchment really was holy scripture, the words surely included the name of God. At this point in his life, Avrum wasn't inclined to chance being sinful. He shoved the letter and picture deep into his pocket. He had other things on his mind, issues that were more immediate and more pressing.

"Abie — is everything ok?" asked Horse. "My feeling is that something is bothering you. Y'know, if you need something, you can still come to me. I don't have to tell you this. It's something you should always know."

"Thanks, Horse. No — I'm fine. Really fine. I'm working."

Behind his eyes, Avrum knew the truth was something else. He was struggling with debts. There were holes in the soles of his shoes, and he had to put off taking them to a shoemaker. A window in the house was broken and he didn't have the money to bring in a glazier. When she complained, Avrum would tell Bella that he needed to wait for his next paycheck.

(35)

The woman in the red coat paused at the card in the window; then she came into the shop and asked about it. Fanny explained that she was the art teacher, that the lessons were given in her house twice a week, that she asked only two dollars for a whole month's tuition, and yes, she would very much like to develop the natural talent that the woman saw in her boy. "He's small and delicate, my little Willy," she said, "and he paints in the most beautiful way.

Willy was truly a gifted little boy. At eleven and a half, the soft cherubic delicacy of his skin, which looked like warm butter tinged with the pink of Damask roses, still lingered. It was the same with almost every other heritage of his infancy. But his small, frightened eyes and the trembling that sometimes came to the corners of his lips played on Fanny's imagination and fantasies. His drawings, his colors, the way he would move his brush, or even the way he would lift the stick of charcoal to his paper, spoke to her of a hypnotic submersion in some deep, hidden, and almost unworldly sensuality. Sometimes she would stand behind him and slip her fingers softly through his hair, hoping the vibrations of her mind would carry through her fingertips to his. Often there were moments — unbearable moments — when she longed for him to cling to her with his head pressing against her breast. She was certain that, given the chance, she could insulate him from all the insidious poisons that so deformed the vision and the values of the aggressive, selfish, and ugly commercial culture of their time.

Her feeling had a chemistry that she followed with trepidation, for all this had happened before. Their names, of course, were different; one might be taller, another shorter, or stouter perhaps, like the so-timid Julian, but she had known them all when their lives were at just that irretrievable moment that recalled for her the dawn hours after a first snowfall. And she tried under her ceiling to create a sanctuary where she might foil the grit and grime waiting to discolor this flush of pure whiteness in their lives.

The children seemed to understand this. Indeed, the only armor she had against the ugly and absurd railings of offended parents was the certainty that their children were left with such riches as even the hardening trials of a lifetime could never diminish its wonder for them. But the parents — the parents and the law — saw her actions as belonging to quite another order of morality.

Once when brought before a judge, she repeated a line from Hesse: "*One of the shortest ways to sanctity may be a life of carnal riot*." Hearing this, on top of the charges against her, the judge had her spend a month in jail advising her to use the library there to investigate less insane philosophies. He also saw fit to add, "And in future, young lady, I would ask you to keep away from all this unbecoming pornography which the French seem to be infesting us with lately. I wouldn't be at all surprised if that remark came to you off the back of one of their naked postcards."

"Herman Hesse is German, not French," Fanny corrected him.

This had delivered the judge to a point where his agitation seemed to make him no longer responsible for his words or actions. "Take this filth away from my eyes immediately," he ordered an officer in the courtroom. For a full minute, he had waved his finger angrily at her.

On the days when Willy came for his lessons, Fanny would wear her flowing and billowy seersucker dress. It was almost the color of his skin, and when she'd stand over his work, leaning across him sometimes to point at something, she liked to see it fall around him, enveloping him in its folds, blending with him, absorbing him into her, as it were. Before the lesson, she would sprinkle a few drops of rosewater over the cloth at her bosom, and at these moments, she would brush her breast like a whisper against his cheek. Sometimes he would turn his cheek into it, and Fanny would have to draw on every ounce of strength in her will to resist delivering her nipple to his mouth.

With the other children, her behavior was only a trifle more restrained lest they believe that her favors were selective or calculated. They too were given to enjoy the smell of her, the feel of her hand on their heads and necks, the kisses on their cheeks and the feel of her dress flowing over them. But she had much more to give Willy. There were moments — and she would feel her heart stirring nervously in the knowledge of what she was about to do — when she would stand in front of him and say something about the way he had mixed his colors. She'd pretend to search for something in his box or she'd prepare new cups of colors and she would stoop and lean forward, talking about one thing or another. Her back would be to the other children, and she would let her dress, which was cut very wide and loose around her neck, fall slowly away. She would be wearing nothing underneath, and by making Willy talk to her, she would bring his head up and present her breasts to his eyes. They would hang freely, and Willy, frozen in his place, would feel himself swimming in their mystery. Willy would always blush fiercely and his words would stay buried in his throat, but Fanny saw that he was a brave little boy.

The first time he couldn't bring himself to look at her at all, and Fanny was anxious about whether he'd report what she'd done to his mother. But he had shown up early for his next lesson, and only a wild impulse drove her against all reason to repeat what she had done. This time Willy allowed himself a furtive glance before dropping his head in shame. "It's OK, Willy, it's OK," she whispered warmly in his ear as she rose.

* * *

Willy didn't come to his next class, or to the one after that. Fanny became increasingly nervous. She might open the door, she imagined, and again find the police there. Or Willy's parents might repeat the unpleasant scenes that other parents had made her endure. He was a very quiet and introverted little boy, but his mother would surely pry from his lips everything that had transpired. While in the States, she had learned from Harry how a glass of whiskey could stop hands from shaking, and these last few days saw her turning with greater and greater frequency to the bottle. The sounds of someone climbing the steps, even when she knew it was most likely one or another of her pupils, terrified her enough to make her heart race painfully. It would take almost half a glass of whiskey to calm her nerves. How fittingly out of character she would think, that while Jews paraded their sobriety before the Gentiles, she couldn't make it to her bed at night until the liquor brought her to the edge of a stupor.

Moreover, she became increasingly careless with her pupils, letting more and more of them see into the neck of her dress. Sometimes, talking to them at their boards, she would let her hand rest at the top of their thighs. Often her breath reeked of the whiskey, and when she sensed that at times the children drew away from her, she took to sprinkling more rosewater over her. Willy never returned.

One afternoon, an older boy by the name of Julian who would come to collect his brother returned to the studio on some pretense, and she let him into her bed. He wasn't shy, and she knew it was all so terribly wrong — but the whiskey was numbing her senses, and her legs weren't supporting her. He groped at her clothes and he wanted her so much. He pleaded with her — it would take so little to make him happy. Her mind was clouded and her capacity to be willful deserted her. She tried to tell him things, to plead, to explain, but soon he was above her, discharging into her. He left her in a rush, but through the haze of her confusion and exhaustion, she saw in the distance disgust and triumph fire in his eyes. The door slammed behind him.

Fanny left the bed to search blindly for the bottle of whiskey. Only when she felt its fires again ravage her throat did she tend to her ablutions.

It may have been ten minutes, it may have been two hours since Julian had left. She felt her strength returning and the haze had lifted from her sense of time and place when she heard a sharp knocking at her door. If it was the police, she thought, they'd be angels to take her away from this room. Instead, it was two hard-looking boys who forced themselves in when she opened the door. It struck her that they were wearing the same black satiny jackets that that young rapist Julian had worn.

They introduced themselves, grinning, saying that so many people had told them such nice things about her, and their club, the Guy Street Dukes, were all great guys and would give her almost anything she'd asked for if she would spend a little time with them that night.

Fanny was now fully alert to their criminal intentions. She struggled in her mind to find some way to diffuse their aggressiveness. "What would I want? And what would they want — your club? Maybe you're looking for somebody else?"

"No, no, it's you," they assured her. And one of the boys took a bold initiative. He reached for her hand and held it with a gentleness which strangely reassured her — but only for an instant. She backed away from them in a rush and shouted for them to leave her alone.

"Listen, we're all great guys, like I said. We'd really like it if you'd come with us. And it's a great place — real private."

Again, she shouted and pleaded for them to go. "I don't know you. I don't know any of you. And I'm expecting people." Fanny withdrew to the table near the sink and struggled to have it shield her from them. Her mind was clouding again.

"That's why we came, miss — we want you to know us." Both laughed.

Fanny shook her head and mumbled, "No. No. Leave me. Just go. Please."

"Look, we'll bring you there. See for yourself what it looks like. We've got these great pictures on the walls and everything. If you say you want to come home, we'll bring you home. Won't we, Stu?"

The boy called Stu nodded, "Sure . . . for sure . . . the minute you say."

Fanny looked for the whiskey bottle. "No. I don't know you, and I don't want to know you. Leave me alone."

"The boys will be disappointed, and we don't want that," said the first boy. A distinct threat hung heavily over his words. He continued, "Maybe you'll change your mind. I tell you, we're all great guys. The Guy Street Dukes have a reputation. We'd also be good for you if you'd trust us. We can pay you. Cash."

"Pay me? Pay me for what?"

The boys exchanged a few quiet words between themselves, then Stu said, "Five bucks."

"Five dollars for what? Oh, God, please, please get out."

Despite herself, Fanny reached for the whiskey bottle, poured herself some and downed it in one swallow.

There was a pause. Then the first boy stepped up close to her, and struck her with a vicious blow to her stomach. The glass flew from her hand and Fanny, gasping for air, dropped to her knees. Stu took a handkerchief from his pocket and crammed it hard into her mouth. Fanny's face contorted with horror and disbelief.

"I don't want to hit you again, lady, but I will until you agree to come with us," said the first fellow, smiling easily. Fanny nodded her head crazily — her mind a wild eruption of panic and pain.

"Will you shout or pull any tricks if we take the handkerchief out?" Fanny shook her head. "Well, you're smart. I was gonna hit you a lot harder the second time. I promised the guys I'd convince you to come, and I'm a man of my word. I mean, I have no choice, y'see?"

"What do y'say, Reg — let's get our piece in now," suggested Stu.

"I was thinking of that. Any objections, Miss?" Fanny was crying and blind with fear and desperation. With one hand on her wrist and the other pressing into her armpit, Reg swung her hard around onto her bed. "You move from that bed," he said to her evenly, "and you'll swallow your teeth." Stu was about to rip her dress off, but Reg cautioned him to "be careful with the buttons — we still got to walk her in the street."

They took their jackets, trousers, and underthings off and stood exposed before her. "Just for warm-ups, this. Now, you listen," warned Reg, "you open your legs as far as you can without me even touching you. Close them for a second, and I swear I'll tie one foot to the window and the other to the stove and I'll ram that friggin' whiskey bottle up you."

"God, please." Fanny's face was the color or chalk.

"Open them, you bitch. Let's see what makes a kike's box so bloody special." Stu said this, but his voice was shaking.

Reg went into her first and pumped furiously. It was over in seconds. "I've had better," he said, climbing off and wiping himself on her bedspread. "You take her, Stu."

But Stu was too excited, and the instant he felt his penis on her body, he splayed his ejaculate everywhere but where he wished to. "Shit," he muttered. "At the last second, I thought what if she had the clap or something."

"Nah, kikes don't get it. But if she gave it to me, I'd kill her."

"Maybe I should have pumped her, then," muttered Stu, hoping he had covered his abject failure.

"Go wipe yourself off, lady, and let's move," said Reg, and Fanny did what he told her. Her stomach hurt unbearably and thick fluids drained from her nose and mouth. If at that moment death would separate her from her tormentors, it would be a blessing.

The clubhouse was an old disused wagon shed under a sprawling warehouse. Smoking nervously, fifteen or twenty young toughs were waiting there for her. Before they left her house, Reg had forced another half glass of whiskey down her throat, and Fanny had become insensible to everything except the relentless pounding in her head. When they came to the door, someone was waiting there to open it, and Reg pushed her roughly in ahead of him. Fanny tripped and tore the skin of her knee on the cement floor. Shakily, she got to her feet and tried to make her way back to the door, but the alcohol had blinded her. Reg blocked her way. He twisted her around and brought her to the middle of the room.

"As of now, she's the property of the Guy Street Dukes," he said importantly. "We own her."

They congratulated him, and Stu said loudly that they had to slip her in a couple of lays to convince her that the Dukes were terrific guys. Someone was burning her neck with a cigarette. Hands reached under her dress. Others pushed her to the back of the room, which was partitioned by a few lengths of old corrugated tin. On the floor was a gray, molding mattress, and hands reached at her from everywhere and tore her clothes away. Then she was pushed down onto the mattress and a body dropped heavily on top of her. Fanny fought him and the boy complained. Reg crossed the room and asked the boy to get off her for a second. Fanny was mumbling incoherently and the boys were uneasy, but Reg said he just had to remind her of their agreement. He helped her to her feet and then took his arm away when she tried to steady herself. She seemed about to lurch against the wall when his fist drove murderously against her jaw and she collapsed with her limbs twisted under her. He straightened her out on the mattress and asked someone to open a bottle of beer. It was in his hands in seconds, and he spilled some across her mouth. Then he spoke to her softly about being nice to them and how they would be nice to her.

Blood showed at the corner of her mouth. He lit a cigarette and pushed it between her lips, but Fanny let it fall away. Reg shook his head. "No sense wasting a good fag," he said, picking it up. He let it hang at the corner of his mouth and motioned with his finger for the boy to get back on top of her.

The faces passed above her in an unreal blur. Then some boys said that they weren't going to put their peckers into that gooey, stinking cesspool. Her belly, crotch, and thighs were coated thickly now with their steamy discharge, and its harsh, acrid smell came up to them. One of the boys said he'd rather jerk off into her mouth, but another cautioned that she might bite. Reg said he'd fix that. He gripped her breast and twisted it hard. He told her that if anyone felt teeth, he personally would kill her.

Fanny rolled her head from side to side, coughing and gagging on her blood and saliva. "Can't have that either, you friggin' whore," said Reg again, and he got behind her and pulled down hard on her hair. Then they kneeled over her and did things to themselves over her mouth. Fanny choked and coughed and spit and swallowed. She could no longer breathe through her nose.

Someone said that the last guys who were let into the club should prove they had real guts by getting into her ass. Reg said that that was a damn good idea, and he was making it part of the Dukes' new initiation rules from that day on. He worked Fanny onto her knees, and then pressed her head down to the mattress. She didn't resist. Between her legs, behind her, hands were spreading her cheeks apart, and suddenly an impossible pain tore into her, ripping and splitting her. A savage unearthly shriek broke through the veil of her stifling numbness, and Reg kicked sharply at her face.

The one who had been inside her complained about the shit that came off on him, and Red said that she'd just have to suck him clean. He sat her up and told her to open her mouth. Fanny heard the words dimly from miles away, and with everything in her body hurting, it hardly mattered that something was being pushed into her mouth. But then it pressed into the throat, and struggling for air, she tried to work free of it. A fist turned and twisted in her hair and held her back. Maddened by the fear and the hopeless, unending torment of it all, Fanny drove her teeth with maniacal fury into the soft meat. A shattering scream exploded above her. Her teeth locked even harder on it then, until a bottle crashed against her skull and brought the quietest of nights down to take her away.

(36)

"I know it's three in the morning, but Christ I got something for you. You can buy it or you can go back to your never never land, but get the wax out of your ears for half a minute."

"Shoot — and hey, even before I hear it, whatever it is, I gotta thank you for keeping me in mind." Simon rubbed the sleep from his eyes and concentrated hard on what he was hearing.

"I got this absolutely naked broad — about twenty-two, twenty-three — stashed behind some garbage pails, spunk coming out of every hole, and I mean every damn hole except maybe her ears. She's got teeth broken and her head's bashed in and full of blood. She's out, but I checked that she's alive. It looks like another bloody gang rape. You want it, it'll cost you a fiver, and you got ten minutes before I call the station."

"Henry, you're the most lovable cop in the business. I'm gonna push you for lieutenant next time around. Make that twenty minutes, OK?" Simon was already into his pants.

"You got fifteen. If you're here in twenty, you'll still get your picture. It's in the lane behind the Luxor Insurance and Royal Bank buildings. If you turn west on Guy behind the buildings, it's about fifty yards up."

Simon kissed the phone.

Fanny's broken and naked body draped lifelessly across some garbage pails filled the bottom half of the *Herald*'s front page the following day. Short brush strokes blackened out her nipples and pubic area, but otherwise, the photograph left little to the imagination. Above it, the headlines screamed *THIRD GANG RAPE THIS YEAR WORST YET*. In print only a fraction smaller, *WILL IT TAKE MURDER BEFORE POLICE CLEAN UP PACKS OF GANG RATS?* Filling the rest of the space were all the lurid details of the hospital report, which included Fanny's full name, age, and address.

At the same hospital, doctors were working through the night repairing the severely mauled penis of a sixteen-year-old boy. It would never be the same.

(37)

Her mother wailed that she was going to kill herself, but in the end, she went to the hospital and cried at Fanny's bed. Fanny was in a coma for four days. Gradually she came to herself and could even smile when her mother related to her about their neighbor, who, while taking a shower, had reached for the shampoo, but because of the steam in the room didn't realize that what he was in fact rubbing into his scalp was the hair remover cream his wife used for her legs. It hurt Fanny to laugh but she laughed weakly. When her father came with flowers after work, they hugged.

But latching herself firmly onto all the right reasons, Bella absolutely refused to see her sister. "Family is family," Bluma tried to explain when she telephoned and asked her daughter to join them at the hospital. "And this is the time we have to show the world where we stand. I'm not going to be ashamed to show my face with my own flesh and blood. Even your father says that in God's eyes the shame is coming to us for the bad things maybe we did to her — I don't have to tell you when. But we're older now, and *dafka* now when she needs somebody, it's not going to be her mother who is going to turn her back on her. I'll find a way to live with my *shprintzileyah* friends. If they feel I'm too low to talk to anymore, then I don't want even to think that they were ever my friends." But Bella wasn't about to be swayed.

"In a million years, I wouldn't change my mind," she said. "And you can tell her that I'll never forgive her."

"You're wrong, *tochter*. When somebody is bleeding — even if she is your worst enemy — you don't make the sore deeper."

"And what about all the deep sores she made in *my* body?"

"*Nu!* Look at what you have and look at what she has. Look at the way you live and at the way she lives."

Bella defended herself. "What good is a fur coat if you can't show your face in it?"

"And what is that supposed to mean? You're still complaining with a fur coat?"

"I have my own serious problems, Mama. My life isn't exactly cherries."

"Look. I didn't call to argue with you. When such a thing happens — you know what to do, or you don't know. It's not something you can learn from a lecture or an argument. It has to come from inside."

"You don't know for a minute what I feel like inside, Mama."

"I try to know."

"Well, you just don't know! When I saw that picture in the paper, it was the end of the world for me. My name was suddenly the dirtiest word in the world."

"You know, maybe it would solve all you problems if you'd remember that your name is Vishinsky now. Your papa, Fanny, and me — it's just us with the dirty name of Finegold."

"Mama!"

"We three have to stick to each other. But if you want, you're free, so don't worry about how your face looks in your fur coat."

Enraged, Bella slammed the receiver down. That was the only answer coming to her, she told herself. Why was it suddenly a crime to own a fur coat? But as the minutes passed, she lost the thread of her own curdled logic and her thoughts increasingly filled with the tumult of accusations that she imagined were certain to be hurled at her. She knew what they would say. Behind her eyes, the image of herself as others might see her assumed the most grotesque and crippling dimensions.

Bella cleared the kitchen table so that her letter would be the first thing (after herself) that would catch the eye of anyone coming into the room. She closed the windows and latched them purposefully. For added effect, she also drew the blinds. Then she set a chair next to the stove and went to the parlor window to wait. At five minutes past five, she spotted Avrum turning the corner. In two to three minutes, he'd be at the door.

Opening the four jets of her gas stove to their maximum, she was about to sit in the chair when the thought came to her that the sight would be infinitely more dramatic if she was to be found sprawled on the floor — in her "condition." So she overturned the chair and adjusted herself on the linoleum . . . and waited.

The smell was quickly becoming unpleasant and she thought perhaps she'd get up and open the window a touch. But then she heard the tinkle of keys, and she knew Avrum was at the door. She stayed where she was and fought to keep her eyes from moving.

Avrum had the key in the door, but at that moment, Mr. Chessik, his neighbor, came up the stairs and asked him if he could make sense of a prescription his doctor had given him. Actually, he already knew what was written — the Doctor had told him — but it didn't hurt to check. And for Mr. Chessik, talking about his bladder sometimes helped it more than the pills.

Bella's eyes weren't moving and neither was anything else when Avrum found her. She was quite dead.

Bella's letter was an unusually neat few lines that scattered blame like shrapnel. It named only Fanny, tearing into her *"for making it impossible for anyone with any real feeling in the family, to look life in the eyes anymore."* A line later described how *"from day one"* she had suffered Fanny being the favorite in the family, getting everything without asking while she had to beg for everything. But a finger pointed to her mother as the catalyst for her act: *"and when the people who should know you the best make you slam the telephone down on them . . ."* For Avrum, she listed her unrewarded virtues *". . . ready to scrub your floors on my knees so that people should have respect when they come into my house."* Summing up, she wrote: *"I am committing suicide not because I am thinking of myself for a single minute . . ."* that she was driven to it *"for the good of my baby, who is too pure to carry such things on his unborn shoulders."*

Wracked with guilt, Bluma suffered a painful and debilitating emotional breakdown. Fanny remained in the unforgiving grip of the depression that insulated her from everything that was happening around her. Four days after Bella's burial, she eased herself off her bed and stepped from her room directly onto the ward's balcony. It was nearing two in the morning and wind carried a soft rain to her eyes. Stretching herself mindlessly on the slippery concrete balustrade, she turned over on her back to look up into the night, and the water blurred the blackness of space. When she dropped from the other side, she might have thought that the sky would catch her.

The canvas that was stretched over the length of the platform where the hospital crated the vegetables from its fields broke Fanny's three-story fall. It didn't tear, but its tension wires gave and bounced her like a rag doll onto the soft, wet earth. She lay there, unconscious, for three hours before a field worker almost stumbled over her.

The original skull fracture had developed further fissures, and shivers of bone were free in her skull. An arm had broken and became dislocated from her shoulder, and from the massive rupture of blood vessels in the middle of her back, it was feared that one of the tension wires way have severed some nerves on her spinal column. On regaining consciousness, Fanny might find that much of her body was paralyzed. The doctors hardly knew where to direct their attention first.

She was still in a coma at the end of the day, and no one was prepared to say how long it might be before she would come out of it, if at all. However, the doctors were cautiously hopeful; they expected that her brain was not damaged, and they were glad to discover that it was the lower left side of her rib cage, and not her spine, that had actually taken the slicing blow of the tension wire. Four ribs had cracked and a piece of the lower one had completely broken away, but while the X-ray had shown it pressing dangerously against a lung, it had stopped short of rupturing it. So far, the signs were all encouraging. They were amazed that, despite all this damage, the girl wasn't done in in the end by the three-hour exposure to the cold and rain while sunk in the mud and in the grip of shock. One of the surgeons who stood over Fanny for better than fourteen hours was able to say to Max that if in the future his daughter would remember that she wasn't a pigeon, there was a good chance that her only souvenir of the day before would be a dime-sized bald patch above her right ear. Overcome, Max kissed the surgeon's hands — the words his heart was pressing to tell him were beyond any language he had ever known.

(38)

The condolences said, the handshakes done, Avrum watched everyone slip back into the stream of their own private lives. Bella was buried, and the memory of her faded even before the period of *shiva* mourning was over; even the picture of her on the dresser somehow couldn't remind him of her. It was a warm, soft face, full of mystery and secret charms — quite unlike anything he had ever known in the woman he married. Bella had enjoyed the picture hugely, saying that it was the first one in her life which showed the real her. In the last month or so of her life, she had taken to looking at herself in the mirror with the picture in front of her, and she would say how much the "sacrifices" she'd had to make left their mark on her looks. Stupidly, Avrum once asked what sacrifices she had in mind, and after that, with every laundry, every housecleaning, and every Friday cooking, she would say, "What sacrifices, eh? You wanted to know what sacrifices? You still want to ask what sacrifices?"

One evening about a month after the funeral, three thickly bearded ultra-orthodox Jews in their satiny black garb appeared at his door and told him that they were from the burial society — the Montreal *Hevra Kadisha.* It was the practice after a death in the family to replace all the *mezuzahs* in the house. They came with half a dozen, and with hammer and nails at the ready. Essentially the mezuzahs were free; Avrum wasn't required to pay any money, unless he wanted something fancy, of course, like hand-carved and polished olive wood. But if he would insist on making a small donation — say, three dollars — they would be pleased to remember Bella's name in their prayers and thus assure her a comfortable place in the next world.

Avrum asked about the mezuzahs that were already affixed to the doorway, which he told them had been there forever.

"Why do they suddenly need changing?"

"When there's a tragedy in a house," said one of the men, speaking in a low voice, as though what he was saying was very personal and confidential, "you always have to check the mezuzahs to see that there isn't some mistake in the spelling — in the spelling or somewhere else. Maybe a microbe got in and ate some of the letters. You never know."

These people annoyed him. Everything about their presence was alien to him. "What spelling? What letters?" he asked not a little aggressively, hoping to keep them at the front door and that they wouldn't linger.

One of the men removed a mezuzah from a box and unscrewed the back. From within it, he withdrew a small, tightly rolled stretch of parchment and told him that inscribed by hand on the parchment were verses from *Sefer Dvarim* — Deuteronomy — that protected the house and everything in the house. He told Avrum that it was far simpler to replace the old mezuzahs with ones that had been thoroughly checked than to start checking every one of the uncertain mezuzahs separately.

"I don't think I need it."

"Take our word for it. You need it. You were visited by the evil eye and you don't want more tragedies in this house."

If this were the house where Horse lived, or even where Cy Green lived, thought Avrum ruefully, these three would long ago have found themselves back on the street. How much longer would it take for him to learn to be more assertive?

“I still don’t think I need it.” He told them but without too much conviction. “What’s there I think maybe you should leave there.”

“It’s free. Why take a chance? We’ll do all the work.”

“How long should this take you?”

“Five minutes at the most.”

“Is fifty cents enough?”

“More than enough.”

* * *

In the pitch black of that same night, Avrum suddenly awoke and threw himself out of his bed. He was in a fright. His heart was pounding furiously and his pajamas were drenched with his sweat. He lit the lamp on the wall above the headboard; the clock showed the hour at a few minutes after three a.m.

He rushed for his trousers on the chair at the foot of his bed, and searched in panic through his pockets. It wasn’t there. He opened the closet door and tried to remember which trousers he had worn when he last met with Horse. Into which pocket had he pushed that letter with the picture that this Larry, or whoever, had sent him? It was so many days ago. What did he do with that letter? Avrum remembered electing not to throw it in the trash, but what *did* he do with it?

It was in none of the pockets — neither the pockets of his trousers, nor in the pockets of his vests or shirts. He paced the room agitated and dumbfounded, pressing his fists into his temples.

Avrum was now virtually in a trance. Something deep within him began to carry him. From the kitchen, he brought a chair to the *boidim*, a low space over the bathroom ceiling where things could be stored. Reaching all the way to the back, ignoring the cobwebs that collected on his fingers, he searched blindly for a small, rectangular wooden box that had metal handles on the narrower ends. A moment later — a span of time that seemed like ages — he found it. Lifting it out, he carried it to the bureau in the bedroom. The image of his mother surfaced slowly in his mind. Soon Avrum felt the grip of her presence there in the room with him. She filled the room. She was there with him, enveloping him.

He found what he was looking for. His hands shook as he fingered the talisman that his mother fitted around his head not an hour before her death. That had been so many years ago, yet he could feel her hands on his head even now. That talisman was a mezuzah — much smaller than what those Jews from the burial society had nailed on his doors, but a true mezuzah nonetheless, a silver capsule stained with the blacks and browns of time, and at that moment, Avrum felt his entire life somehow linked to it. He studied its construction . . . the embossed Hebrew letter *shin* for *Shaddai*, and an image of the tabernacles, with specks of blue stone fitted above them. He had only to pull hard on the top and the bottom edge to separate the halves and expose its interior.

There it was: the parchment, rolled so tightly he had to use the nail of his little finger to open it. And on the parchment, in the smallest letters, was the same sharply etched script he had seen only hours earlier.

But where was the envelope, with the message and photograph?

There were almost two hours until daybreak. Avrum glanced out the window to the cold and empty street. Made restless by his frustration at not having better studied the image in the photograph and not having worked harder to decipher the writing, the feeling that was overtaking him at that moment was that his very life was slipping away from him. Nothing lent itself to explanation. The image of his mother diminished rapidly and left him with a terrifying sense of loneliness and emptiness. He was so utterly and completely alone in the world, and the anguish that pressed so heavily on his heart at this time might have delivered an ocean of tears had his mother still been there to receive them.

His thoughts were jumbled, and the cacophony of groans, whistles, and mumbled voices that came to his ears numbed his faculties for concentration and rational thought. It occurred to him that he might be going mad. He put some old coffee on the massive black and yellow Gurney stove Bella had purchased without asking him. He waited for the water to heat up. At least there were still some sacks of coal in the shed; the stove would need a full shovel if not more to keep it hot for the day.

He dressed slowly. It would be cold in the shed, but it was a feeling he would now invite. The colder it was the more it would cleanse him, he felt. But as he opened the door to the shed, he suddenly stiffened and froze as though in the throes of a catatonic episode. There was a moment of intense concentration before a massive wave of exhilaration and excitement overtook his mind. He knew now where that envelope was. He knew *exactly* where that envelope was.

Swiftly shutting the door, he sat down on a kitchen chair and hurriedly removed the shoe on his right foot. There it was — the envelope, still with the papers folded inside it. Avrum had sandwiched it between two pieces of leather and used it to cover the hole in the sole of that shoe. Clearly, God forgave his compounded transgression when he'd placed His name in that lowly shoe and then put his heavy foot down over it. Avrum rushed to the table with the envelope and opened it. He set the photograph of the paper or parchment, which showed four pins at its corners apparently to keep it from rolling up, next to the parchment from his talisman.

They were identical. Absolutely identical. The lines, the spacing, the letters that stretched in bolder lines — everything matched perfectly.

It was Hershel. He found him at last.

Then he recalled something Kapitolnik had said about Hershel finding *him*. A smile played at his lips, then a laugh escaped him. Kapitolnik was everything Freidle Kaplan said he was.

Avrum studied the scrawl again. The name written there was not Larry or Jerry: it was *Harry*. Harry was the English name for Hershel. Old man Stein, who sold candy and made milkshakes in his store across from the factory, was called Harry. But his wife still called him Hershel. So did Myer.

Avrum still could not fathom the sentences, but it didn't matter. Hershel was alive. They were home.

* * *

"Who is calling long distance at this hour? Is this an emergency?"

When the clock showed seven-fifteen that morning, Avrum could no longer contain his need to get through to the number on the paper. He dialed the long distance operator, who called him back ten minutes later. He had asked to make a person-to-person call to Harry Vishinsky, and now heard from that operator that no one by that name lived at that number.

"So, let me talk to anybody at that number," said Avrum, suddenly feeling at a loss and on the verge of despair. "Don't hang up, operator. Please. Try calling them again."

A few minutes later, the connection was renewed and Avrum found a throaty woman with a chronic cough at the other end.

"I'm looking for a Harry Vishinsky. He gave me this number to call."

"Well, no Harry Vishinsky lives here. I just told the operator that. Goodbye."

"But he gave me this number."

"Well, it's a mistake. It happens all the time. I'm sorry."

"WAIT. Wait please. Maybe the name is Larry?" Avrum was scrambling desperately for something to hold on to.

"No Larry here either." The woman cleared her throat and sounded decidedly impatient. "Does he owe you money?"

"Money?"

"Yes. Well, no one by that na—" She coughed violently now, and without letup.

"Please. He's my brother."

But she had already replaced the receiver.

(39)

The quiet in the house became enervating. Avrum quit his job as a watchman and the nights were his again, only now, they were heavy with an air of desertion and abandonment. A heavy pervading loneliness infiltrated all the empty stretching hours. One evening, quite on the spur of the moment, Avrum bathed, changed into fresh clothes, and went to visit Fanny at the hospital. At the gate to the hospital, an old man was selling flowers, and with a small bouquet of red roses in hand, Avrum found her room and let himself in. There were four other patients there and visitors stood around every bed, but he instantly recognized Max and Bluma Finegold, and guessed that the body next to them bundled in casts and miles of gauze had to be Fanny. Except for her lips, nostrils, and eyes, her entire head was taped over. One arm was partially free and her legs were covered; otherwise, she seemed lost in a husk of white cement. The sight shocked him.

Suddenly the flowers were an embarrassment. Avrum was uncertain how to explain his visit, when his wife — their daughter — was barely a month in the ground. The Finegolds walked over and embraced him, thanking him for coming. They also thanked him for the flowers. Fanny followed him with her eyes.

Avrum returned a week later, and again the week after that. Soon he was showing up three and even four times a week. Eventually, most of the bandages below her forehead were removed, and Fanny began responding to his words, although in a low, gravelly voice. Sometimes she would get the nurse to pat a touch of powder on her nose and paint a faint blush into her cheeks. Avrum always noticed her efforts and complimented her enthusiastically.

Then there was the visit when he told her of Hershel's message and the telephone number that led nowhere. Fanny asked to see the note, and Avrum set it in her hands the very next day.

Fanny's eyes seemed to explode from within and her lips puckered tightly. "I know this writing," she blurted. "I know it well. It's Harry's . . . Harry Weiss — that's my so-called friend . . . the artist — the monk I was telling you about. That's if you remember. Do you remember?"

"Harry Weiss? A monk? A Christian?"

"Harry Weiss! Yes, Harry Weiss. That's his handwriting for sure. That's also how he writes his name. I've seen it a hundred times. And the message he wrote is: *If you know what is in the picture, you know who I am and that I'm alive.* And that telephone number — I know it by heart. I called it myself so often. It's Laura Victor's place. Harry stays there when he's in the city. Do you have any idea how much his paintings are worth today? He's a top Dadaist. All the museums are running after him."

* * *

"My name is Avrum Vishinsky, and I'm calling again from Montreal. The man I am looking for — his name is Harry WEISS . . . WEISS. That's how he calls himself now."

"You called last a few weeks ago — maybe a month. Am I right?" Laura Victor was trying to put the pieces together.

"Yes, I called you and you said he didn't live there."

"Well, you didn't ask for Harry *Weiss*, now did you? You gave me another name. Maybe some people are good at mind reading, but I'm not. Anyways, I think I know who you are." Her last words led into an extended spate of hacking, throat clearing, and spitting. Avrum waited.

"I am his brother." Avrum spoke in a weak, almost pleading voice. "We were separated a long time ago."

"The wrestler, yes? From the newspaper, yes?"

"Yes." This time he almost shouted his reply. "Yes, that's me exactly!"

"Well, you really hurt him, y'know. You hurt him really bad." Again, coughing ended her words.

"Hurt him? How could I have hurt him? What are you saying?" Avrum's mind raced in panic. What had he missed?

"Your brother sent you the letter, and every day for a month and a half, he sat next to the telephone. He wouldn't leave the house. Not for a minute. He wouldn't even leave the room. He waited all that time for your call, which never came. Walking back and forth, back and forth, every five minutes checking to see that the phone was working. It made him sick."

"He sent that letter to a promoter. I don't wrestle anymore. The letter got to me very very late." In his sinking heart, Avrum knew that that was a lame excuse. Had he called the number the same day Horse had delivered the letter, chances are he might still have found him.

"Can I speak with him now?"

"It's at least three weeks that he's away."

"Away where? Where can I find him?"

"I have no idea. He comes and goes."

"When is he coming back?"

"Your guess is as good as mine. I never know until he shows up at the door."

Laura Victor suffered another spell of heavy coughing, but Avrum got her to give him her address in Newark, New Jersey — which was the same address Fanny had had. He bade her write down his own address and the phone numbers at his home and at the Sweet Mode Dress factory. She promised that she would deliver this information to him the moment he stepped through the door. "In the meantime," she said, "there's nothing you can do but wait."

* * *

Three weeks later, the doctors let Fanny sit in a wheelchair, and Avrum took her downstairs and out to the gardens. The first time down, she asked to be wheeled around to the back to see where and how far she had fallen. Avrum hesitated. Max and Bluma were with them at the time and they looked at each other uncertainly, but Fanny reassured them and they took her there. It was impossible to know what thoughts surfaced behind her eyes.

Her parents began to space their visits over greater intervals. Max had trouble with his disk and Bluma suffered from pressure and swelling in her legs. Teitleman, the doctor, had advised both of them to keep off their feet as much as possible. Bluma would show up some afternoons, but Fanny and Avrum had the evenings to themselves. By this time, Avrum was visiting every day.

They opened themselves to each other, freely confessing that somewhere in their lives their hearts had deceived their minds. Perhaps the truth was the other way around, but Fanny decided that it had to be the heart. "Just think how it deceives *death* from one beat to the next."

Fate became a favorite subject of conversation. Avrum told her of Kapitolnik and his search for Hershel, and Fanny related the incident back in Biranovici when Manya and Viktor had come upon her.

"You know, even before she told me that she was my mother, I just knew that there was something between us, something very mysterious. Maybe it was the way she looked at me, or maybe my brain collected what my eyes were seeing before my consciousness could frame it. We had the same forehead, the same eyes, the same chin — then, of course, my mother's reaction put the final stamp of truth on this woman's story."

"She admitted it?"

"God no! She just became hysterical, and that was confession enough."

"How did you father react?"

"Oh, he had time to invent a good story. It really was a good story, and he wanted so much for me to believe it. But suddenly, nothing was black and white anymore. My eyes and ears pulled one way, my heart another. I didn't know if truth and honesty were one and the same anymore. I spent my life looking for the answer."

"Was there one?"

* * *

Standing in line for tickets at an uptown music hall on a Saturday night, her arm linked in Harry's, they were watching the way the couple ahead of them, at least the woman, kept rubbing her knee against her partner's leg. Both were somewhat too elegantly dressed for those surroundings, but what was most incongruent about the picture was the very formal way they addressed each other in the most refined Polish — the classical, literary Polish one almost never heard in the streets those days.

Perhaps the woman caught their stares. Maybe it was a vibration of another order. But what did the reason matter; she turned to look at them. The instant she turned around, everything paled. The woman was Manya.

"Manya?" Somehow the name broke through Fanny's shock and confusion. It was hardly louder than a whisper.

"Yes? We know each other?" From the way the color had risen to her face, it was plain that they did. Her gentleman now turned, or half-turned, to look at her.

"I'm Fanya — Fanya . . . from Bir—" But the woman cut abruptly into her words.

"Yes, Fanya, of course. It is so very very nice to see you. I see everyone has found some excuse to come to the United States. I trust your life is in order?"

What talk was this, thought Fanny; why the imperious manner?

"Manya . . ."

"We must have a chat my dear — sometime. Look, come with me over to the lamp and let me write down your address. I have this dreadful headache, otherwise I'd chat with you now. I'm afraid we shall not even stay for the performance."

Under the lamp and away from the men, Manya very quickly said to her, "Dearest, it is so nice to see you. Here, write your address on this paper, clearly and in detail. You have a telephone? Yes? Please write that, too. But let me explain in a word. Under no circumstances are you to let out what we are to each other. Do you understand? It would ruin me. That man is none other than Count Casimir Kozinski, whose blood traces back to Sobiesky himself, and we are to be married. If he knew that I had a daughter in some backwater town like Biranovici, it would destroy my whole world. After all I've invested, I can't let this happen to me. Dearest, I will call you, and when we meet, I will explain everything. Please?" Fanny could only nod dumbly.

Manya and her gentleman withdrew from the line, and Fanny never heard from her again.

* * *

Fanny shared with Avrum everything she could remember of Hershel. He was a painter, today a leader in the school they called Dadaism.

"They start out by painting something you see and think you know," she explained, "and then it changes into something that could be the very opposite — like a square coming out of a circle . . . like the motor of a machine instead of a brain coming out of the head of a man."

Hershel also had some serious emotional and maybe mental problems. "In everything, he could see something that could hurt him. He was always saying that there was someone who wanted to kill him. He could hear knocking on the door when there was no knocking."

Despite all his difficulties, Fanny could describe him as a true genius and said that if he wanted her to stay with him, she would never say no. "It was as though he was a hundred years old and five years old at the same time. But he was like a frightened deer all the time. I could never know from this minute to the next where he would be, what he would say, or what he would do. He would go out for cigarettes and forget to come back. I never left him. He was always leaving me."

* * *

Fanny talked of books and writers. They would talk about Plato and Aristotle and argue about whether they were right when they said that twenty years was the ideal difference between the ages of a husband and wife.

Fanny had a nurse buy a set of watercolors, and presented Avrum with them. She showed him how to use them, and if there was an hour of light, Avrum would sit on the balcony with her and paint something of the scenery. Fanny was always effusive in her praise of his efforts. He even began to believe them himself.

Once she asked him to bend over so that she could whisper something in his ear. Instead of a whisper, she kissed him. Avrum was overcome with joy and not a little gratitude. For the very first time, he felt that something very deep and very vital within him was finding its first roots in this new world.

(40)

The call came for Avrum at the factory just before noon. Shirley, who was back at her old job, called to Avrum and told him to take the call in the showroom. He opened the door there to find Myer and Florence looking through some catalogs and examining swatches of textiles.

"I got a call," he explained to them, going for the phone.

"If it's private, it couldn't wait until your lunch hour?" Thus Myer.

Florence frowned at him and raised her open palms. "Myer!" was all she said. Her husband instantly retreated with his eyes and the turn of his mouth asking "So what did I do now?"

Lifting the receiver off the hook and raising the mouthpiece in the direction of his lips, he spoke. "Hello?"

It was Hershel.

Myer gasped. He jumped out of his chair, rushed around the table, brought Avrum one of the leather seats reserved for customers, and pushed him into it. Florence went to his side, got down on one knee and rested the tips of her shaking fingers on his arm. Her lips trembled and tears cascaded down her face.

* * *

"The watched pot never boils," Fanny would remind Avrum. The more you'll expect him, the longer it will be before he shows up."

Avrum was at Fanny's bedside every evening now. He would return from the factory, shower, dab some brilliantine in his hair, and put on a shirt that would just have come from the Chinese laundry. From the flower girl at the entrance to the hospital, he'd pick out a few sweet carnations.

"He spoke about a hospital," said Avrum. "Maybe he needs me there. I called him the next day, and this Laura Victor tells me he went for an examination and that it will take a few days."

Fanny told him that Hershel, or Harry, was probably at the psychiatric hospital — that he had been really sick for the longest time. "I didn't want to tell you this before, but on different days, he could be different people with different names. He could be Harry, or he could be Peter. I think he became a monk to get away from this imaginary Peter."

"Piotr," Avrum corrected her. "Not *Peter* — *Piotr*."

At her bedside only hours after receiving the call from Hershel, Avrum had endlessly repeated the exchanges that had Hershel shouting into the mouthpiece from his end and Avrum from his. At one point, it appeared that Hershel had fainted; Laura Victor got on the phone and asked Avrum to wait a minute or two until Hershel could get back to himself.

The conversation between them was not always very clear, coherent, or fluid. The line connection was heavy with static. Avrum kept asking Hershel if he was still alive and if he believed in miracles, and Hershel needed immediately to know all the details of how Avrum managed to escape the woman and that house. There were long stretches of silence. Each merged in the last remembered image of the other. Hershel cried openly, and Avrum, choking back his own tears, promised that they would be a family again. Avrum insisted on going to Newark that same evening, and Hershel promised to be on the next train to Montreal.

"Well, maybe not on the next train. You see, I'm not so well. I had my nervous troubles, but I'm a hundred percent now. I'm a thousand percent now! I just have an appointment to see my doctor in New York first — a hospital, actually — and then I'll come immediately. A few days at the most."

Avrum mentioned Fanny's name and told him that he had been married to her sister. "She knows you." Hershel was incredulous. A baseball bat slamming into his head would have surprised him less.

"FANNY? FANNY THE ART TEACHER? Fanny with the children?" Silence. "Sure. From Canada. Sure. Sure. Would you believe it that I was once even in her house?" Silence. "SO WHY COULDN'T SHE TELL ME THAT SHE KNOWS YOU? FOR GOD'S SAKE, WHY COULDN'T SHE SAY ONE WORD? Something? And what? You married her sister?" A silence of many seconds followed. Everything seemed to freeze. In a softer and undecided tone of voice, he continued. "So maybe we're not really talking about the same Fanny? Are you sure?"

"She told me that if it were you, that you changed your religion — that you're a monk. Is this true?"

"A monk?"

"A monk. That's what she said."

"NO, NO. Oh, no. I'm not a monk. And thank God I'm still a hundred percent Jewish. Maybe sometimes I rent a room there. That's all. They just protect me. They let me paint there. To pay them, I work in their gardens."

Avrum told him that Fanny had had a bad accident and that she was now a patient at the Montreal General Hospital . . . that he was seeing her almost every evening . . . that it was she who managed to read his message.

There were also strings of conversation that led nowhere. Avrum asked Hershel if he remembered Shloimke Plotkin, and Hershel spoke about how paints and canvasses were getting more and more expensive. Avrum asked why he sent a photo of the parchment and not of the mezuzah, which he would have linked to him immediately. Hershel's reply was unclear. (Later, Fanny told him that at the psychiatric hospital, they took away everything he carried that he could use to hurt himself. The chain certainly. He was probably allowed to keep only the parchment. Perhaps they thought he would find a way to cut his wrists with the metal.)

In the end, they made kissing noises into their phones' mouthpieces and lowered the receivers, crying softly in Yiddish, "*Lebst noch, mein bruder* — you're still alive, my brother . . . you're still alive." When the busy signal came on, Avrum was still holding the receiver. He pressed it gently over his heart before replacing it. Florence kissed him on the top of his head and Myer patted him on the shoulder.

(41)

It was at that time that Avrum stopped as he always did after work to pick up his newspaper, and an item in another paper that the kiosk's owner had strung up and secured with a clothespin burned harshly into his eyes. A judge had let lawyers representing some members of the Guy Street Dukes convince him that Fanny had not been raped after all — but had actually invited all the perverse sexual unions the police had claimed were forced upon her. The fracture of her skull was surely an unfortunate accident, but it was the result of her own drunken and inciting behavior. The lawyers produced Fanny's past sexual misdemeanors as a matter of record to show that "the youths could not have been imposing their will on an entirely blameless and resisting virgin."

Avrum's eyes shifted crazily back and forth across the page and he felt the tensions and frustrations of the last days collide powerfully with the strange and otherworldly chemistry which was fast overtaking him. At first, he could distinguish nothing outside the cloudiness that had stricken his mind and electrified him so that his body shook and trembled as he stood there. But words, initially disconnected and incoherent, rushed up to him from a great distance.

"I have seen the winter rise before the sun and engulph the summer for a day."

He knew them.

Then he heard the rifle shots. Cold air with the acrid smell of gunpowder again filled his lungs. Swords flashed everywhere. He heard the terrified cries to God, the shrieks and the desperate wailing that pierced the thick clouds of dust and smoke. He could still feel his body pressing Hershel's into the ground beneath the bushes while horses' hooves sliced powerfully into the ground only inches away from them.

". . . and this is your inheritance I deliver; measure it not against the cedar and stone of kings . . .

"Your inheritance . . . a covenant yea of vengeance but vivid with love."

What was happening? It was as if his very soul was being invaded. Dizzily, he stepped around the side of the kiosk and fell against it, bringing his hands to his head. Behind his eyes, the lifeless body of his mother lay before him, with the bloodied body of his father lying face down across her feet.

The voice was now clear and sure. It recalled his destiny with an ancient promise. And as though etched in his soul, it would not release him.

"And Avrum . . . Avrum, my firstborn . . . you are a multitude of one and a multitude apart. Your heritage will be delivered unto you violated and defiled, for it is the land of Canaan. Then the pestilence born from their dogs will overtake your armor — for your shield that was resignation and your sword that was perseverance shall wither. But until that day, you shall proceed not by mortal will but by distant design."

Again:

". . . the pestilence born from their dogs will overtake your armor — for your shield that was resignation and your sword that was perseverance shall wither.

"And then . . .

"And then . . . shall you shed your tired armor and embrace what you have learned from your enemies. AND YOU SHALL SMITE THEM."

* * *

He didn't go to Fanny that evening, but took the streetcar downtown to St. Catherine and Bleury, and another from there westward to Guy Street. It was a short walk from there to the clubhouse of the Dukes. He found it empty. To pass an hour and a half, he stepped into a nearby movie house, but the only pictures that captured his mind was of the carnage that night on the road to Lvov. When he returned to their clubhouse, it was after nine, and the lights were on inside. Laughter reached outside to the lane.

He tried the door, but it was locked. Over the talk and the laughter, someone asked who it was and the answer came from Avrum's foot, which drove into the lock and splintered the rotted frame. The door swung away. A sudden electrified silence froze everything where it was, but an instant later, the boys sprang to their feet. Switchblades flashed open and Avrum looked down at them. One of the boys motioned for the others to spread out, and Avrum guessed that he might be the one Fanny remembered as their leader — the one called Reg. He approached Avrum, deftly holding the blade in front of him and turning it slowly over and over in the flat of his palm.

"What the freaking hell you think you're doing here, mister?"

"I'm looking for Mr. Reg and his friends."

"Get the hell out'a here before we bleed you, for Chris-sake."

Avrum took his bearings slowly. There were at least twenty of them — maybe twenty-five. Most had knives, but some were wielding broken bottles, and one of them was swinging a bicycle chain.

"I've come for Mr. Reg and his friends." Avrum stepped slowly inside and Reg quickly stepped back, too. The blood drained from his face and he stopped playing with his knife.

"You crazy, mister? You want us to spread your guts out on the floor?"

"You better hold on to your toys, because I'm sending you all to the hospital. I'm going to kill as many of you as I can." Avrum said this matter-of-factly.

"What the friggin hell we do to you?" wailed Reg. "Any-body here know this guy?" One boy answered by dashing out the door.

"I'm just a simple messenger. You have some unfinished business with a lady named Fanny Finegold."

Someone called out, "The judge let us go. We were innocent."

"Not this judge." Avrum pointed at himself.

"WHEN I GIVE THE WORD, WE JUMP HIM!" shouted Reg.

Avrum grabbed a chair and swung it at Reg, who backed away in time but shouted for his friends to attack. A few lunged forward, and the chair slammed into two of them. First blood was drawn. Avrum kicked a third in the chest, but the fourth got his bottle into Avrum's chin and neck. Avrum lifted him off the ground, catching him by the jacket, and threw him like a broken toy to crash against the wall. He felt the blood beginning to drain under his shirt now, and his face burned. The one with the chain swung it and it caught him on the shoulder, but Avrum had his eye fixed on Reg, who backed away to the wall. Someone threw a knife at Avrum — inexpertly. The handle hit him over an eye; more blood was drawn, but the wound was superficial and Avrum moved relentlessly ahead.

Reg made his move, spitting and throwing an old can at Avrum's face, hoping it would distract Avrum long enough for him to close in with his knife. Avrum sidestepped the lunge and caught Reg by his wrist and chin. With a sudden vicious smash against the wall, he shattered Reg's wrist; the knife dropped to the floor. Reg howled. Avrum broke a leg off a chair and hammered it unmercifully against Reg's mouth and at those trying to get at his back. They fell like flies; those not on the floor raced to get out. Another single blow demolished Reg's nose, flattening the bone and cartilage so that his face lost every semblance of human proportion. The shapeless, disfigured mass dropped unconscious to the floor. Avrum wouldn't let up the fury of his charge and delivered a vicious kick squarely between the legs of the crumpled, broken, prostrate body. A large pool of blood quickly collected where the body lay.

A knife plunged into his shoulder near his neck and stayed there. Avrum caught the hand that had driven it there and broke it instantly at the elbow. It snapped like a dry twig. He worked a bottle out of the hand of another boy and threw it hard at those who were rushing for the door. It caught one of them on his ear, and when the bottle fell, the side of the boy's face was half torn away. The chain came down again on his back, and another knife cut his arm. Avrum was able to latch onto the boy with the knife; only then did Avrum remove the knife that was still in his shoulder with his free hand; he knew he was bleeding heavily. The boy in his grip howled and pleaded for his life. Lifting him over his head, Avrum threw him hard across the room into the one who still had the chain, and both crashed to the floor. There was no one left moving in the room then but them, and Avrum kicked at their faces and bodies until they, too, stopped moving.

* * *

The taxi pulled up at the hospital and Avrum handed the driver all the money he had in his pocket. "I'm sorry about the blood," he apologized. He refused the change and the driver asked if he needed help, but Avrum assured him that he could manage.

The astounded nurses tried to steer him to the emergency wing in the outpatient ward, but he shook them off and headed for the stairs. They called for help and rushed after him. Blood spilled from his shoes, but he made it to Fanny's room. People were everywhere, looking at him while horror registered on their faces — but now he could tell Fanny that he knew a thing about punishment and justice and guilt and reward. He'd tell her that her nightmare was in the weave of his heritage, and that now it had been played out and ended. He would tell her that he was immersed in the flow of his true destiny, and that he was no longer a separate man.

He heard Fanny scream. Someone standing near her bed rushed over and gripped him. Again, he heard Fanny's voice crying shrilly out to him, but the cacophony of whines and whistles and the relentless throbbing in his head mixed with her words had made it seem that they were falling upon him from everywhere. Still, he heard, "Abie . . . it's Harry . . . Oh God, Abie . . . it's Harry Weiss . . . your Hershel . . . He's here . . . He's right here. God help him — somebody help him, please."

"And on that day, the artery that was rent shall be healed, the tree shall be resurrected, and you shall have inherited the land."

Avrum knew in his heart that he wasn't dying, but before he lost consciousness, he looked around at the man who was holding him. He would have known him anywhere.

* * *

Hot twisting winds lifted the desert sands over the crest of the mountain, and Avrum cupped his eyes and shivered with cold. Below, he could see the slashed slopes dropping into an ocean of turbulent cloud, and it was not his own will that fixed his eyes on the pitching currents. Suddenly, in a burst, it collected into the images of Iannuk, the Doctor, and Grigor, and they rose massively up to him. They had never left him, he thought, nor would they ever. Voices issued from the cloud, but they boomed and echoed all around him. The first that he could hear clearly belonged to Iannuk. "Never expect," it said. "Never . . ."

His image became overtaken by that of the Doctor, who spat, "Never trust, you fool."

"And never lose your hold." Now it was Grigor, who might have been laughing.

The cloud dropped away and rested, and the faces dissipated into nothing. Abruptly, the winds grew hotter. They pummeled and pitched the cloud more terribly than before, and Avrum waited for the other images he knew would emerge. It wasn't until their swell rushed up again to him that he recognized them, and just as suddenly, they were lost. But their voices lingered. "Consider nothing," said Myer Goldenberg. Before the echo was lost, Horse and Strulevitch spoke almost together, but their words were garbled. The smoke from Strulevitch's cigar filled his nostrils.

The cloud didn't drop away, and Avrum felt the last warmth seep from his body. He could no longer feel anything of his body beyond the cold. From the darkness of the shadows, Bella rose in an evil fury, her face a grotesque contortion of the picture of her that she so liked. An instant later, the image of a warm and welcoming Fanny, her hands outstretched, replaced Bella. Then all the images receded and only a voice — a voice he knew so well — reached his ears. In low, hoarse, rumbling tones, he heard: "You never forgot me, my brother. You never forgot me."

There was a rumbling from a great distance, and it seemed as if every current in the cloud turned to sweep at him. They lashed him and rocked him. Icicles hung from his hair and crystals caked his face. He tried to move his toes, but it was as though they were no longer a part of him.

Suddenly, the winds shifted and the cloud pulled away and rose even higher. Avrum feared he'd lose his balance, but from nowhere, warmth was returning to him. A shaft of sunlight almost broke through, and a final great swirl brought forth the image of his mother.

"Mama!"

Avrum fell to the ground and the image grew over him. It spoke slowly, through a hollowness as deep as the universe.

"I am . . . Hassia from the House of Neiditch. I am . . . the burden and the pledge that is Faith. I am . . ."

And then sunlight overwhelmed the sky and swallowed the cloud. Calamity threw Avrum onto his back, and a multitude of colors filled his eyes. Sounds reached his ears. And voices.

"We'll give him another half pint, nurse. I think that should do it."

"I think so, too. A half pint at the most."

GLOSSARY

baitzes: vernacular reference to testicles; balls

bankis: heated suction cups (medicinal)

bobehmysehs: a grandmother's fairy tale

boyehle: a timid mama's boy

cheder: school; classroom

chupeh: canopy under which the marriage ceremony is performed

dafka: on purpose; intentionally; in spite

drek: dirt; anything deemed worthless

eechs: disgusting

Eretz Yisrooel: Israel

feigeleh: homosexual

Frantzoizen: Frenchies; French community

gans git: all is well

Gehenom: hell, Satan's domain

goy: non-Jew

groshen: the equivalent of a penny

Hevra Kadisha: Jewish burial society

hometz: food that is leavened (e.g. bread)

kehila: community

Keneder Adler: the *Canadian Eagle* newspaper

kourveh: prostitute

ktuba: marriage contract

kugel: baked noodle pie

landsman: someone from the same place in the old country

loz mir (from *loz mir alain*): leave me alone

latkes: potato pancakes

Madim: the planet Mars

mazel-tov: good luck; good fortune

menshlichdik: honorable; proper

meshugosim: individuals who are mentally deranged

mezuzah, mezuzot(pl.): hollow capsule containing parchment with prayer inscribed, usually affixed to the frame of a doorway identifying the residence of a Jew.

nu shoin: equivalent of "come on," or "hurry up, I'm waiting."

oif kapurus: "Let this be sacrificed so that more important things may be spared."

plotchkeh: the skin that collects on the surface of boiled milk

putz: penis; fool

reb: a respectful manner of addressing a Jew who is assumed to be learned

Shabbes Koidesh: the holy Sabbath

Shabbtai: the planet Saturn

Shaddai: Jehovah

shaygitz: non-Jew; rascal

shiva: literally "seven," referring specifically to the ritual mourning period of seven days.

shlep: drag; move heavily

shmaltz herring: marinated herring

shmattes: rags, cheap clothing

shmuk/shmuck: dumb bimbo; sap; sucker; fall guy; sometimes intended as a reference to the penis

shmutzik: dirty

shnapps: whiskey

shochet: ritual slaughterer

shprintzileah: capricious; flighty (refers specifically to girls or women)

shtick: antics

shuleh: small synagogue or Jewish religious school

shvartzer: a black person

smootch: dollars (archaic)

stamm: without reason; without cause

Tehillim: Book of Psalms

tochter: daughter

tzitzes: vernacular reference to breasts; boobs

yiddeleh: normally a complimentary reference to a simple Jew

yiddineh: a Jewish and somewhat conventional thinking woman

Yiddisher Forvertz: the *Jewish Forward* newspaper

yiddishkeit: of a Yiddish nature

Zedek: the planet Jupiter

zjlob: a heavyset, dimwitted bum

zunneleh: a small son, as addressed by a parent